ANN M. MARTIN

THE BABY-SITTERS CLUB®

CLAUDIA AND THE BAD JOKE

A GRAPHIC NOVEL BY

ARLEY NOPRA

WITH COLOR BY K CZAP

An Imprint of
SCHOLASTIC

This book is in memory of Lyman Chamberlain Martin —
Grandpoppy — who always liked a good joke
A. M. M.

For my family, who never stopped believing in me.
For my grandmas, who I fondly thought of during the making of this book.
For Thao, who I could always count on to have my back.
To everyone who reminded me to drink water, thank you!

And for Bengee, who cheered me up when I needed it the most.
You made me laugh and you are infinitely awesome for that.
A. N.

Text copyright © 2024 by Ann M. Martin
Art copyright © 2024 by Arley Nopra

Library of Congress Control Number: 2023934544

ISBN 978-1-338-83551-9 (hardcover)
ISBN 978-1-338-83550-2 (paperback)

10 9 8 7 6 5 4 3 2 1   24 25 26 27 28

Printed in China   62
First edition, January 2024

Edited by Cassandra Pelham Fulton
Book design by Shivana Sookdeo
Creative Director: Phil Falco
Publisher: David Saylor

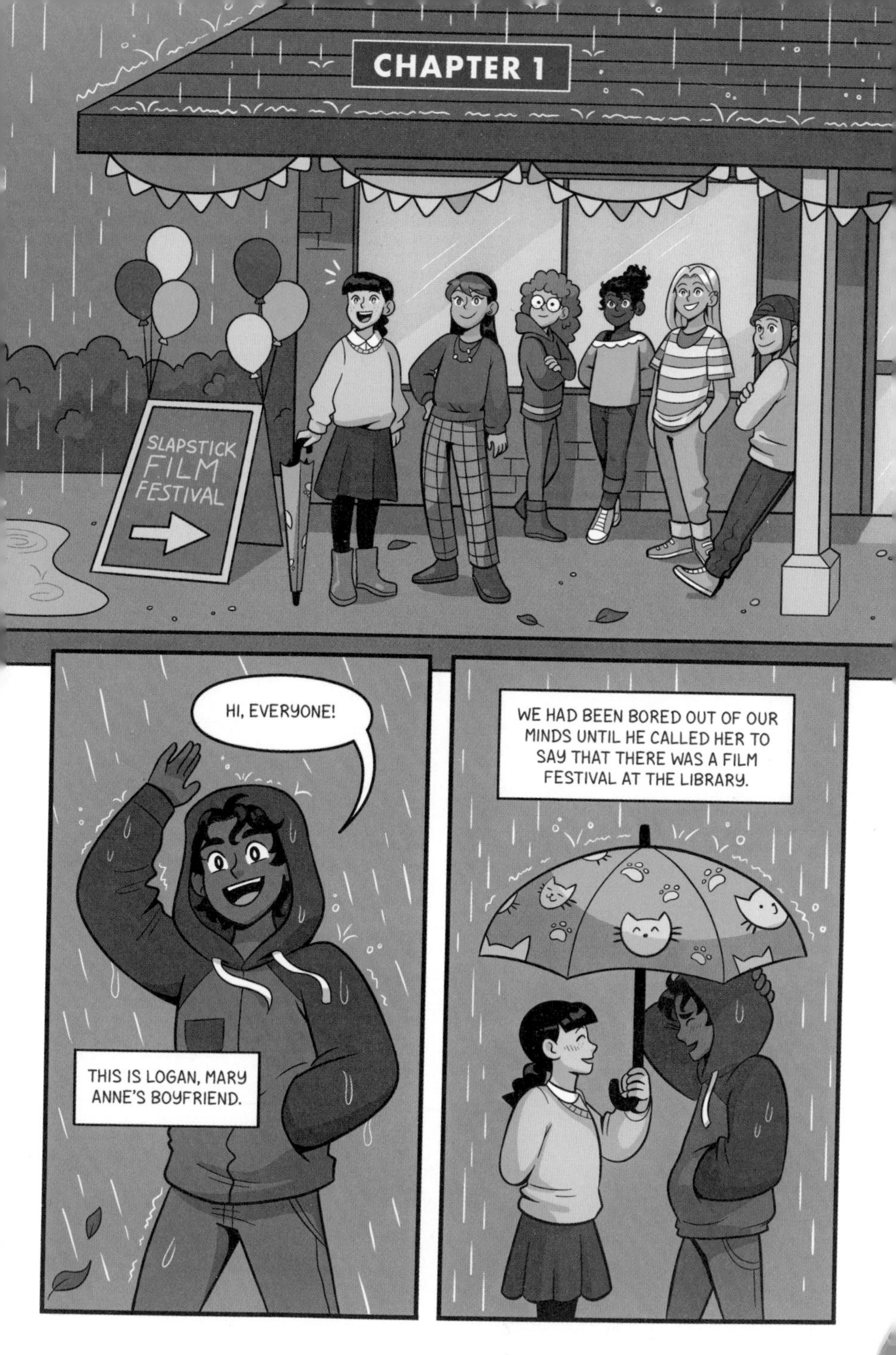
CHAPTER 1
SLAPSTICK FILM FESTIVAL
HI, EVERYONE!
THIS IS LOGAN, MARY ANNE'S BOYFRIEND.
WE HAD BEEN BORED OUT OF OUR MINDS UNTIL HE CALLED HER TO SAY THAT THERE WAS A FILM FESTIVAL AT THE LIBRARY.

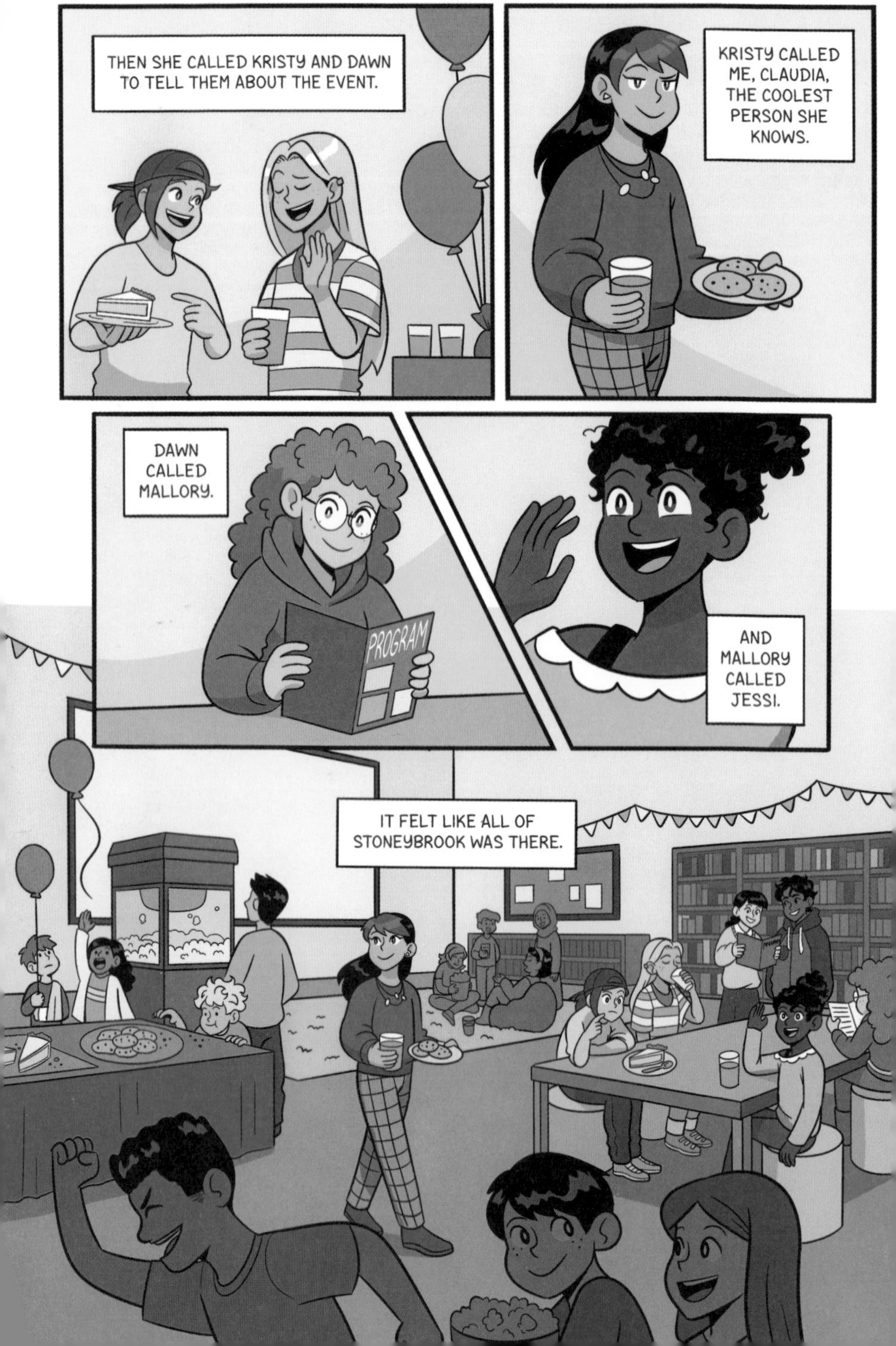
THEN SHE CALLED KRISTY AND DAWN TO TELL THEM ABOUT THE EVENT.
KRISTY CALLED ME, CLAUDIA, THE COOLEST PERSON SHE KNOWS.
DAWN CALLED MALLORY.
PROGRAM
AND MALLORY CALLED JESSI.
IT FELT LIKE ALL OF STONEYBROOK WAS THERE.

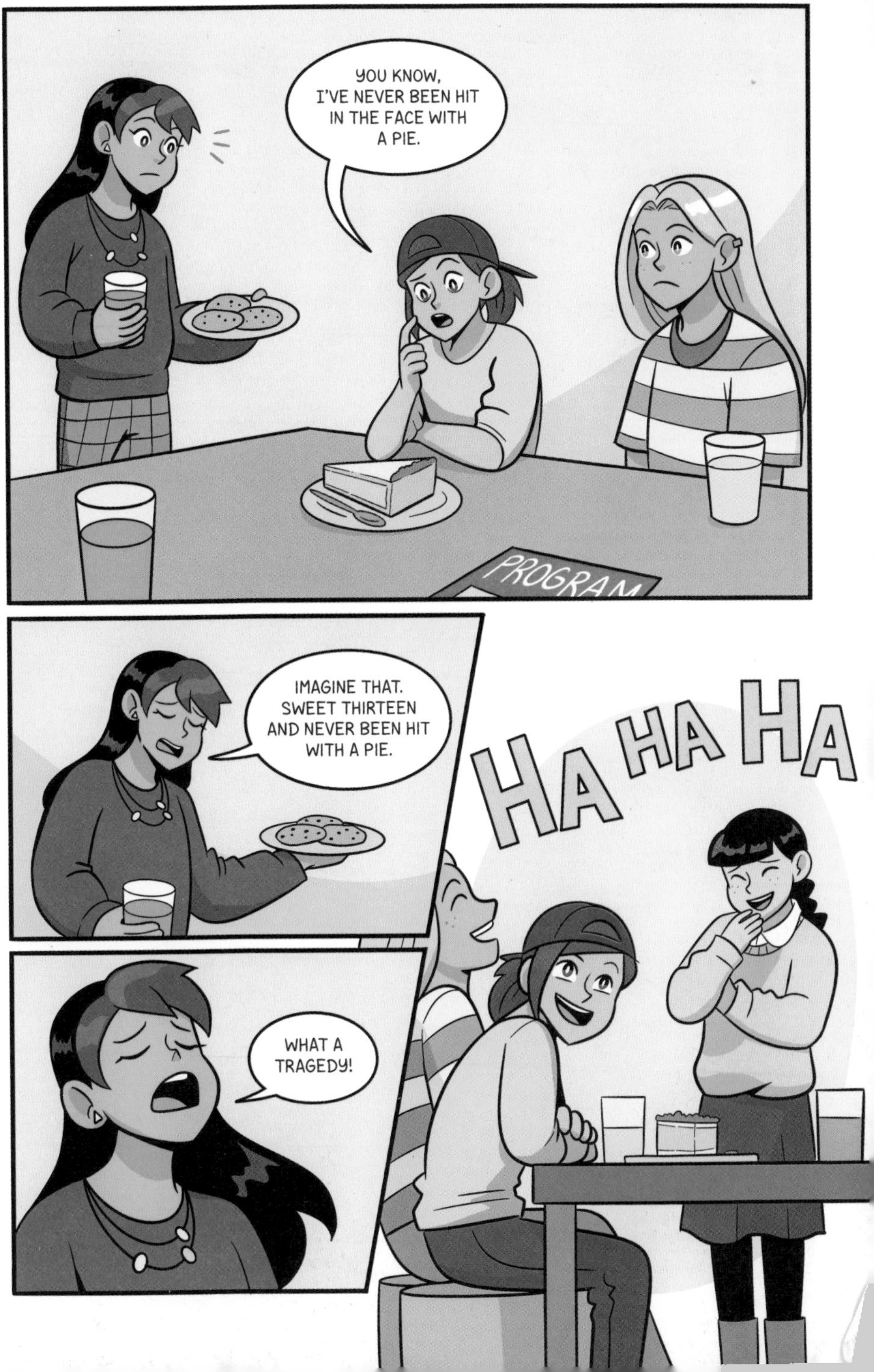
YOU KNOW, I'VE NEVER BEEN HIT IN THE FACE WITH A PIE.
PROGRAM
IMAGINE THAT. SWEET THIRTEEN AND NEVER BEEN HIT WITH A PIE.
WHAT A TRAGEDY!
HA HA HA HA

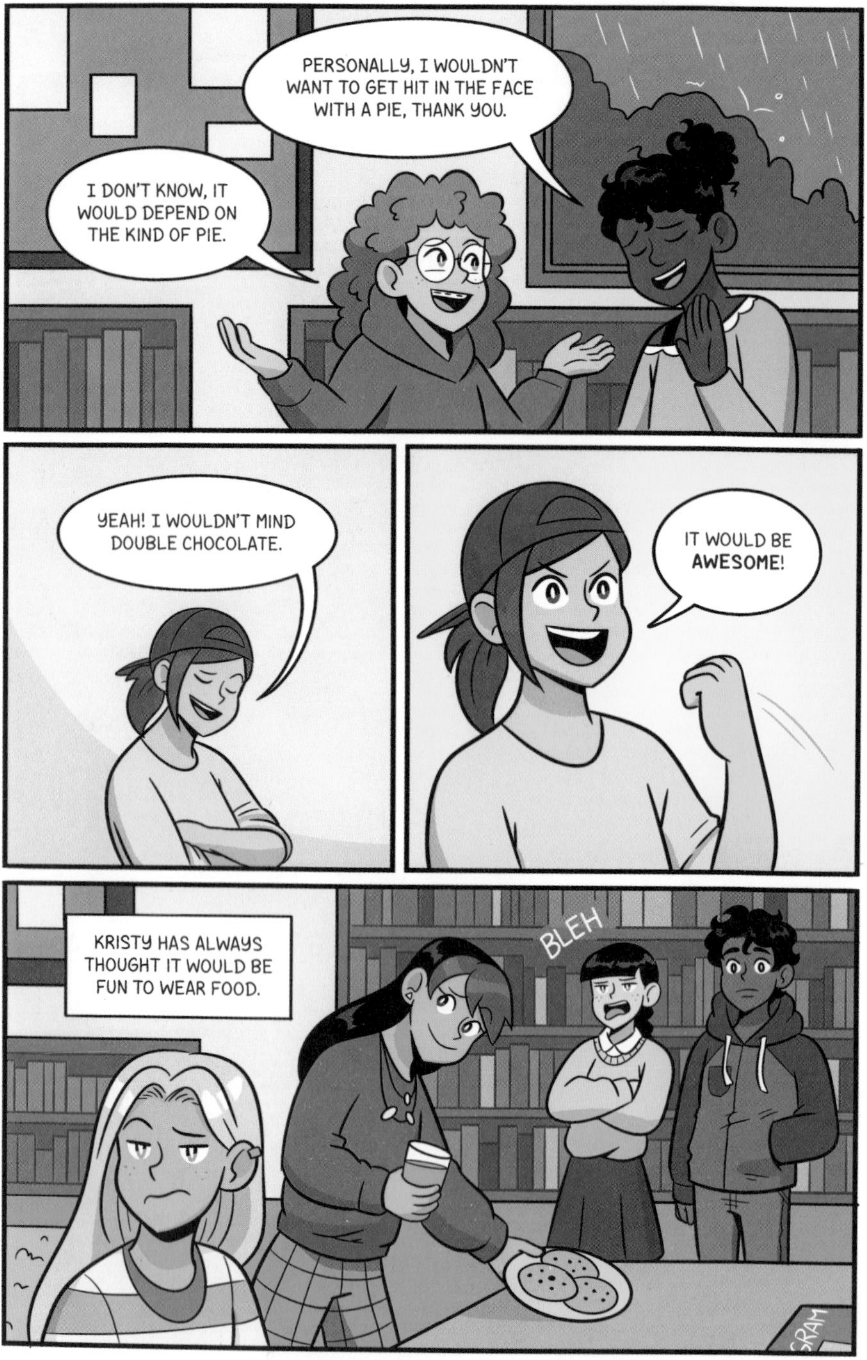
PERSONALLY, I WOULDN'T WANT TO GET HIT IN THE FACE WITH A PIE, THANK YOU.
I DON'T KNOW, IT WOULD DEPEND ON THE KIND OF PIE.
YEAH! I WOULDN'T MIND DOUBLE CHOCOLATE.
IT WOULD BE **AWESOME!**
KRISTY HAS ALWAYS THOUGHT IT WOULD BE FUN TO WEAR FOOD.
BLEH

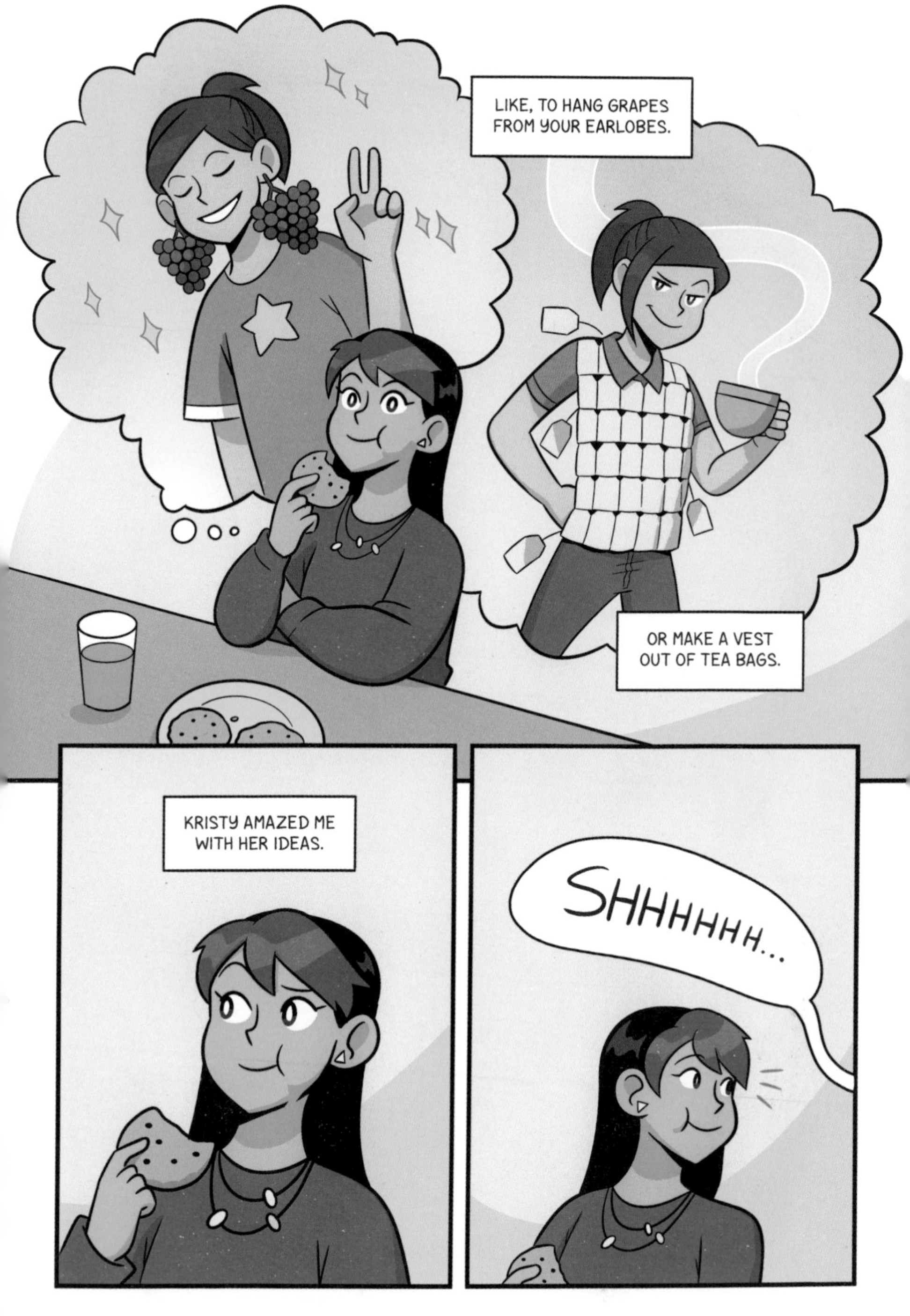
LIKE, TO HANG GRAPES FROM YOUR EARLOBES.
OR MAKE A VEST OUT OF TEA BAGS.
KRISTY AMAZED ME WITH HER IDEAS.
SHHHHHH...

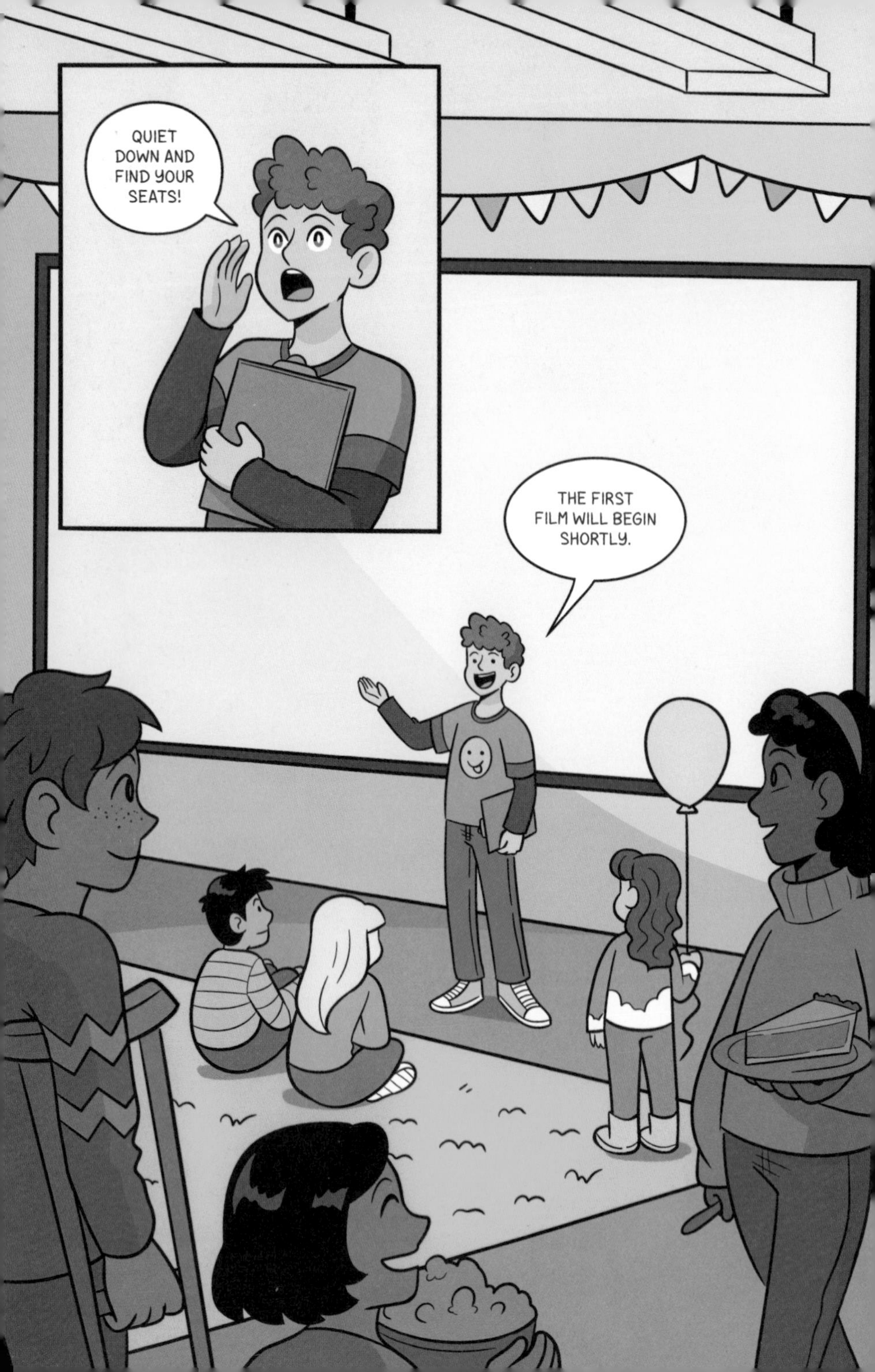
QUIET DOWN AND FIND YOUR SEATS!
THE FIRST FILM WILL BEGIN SHORTLY.

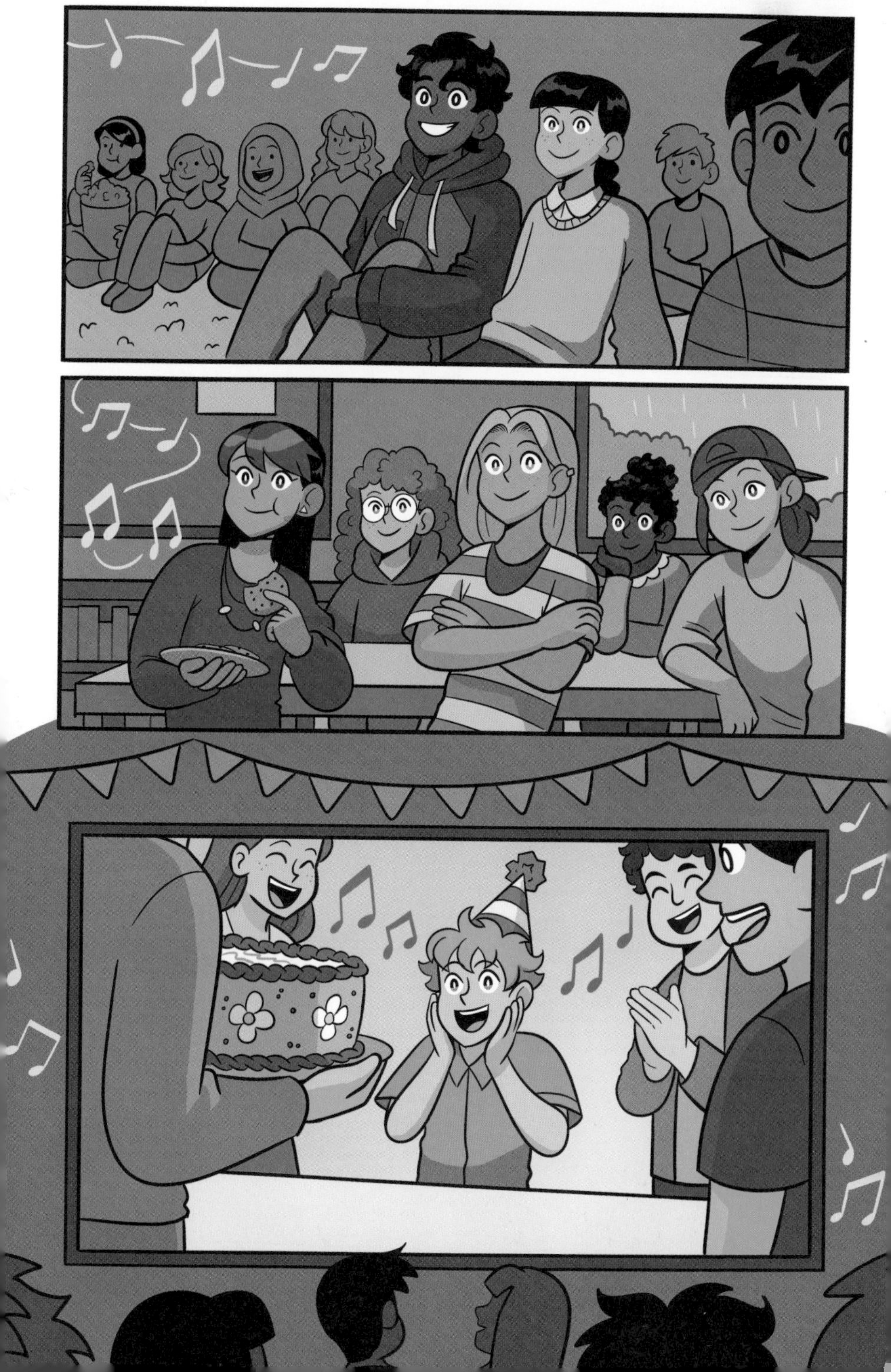

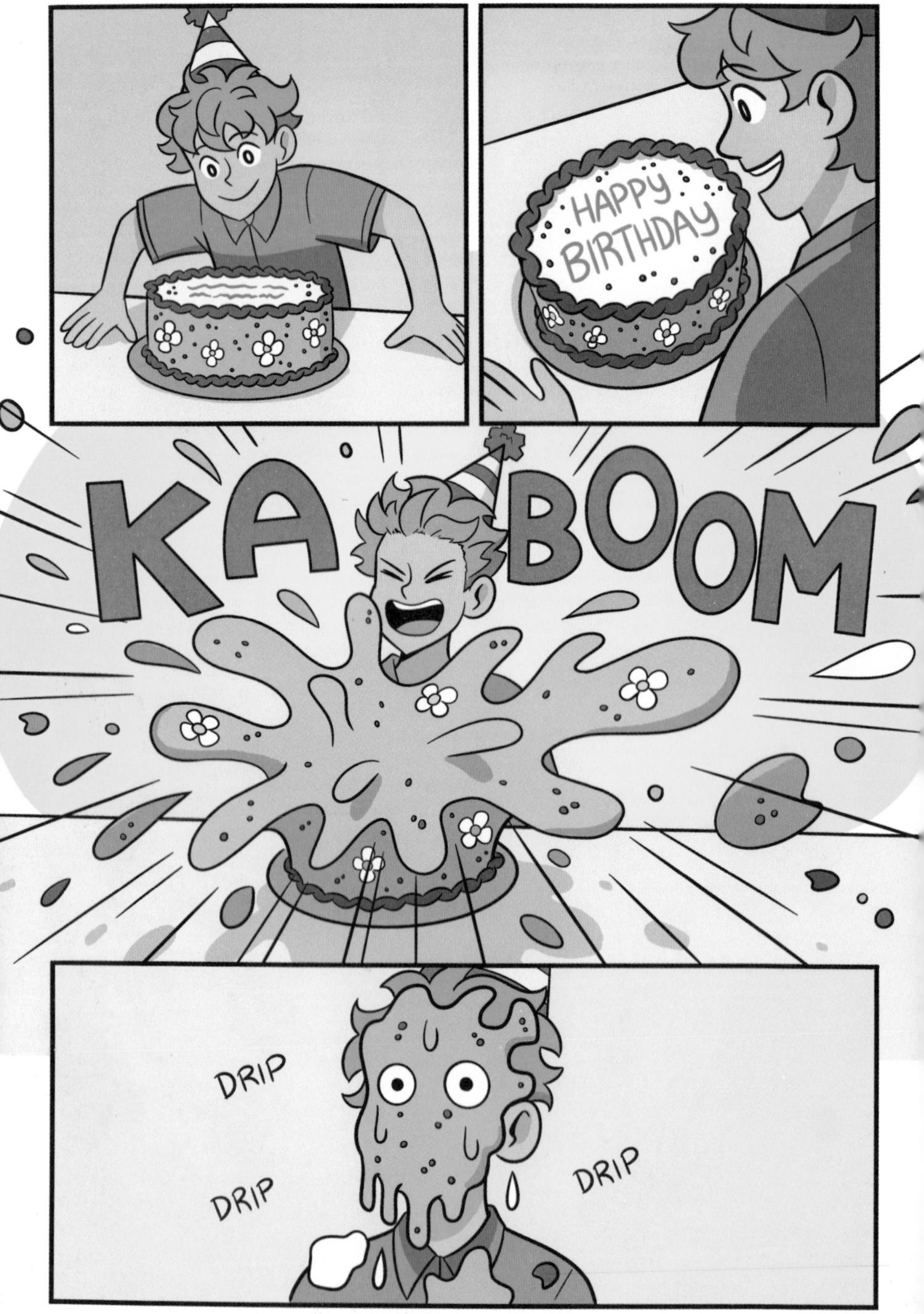
HAPPY BIRTHDAY
KA BOOM
DRIP
DRIP
DRIP

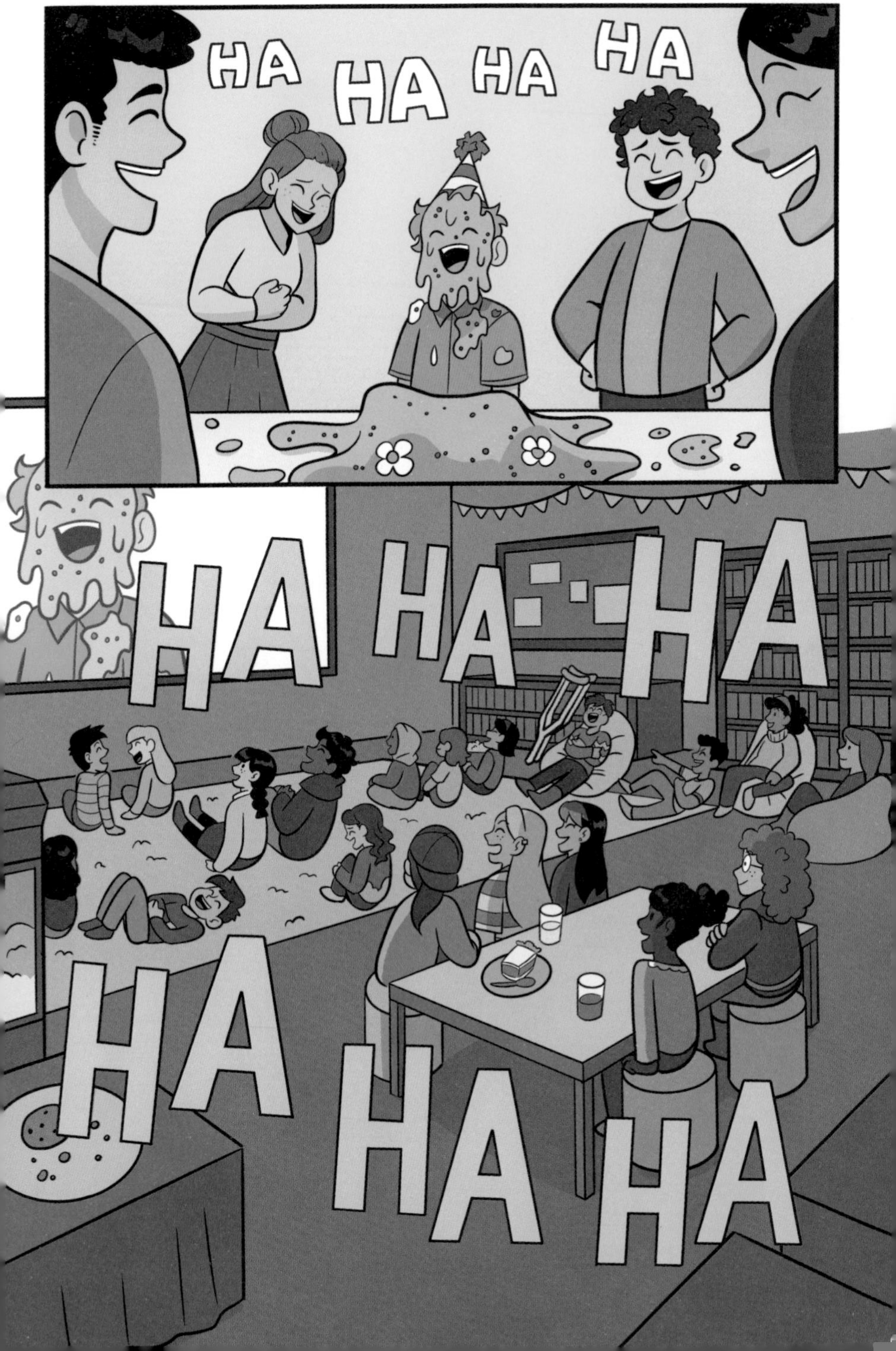
HA HA HA HA
HA HA HA
HA HA HA

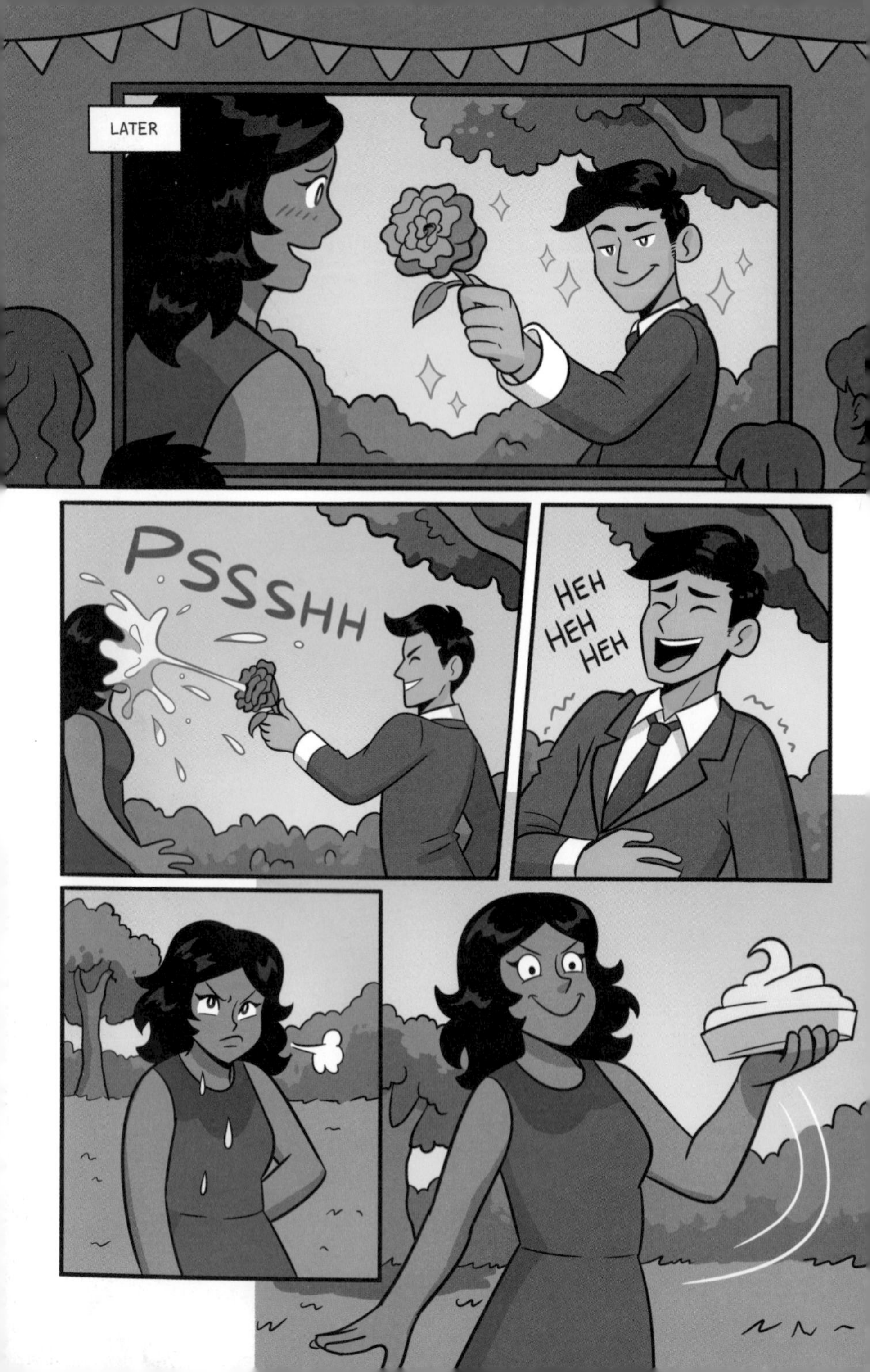
LATER
PSSSHH
HEH
HEH
HEH

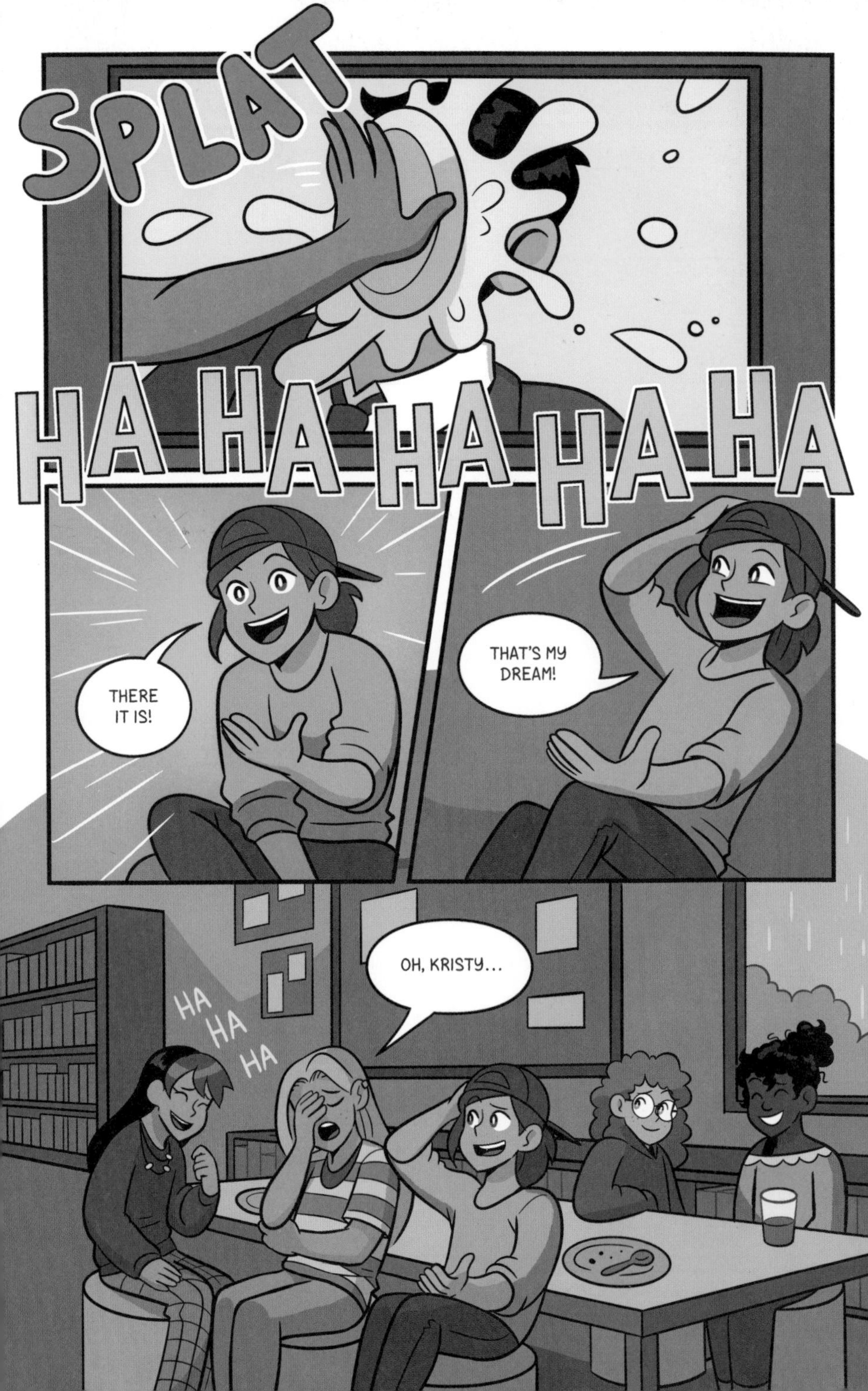
SPLAT
HA HA HA HA HA
THERE IT IS!
THAT'S MY DREAM!
HA
HA
HA
OH, KRISTY...

CHAPTER 2

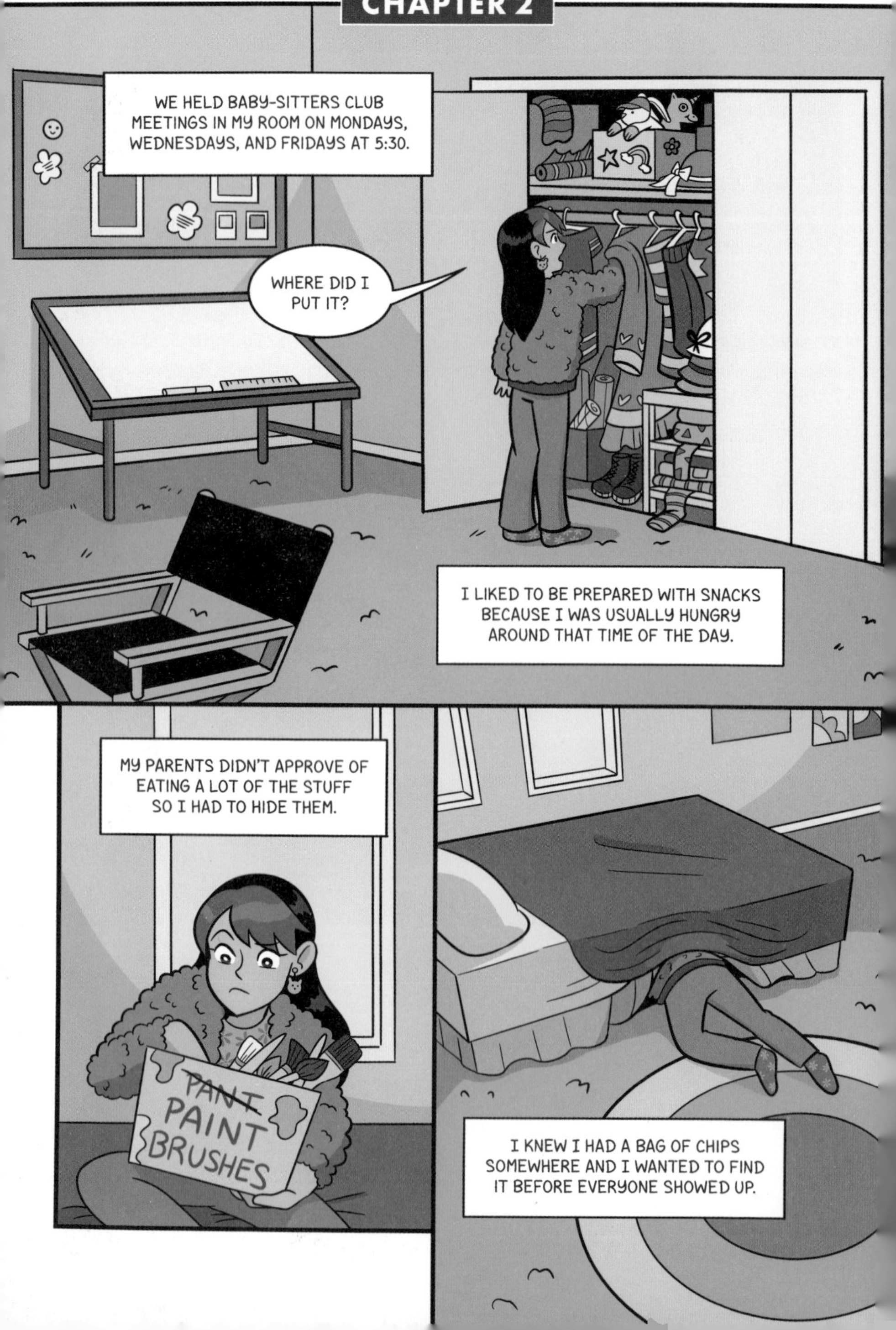
WE HELD BABY-SITTERS CLUB MEETINGS IN MY ROOM ON MONDAYS, WEDNESDAYS, AND FRIDAYS AT 5:30.
WHERE DID I PUT IT?
I LIKED TO BE PREPARED WITH SNACKS BECAUSE I WAS USUALLY HUNGRY AROUND THAT TIME OF THE DAY.
MY PARENTS DIDN'T APPROVE OF EATING A LOT OF THE STUFF SO I HAD TO HIDE THEM.
PANT PAINT BRUSHES
I KNEW I HAD A BAG OF CHIPS SOMEWHERE AND I WANTED TO FIND IT BEFORE EVERYONE SHOWED UP.

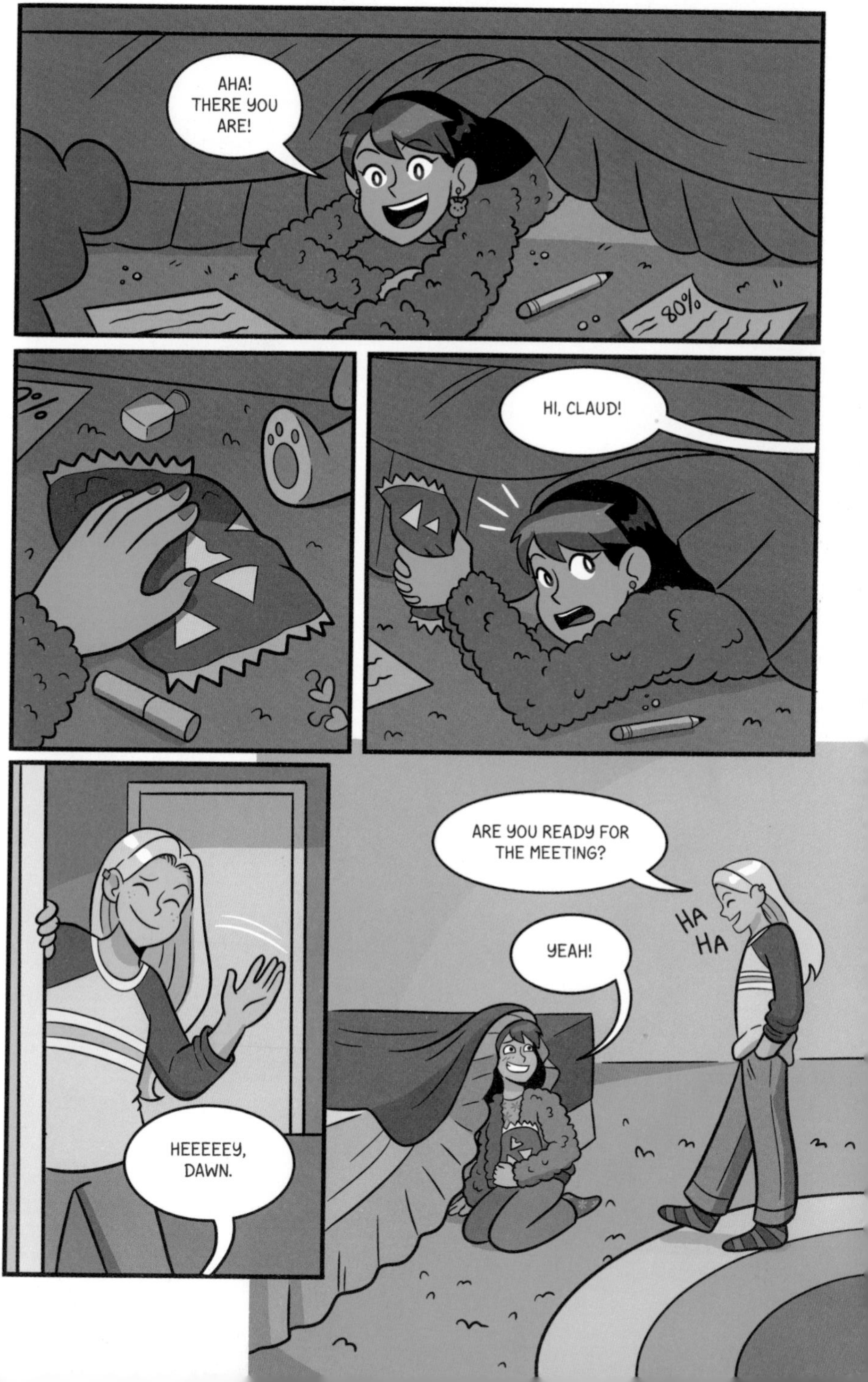
AHA! THERE YOU ARE!
80%
HI, CLAUD!
HEEEEEY, DAWN.
ARE YOU READY FOR THE MEETING?
HA HA
YEAH!

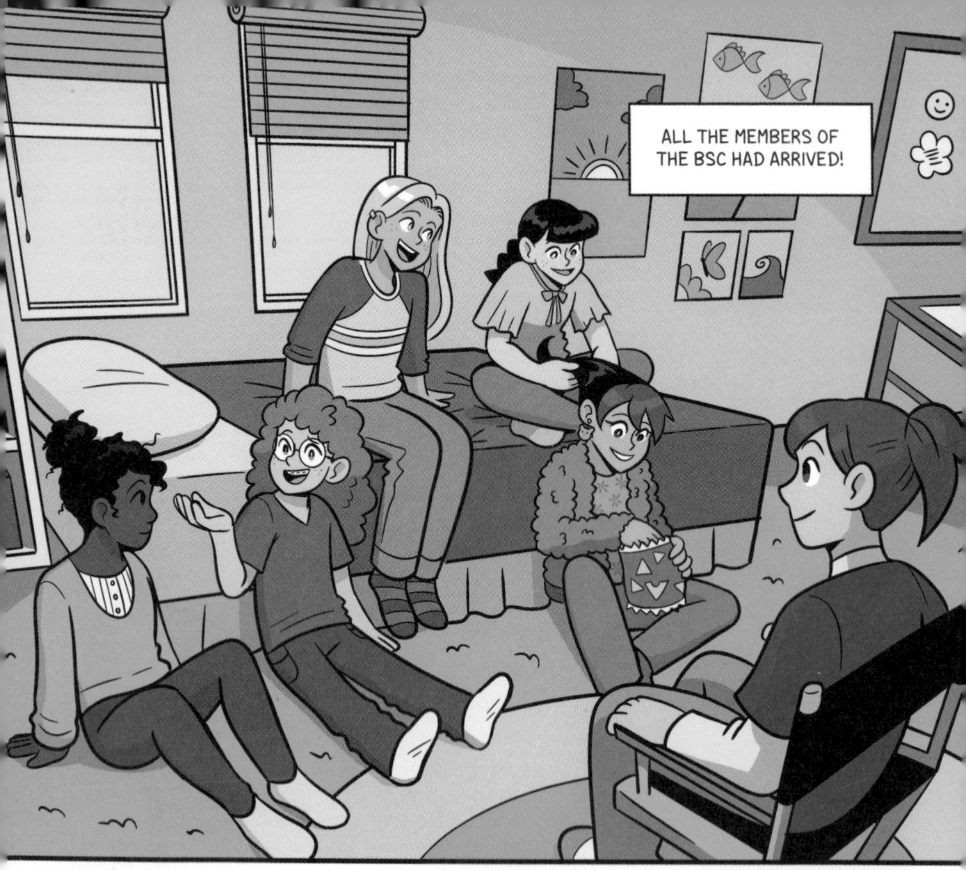
ALL THE MEMBERS OF THE BSC HAD ARRIVED!
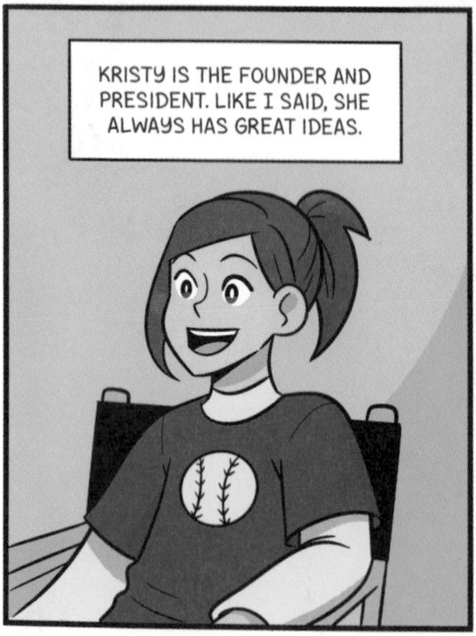
KRISTY IS THE FOUNDER AND PRESIDENT. LIKE I SAID, SHE ALWAYS HAS GREAT IDEAS.
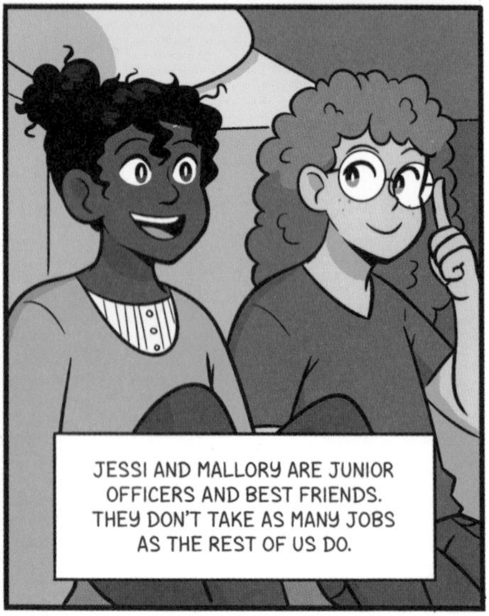
JESSI AND MALLORY ARE JUNIOR OFFICERS AND BEST FRIENDS. THEY DON'T TAKE AS MANY JOBS AS THE REST OF US DO.

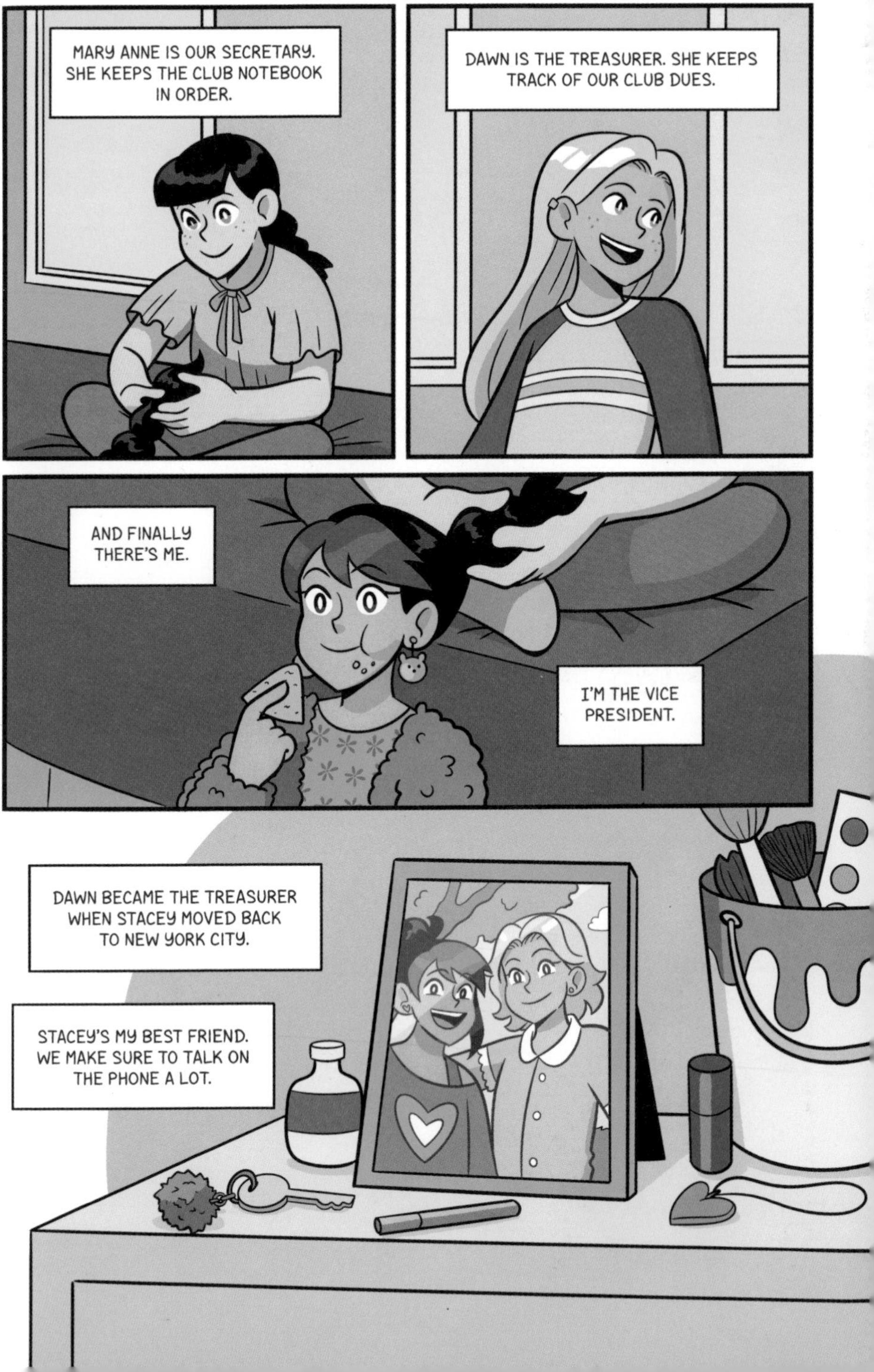
MARY ANNE IS OUR SECRETARY. SHE KEEPS THE CLUB NOTEBOOK IN ORDER.
DAWN IS THE TREASURER. SHE KEEPS TRACK OF OUR CLUB DUES.
AND FINALLY THERE'S ME.
I'M THE VICE PRESIDENT.
DAWN BECAME THE TREASURER WHEN STACEY MOVED BACK TO NEW YORK CITY.
STACEY'S MY BEST FRIEND. WE MAKE SURE TO TALK ON THE PHONE A LOT.

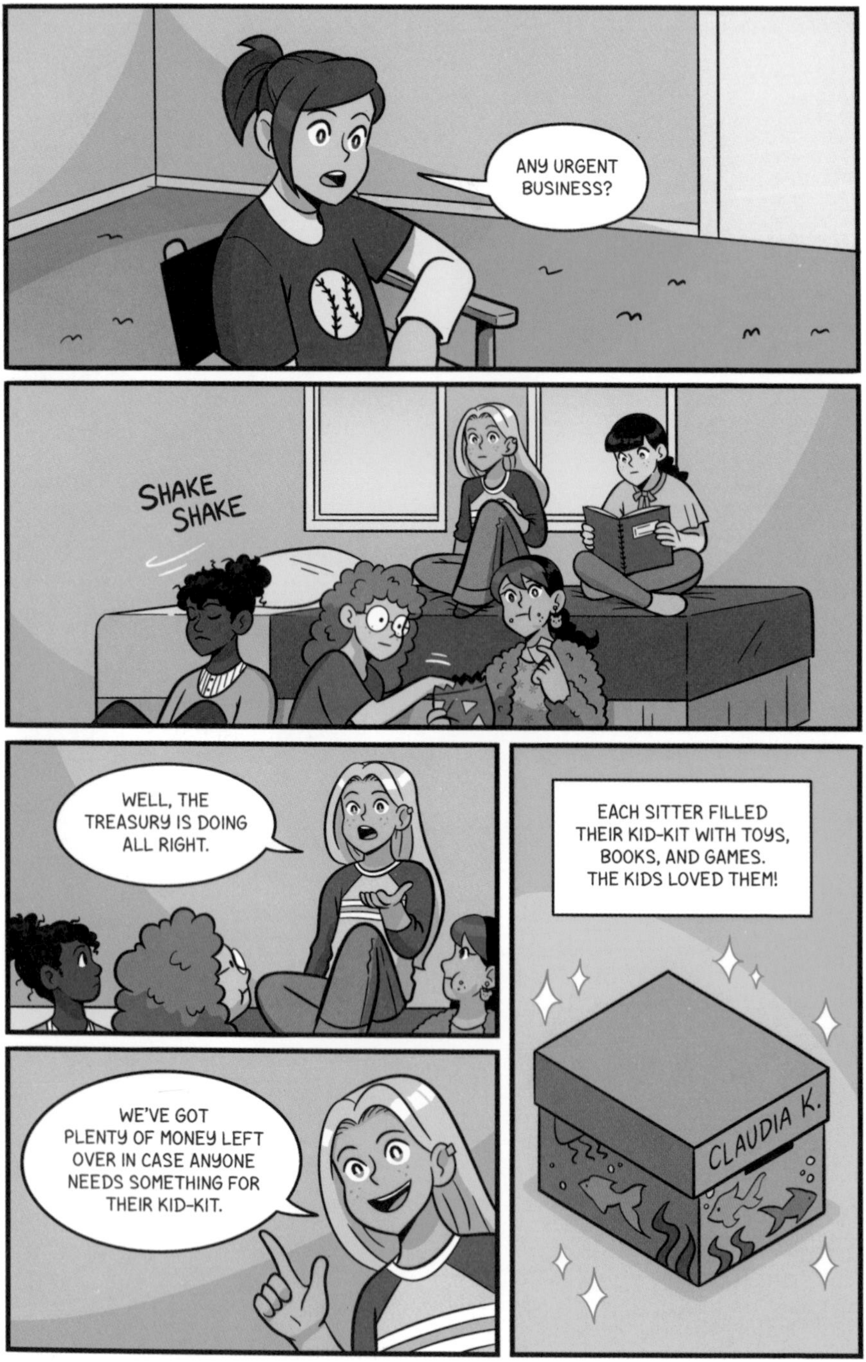
ANY URGENT BUSINESS?
SHAKE SHAKE
WELL, THE TREASURY IS DOING ALL RIGHT.
WE'VE GOT PLENTY OF MONEY LEFT OVER IN CASE ANYONE NEEDS SOMETHING FOR THEIR KID-KIT.
EACH SITTER FILLED THEIR KID-KIT WITH TOYS, BOOKS, AND GAMES. THE KIDS LOVED THEM!
CLAUDIA K.

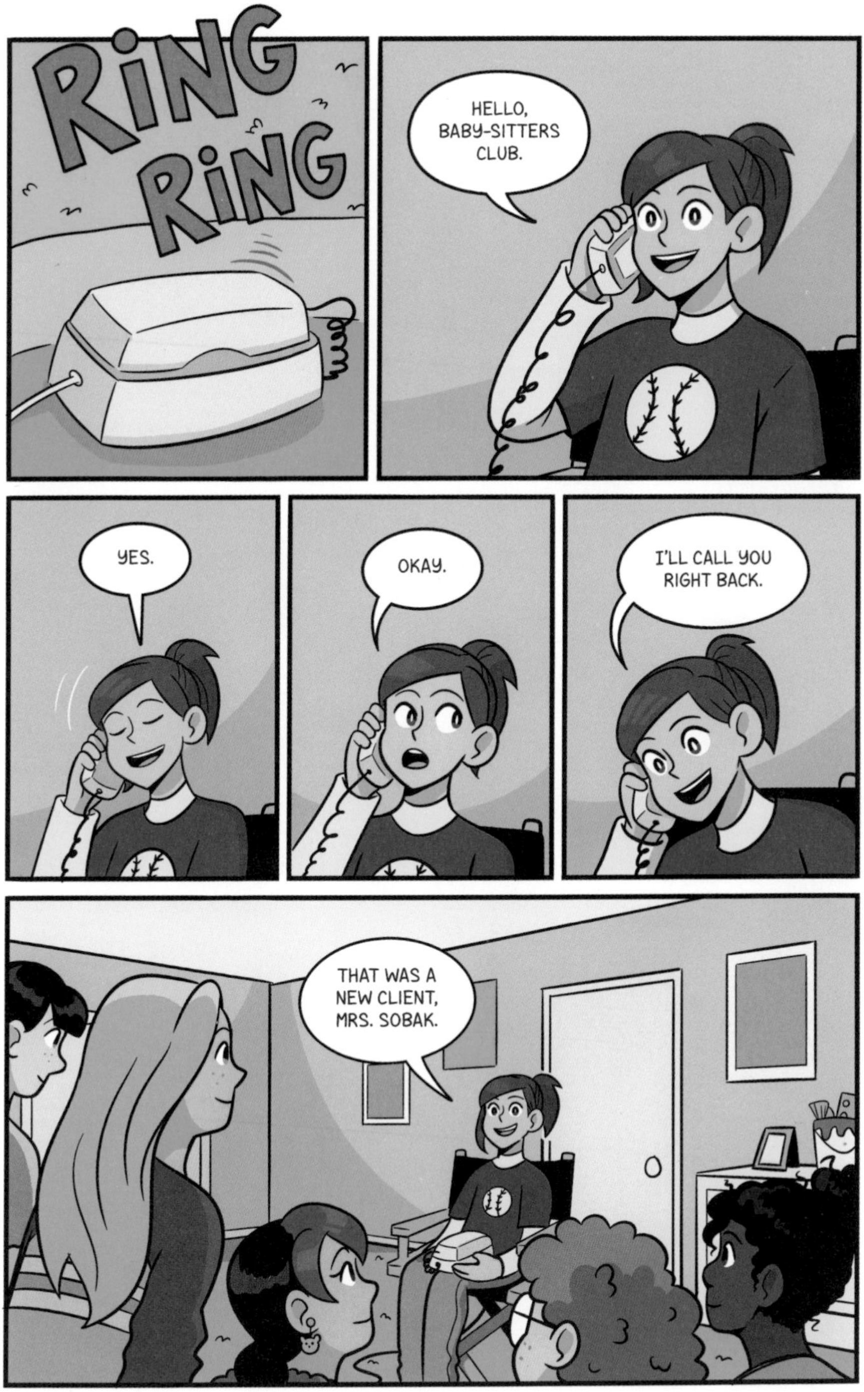
RING
RING
HELLO, BABY-SITTERS CLUB.
YES.
OKAY.
I'LL CALL YOU RIGHT BACK.
THAT WAS A NEW CLIENT, MRS. SOBAK.

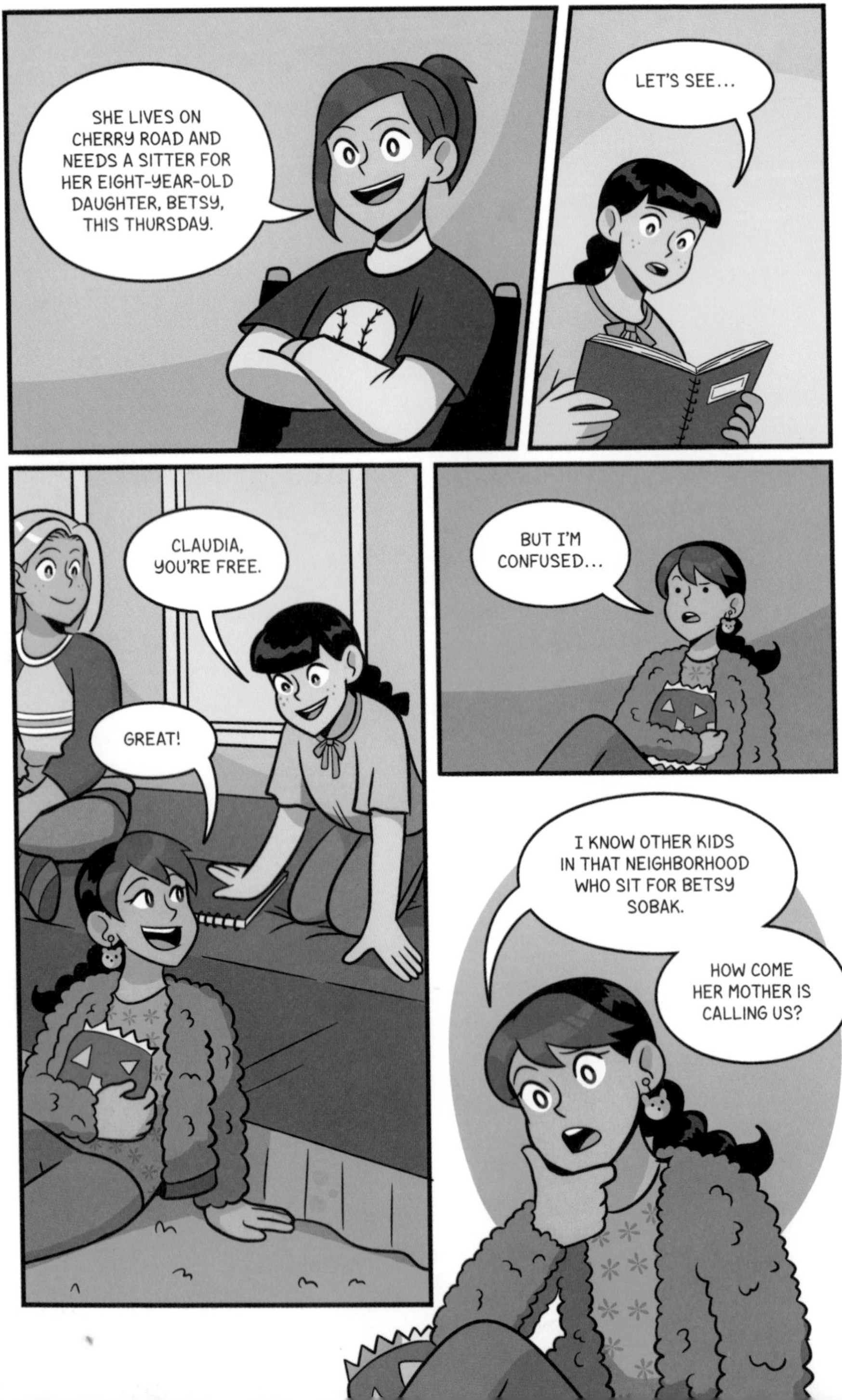
SHE LIVES ON CHERRY ROAD AND NEEDS A SITTER FOR HER EIGHT-YEAR-OLD DAUGHTER, BETSY, THIS THURSDAY.
LET'S SEE...
CLAUDIA, YOU'RE FREE.
GREAT!
BUT I'M CONFUSED...
I KNOW OTHER KIDS IN THAT NEIGHBORHOOD WHO SIT FOR BETSY SOBAK.
HOW COME HER MOTHER IS CALLING US?

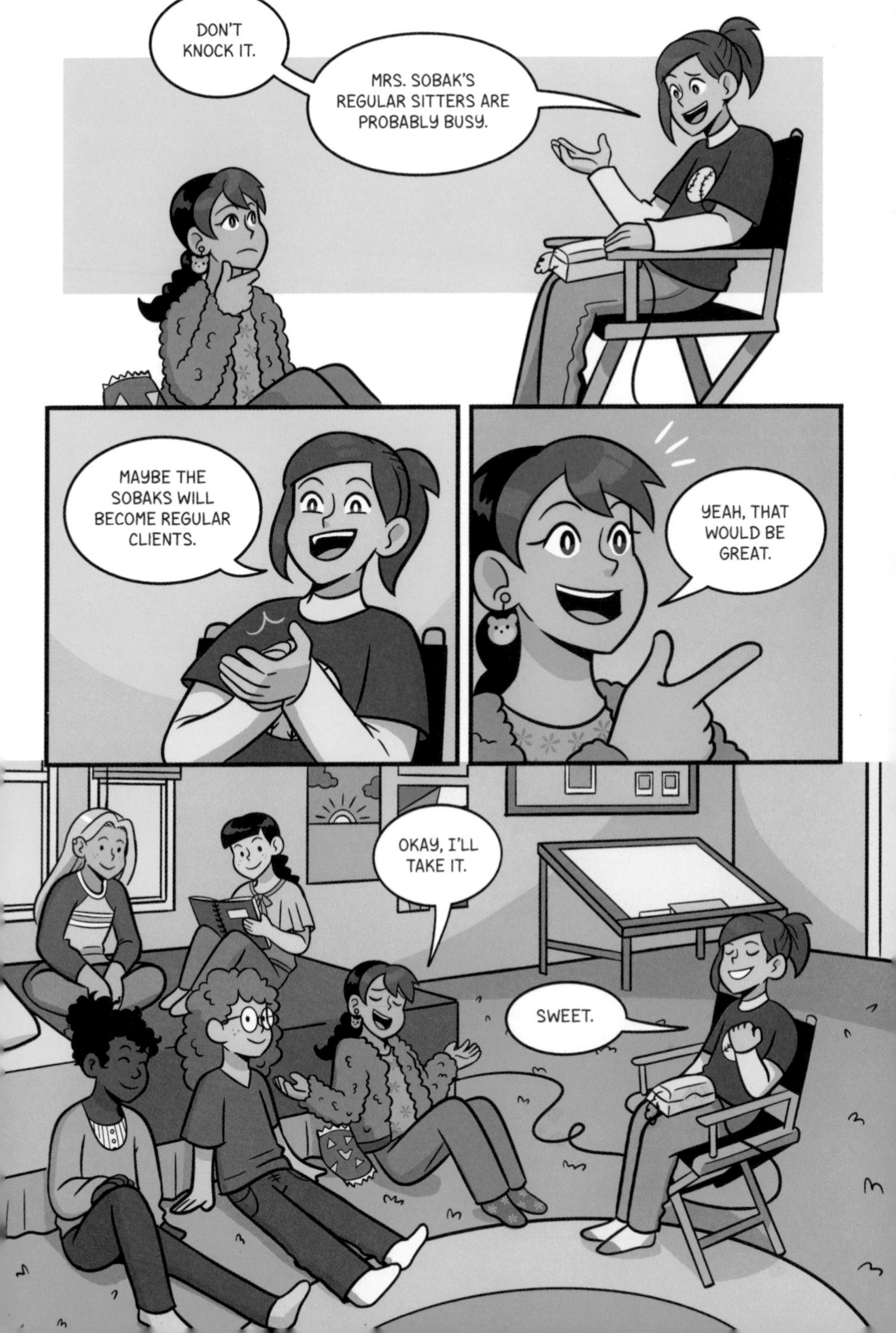
DON'T KNOCK IT.
MRS. SOBAK'S REGULAR SITTERS ARE PROBABLY BUSY.
MAYBE THE SOBAKS WILL BECOME REGULAR CLIENTS.
YEAH, THAT WOULD BE GREAT.
OKAY, I'LL TAKE IT.
SWEET.

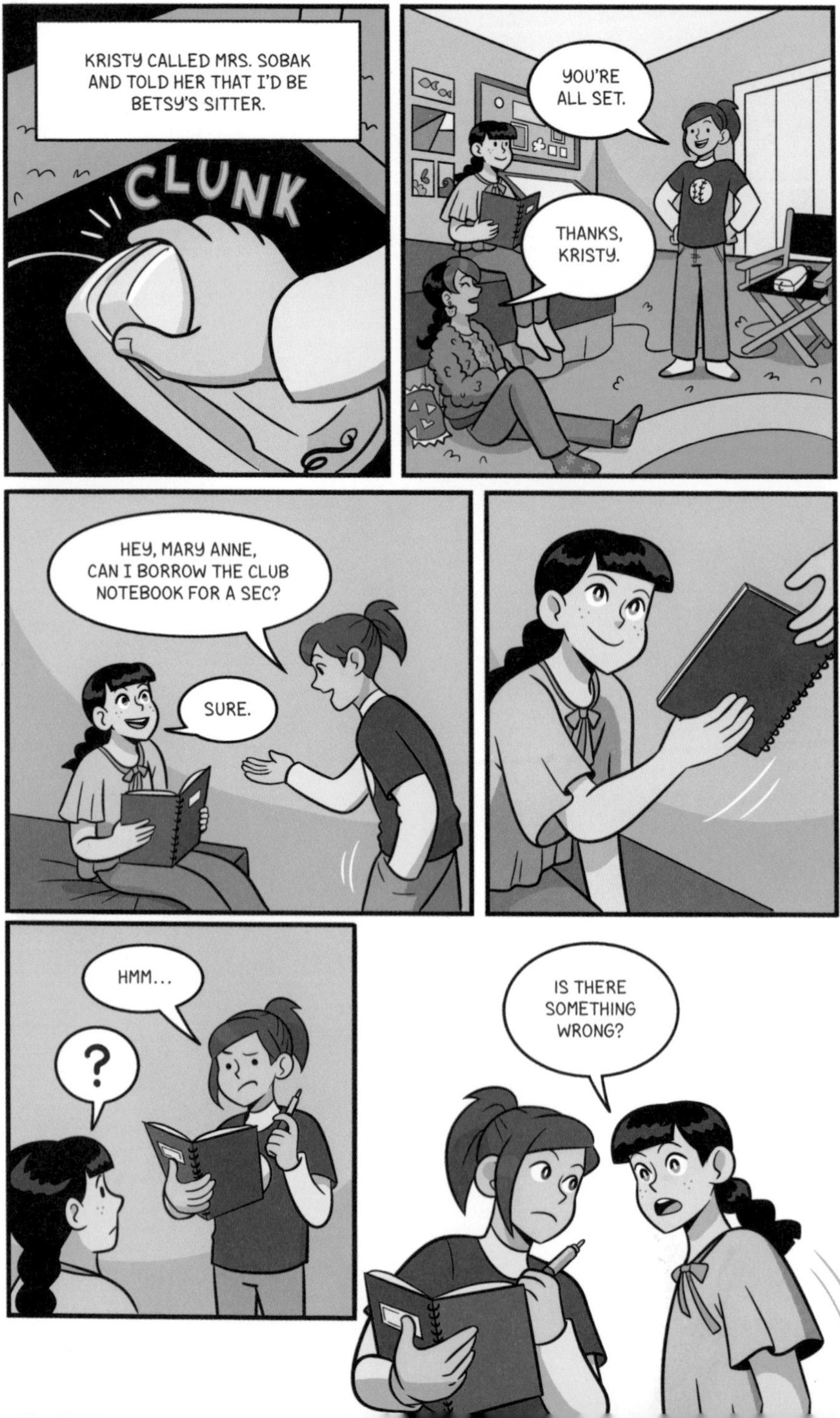
KRISTY CALLED MRS. SOBAK AND TOLD HER THAT I'D BE BETSY'S SITTER.
CLUNK
YOU'RE ALL SET.
THANKS, KRISTY.
HEY, MARY ANNE, CAN I BORROW THE CLUB NOTEBOOK FOR A SEC?
SURE.
HMM...
?
IS THERE SOMETHING WRONG?

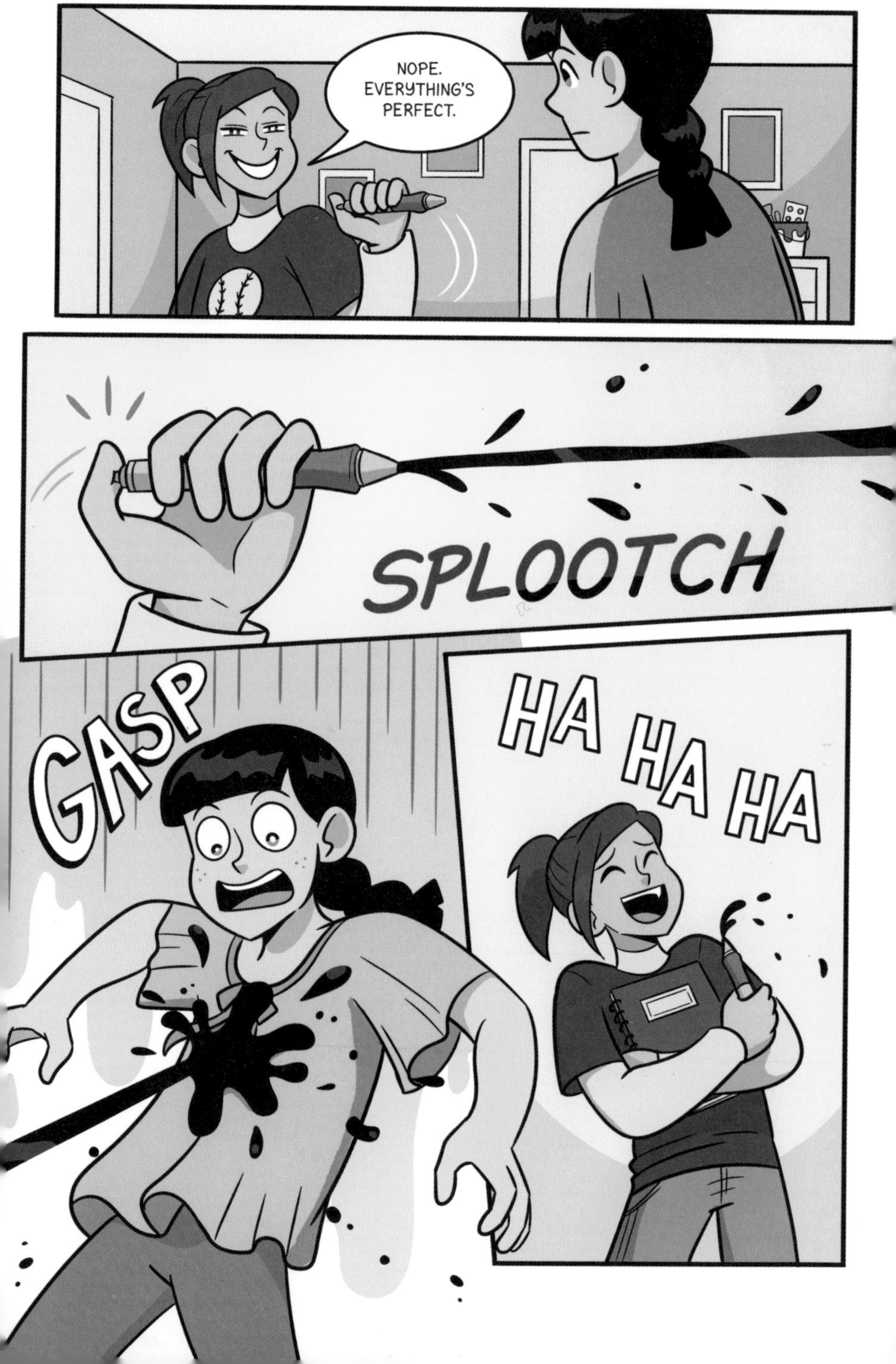
NOPE. EVERYTHING'S PERFECT.
SPLOOTCH
GASP
HA HA HA HA

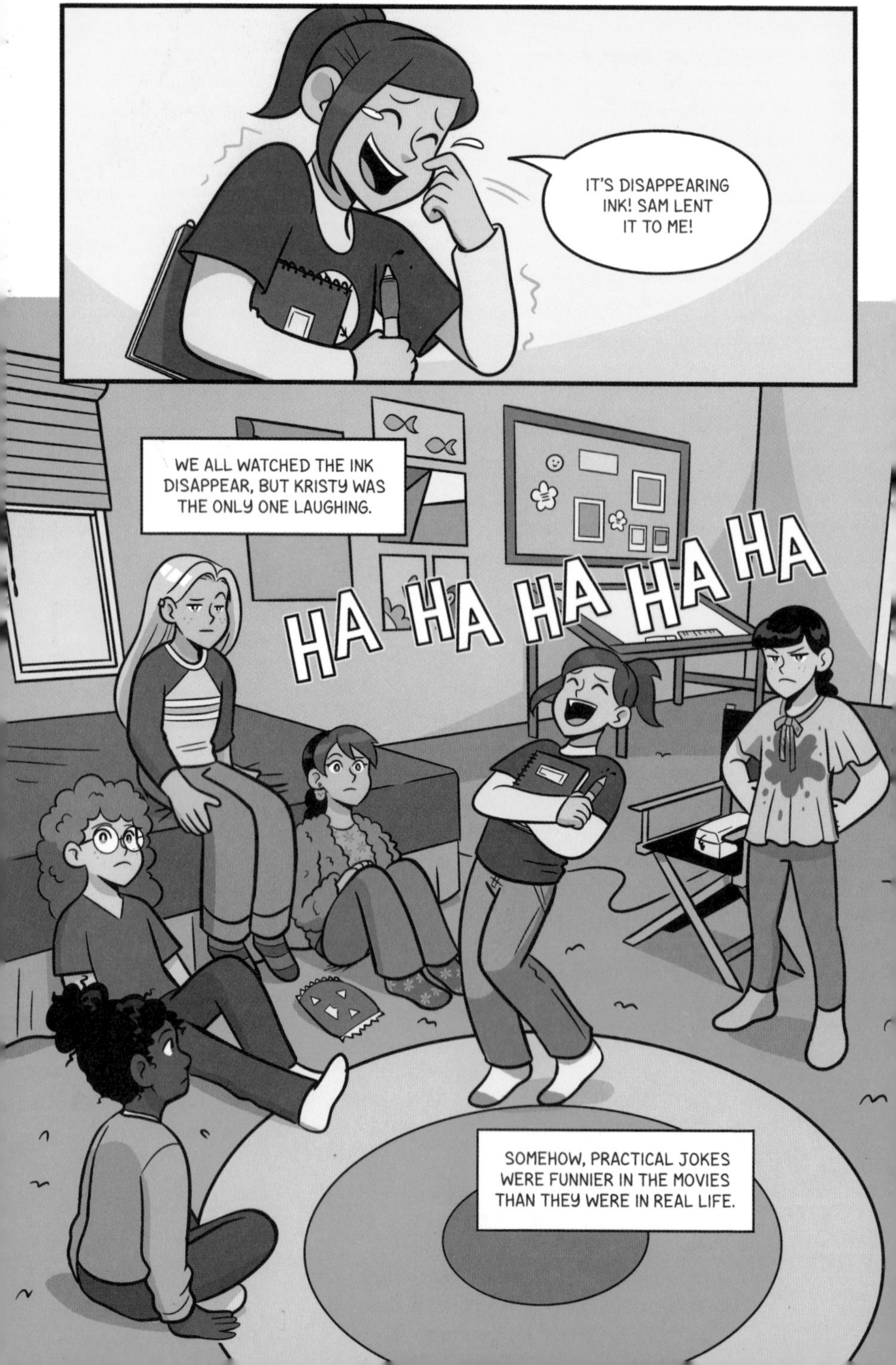
IT'S DISAPPEARING INK! SAM LENT IT TO ME!
WE ALL WATCHED THE INK DISAPPEAR, BUT KRISTY WAS THE ONLY ONE LAUGHING.
HA HA HA HA HA HA
SOMEHOW, PRACTICAL JOKES WERE FUNNIER IN THE MOVIES THAN THEY WERE IN REAL LIFE.

CHAPTER 3

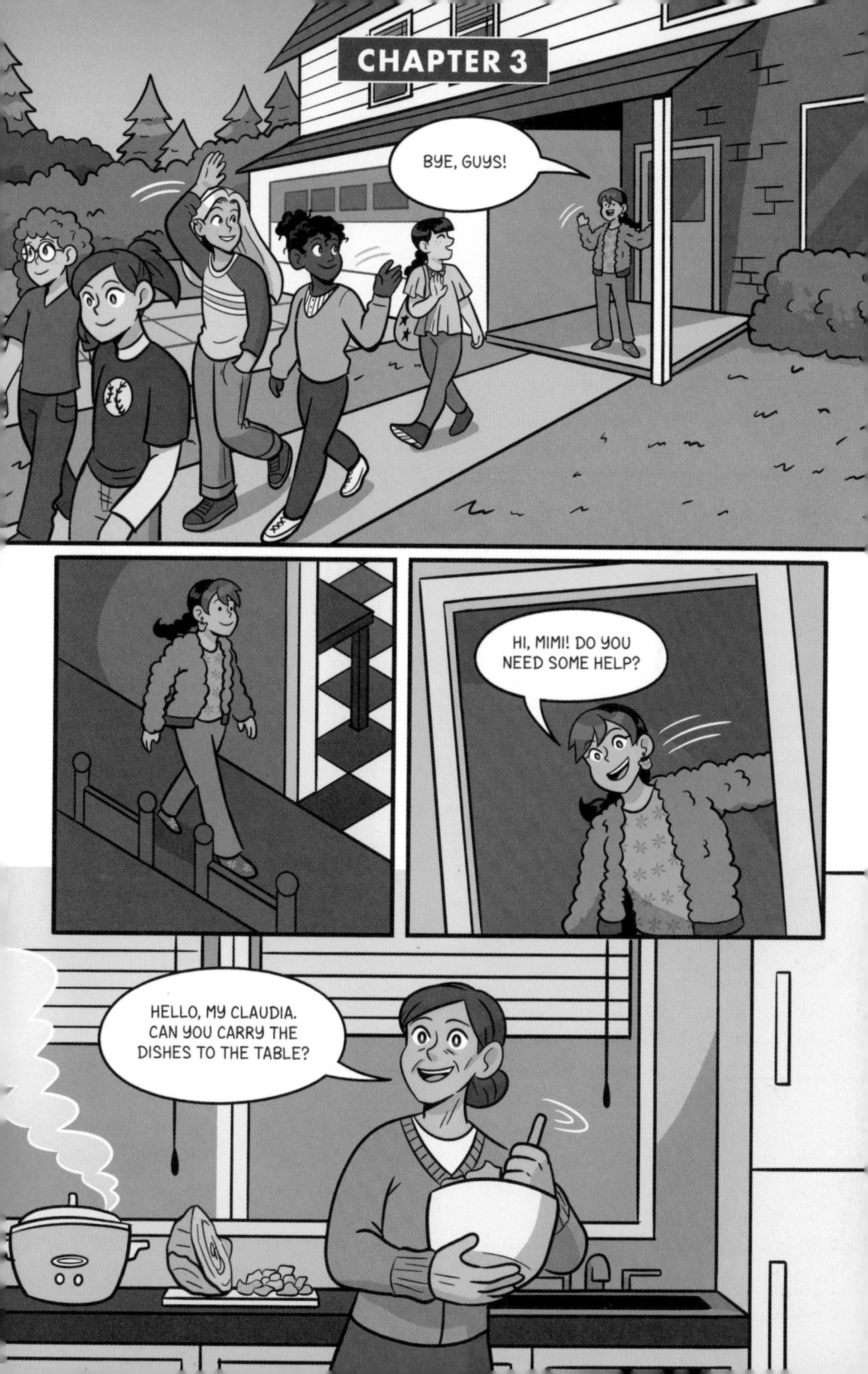
BYE, GUYS!
HI, MIMI! DO YOU NEED SOME HELP?
HELLO, MY CLAUDIA. CAN YOU CARRY THE DISHES TO THE TABLE?

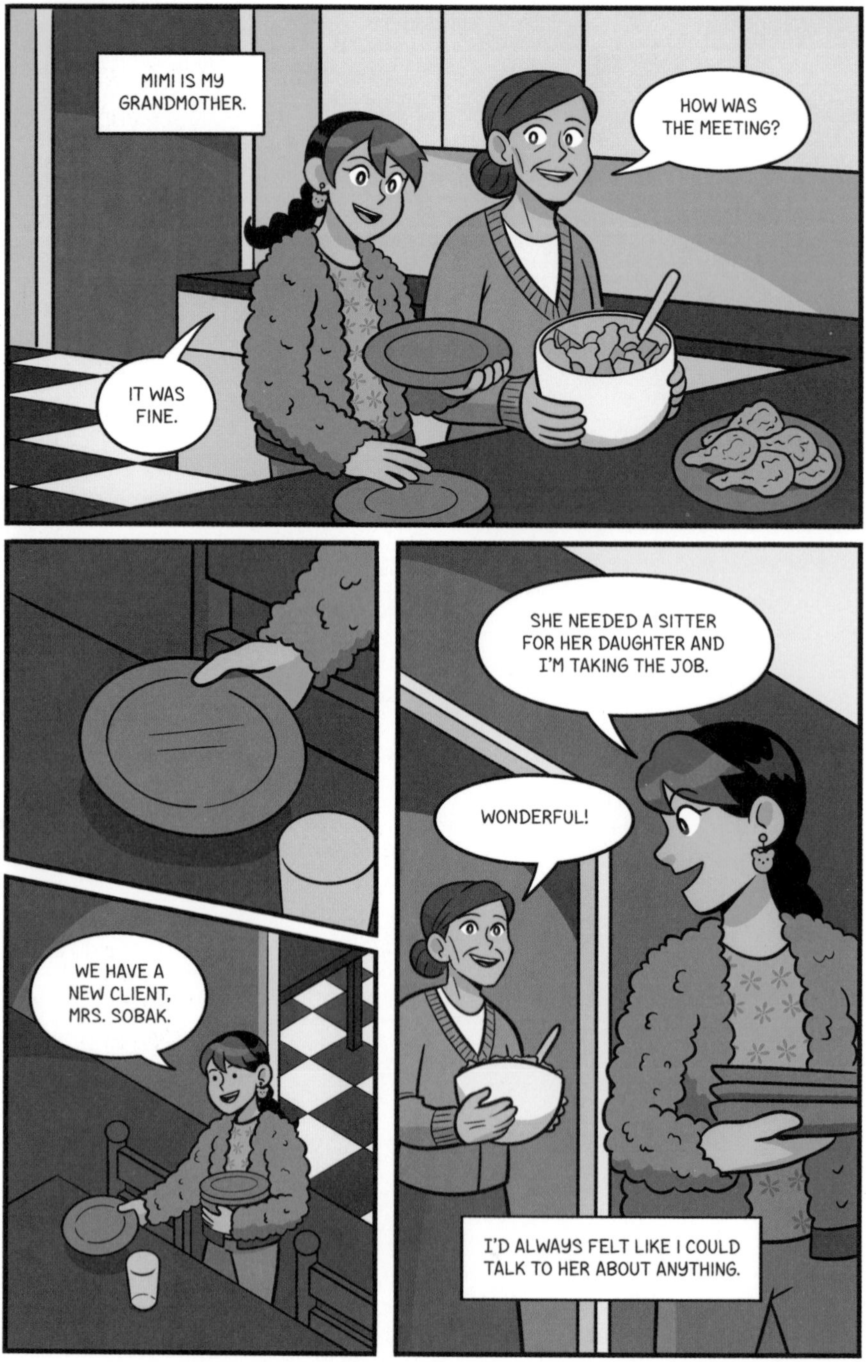
MIMI IS MY GRANDMOTHER.
HOW WAS THE MEETING?
IT WAS FINE.
WE HAVE A NEW CLIENT, MRS. SOBAK.
SHE NEEDED A SITTER FOR HER DAUGHTER AND I'M TAKING THE JOB.
WONDERFUL!
I'D ALWAYS FELT LIKE I COULD TALK TO HER ABOUT ANYTHING.

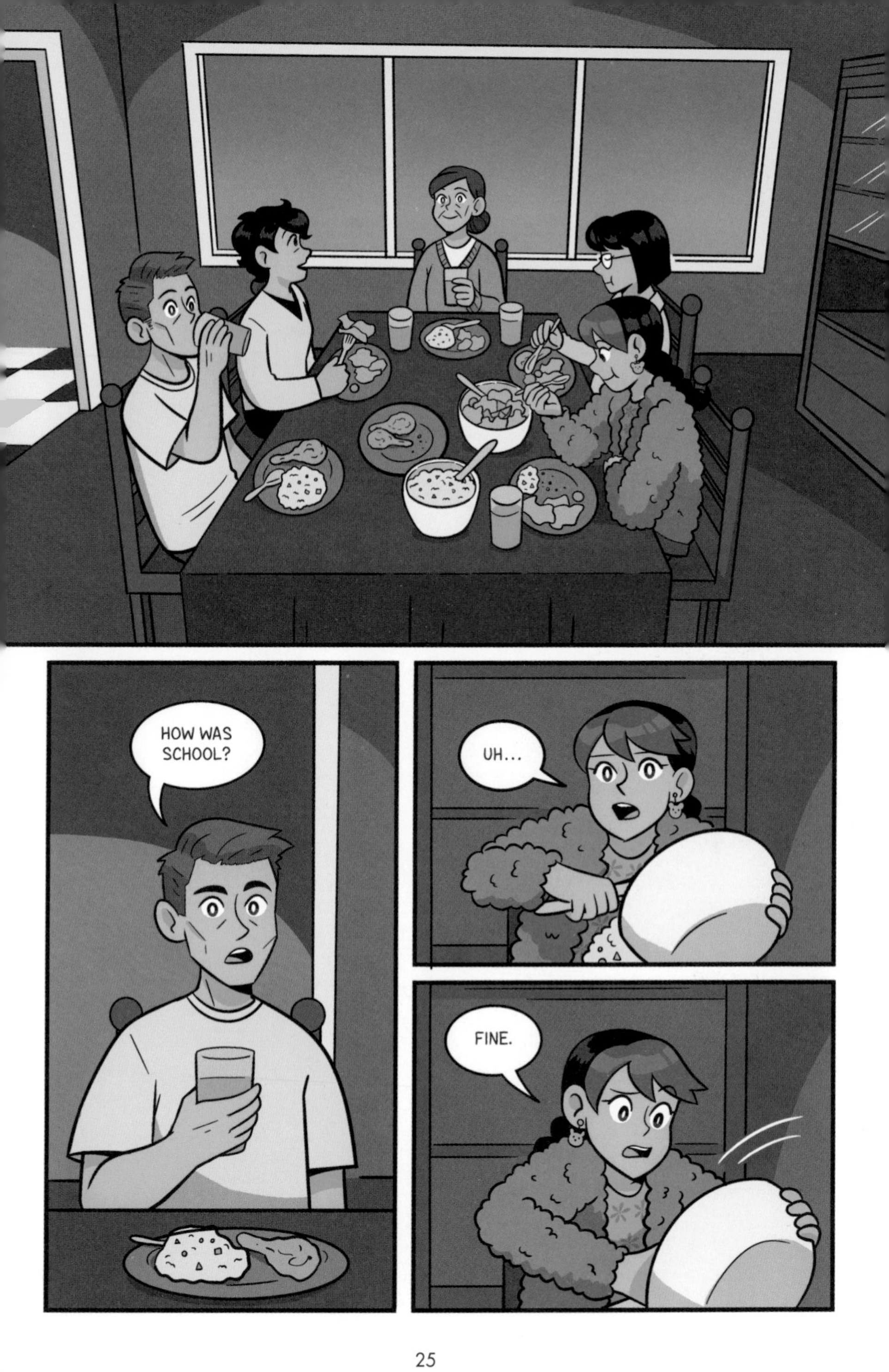
HOW WAS SCHOOL?
UH...
FINE.

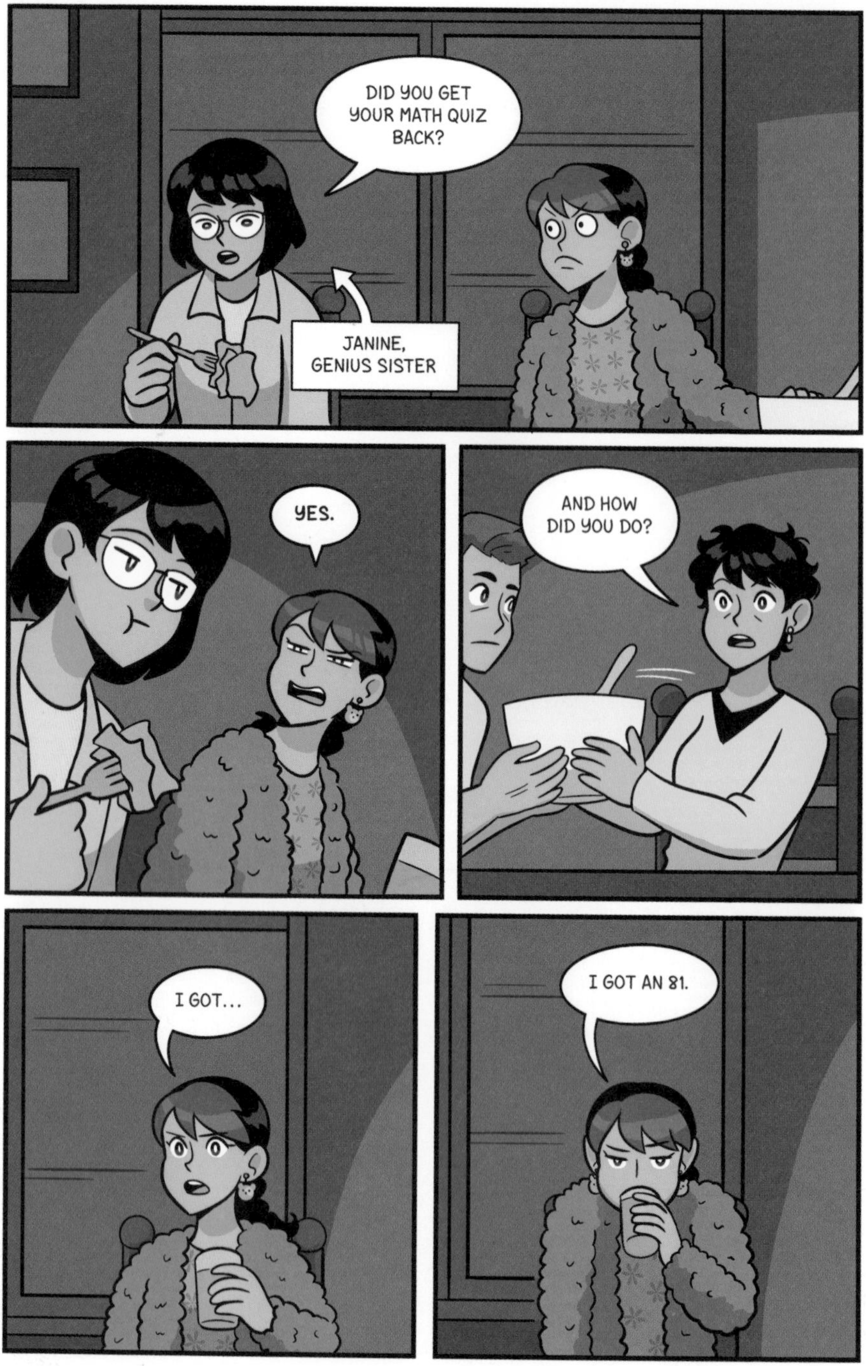
DID YOU GET YOUR MATH QUIZ BACK?
JANINE, GENIUS SISTER
YES.
AND HOW DID YOU DO?
I GOT...
I GOT AN 81.

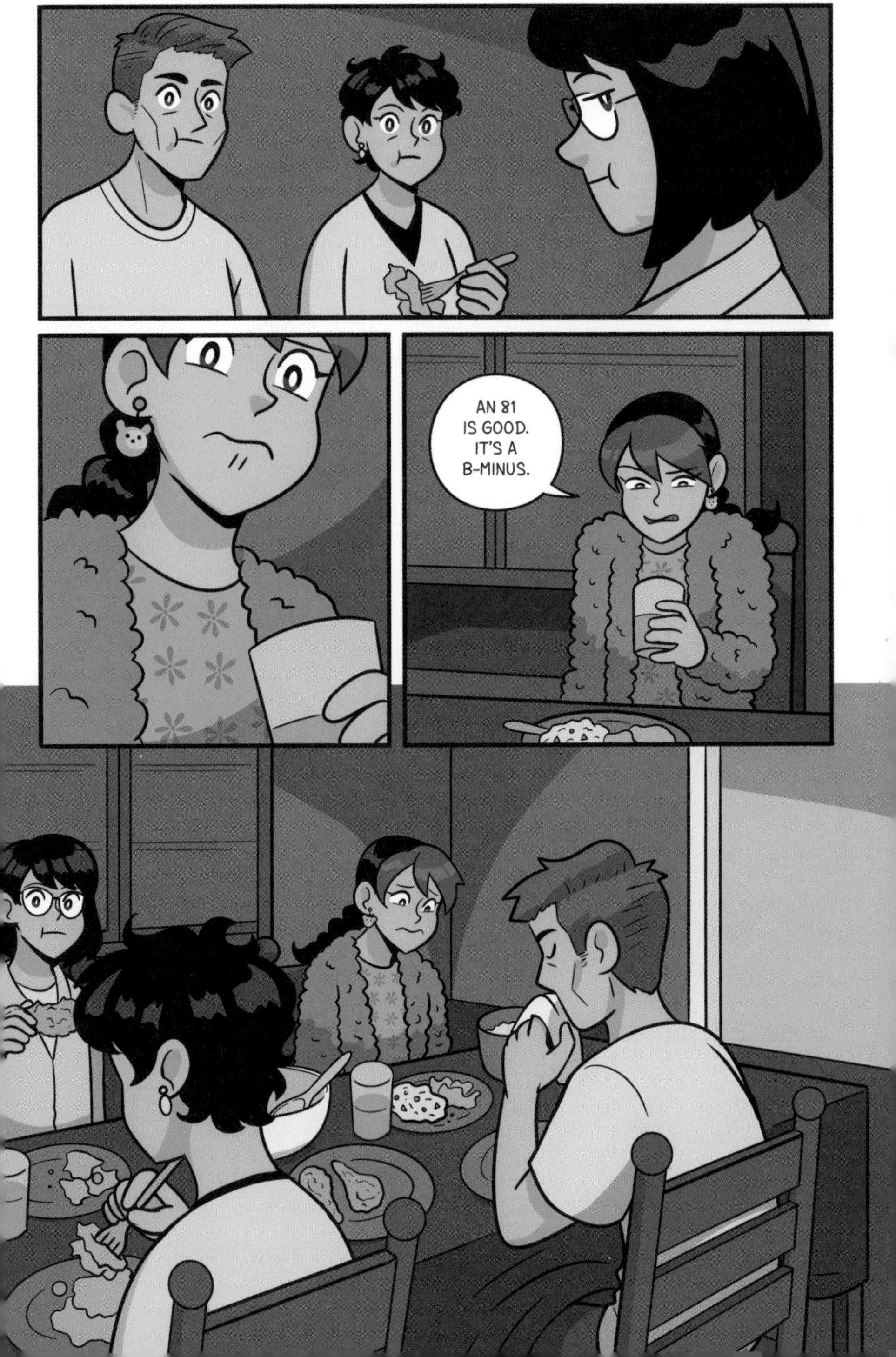
AN 81 IS GOOD. IT'S A B-MINUS.

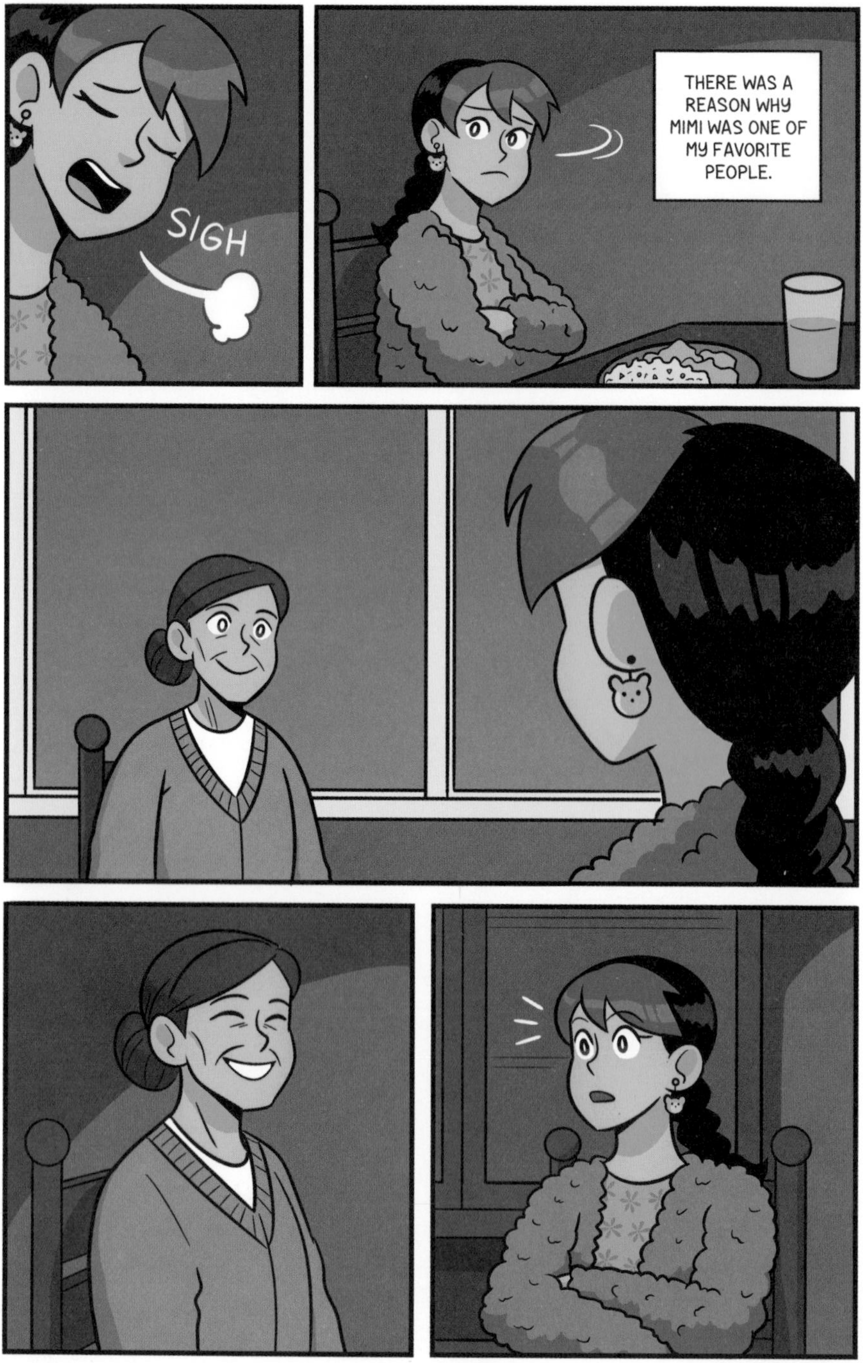
SIGH
THERE WAS A REASON WHY MIMI WAS ONE OF MY FAVORITE PEOPLE.

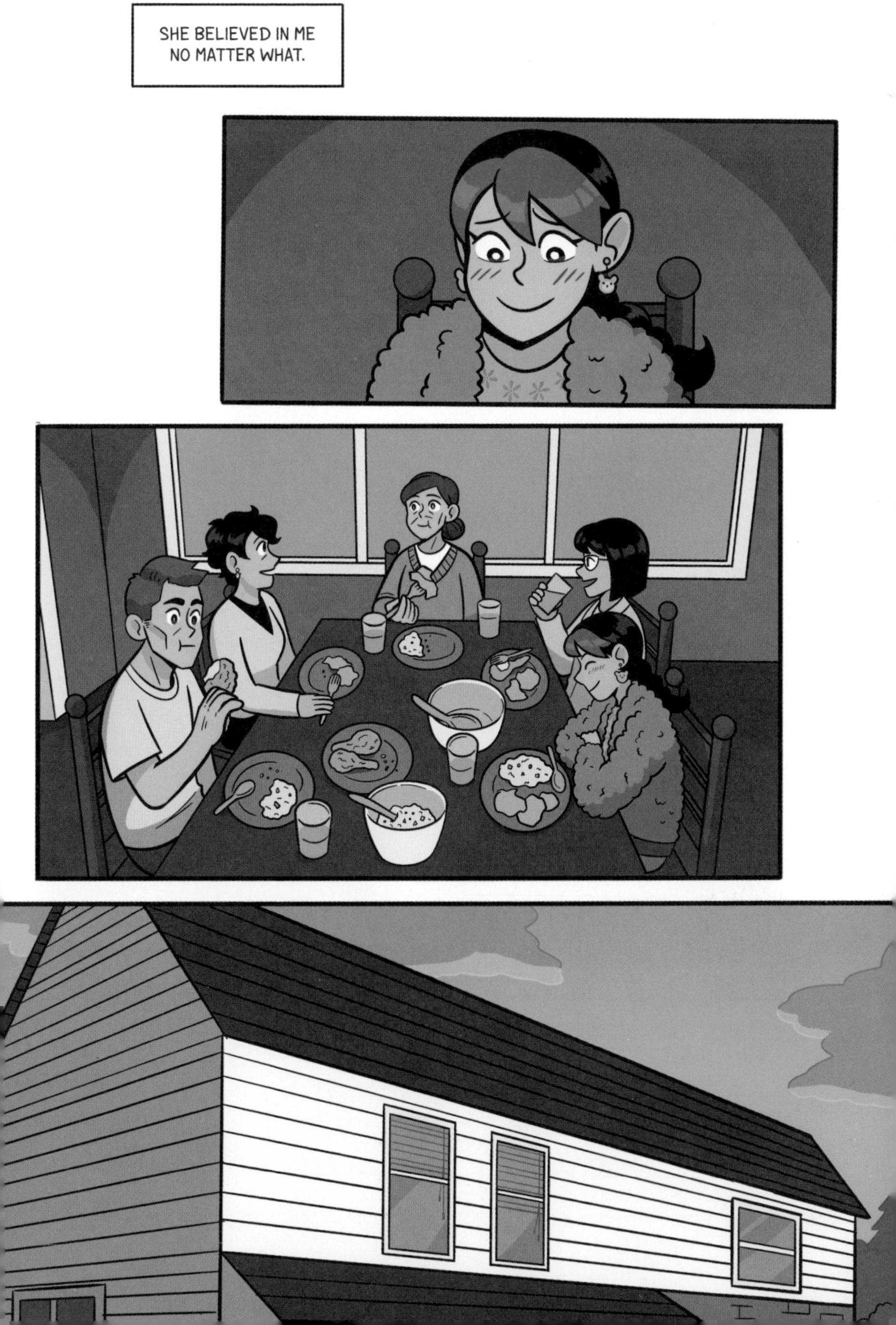
SHE BELIEVED IN ME NO MATTER WHAT.

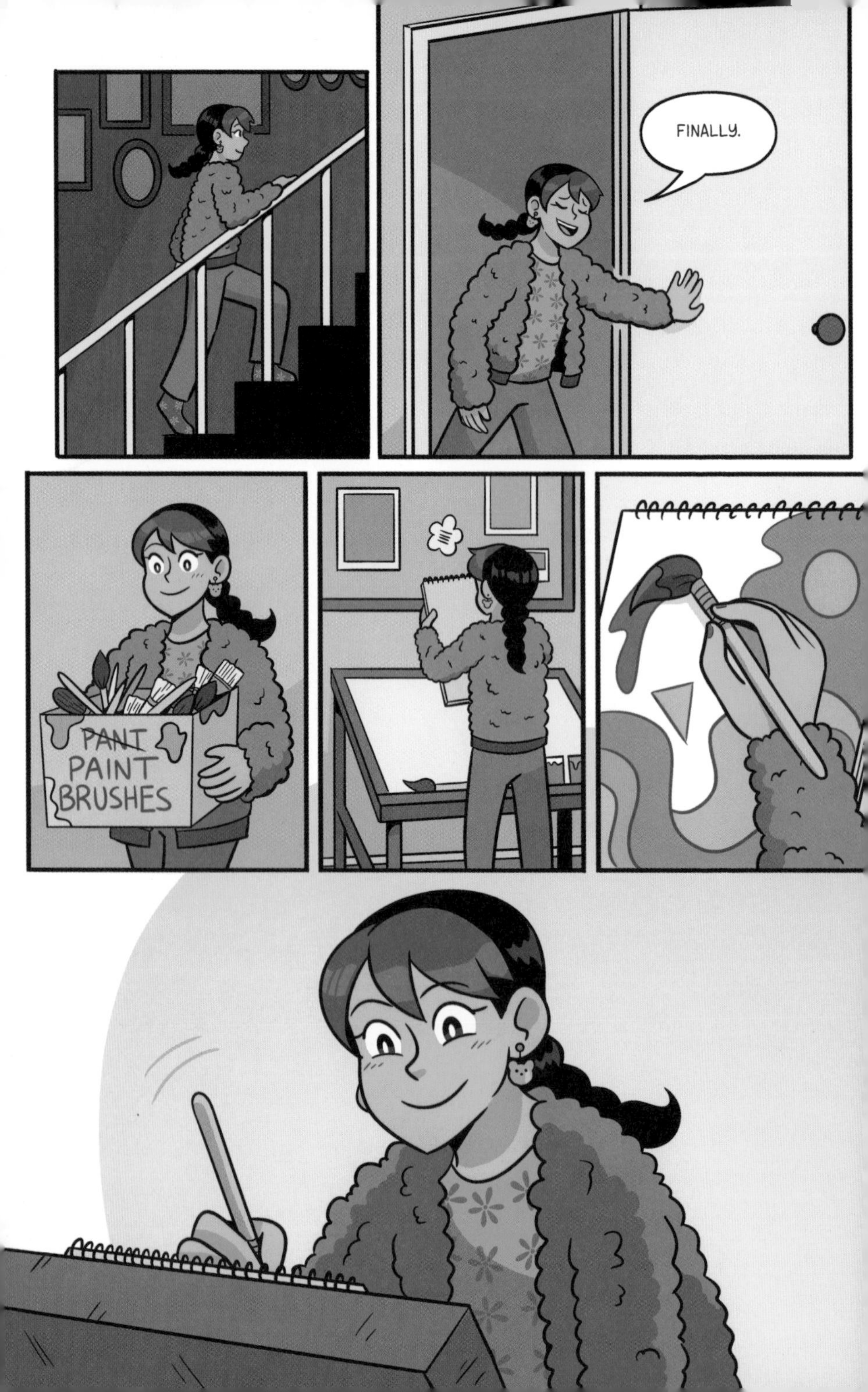
FINALLY.
PANT
PAINT
BRUSHES

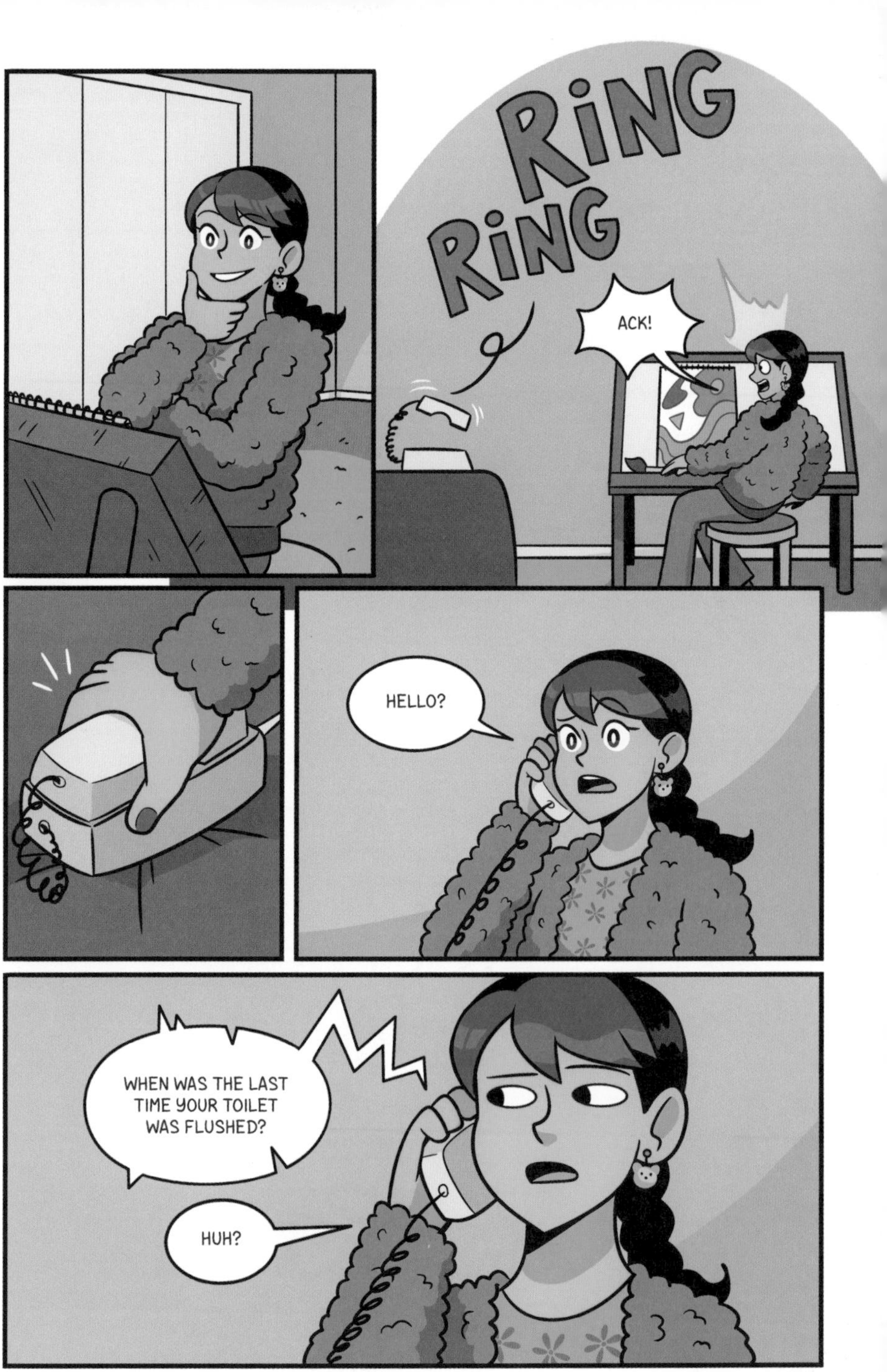
RING
RING
ACK!
HELLO?
WHEN WAS THE LAST TIME YOUR TOILET WAS FLUSHED?
HUH?

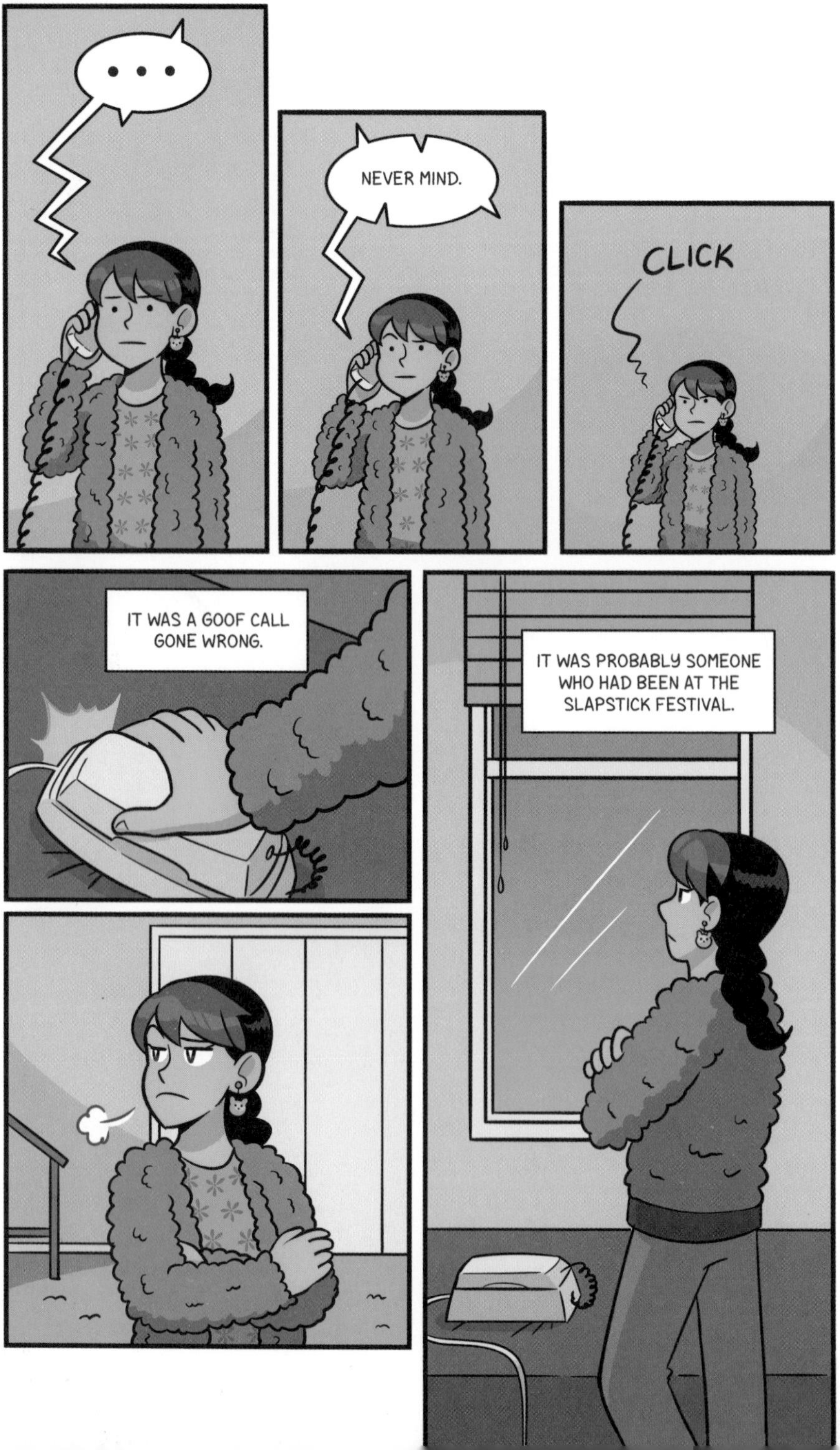
. . .
NEVER MIND.
CLICK
IT WAS A GOOF CALL GONE WRONG.
IT WAS PROBABLY SOMEONE WHO HAD BEEN AT THE SLAPSTICK FESTIVAL.

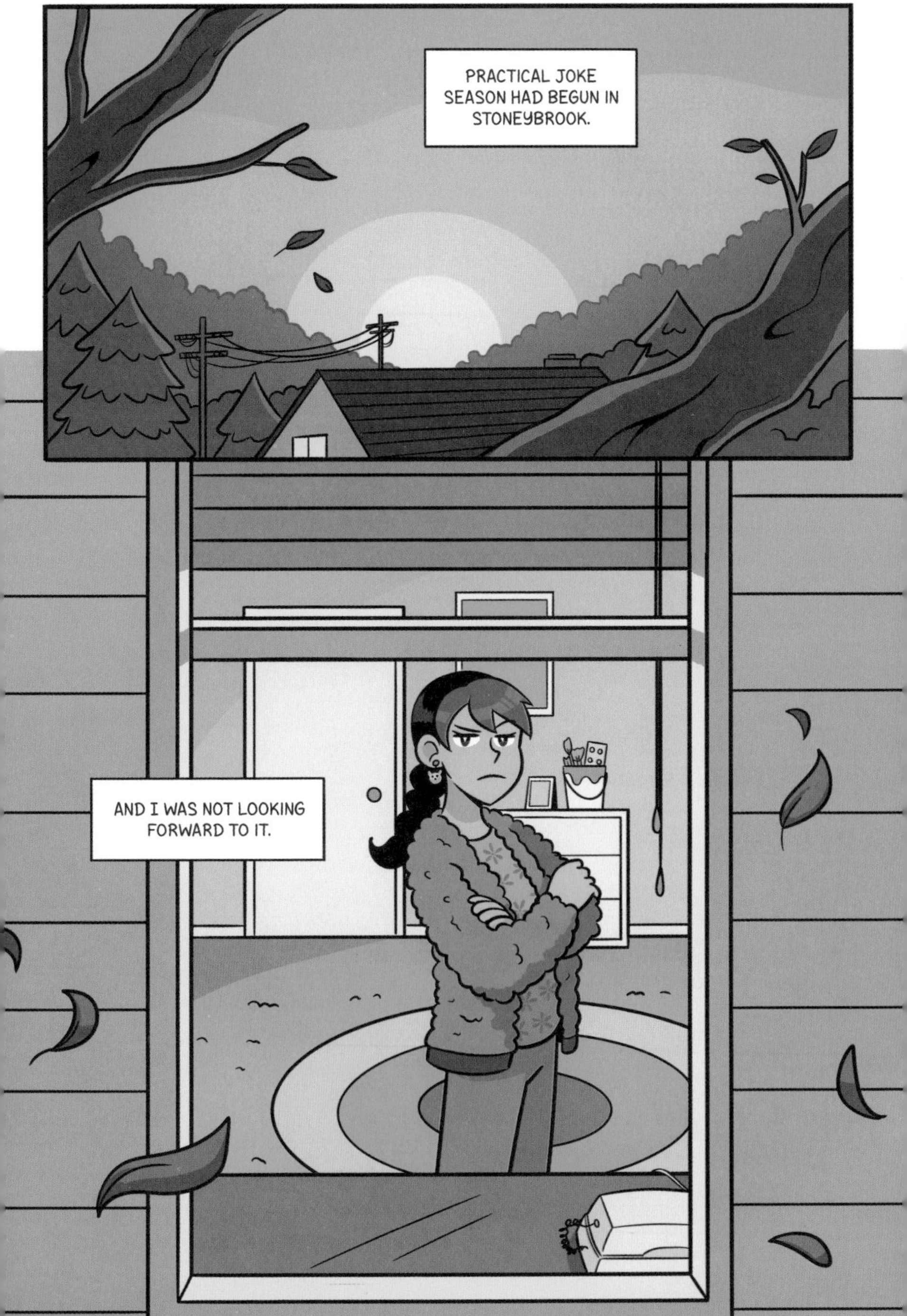
PRACTICAL JOKE SEASON HAD BEGUN IN STONEYBROOK.
AND I WAS NOT LOOKING FORWARD TO IT.

CHAPTER 4

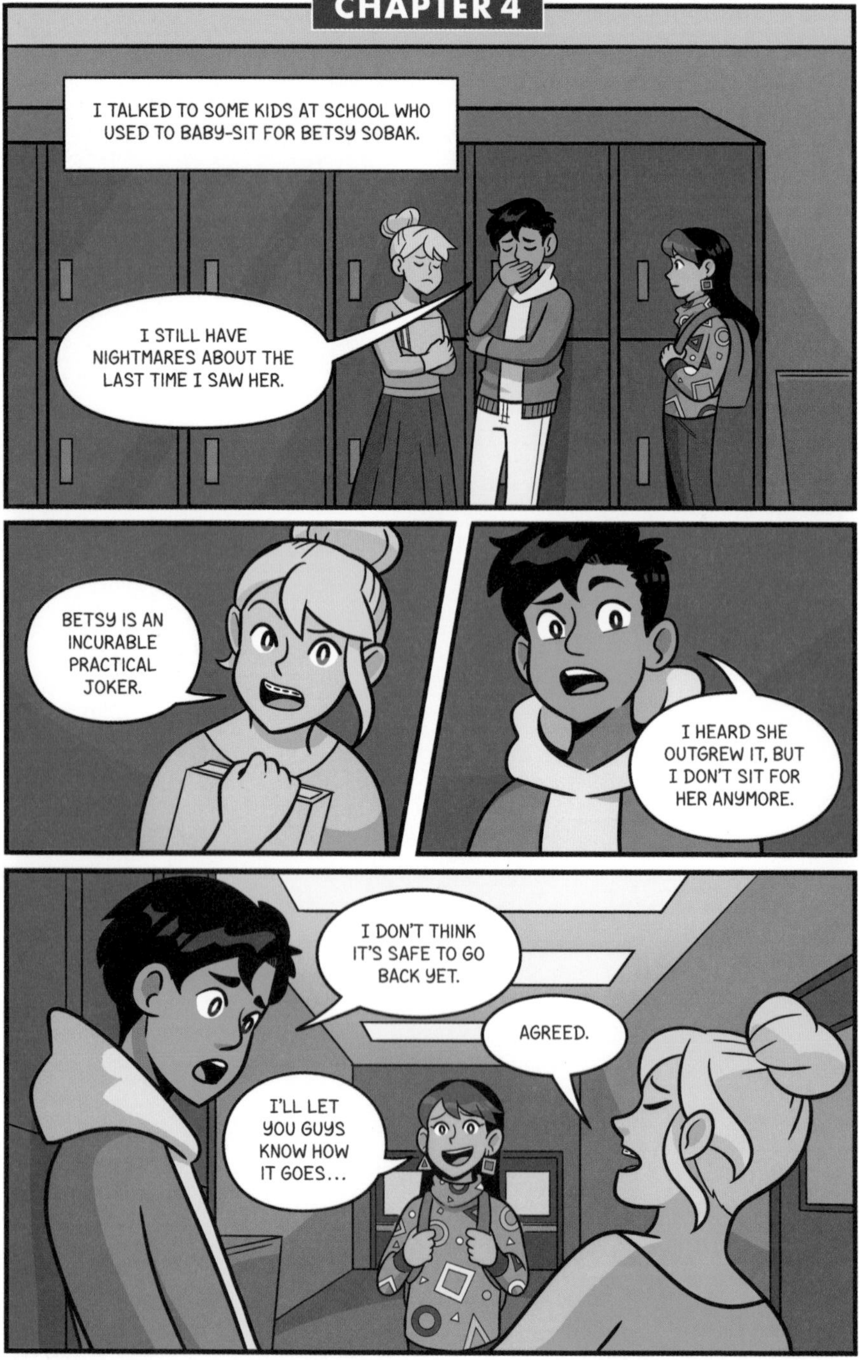
I TALKED TO SOME KIDS AT SCHOOL WHO USED TO BABY-SIT FOR BETSY SOBAK.
I STILL HAVE NIGHTMARES ABOUT THE LAST TIME I SAW HER.
BETSY IS AN INCURABLE PRACTICAL JOKER.
I HEARD SHE OUTGREW IT, BUT I DON'T SIT FOR HER ANYMORE.
I DON'T THINK IT'S SAFE TO GO BACK YET.
AGREED.
I'LL LET YOU GUYS KNOW HOW IT GOES...

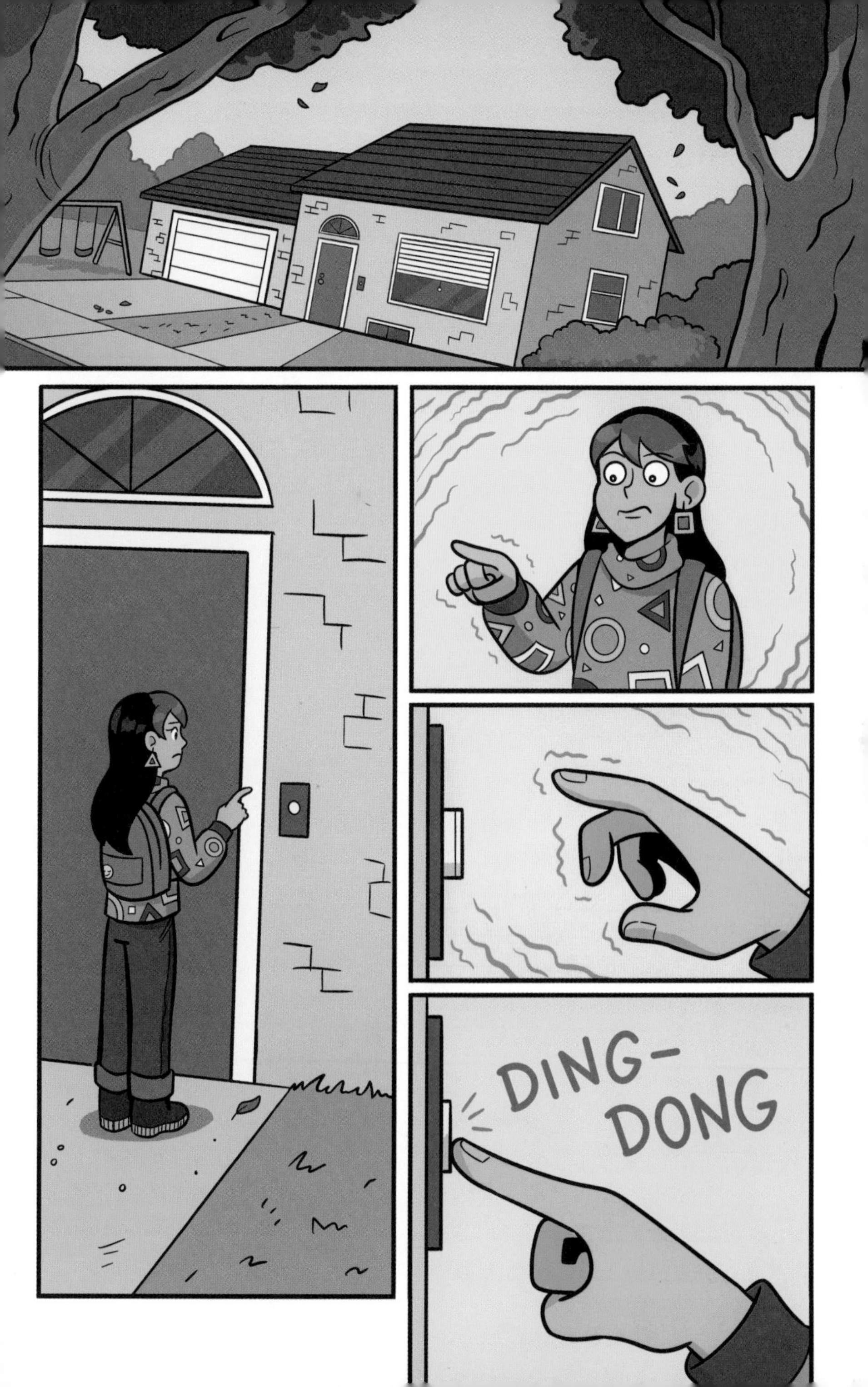
DING-
DONG

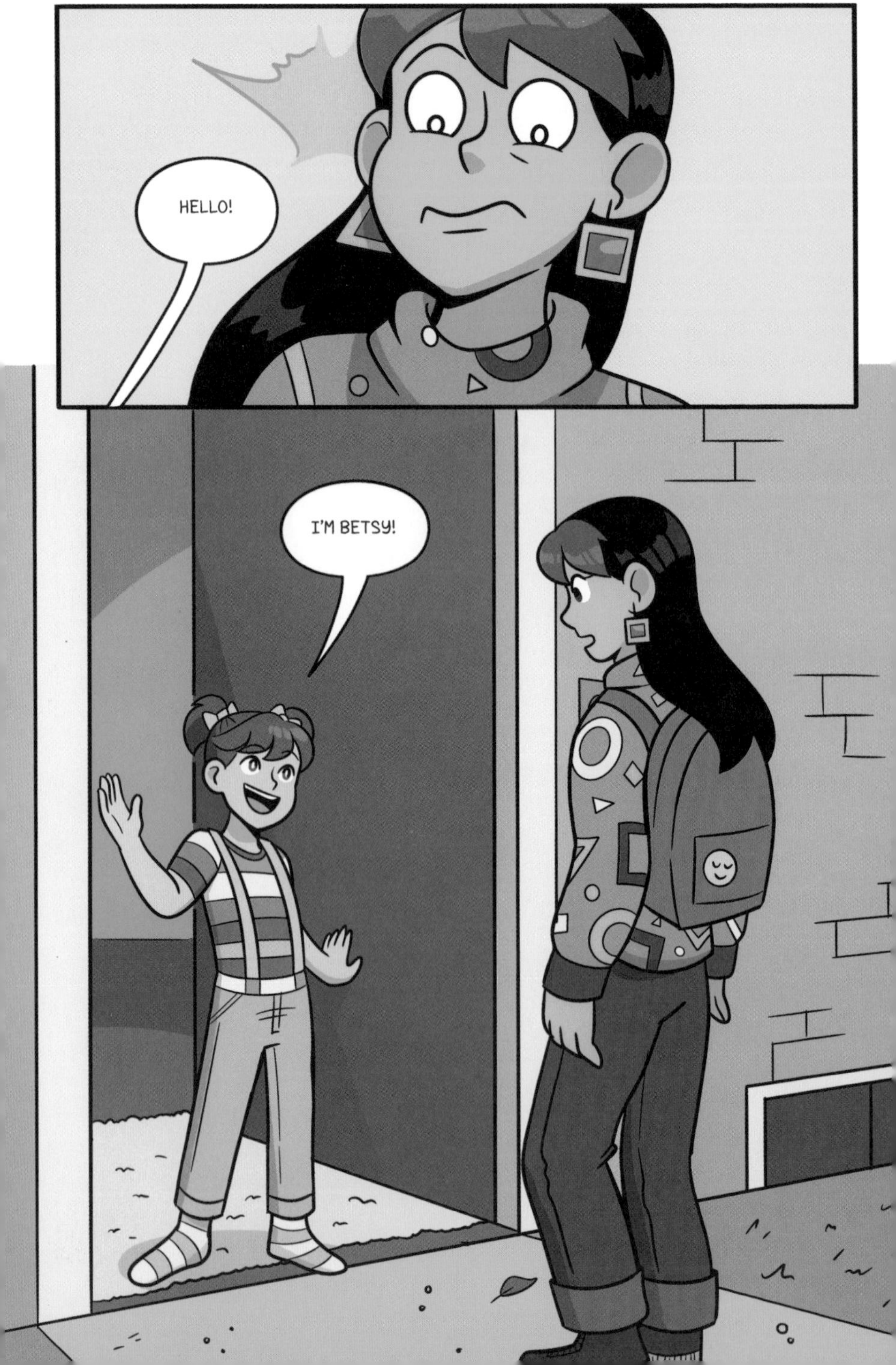
HELLO!
I'M BETSY!

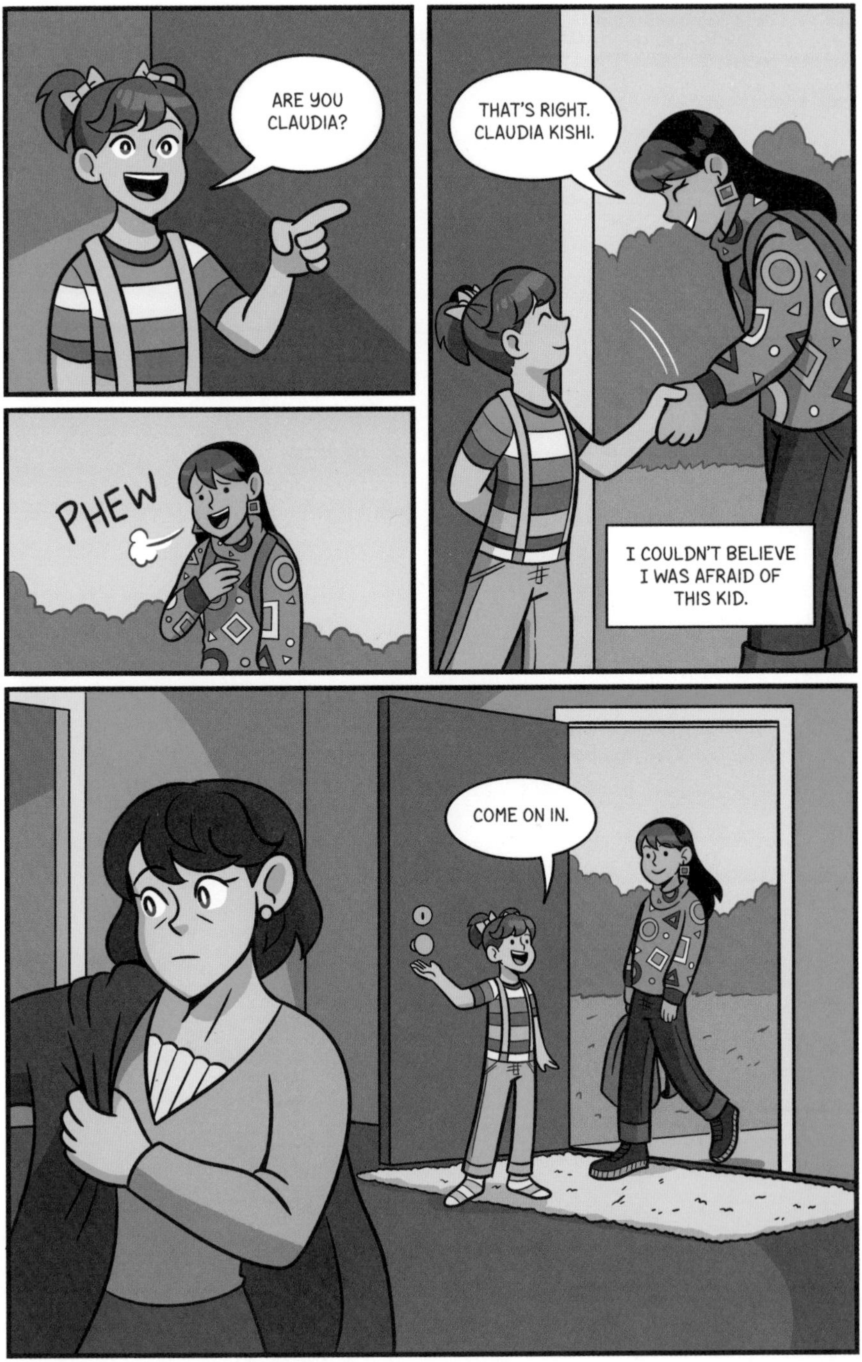
ARE YOU CLAUDIA?
THAT'S RIGHT. CLAUDIA KISHI.
PHEW
I COULDN'T BELIEVE I WAS AFRAID OF THIS KID.
COME ON IN.

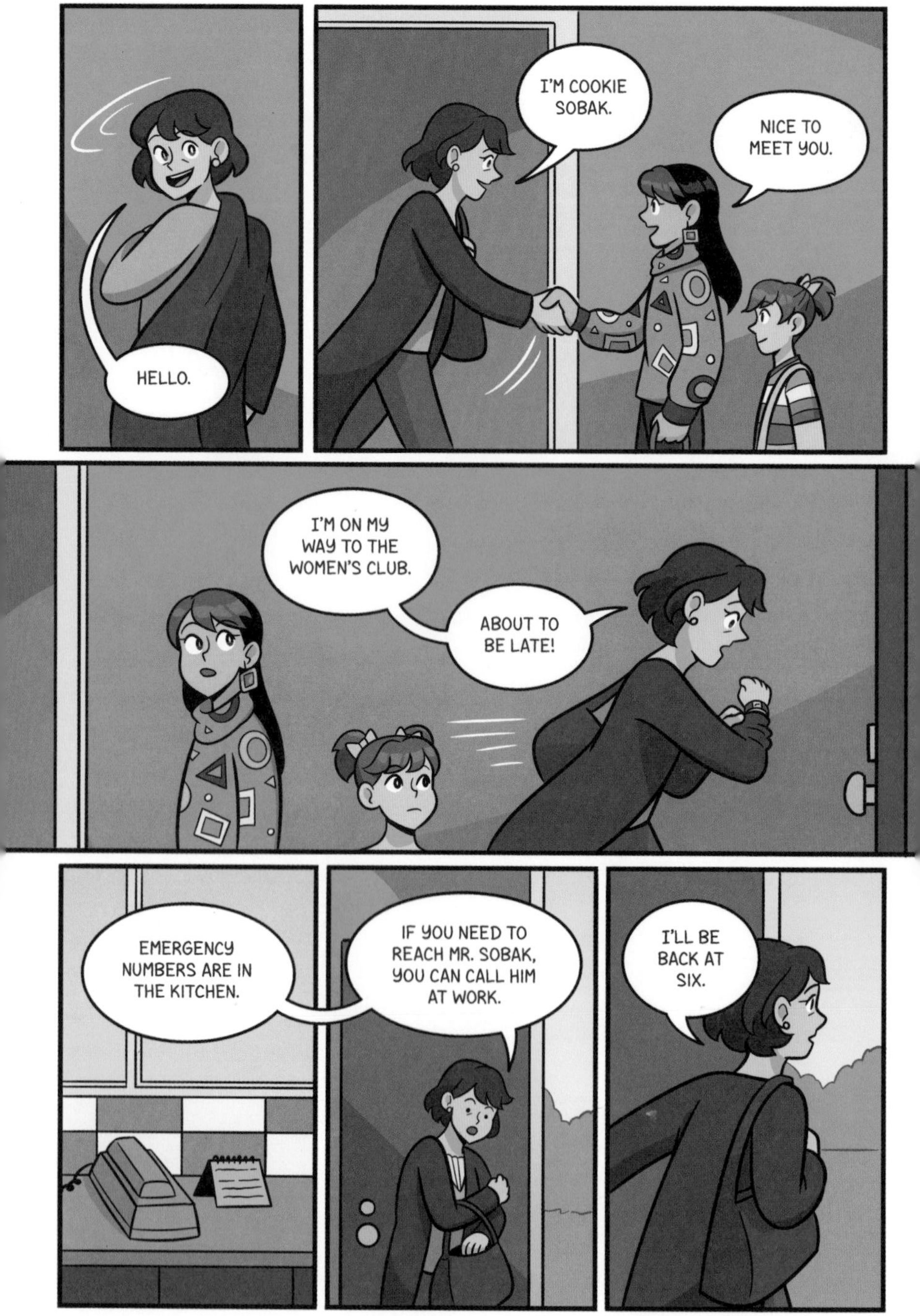
HELLO.
I'M COOKIE SOBAK.
NICE TO MEET YOU.
I'M ON MY WAY TO THE WOMEN'S CLUB.
ABOUT TO BE LATE!
EMERGENCY NUMBERS ARE IN THE KITCHEN.
IF YOU NEED TO REACH MR. SOBAK, YOU CAN CALL HIM AT WORK.
I'LL BE BACK AT SIX.

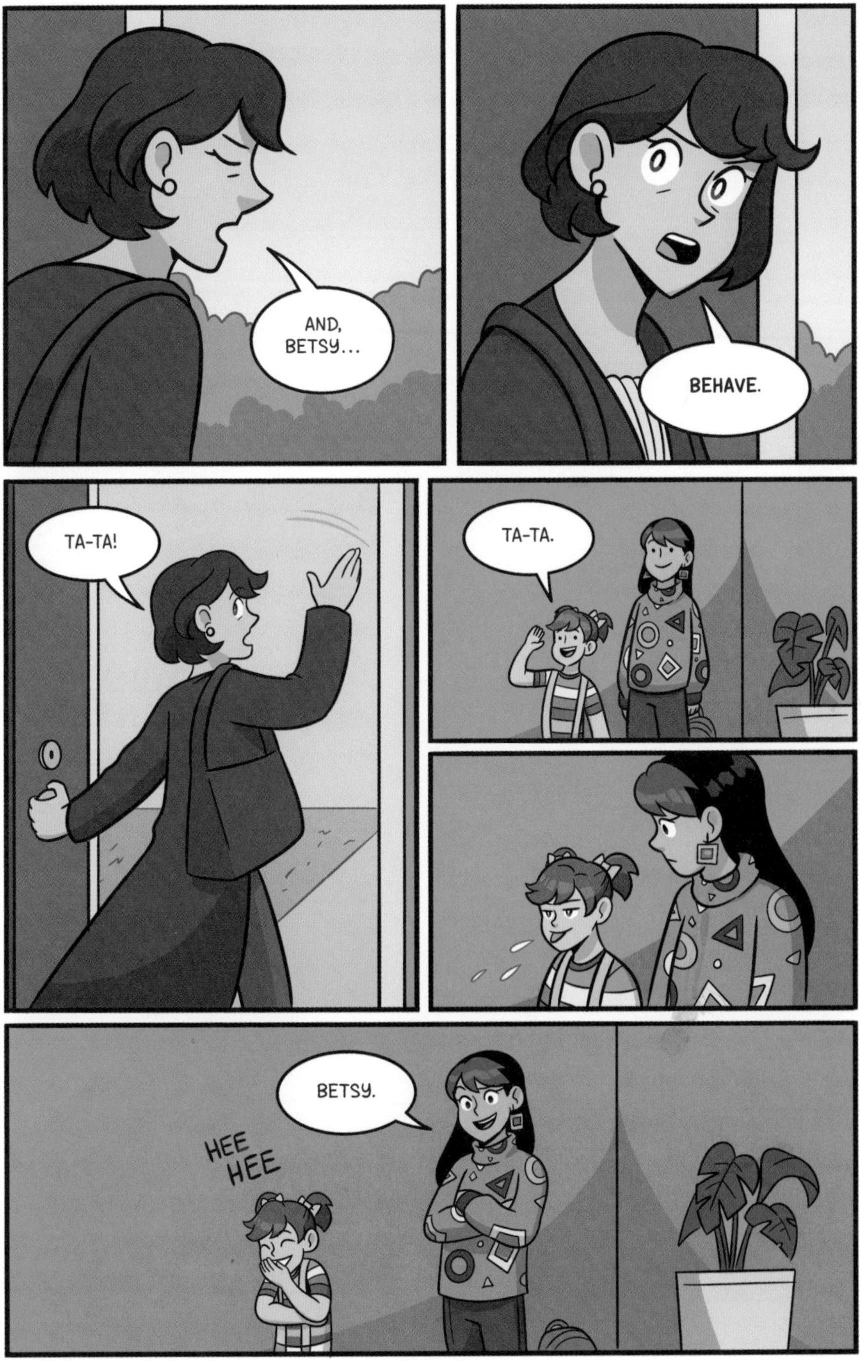
AND, BETSY...
BEHAVE.
TA-TA!
TA-TA.
BETSY.
HEE HEE

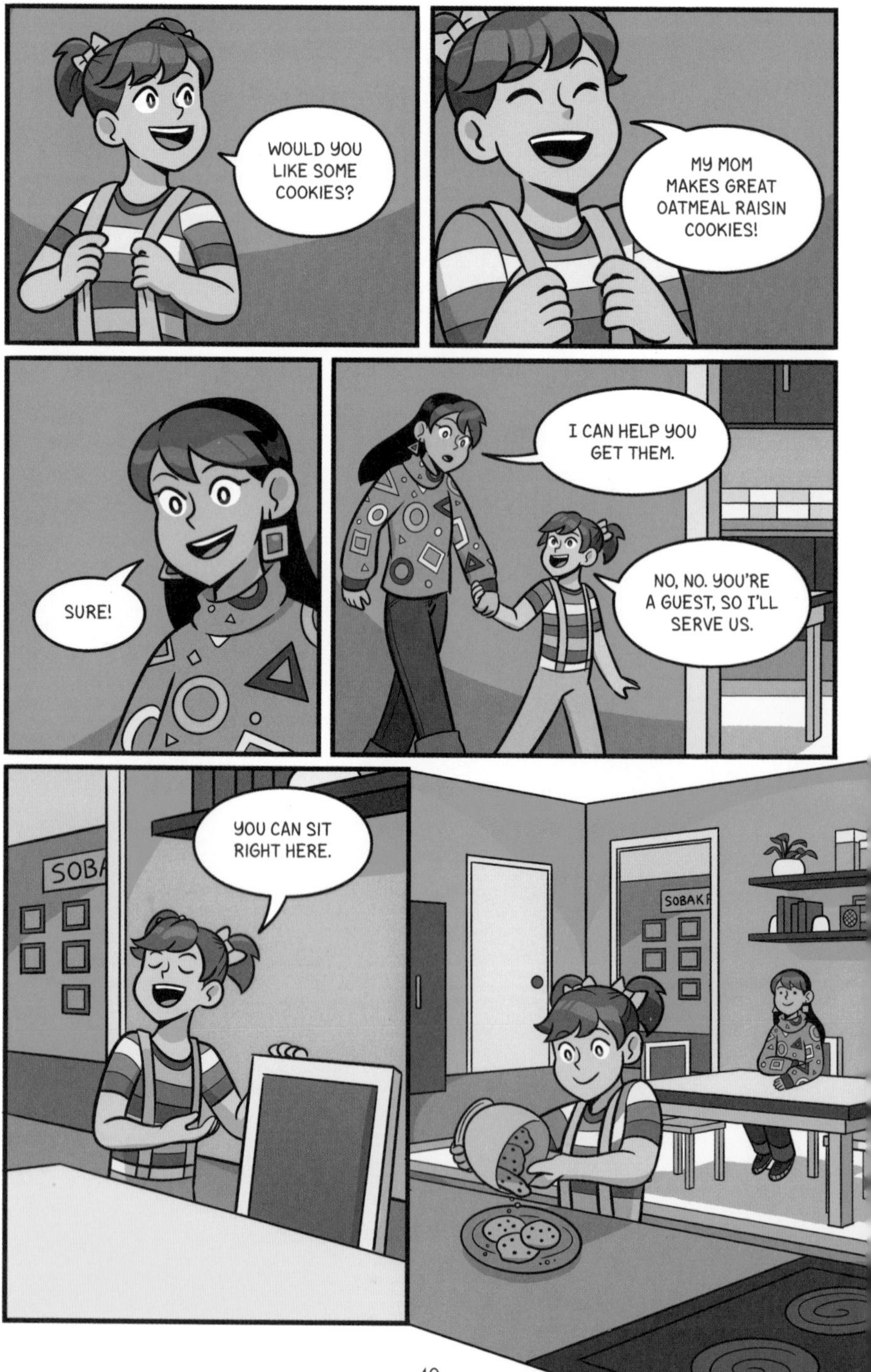

WOULD YOU LIKE SOME COOKIES?
MY MOM MAKES GREAT OATMEAL RAISIN COOKIES!
SURE!
I CAN HELP YOU GET THEM.
NO, NO. YOU'RE A GUEST, SO I'LL SERVE US.
YOU CAN SIT RIGHT HERE.
SOBA
SOBAK

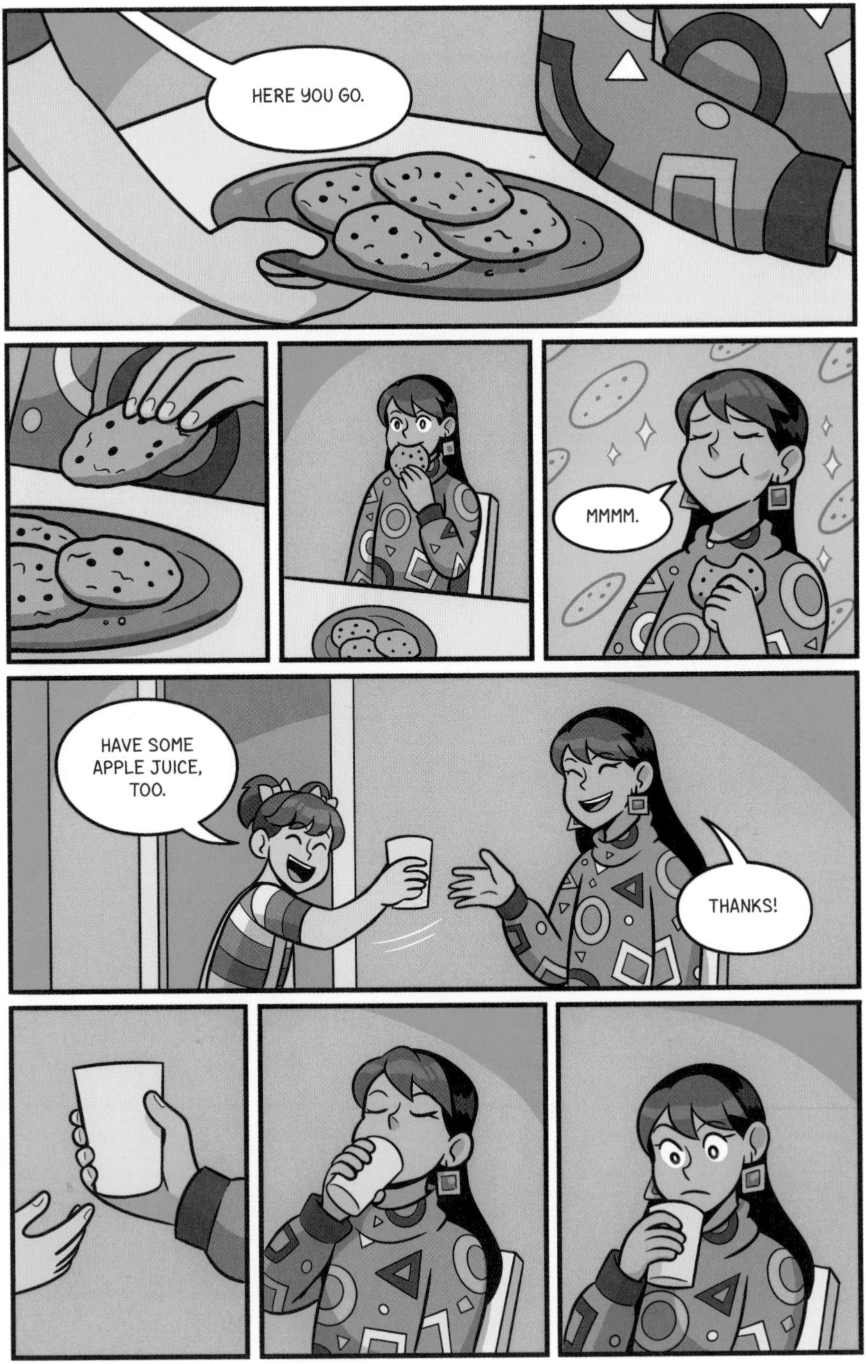
HERE YOU GO.
MMMM.
HAVE SOME APPLE JUICE, TOO.
THANKS!

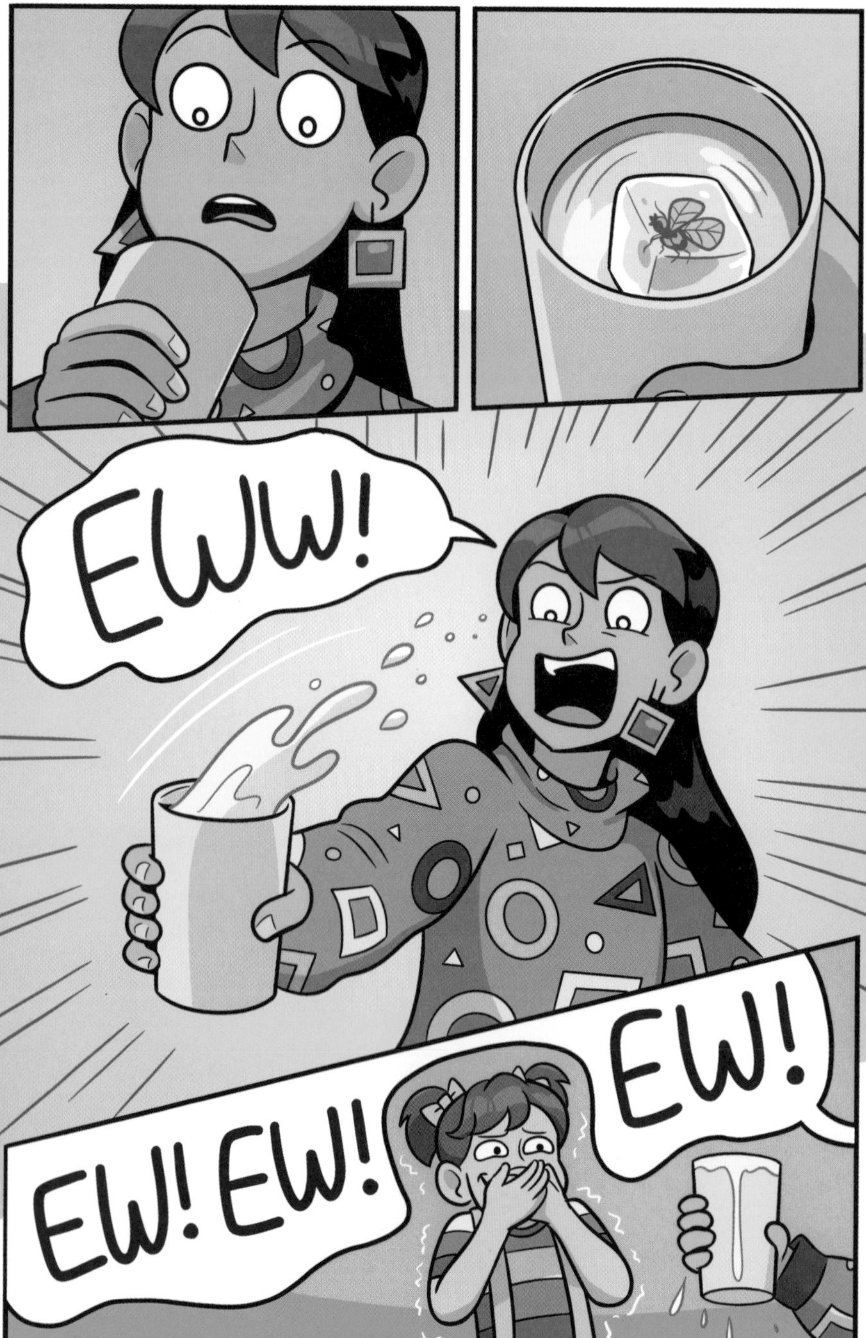
EWW!
EW! EW!
EW!

HA HA HA HA HA HA
GOTCHA!
THE FLY IS FAKE! IT'S IN A FAKE ICE CUBE!
WELL, THAT'S JUST GREAT, BETSY. NOW I'VE GOT APPLE JUICE ON MY FAVORITE SWEATER.

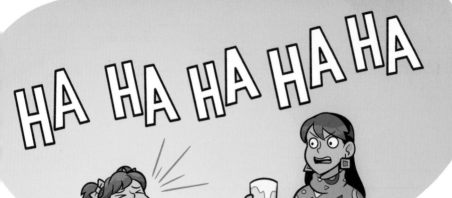

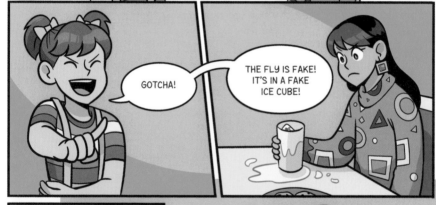

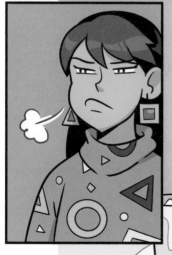

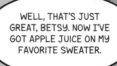

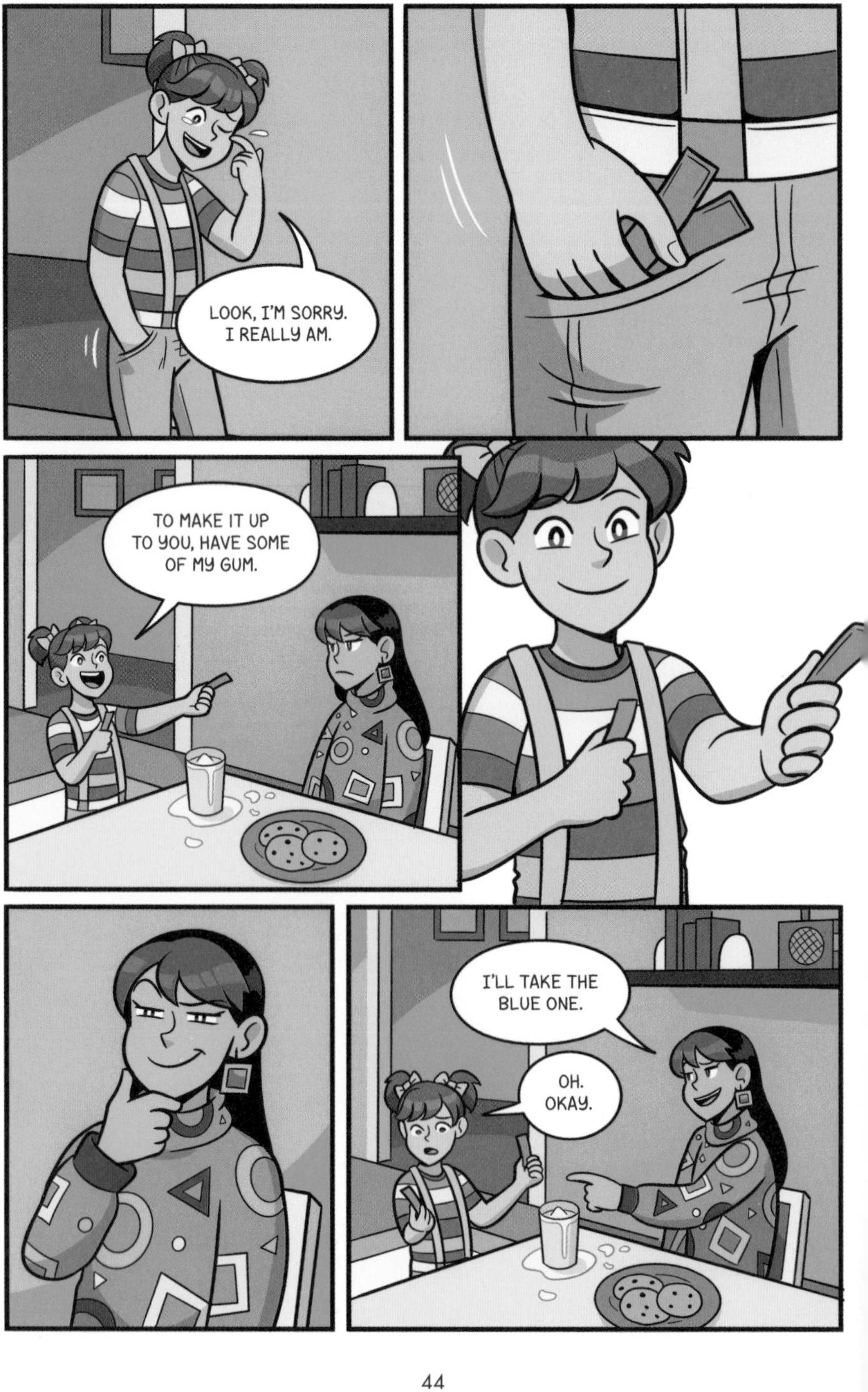
LOOK, I'M SORRY. I REALLY AM.
TO MAKE IT UP TO YOU, HAVE SOME OF MY GUM.
I'LL TAKE THE BLUE ONE.
OH. OKAY.

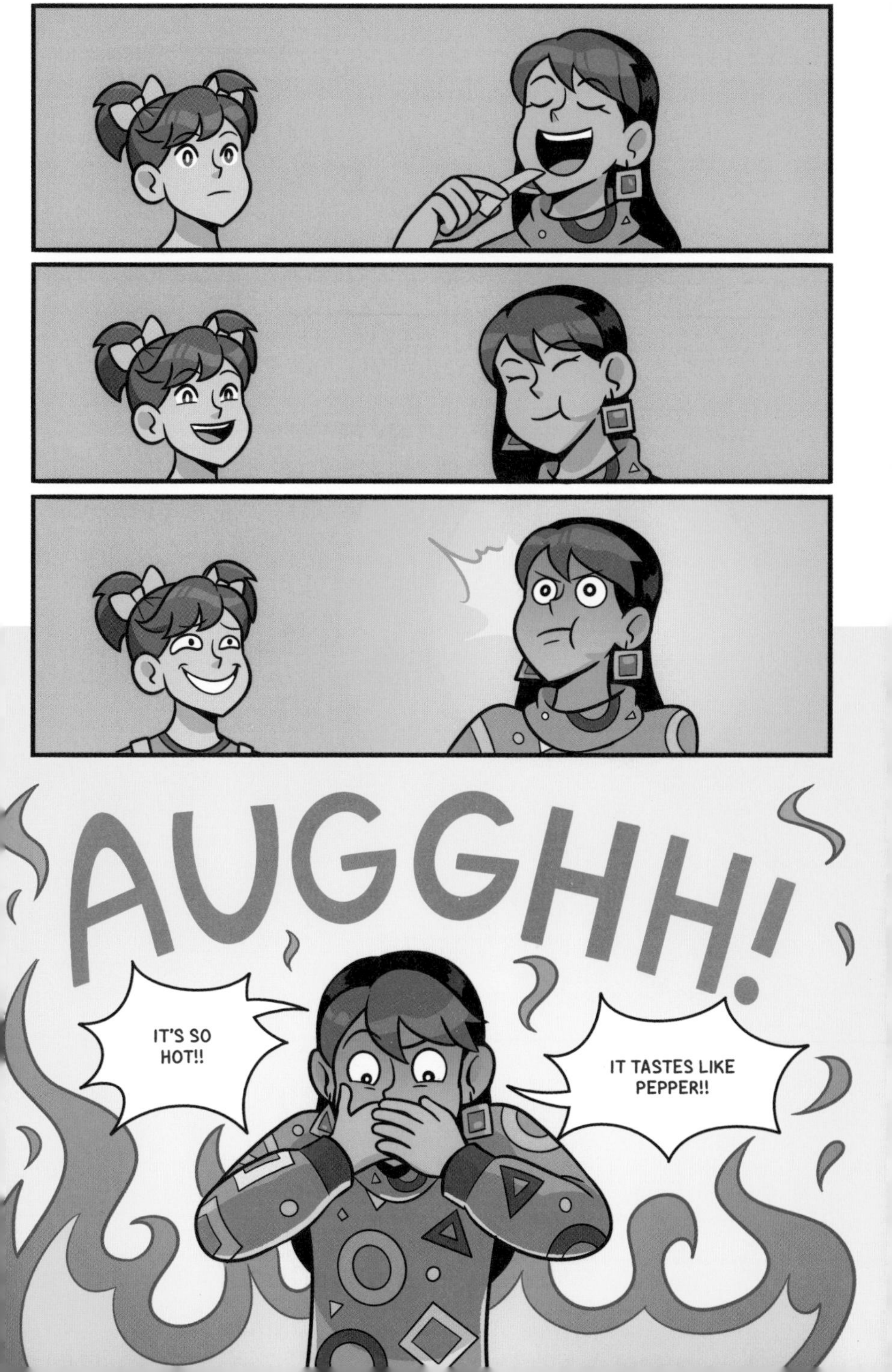
AUGGHH!
IT'S SO HOT!!
IT TASTES LIKE PEPPER!!

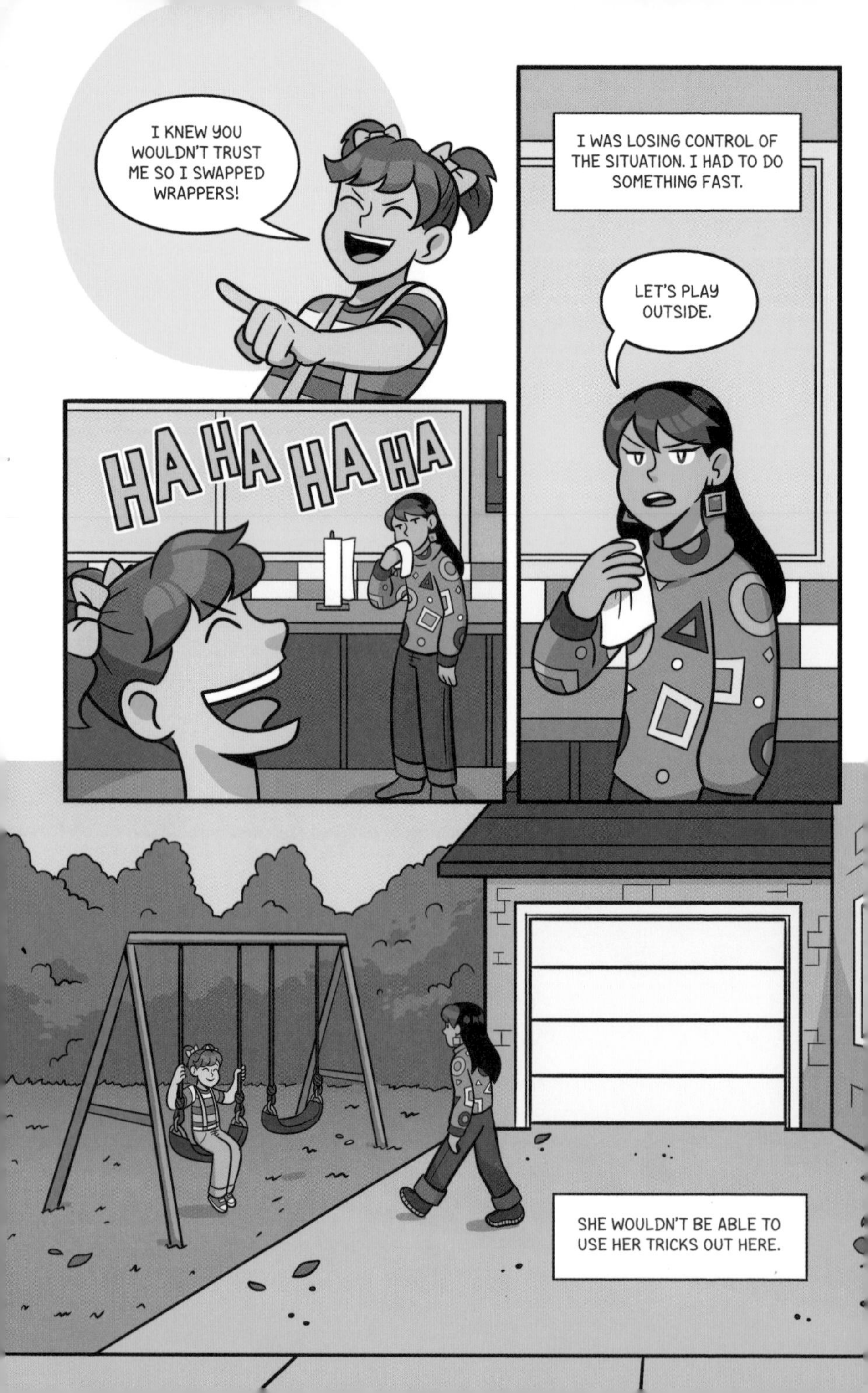
I KNEW YOU WOULDN'T TRUST ME SO I SWAPPED WRAPPERS!
HA HA HA HA
I WAS LOSING CONTROL OF THE SITUATION. I HAD TO DO SOMETHING FAST.
LET'S PLAY OUTSIDE.
SHE WOULDN'T BE ABLE TO USE HER TRICKS OUT HERE.

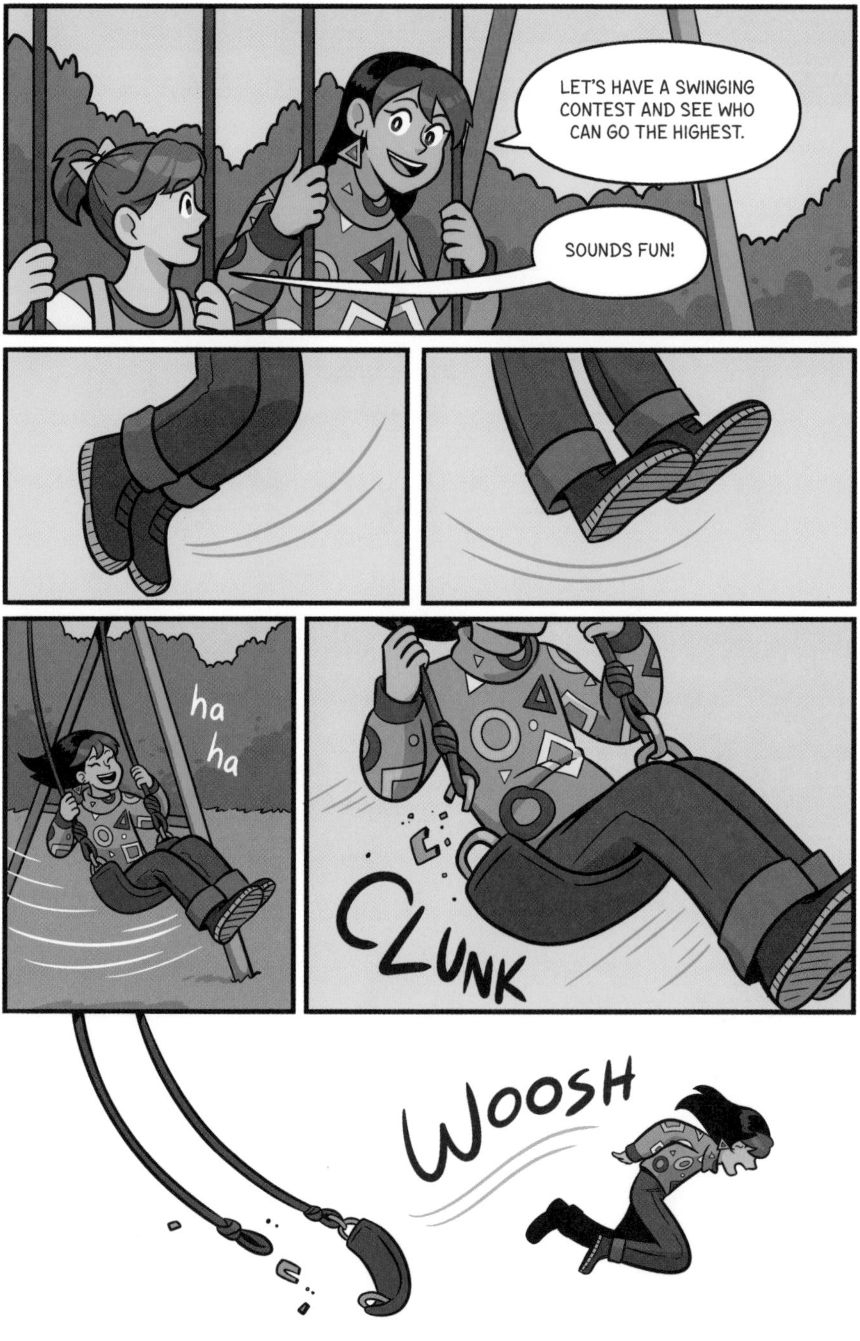
LET'S HAVE A SWINGING CONTEST AND SEE WHO CAN GO THE HIGHEST.
SOUNDS FUN!
ha
ha
CLUNK
WOOSH

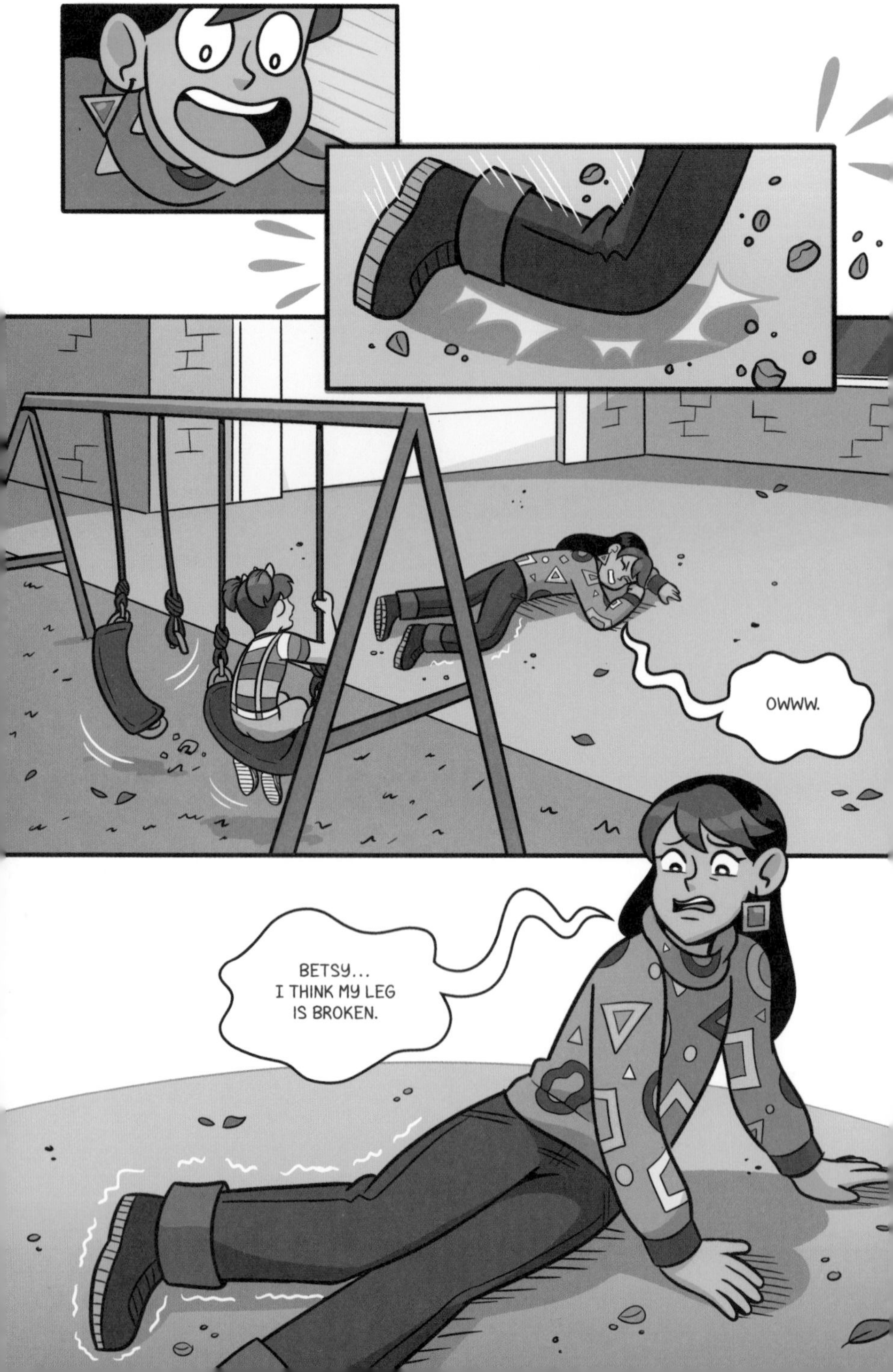
OWWW.
BETSY... I THINK MY LEG IS BROKEN.

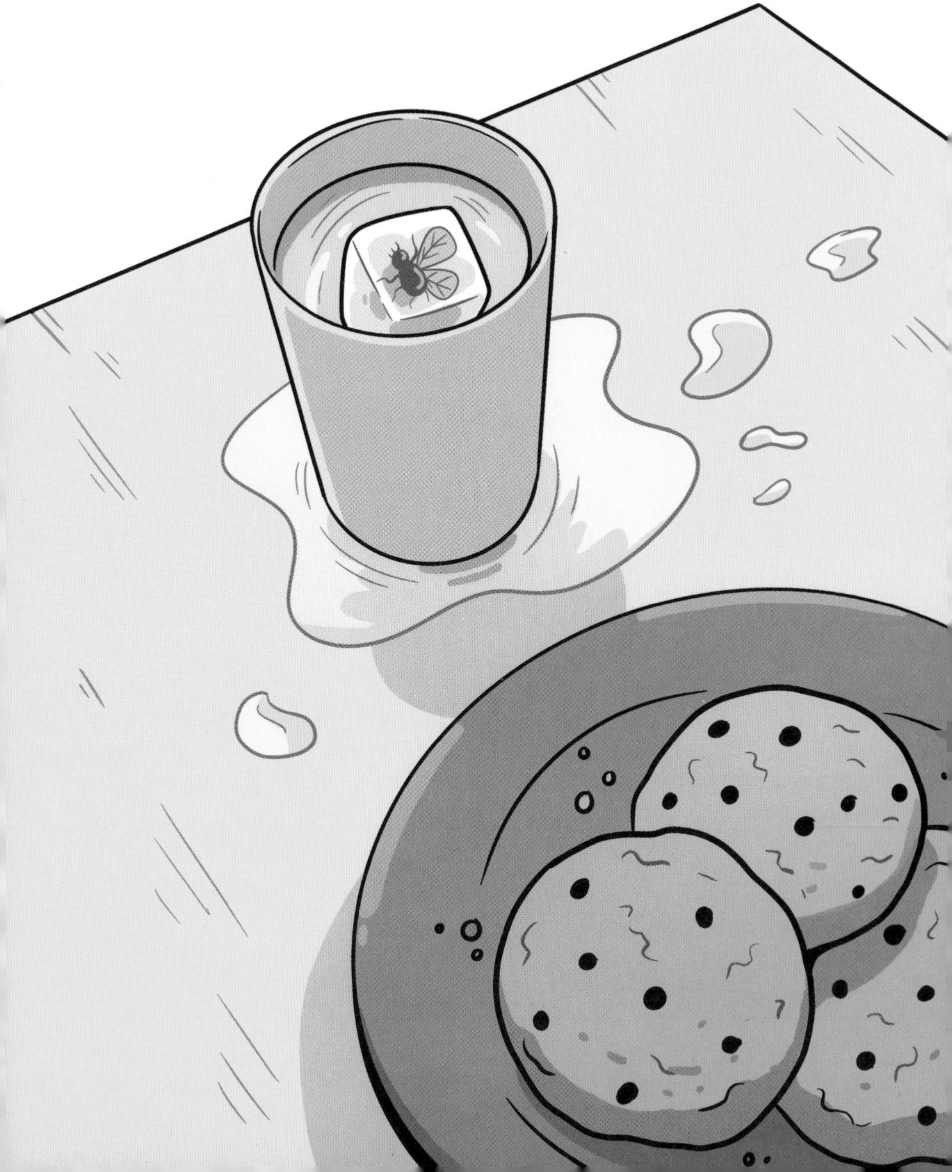

CHAPTER 5

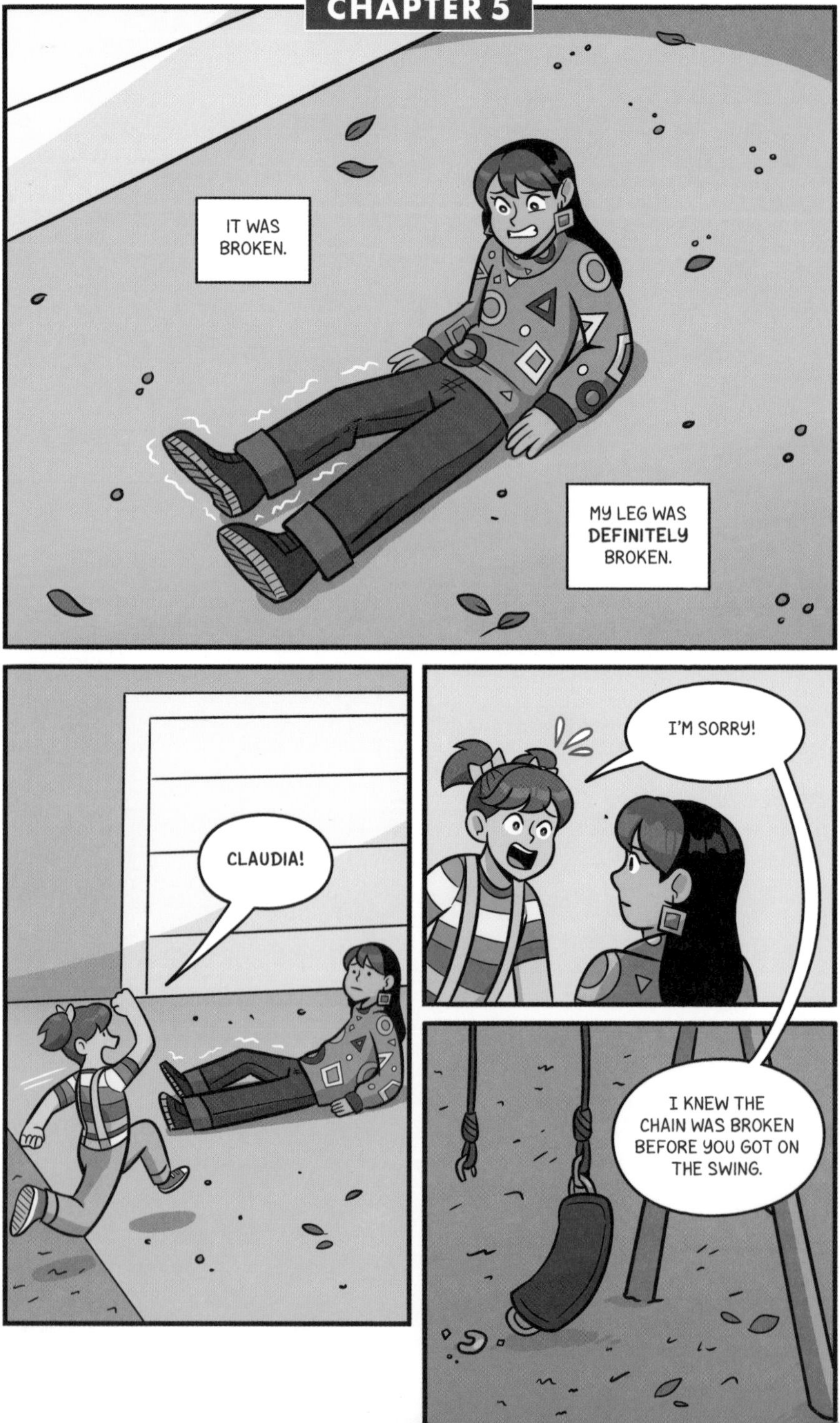
IT WAS BROKEN.
MY LEG WAS DEFINITELY BROKEN.
CLAUDIA!
I'M SORRY!
I KNEW THE CHAIN WAS BROKEN BEFORE YOU GOT ON THE SWING.

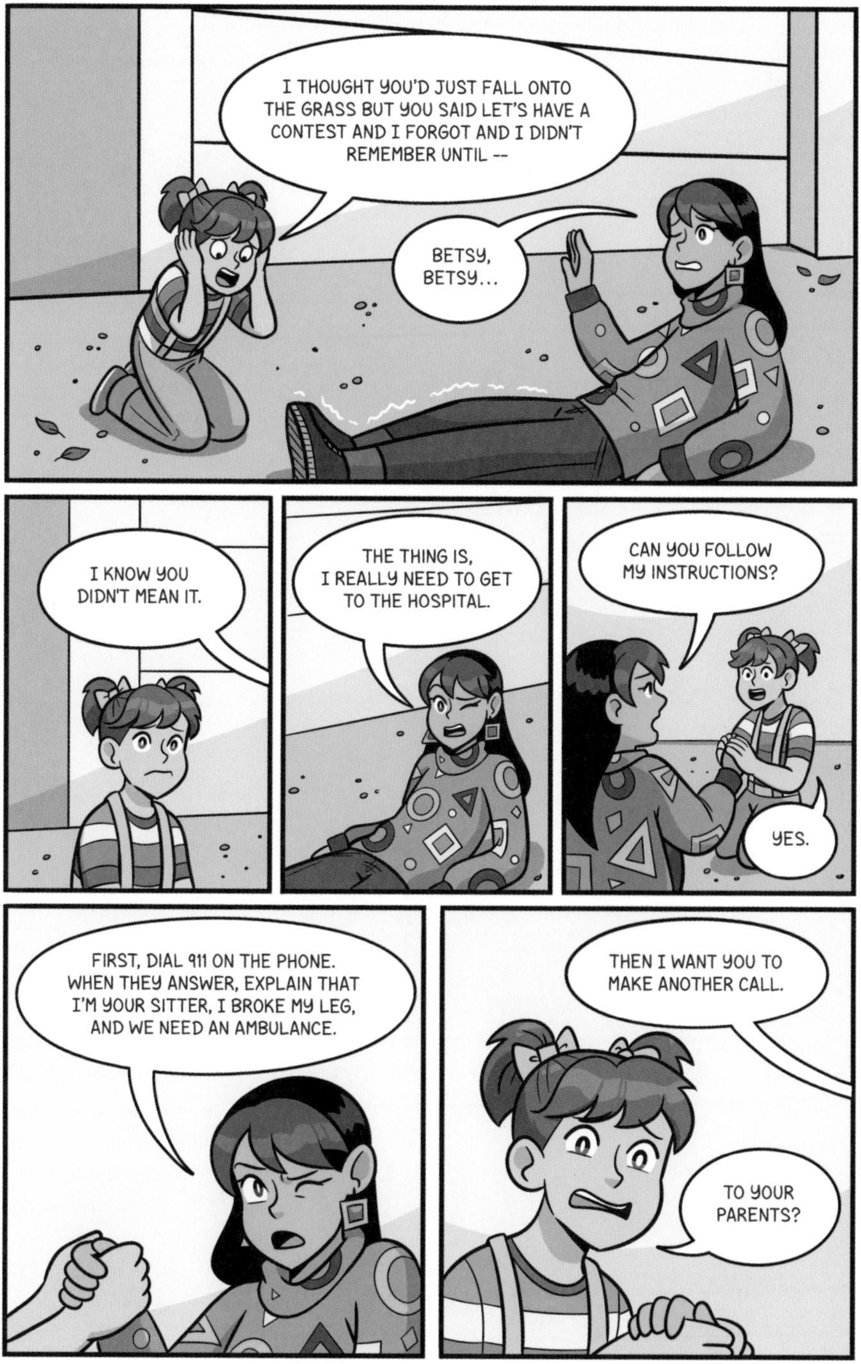
I THOUGHT YOU'D JUST FALL ONTO THE GRASS BUT YOU SAID LET'S HAVE A CONTEST AND I FORGOT AND I DIDN'T REMEMBER UNTIL --
BETSY, BETSY...
I KNOW YOU DIDN'T MEAN IT.
THE THING IS, I REALLY NEED TO GET TO THE HOSPITAL.
CAN YOU FOLLOW MY INSTRUCTIONS?
YES.
FIRST, DIAL 911 ON THE PHONE. WHEN THEY ANSWER, EXPLAIN THAT I'M YOUR SITTER, I BROKE MY LEG, AND WE NEED AN AMBULANCE.
THEN I WANT YOU TO MAKE ANOTHER CALL.
TO YOUR PARENTS?

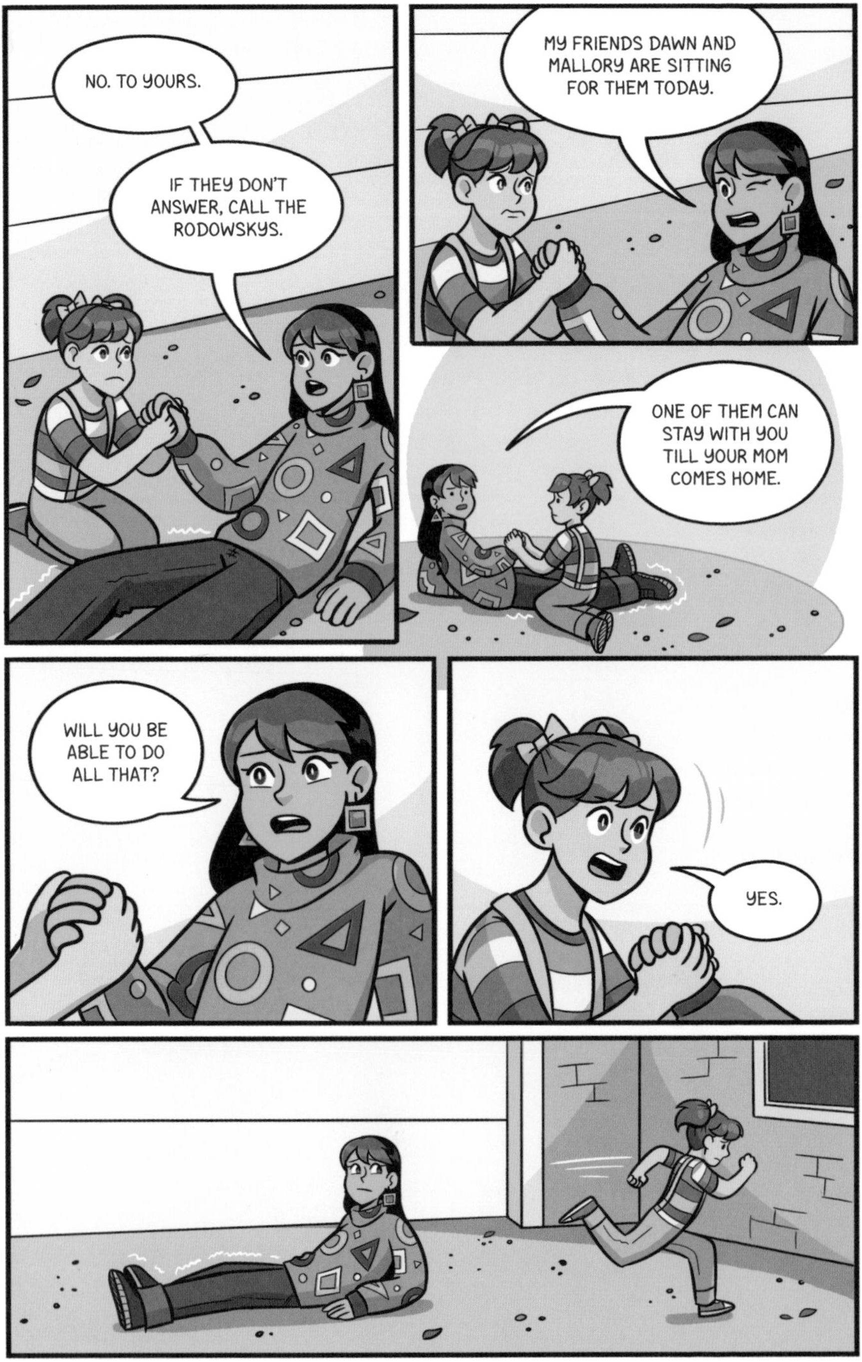
NO. TO YOURS.
IF THEY DON'T ANSWER, CALL THE RODOWSKYS.
MY FRIENDS DAWN AND MALLORY ARE SITTING FOR THEM TODAY.
ONE OF THEM CAN STAY WITH YOU TILL YOUR MOM COMES HOME.
WILL YOU BE ABLE TO DO ALL THAT?
YES.

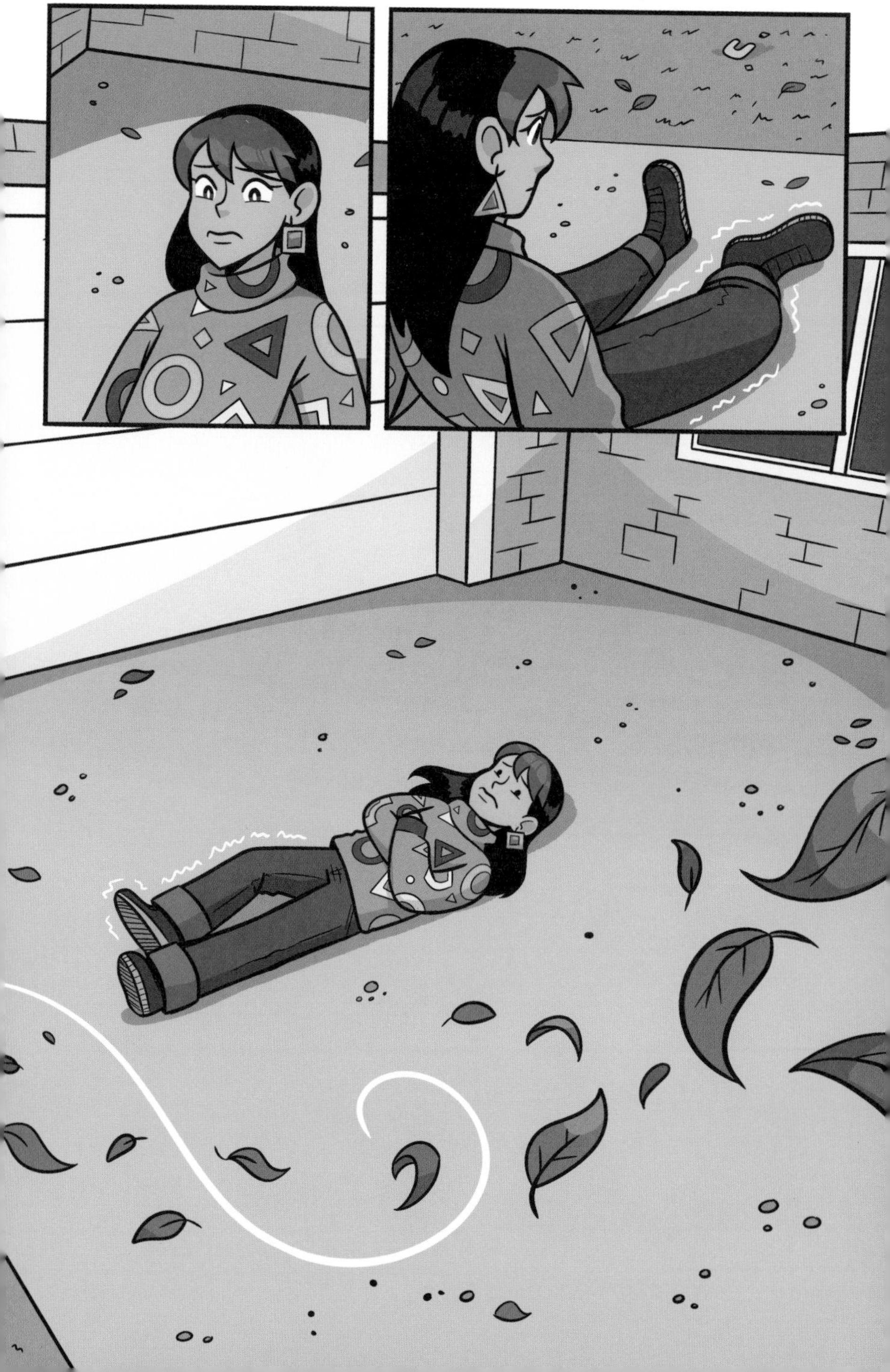

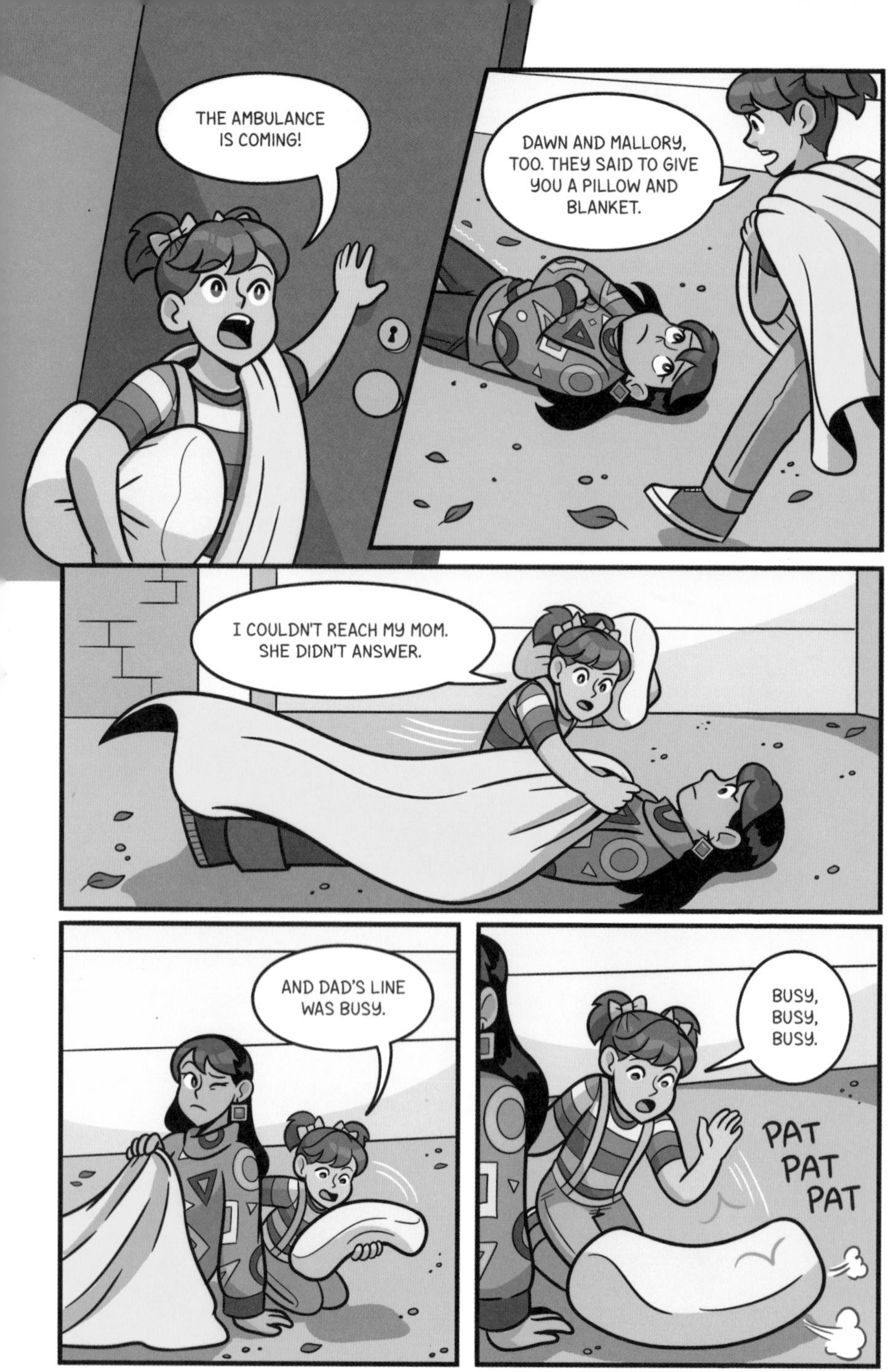
THE AMBULANCE IS COMING!
DAWN AND MALLORY, TOO. THEY SAID TO GIVE YOU A PILLOW AND BLANKET.
I COULDN'T REACH MY MOM. SHE DIDN'T ANSWER.
AND DAD'S LINE WAS BUSY.
BUSY, BUSY, BUSY.
PAT PAT PAT

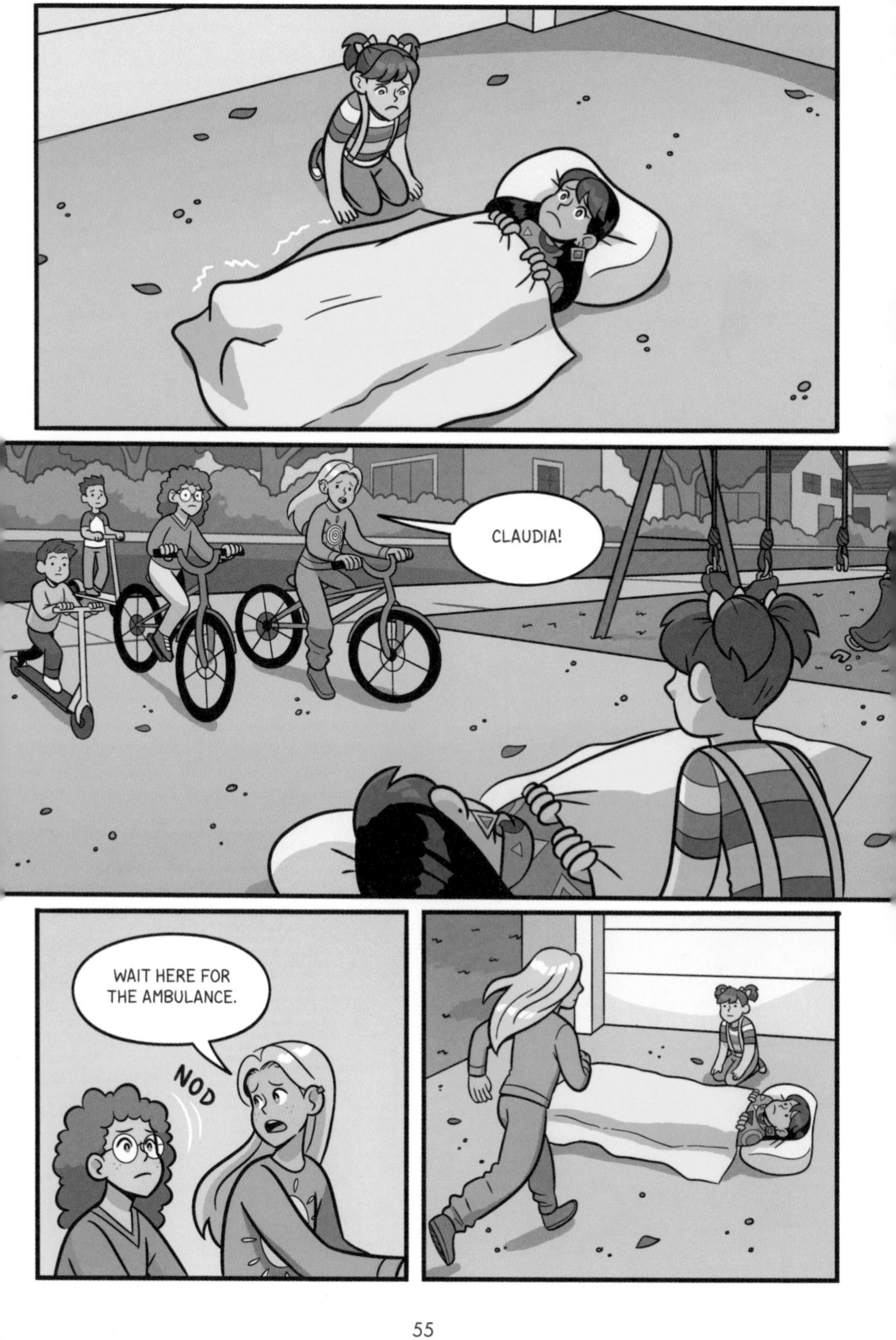
CLAUDIA!
WAIT HERE FOR THE AMBULANCE.
NOD

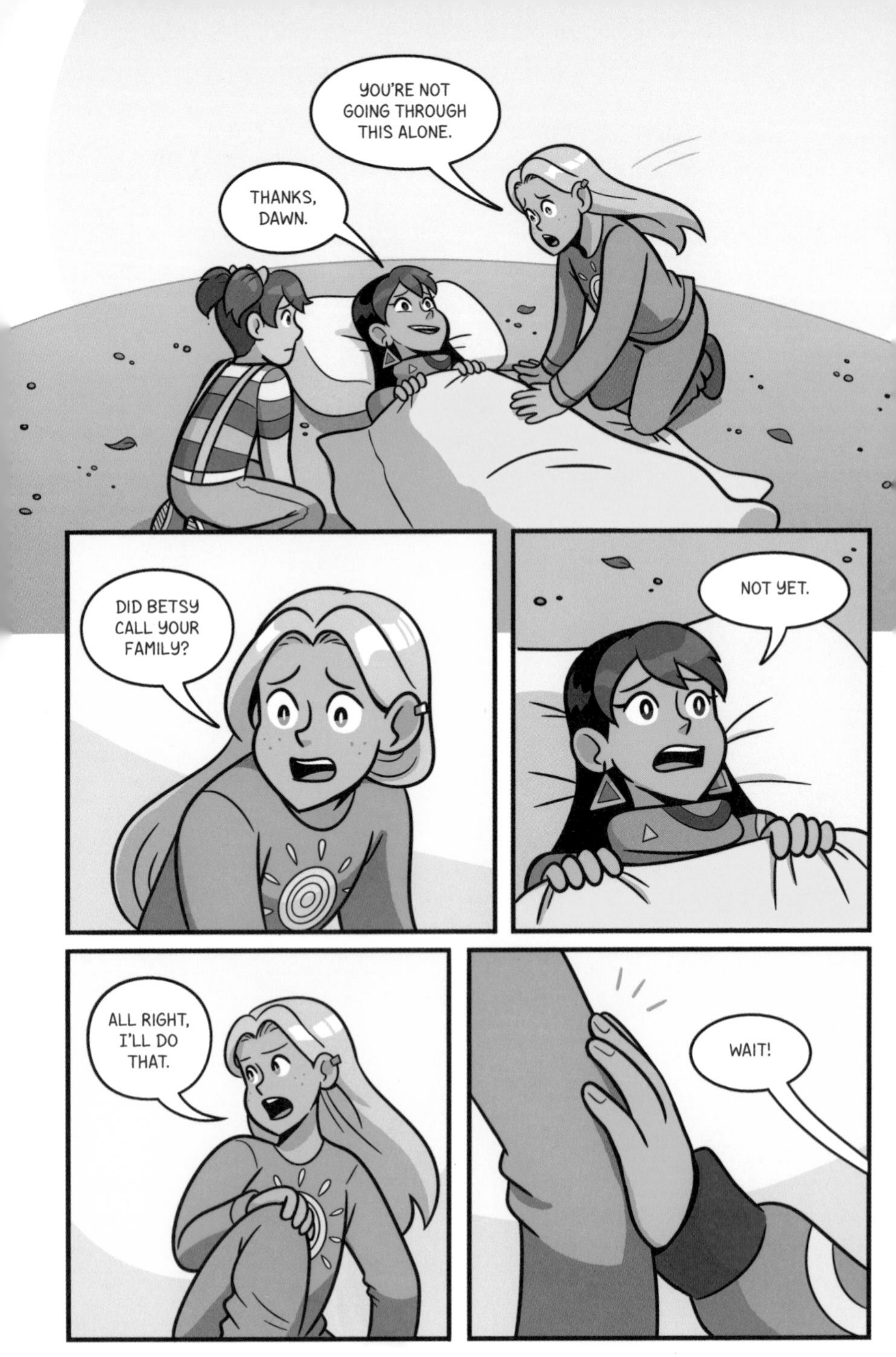
YOU'RE NOT GOING THROUGH THIS ALONE.
THANKS, DAWN.
DID BETSY CALL YOUR FAMILY?
NOT YET.
ALL RIGHT, I'LL DO THAT.
WAIT!

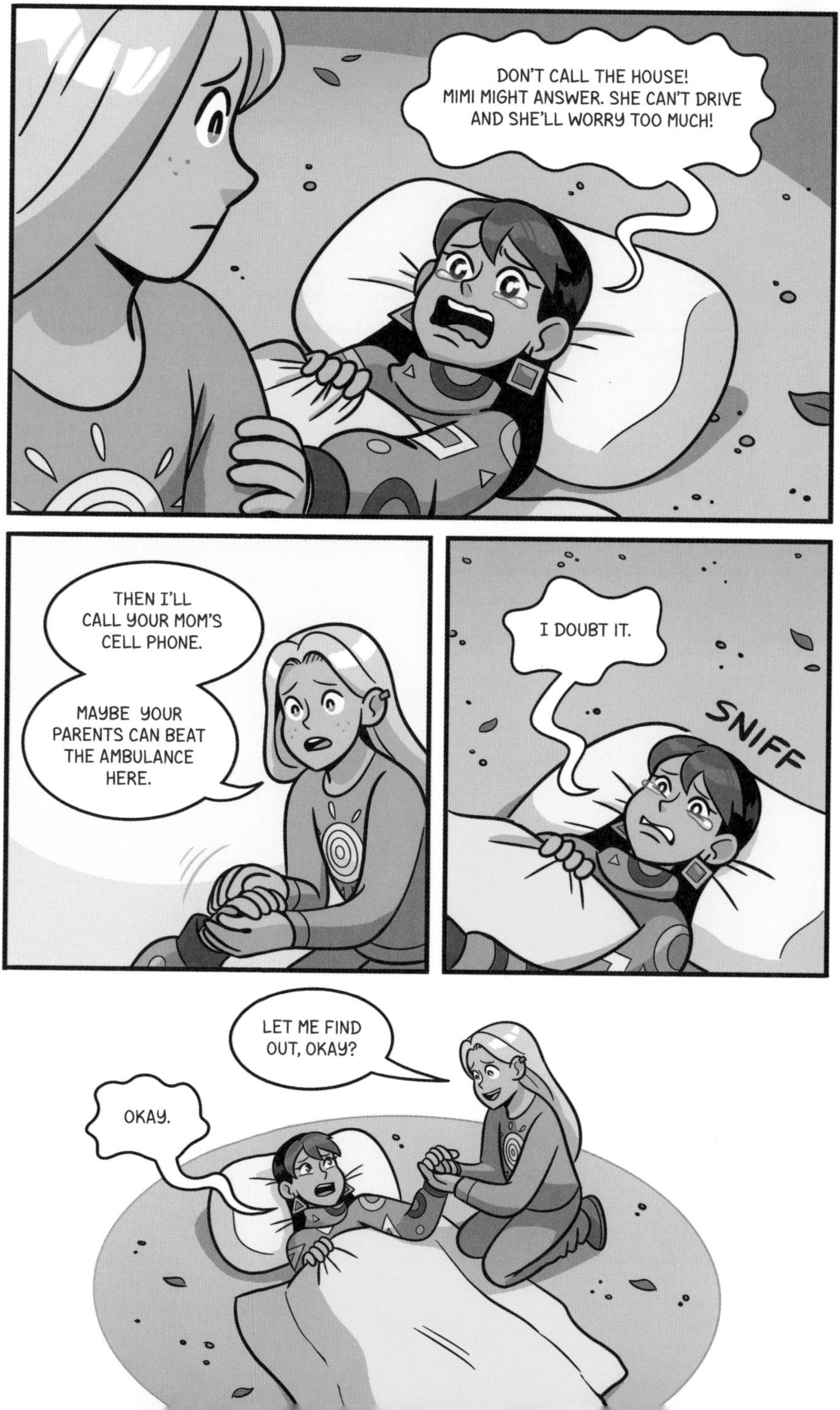
DON'T CALL THE HOUSE! MIMI MIGHT ANSWER. SHE CAN'T DRIVE AND SHE'LL WORRY TOO MUCH!
THEN I'LL CALL YOUR MOM'S CELL PHONE.
MAYBE YOUR PARENTS CAN BEAT THE AMBULANCE HERE.
I DOUBT IT.
SNIFF
LET ME FIND OUT, OKAY?
OKAY.

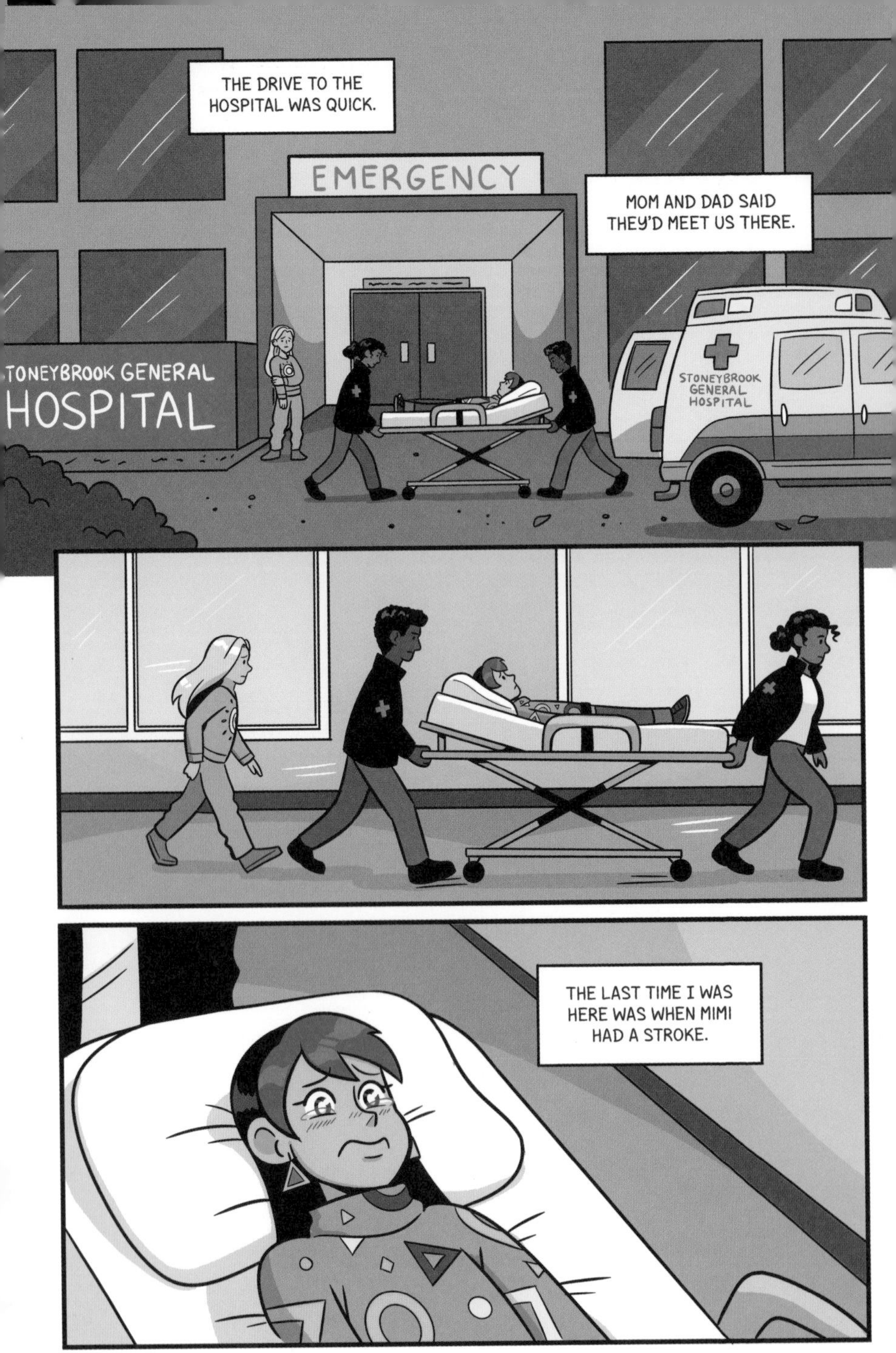
THE DRIVE TO THE HOSPITAL WAS QUICK.
EMERGENCY
MOM AND DAD SAID THEY'D MEET US THERE.
STONEYBROOK GENERAL HOSPITAL
STONEYBROOK GENERAL HOSPITAL
THE LAST TIME I WAS HERE WAS WHEN MIMI HAD A STROKE.

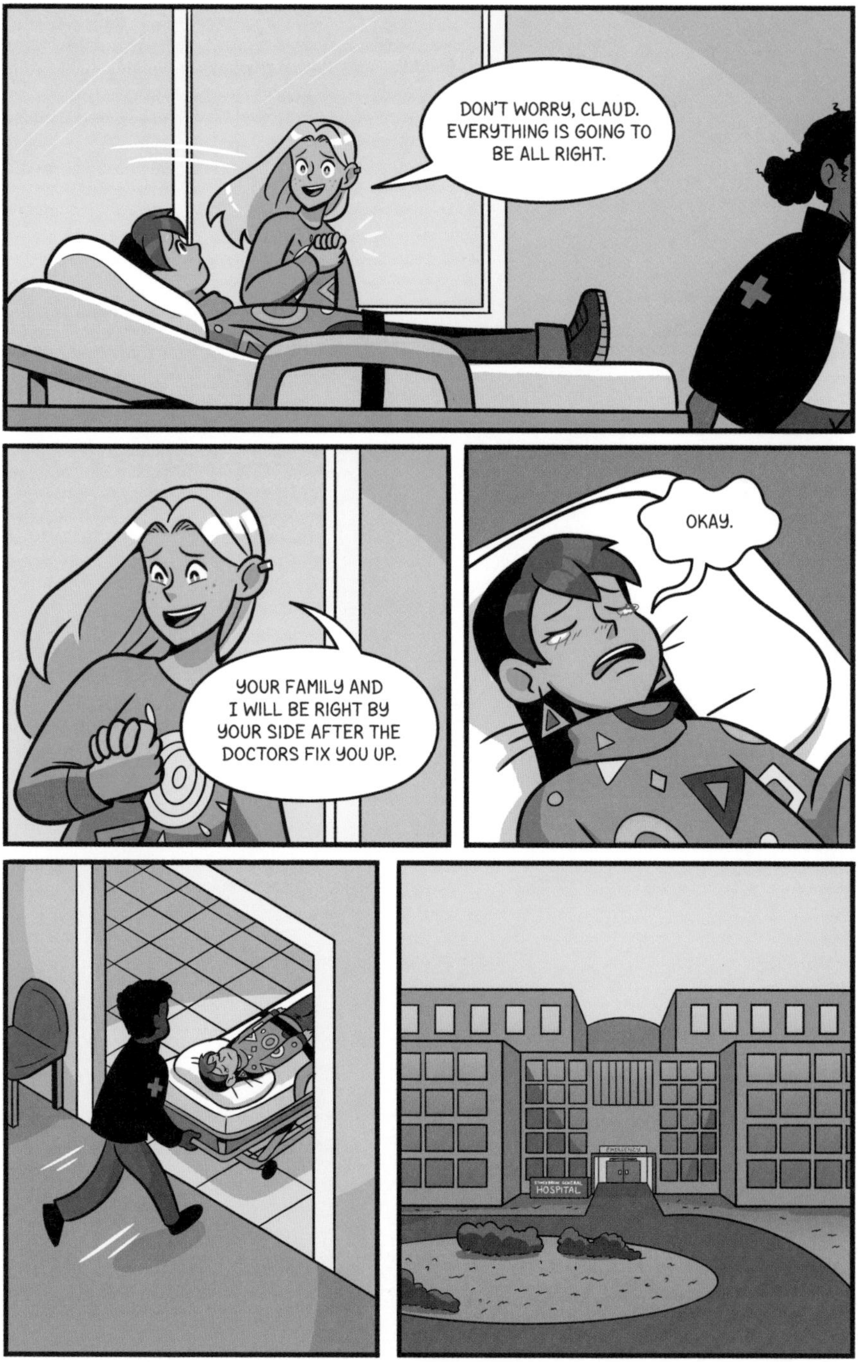
DON'T WORRY, CLAUD. EVERYTHING IS GOING TO BE ALL RIGHT.
YOUR FAMILY AND I WILL BE RIGHT BY YOUR SIDE AFTER THE DOCTORS FIX YOU UP.
OKAY.
HOSPITAL

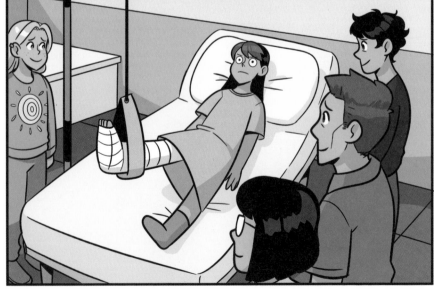

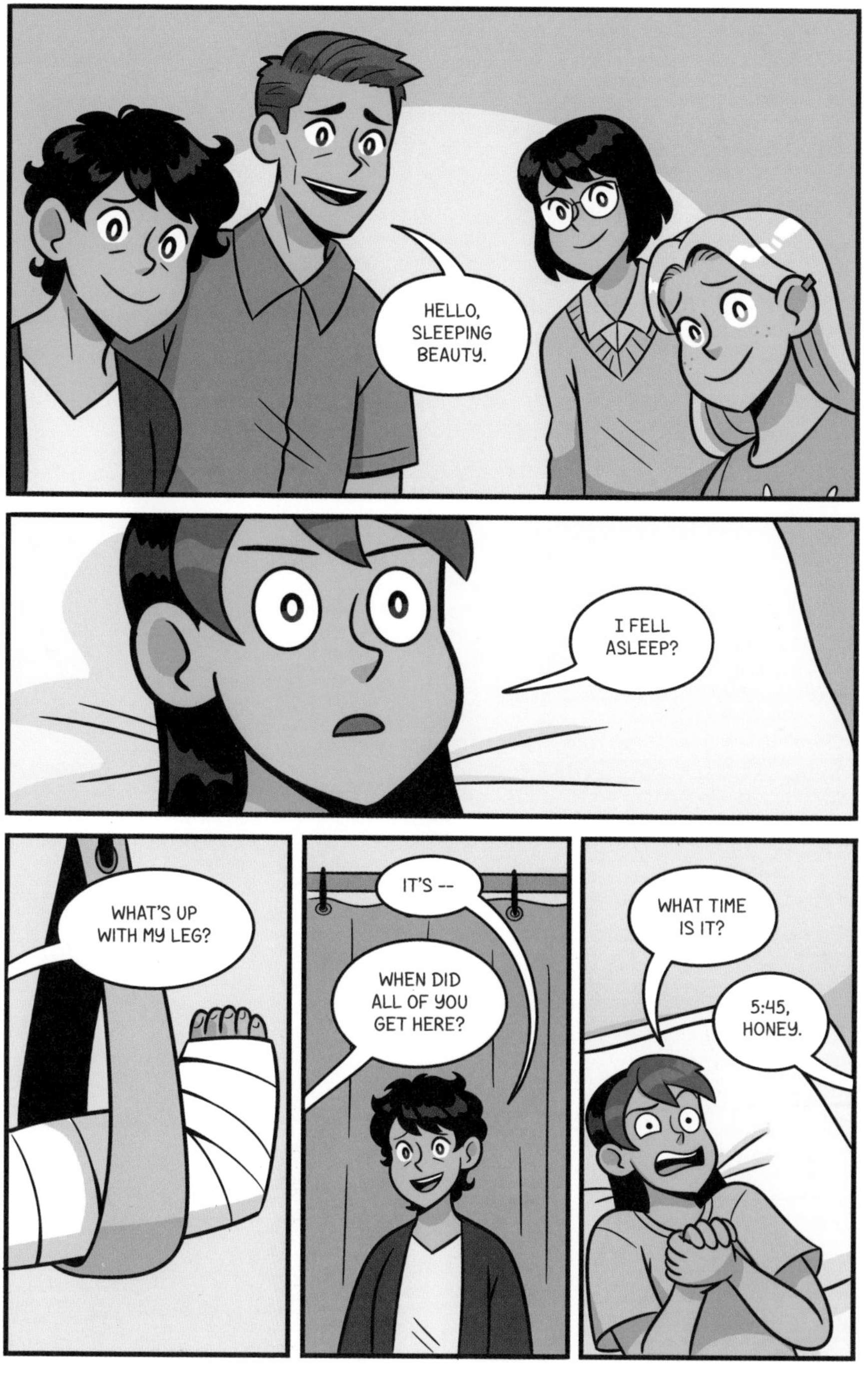
HELLO, SLEEPING BEAUTY.
I FELL ASLEEP?
WHAT'S UP WITH MY LEG?
IT'S --
WHEN DID ALL OF YOU GET HERE?
WHAT TIME IS IT?
5:45, HONEY.

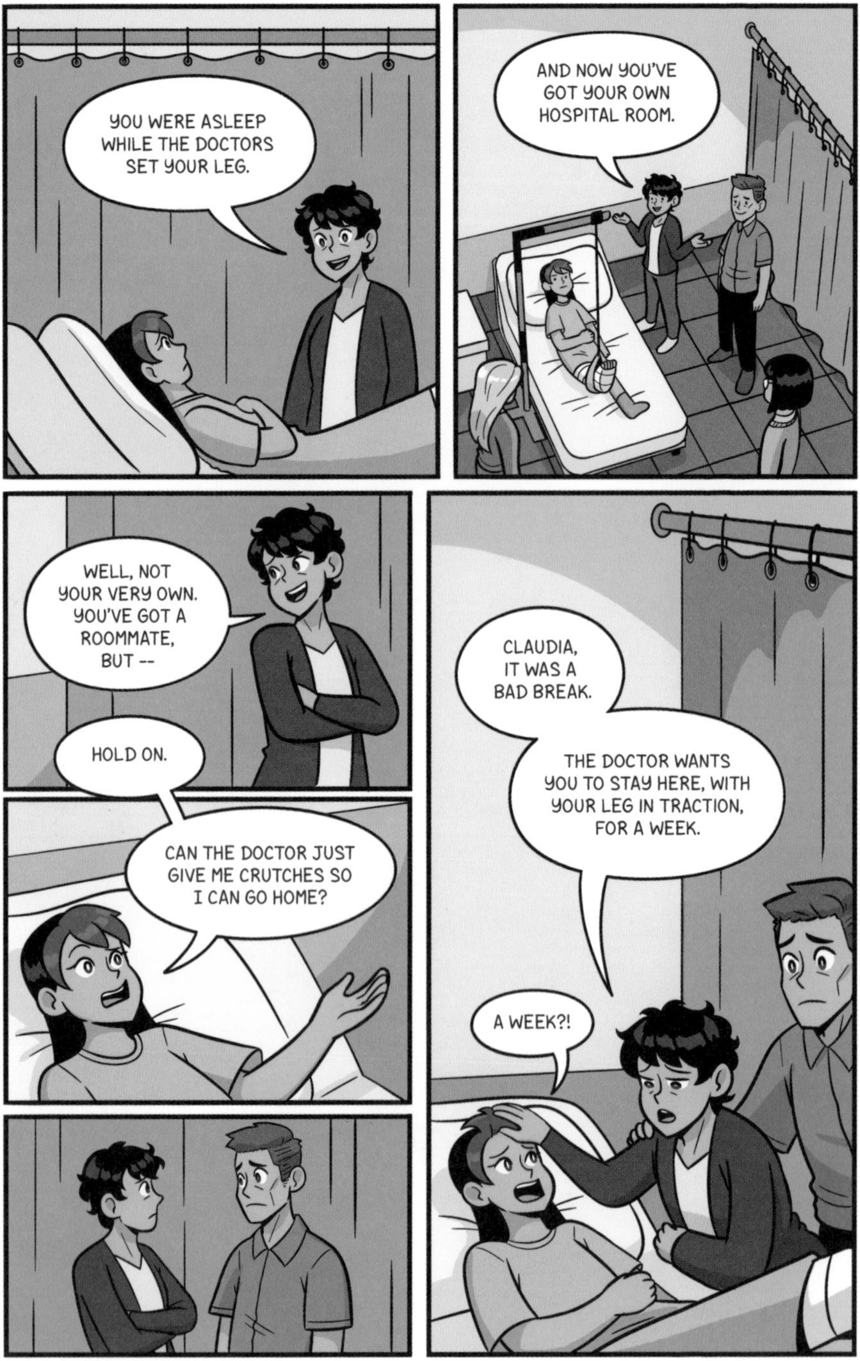
YOU WERE ASLEEP WHILE THE DOCTORS SET YOUR LEG.
AND NOW YOU'VE GOT YOUR OWN HOSPITAL ROOM.
WELL, NOT YOUR VERY OWN. YOU'VE GOT A ROOMMATE, BUT --
HOLD ON.
CAN THE DOCTOR JUST GIVE ME CRUTCHES SO I CAN GO HOME?
CLAUDIA, IT WAS A BAD BREAK.
THE DOCTOR WANTS YOU TO STAY HERE, WITH YOUR LEG IN TRACTION, FOR A WEEK.
A WEEK?!

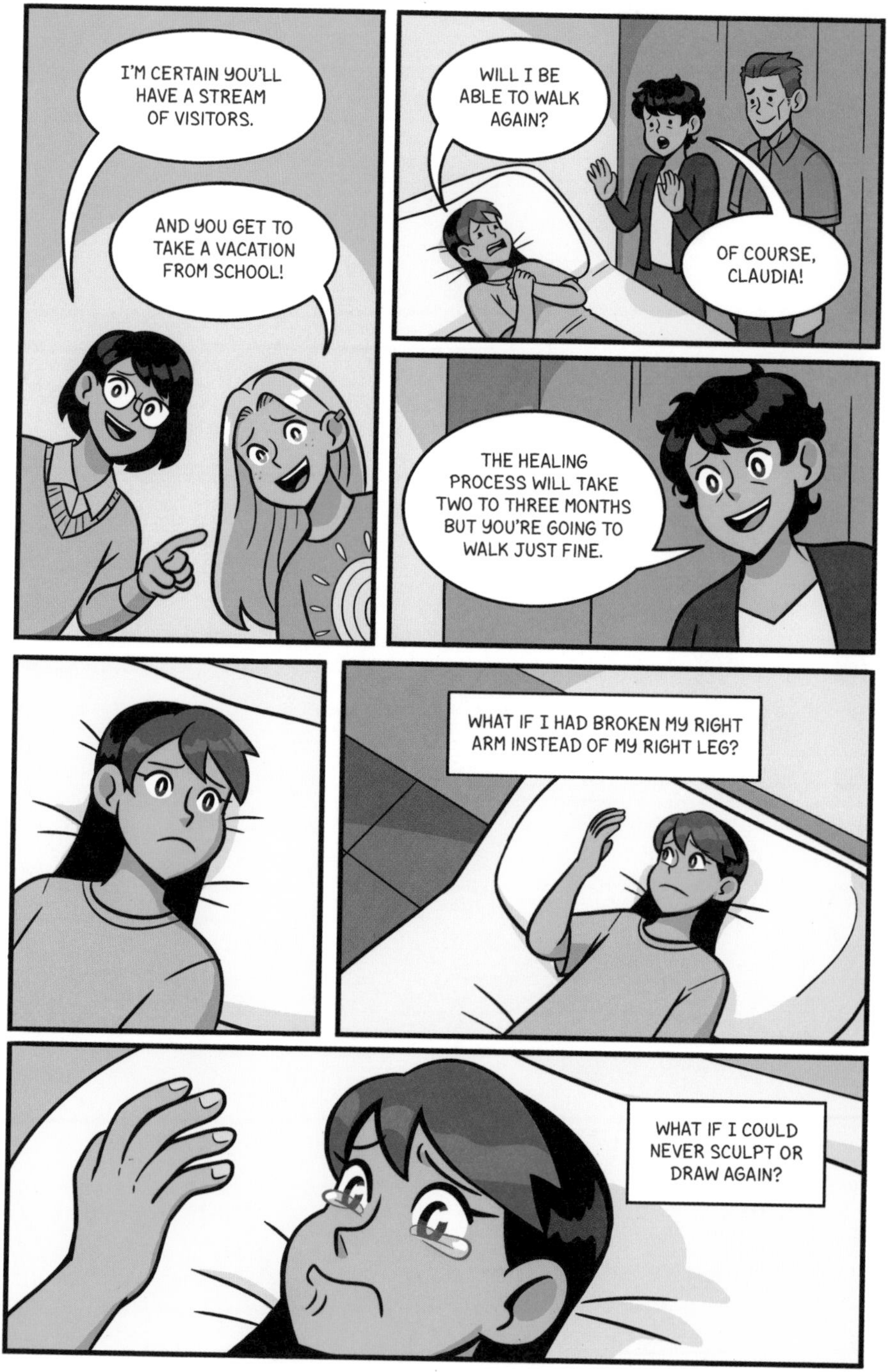
I'M CERTAIN YOU'LL HAVE A STREAM OF VISITORS.
AND YOU GET TO TAKE A VACATION FROM SCHOOL!
WILL I BE ABLE TO WALK AGAIN?
OF COURSE, CLAUDIA!
THE HEALING PROCESS WILL TAKE TWO TO THREE MONTHS BUT YOU'RE GOING TO WALK JUST FINE.
WHAT IF I HAD BROKEN MY RIGHT ARM INSTEAD OF MY RIGHT LEG?
WHAT IF I COULD NEVER SCULPT OR DRAW AGAIN?

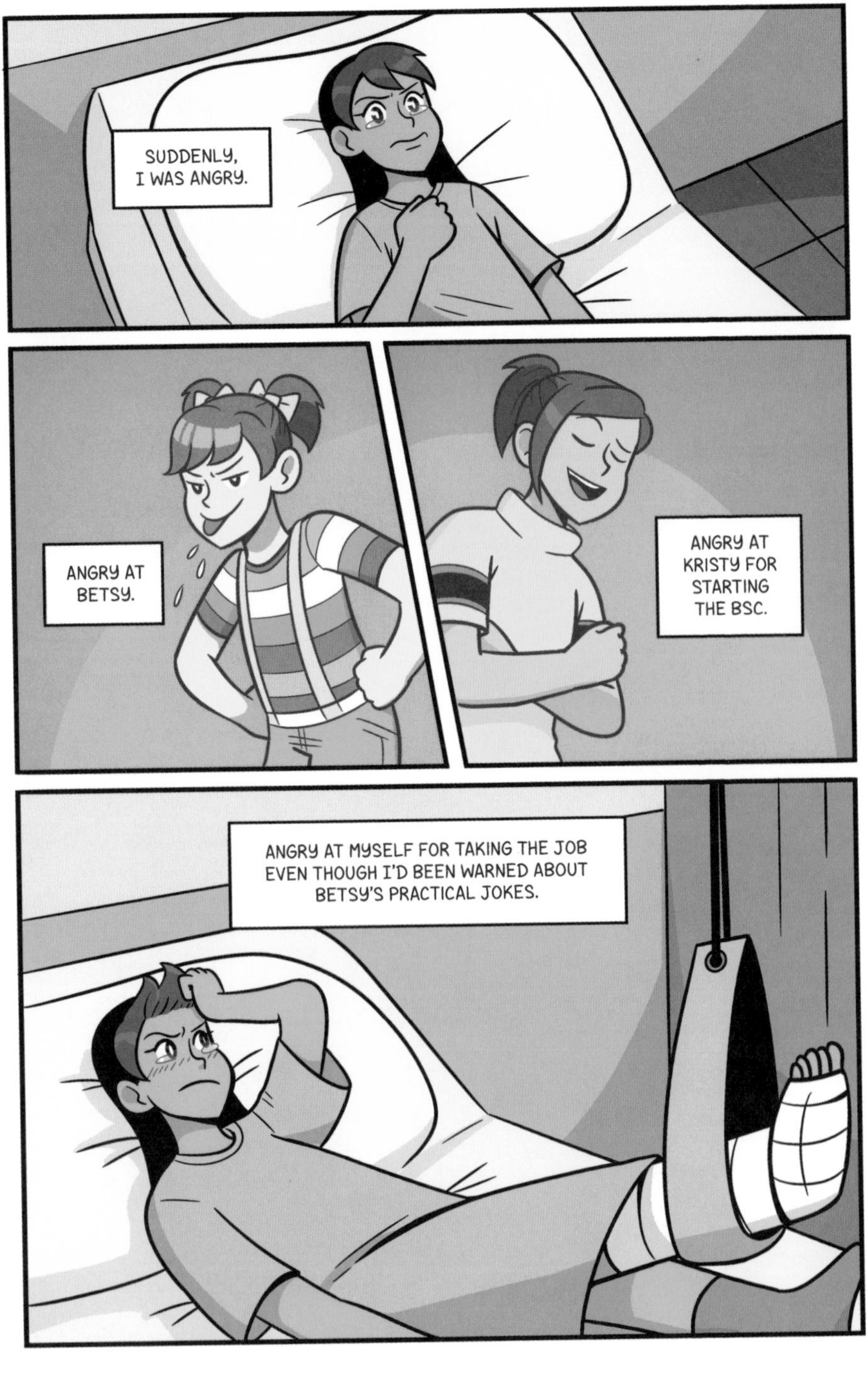
SUDDENLY, I WAS ANGRY.
ANGRY AT BETSY.
ANGRY AT KRISTY FOR STARTING THE BSC.
ANGRY AT MYSELF FOR TAKING THE JOB EVEN THOUGH I'D BEEN WARNED ABOUT BETSY'S PRACTICAL JOKES.

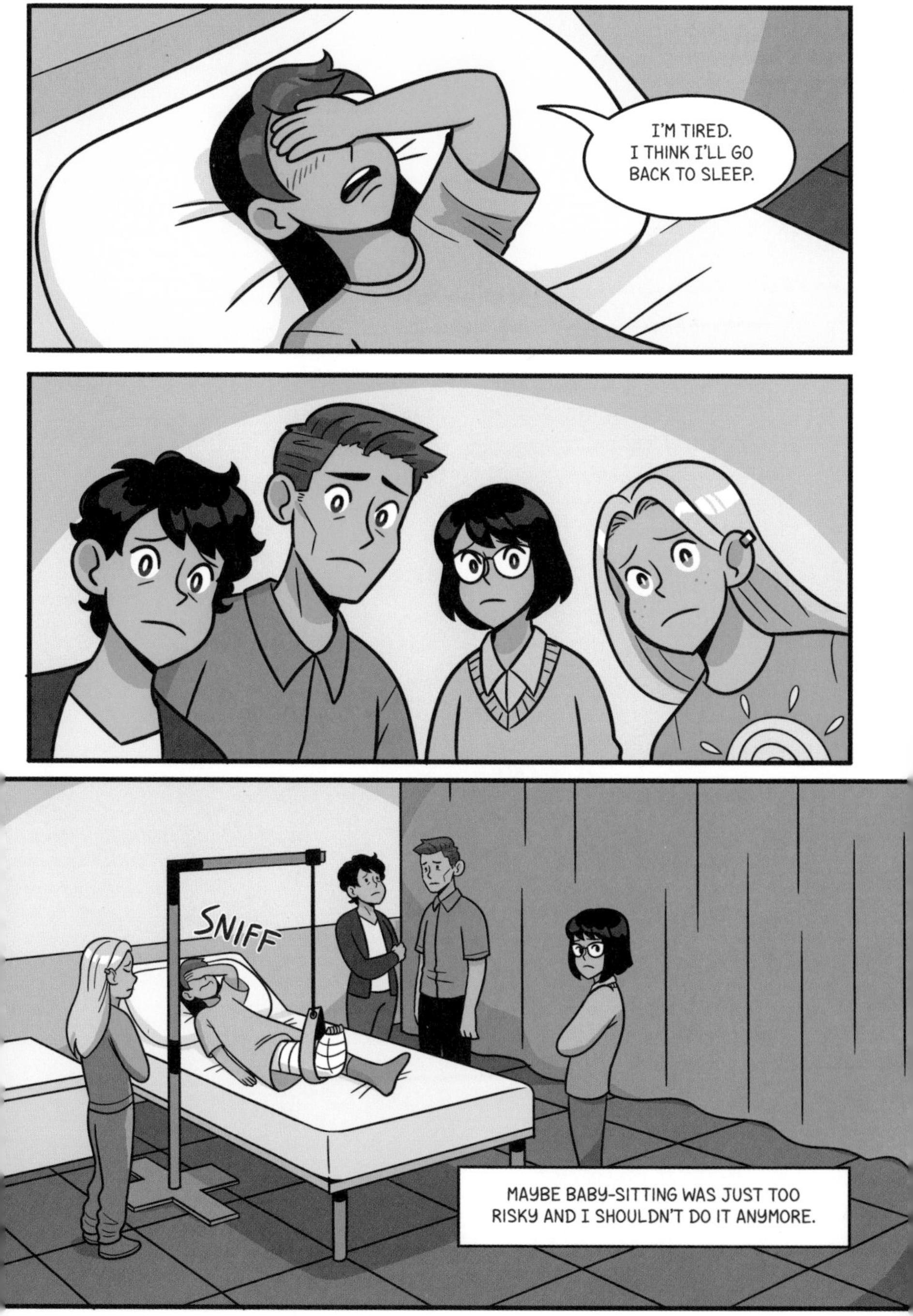
I'M TIRED. I THINK I'LL GO BACK TO SLEEP.
SNIFF
MAYBE BABY-SITTING WAS JUST TOO RISKY AND I SHOULDN'T DO IT ANYMORE.

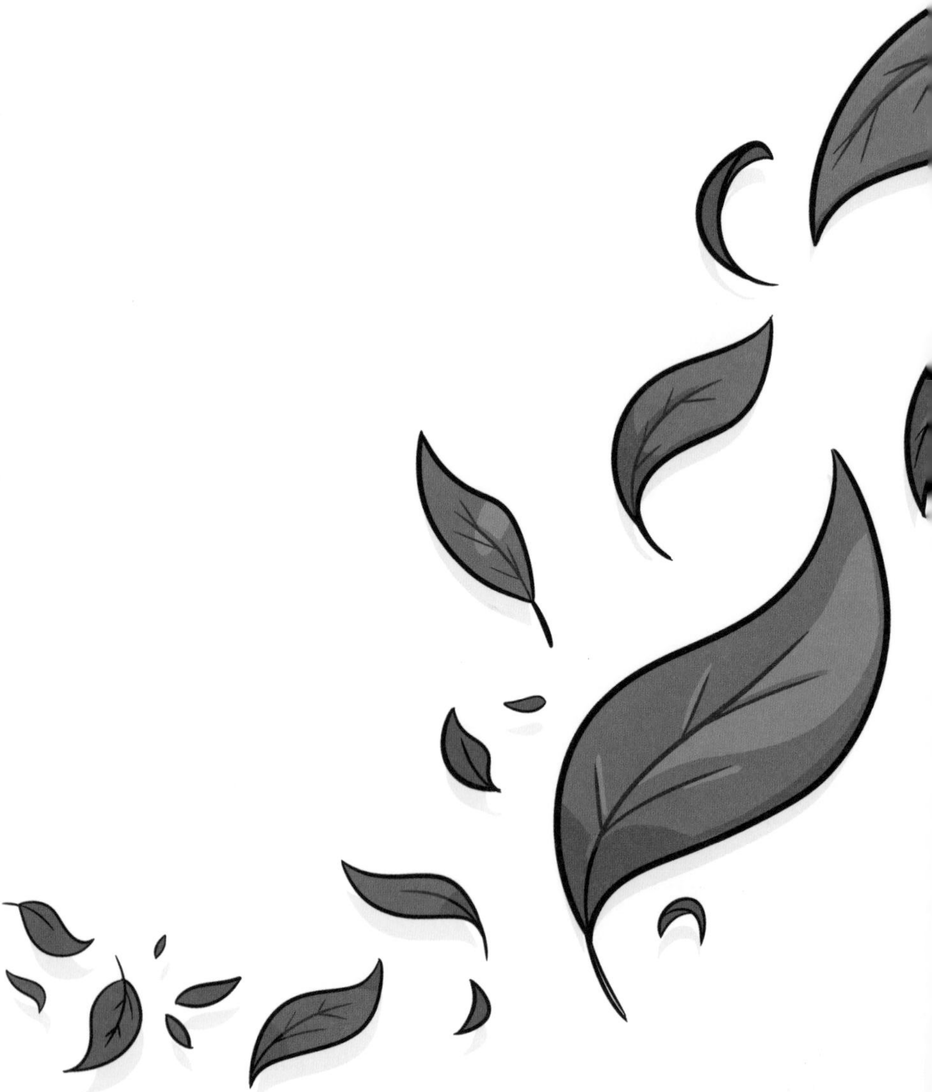

CHAPTER 6

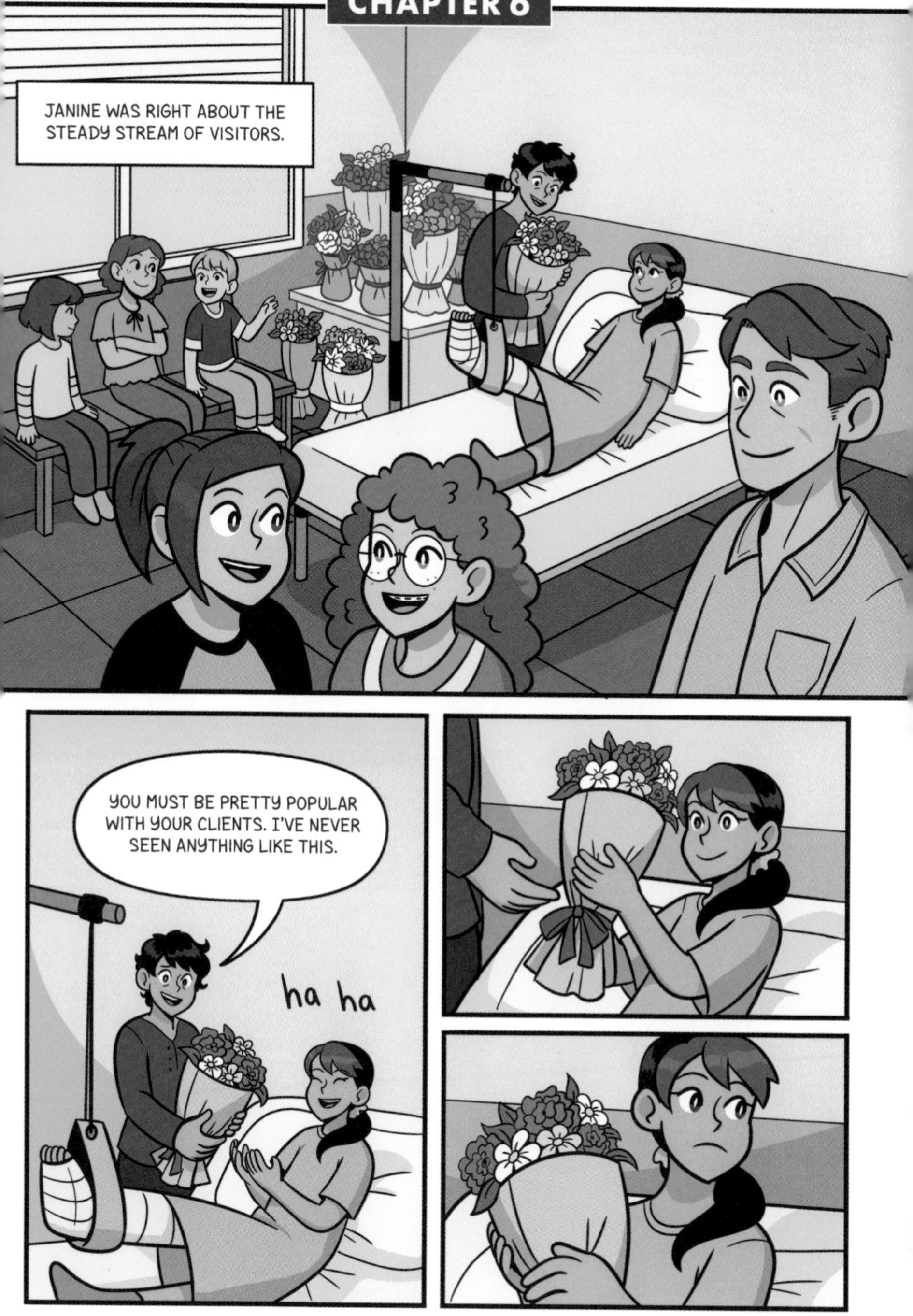

JANINE WAS RIGHT ABOUT THE STEADY STREAM OF VISITORS.
YOU MUST BE PRETTY POPULAR WITH YOUR CLIENTS. I'VE NEVER SEEN ANYTHING LIKE THIS.
ha ha

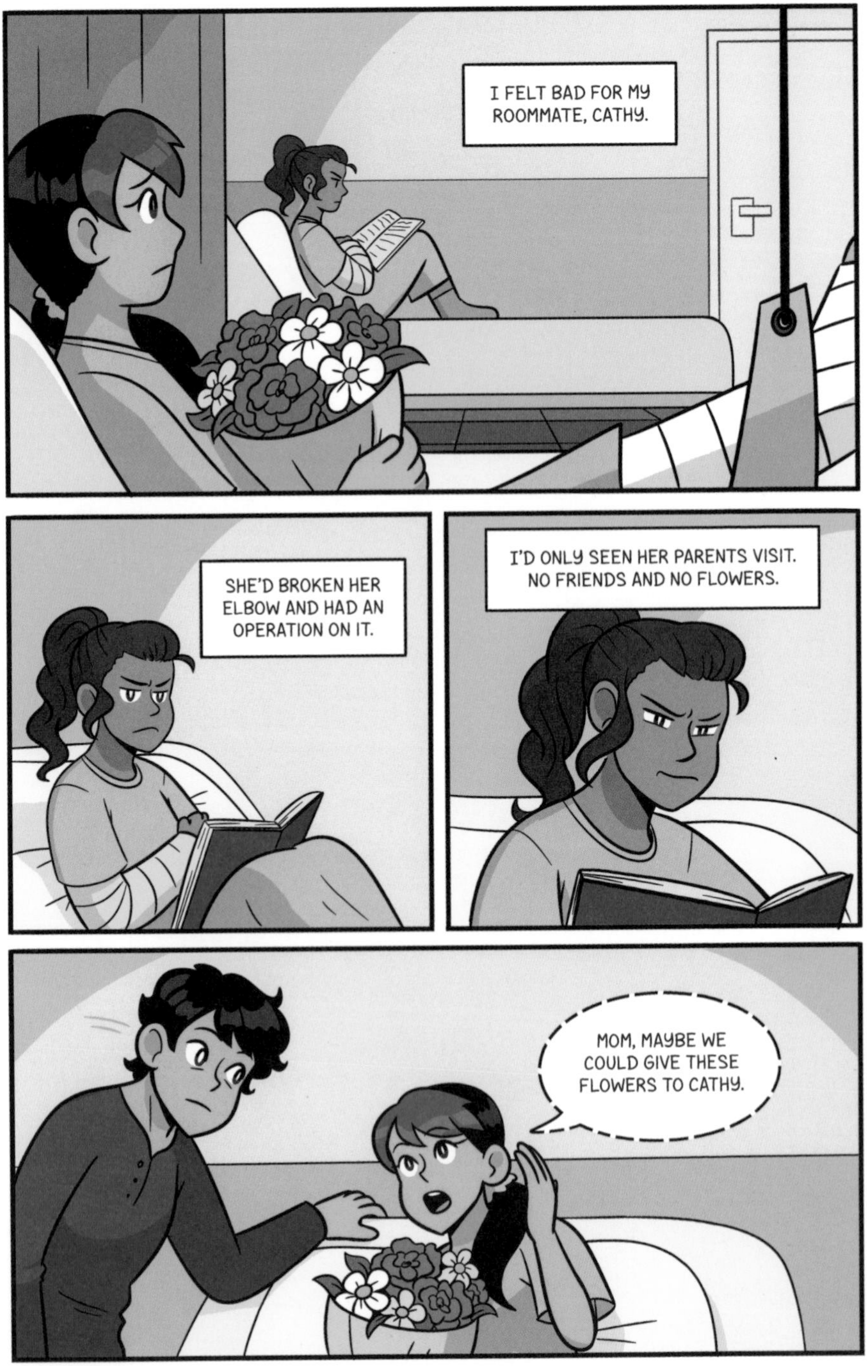
I FELT BAD FOR MY ROOMMATE, CATHY.
SHE'D BROKEN HER ELBOW AND HAD AN OPERATION ON IT.
I'D ONLY SEEN HER PARENTS VISIT. NO FRIENDS AND NO FLOWERS.
MOM, MAYBE WE COULD GIVE THESE FLOWERS TO CATHY.

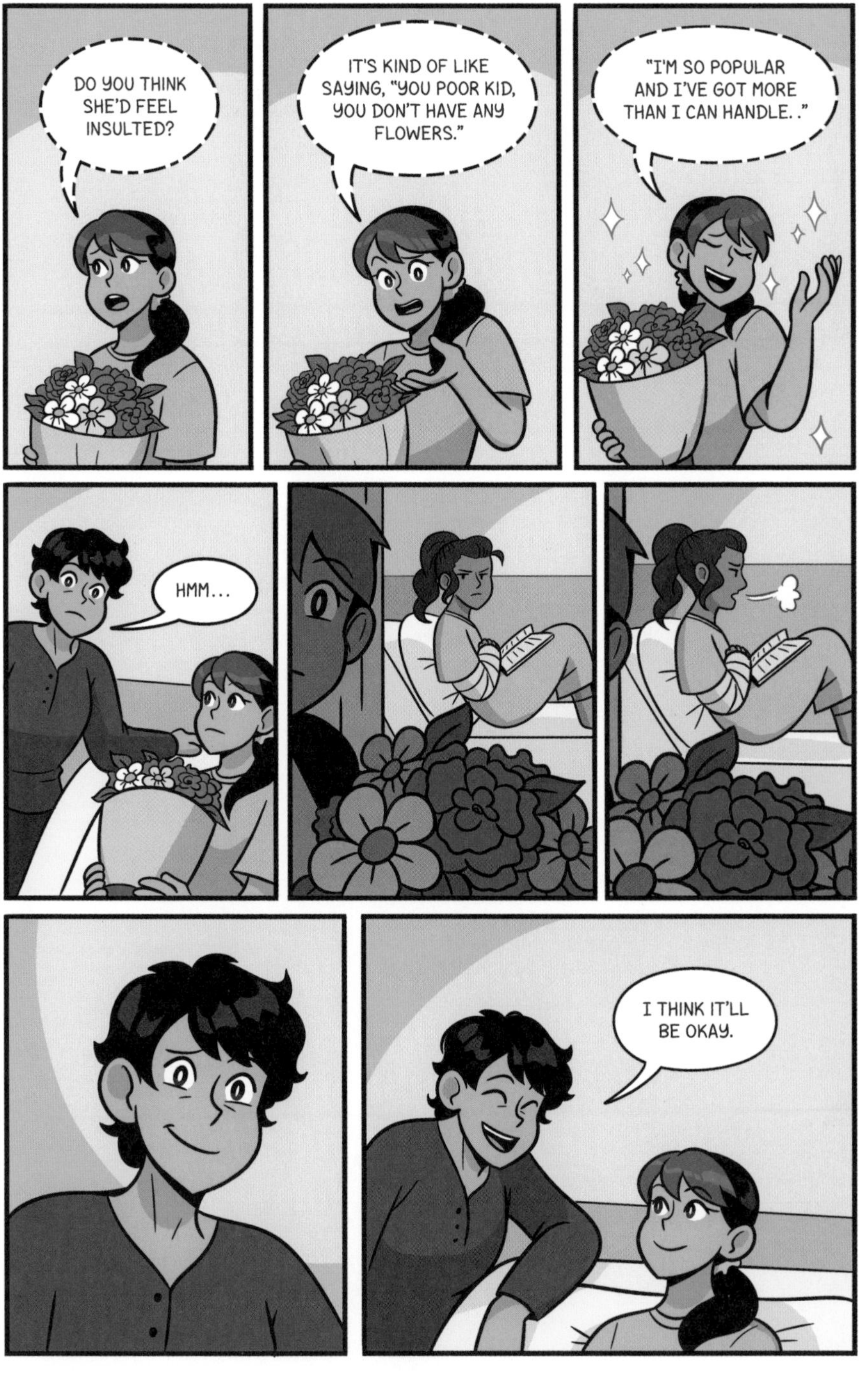
DO YOU THINK SHE'D FEEL INSULTED?
IT'S KIND OF LIKE SAYING, "YOU POOR KID, YOU DON'T HAVE ANY FLOWERS."
"I'M SO POPULAR AND I'VE GOT MORE THAN I CAN HANDLE.."
HMM...
I THINK IT'LL BE OKAY.

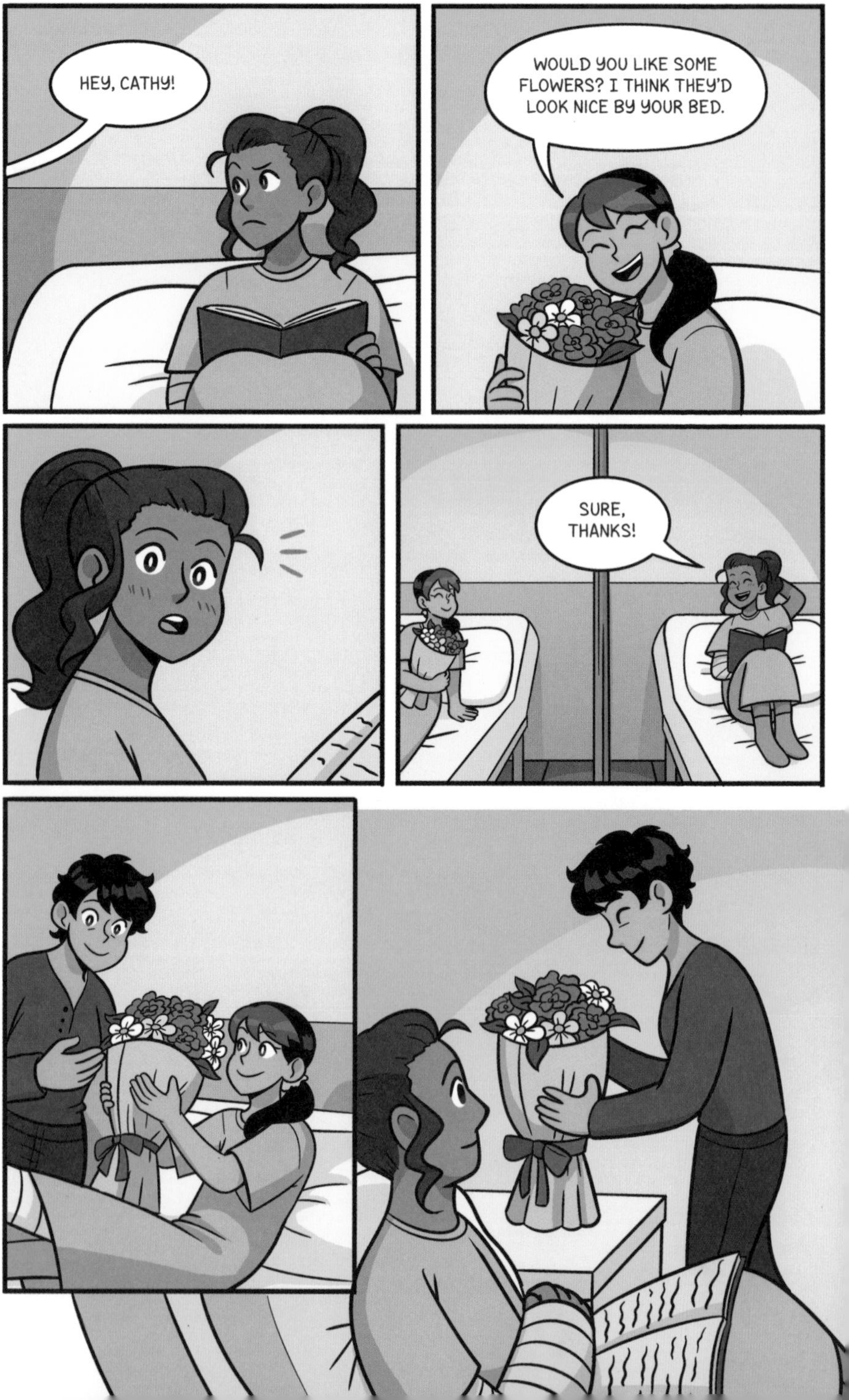
HEY, CATHY!
WOULD YOU LIKE SOME FLOWERS? I THINK THEY'D LOOK NICE BY YOUR BED.
SURE, THANKS!

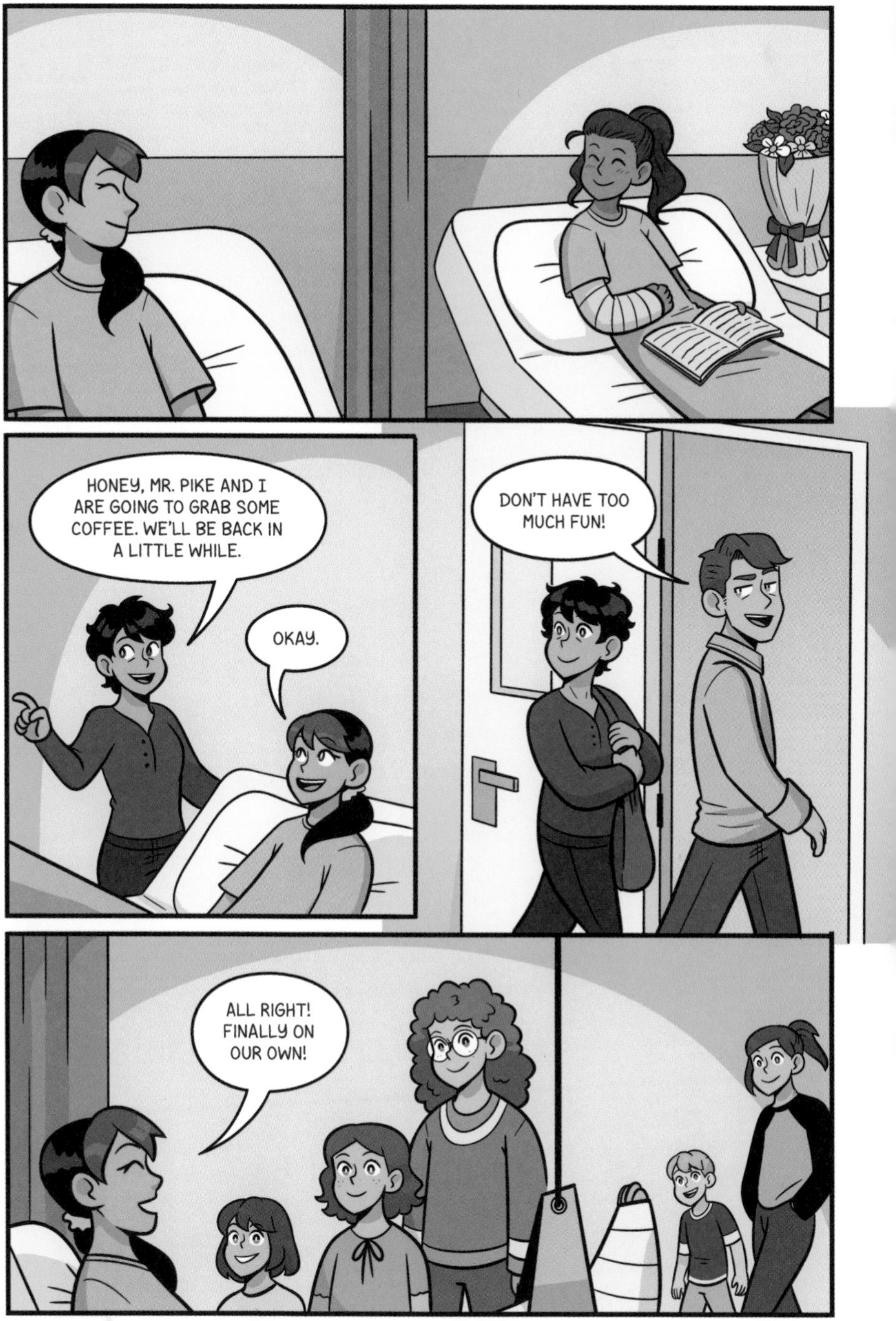
HONEY, MR. PIKE AND I ARE GOING TO GRAB SOME COFFEE. WE'LL BE BACK IN A LITTLE WHILE.
OKAY.
DON'T HAVE TOO MUCH FUN!
ALL RIGHT! FINALLY ON OUR OWN!

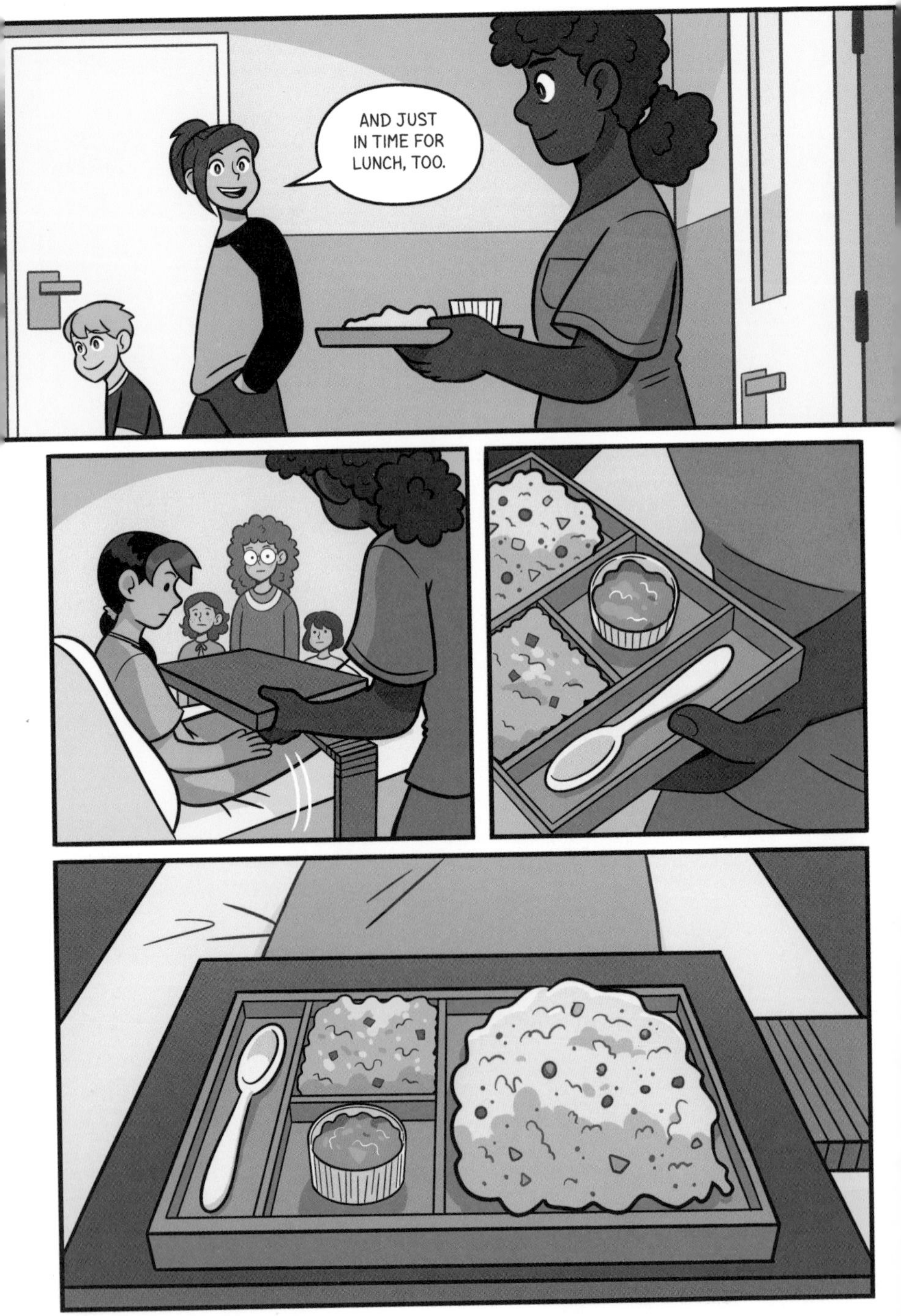
AND JUST IN TIME FOR LUNCH, TOO.

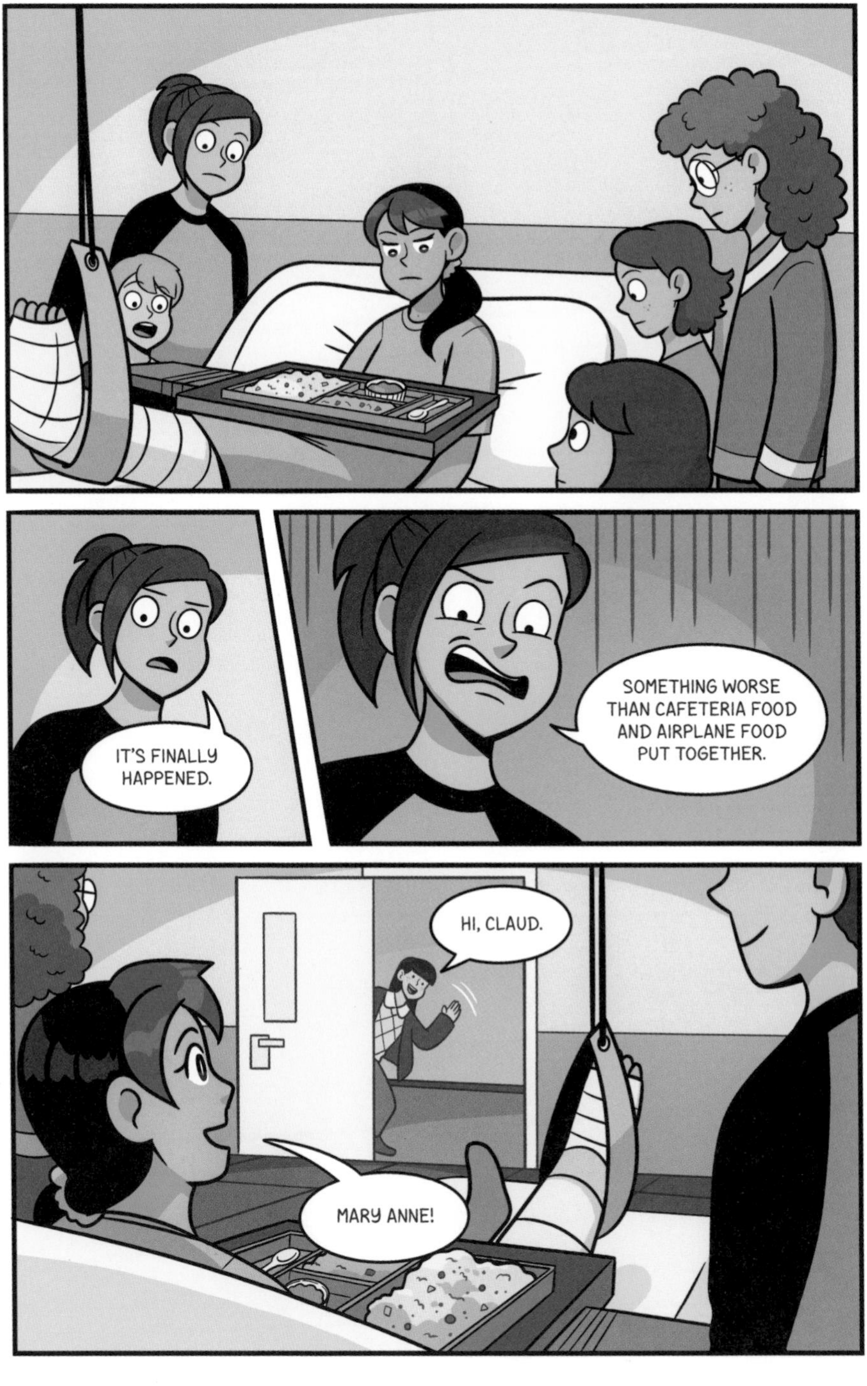
IT'S FINALLY HAPPENED.
SOMETHING WORSE THAN CAFETERIA FOOD AND AIRPLANE FOOD PUT TOGETHER.
HI, CLAUD.
MARY ANNE!

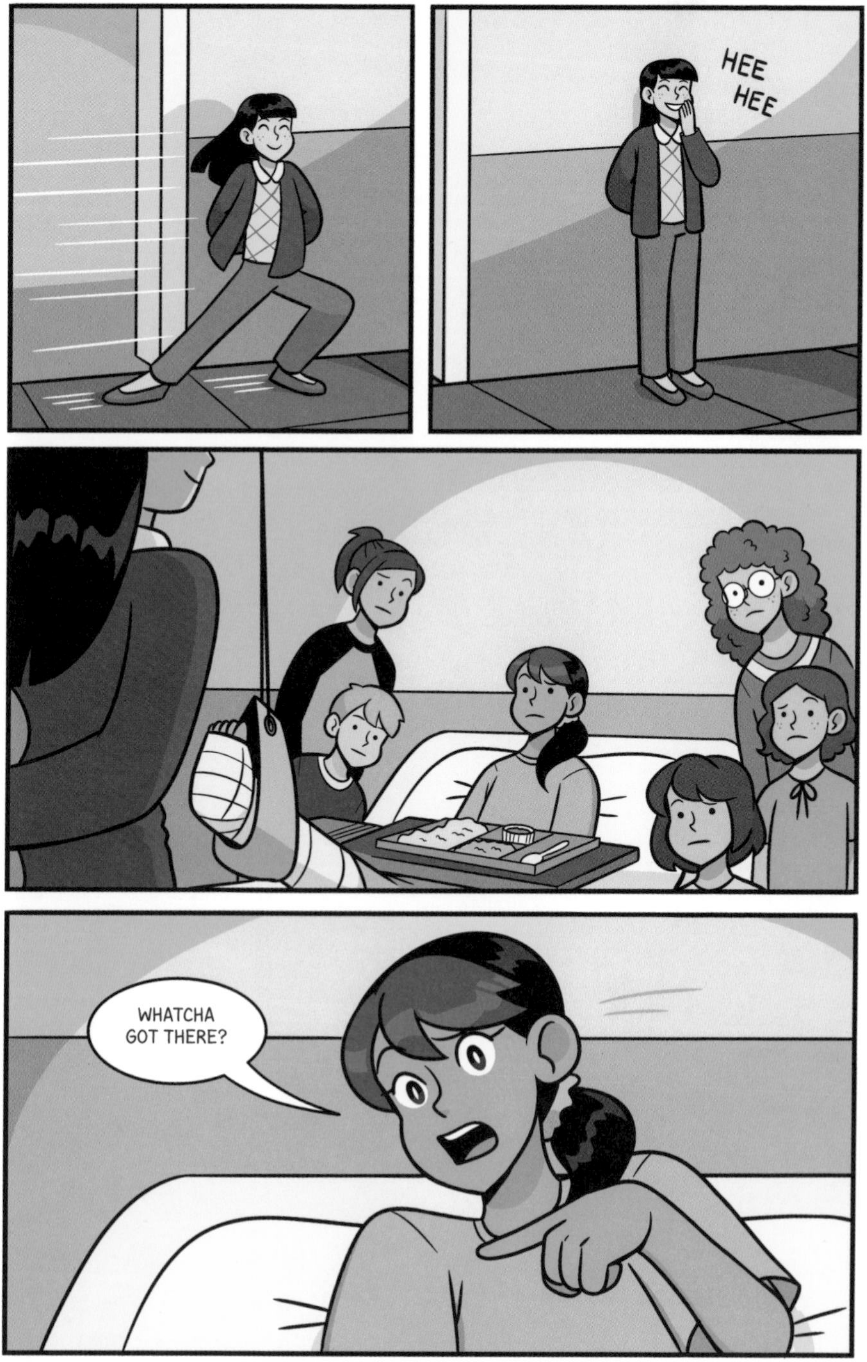
HEE HEE
WHATCHA GOT THERE?

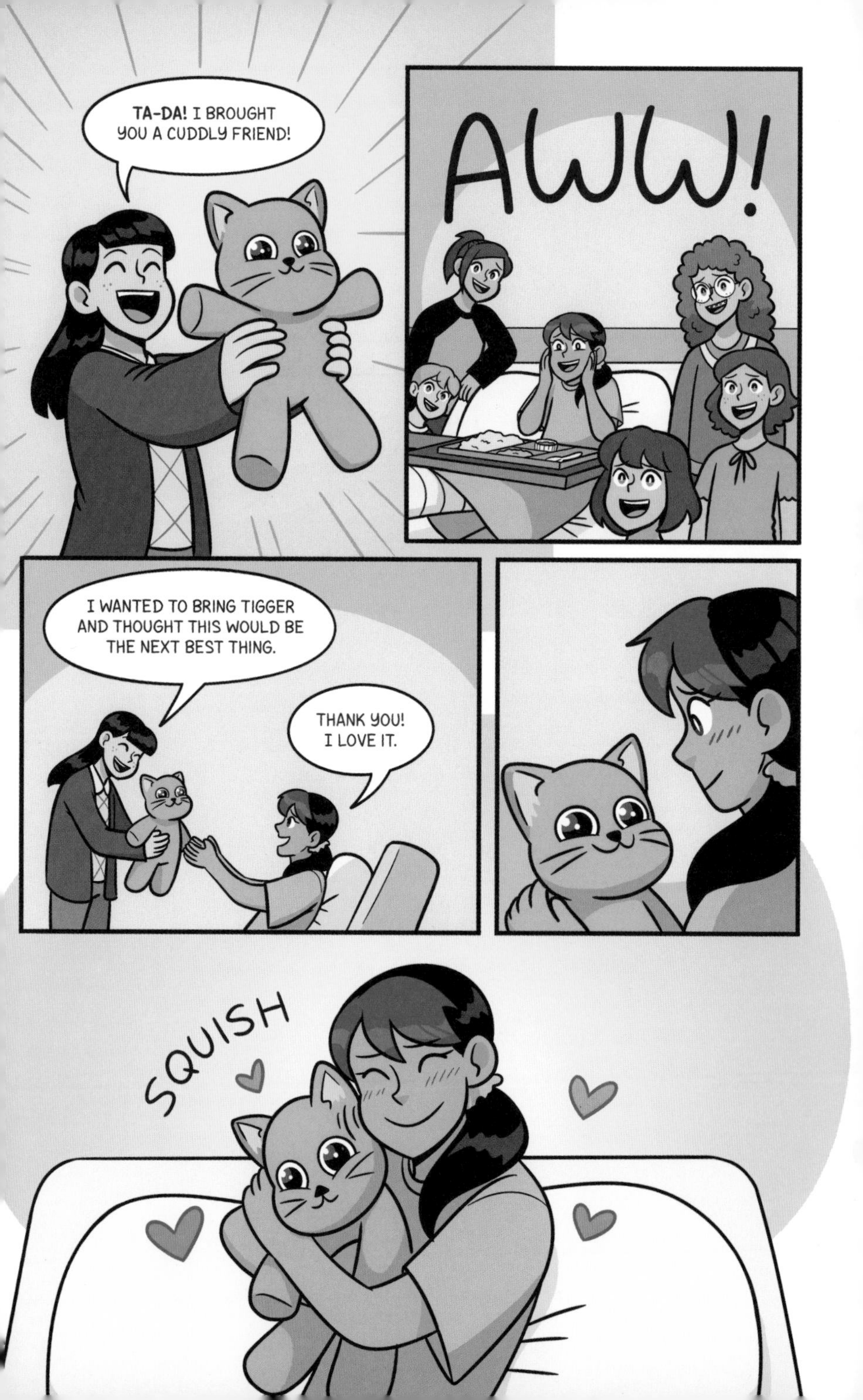
TA-DA! I BROUGHT YOU A CUDDLY FRIEND!
AWW!
I WANTED TO BRING TIGGER AND THOUGHT THIS WOULD BE THE NEXT BEST THING.
THANK YOU! I LOVE IT.
SQUISH

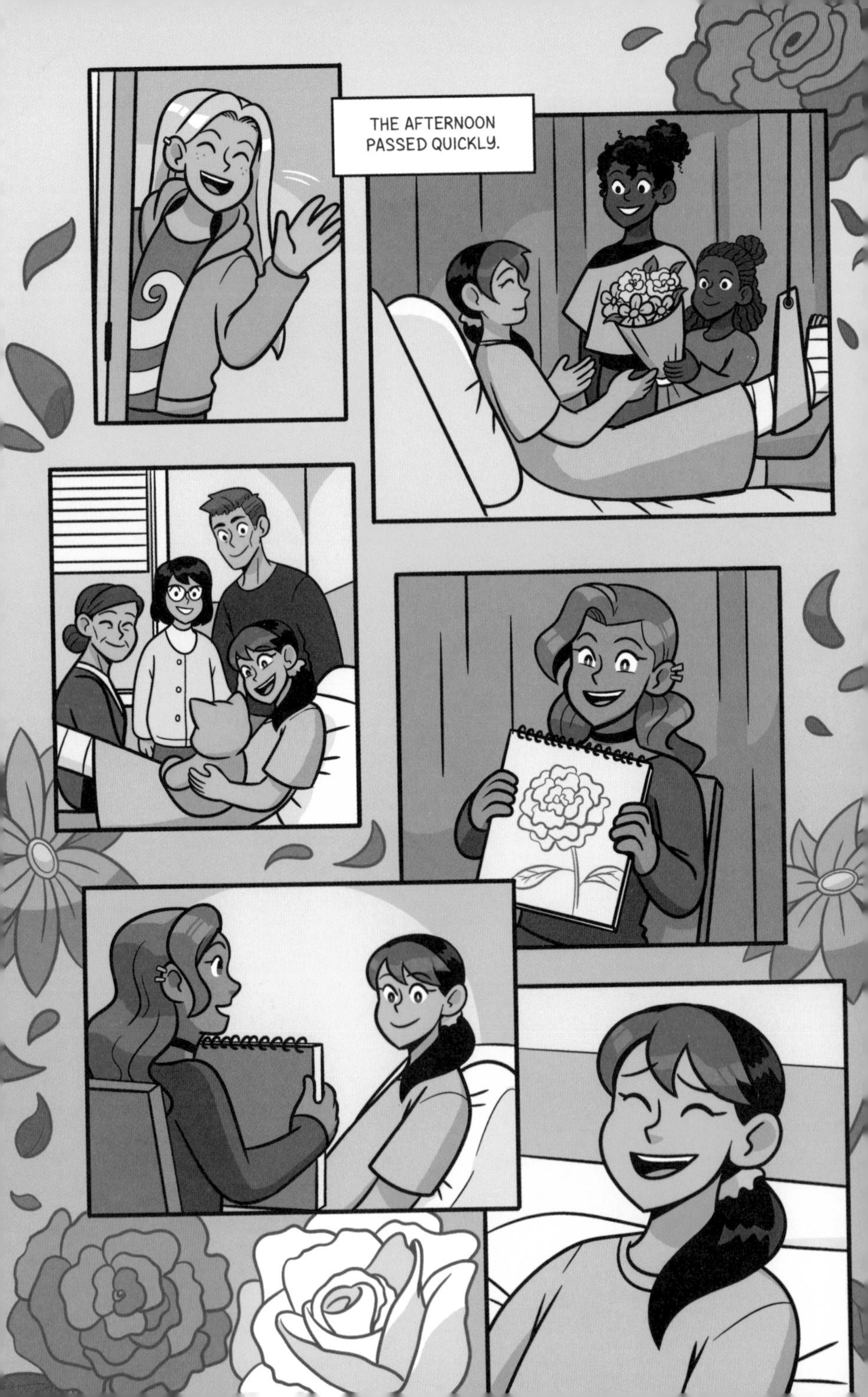
THE AFTERNOON PASSED QUICKLY.

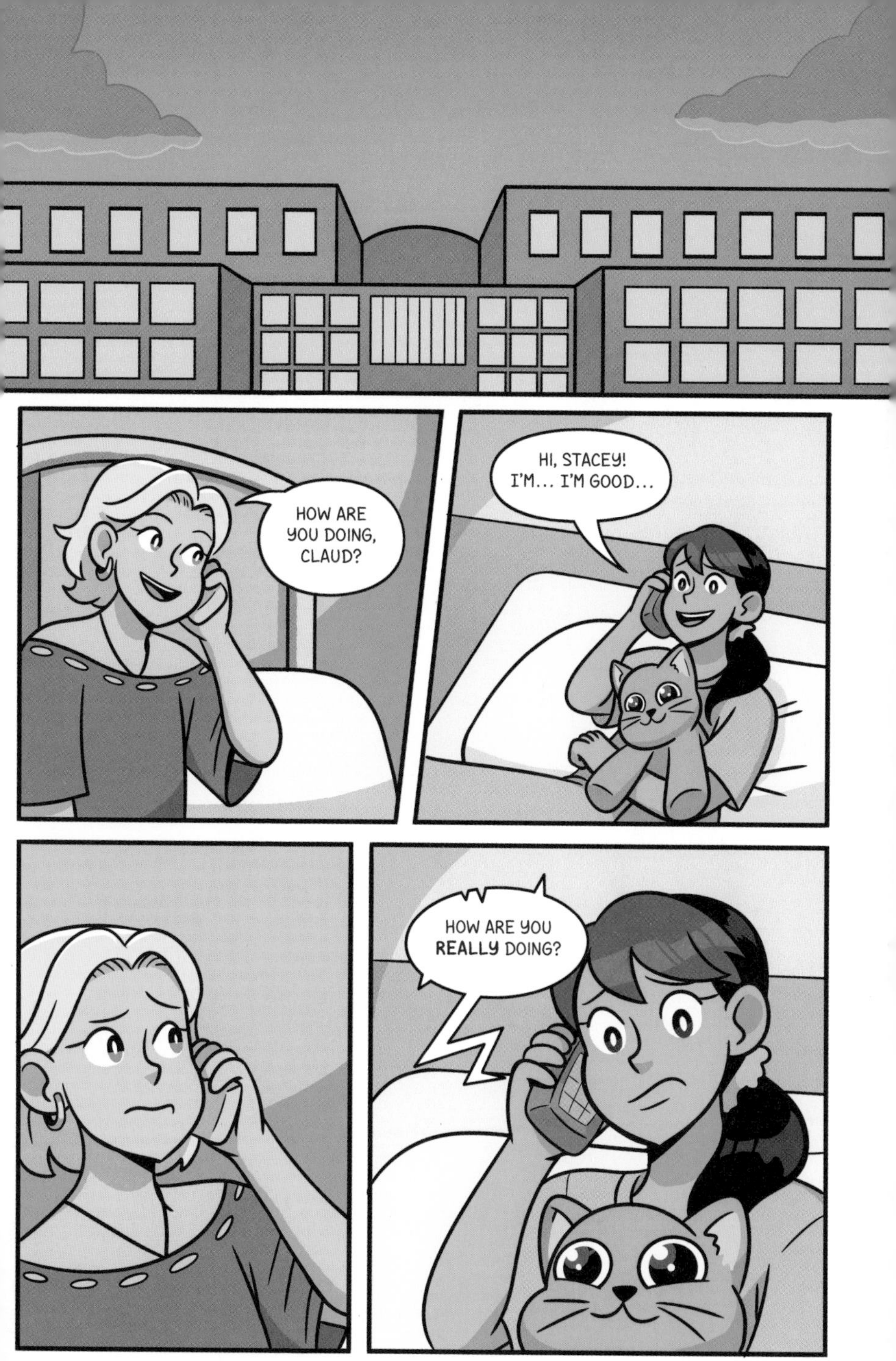
HOW ARE YOU DOING, CLAUD?
HI, STACEY! I'M... I'M GOOD...
HOW ARE YOU **REALLY** DOING?

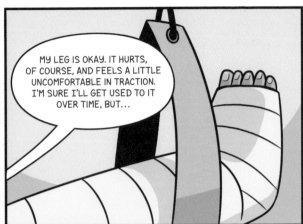

MY LEG IS OKAY. IT HURTS, OF COURSE, AND FEELS A LITTLE UNCOMFORTABLE IN TRACTION. I'M SURE I'LL GET USED TO IT OVER TIME, BUT...

UM...

WHAT'S WRONG?

I'VE BEEN DOING A LOT OF THINKING AND I KEEP GOING BACK TO THIS ONE THING.

WHAT IF I HAD SEVERELY BROKEN MY HANDS OR ARMS WHEN I FELL?

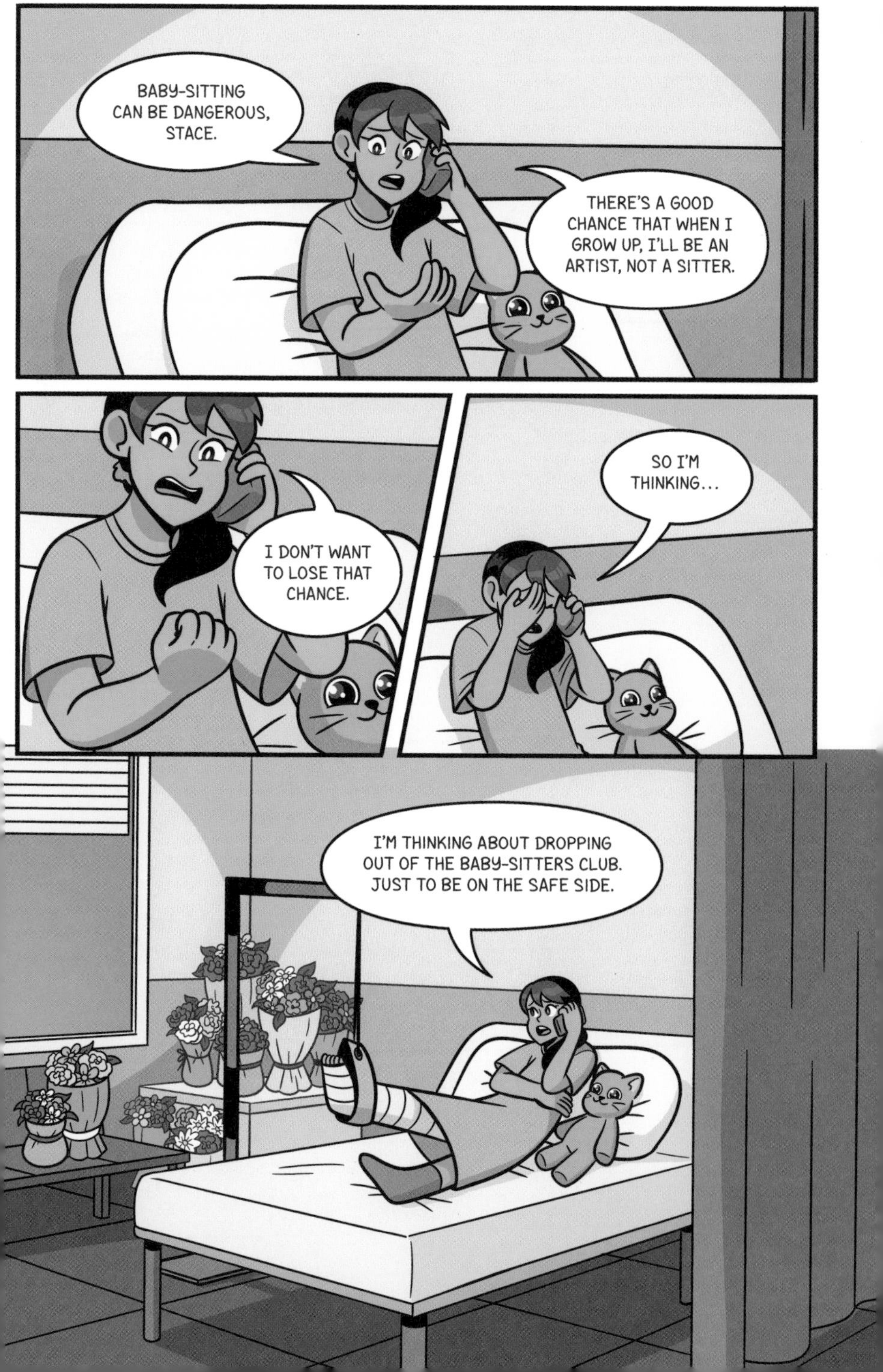
BABY-SITTING CAN BE DANGEROUS, STACE.
THERE'S A GOOD CHANCE THAT WHEN I GROW UP, I'LL BE AN ARTIST, NOT A SITTER.
I DON'T WANT TO LOSE THAT CHANCE.
SO I'M THINKING...
I'M THINKING ABOUT DROPPING OUT OF THE BABY-SITTERS CLUB. JUST TO BE ON THE SAFE SIDE.

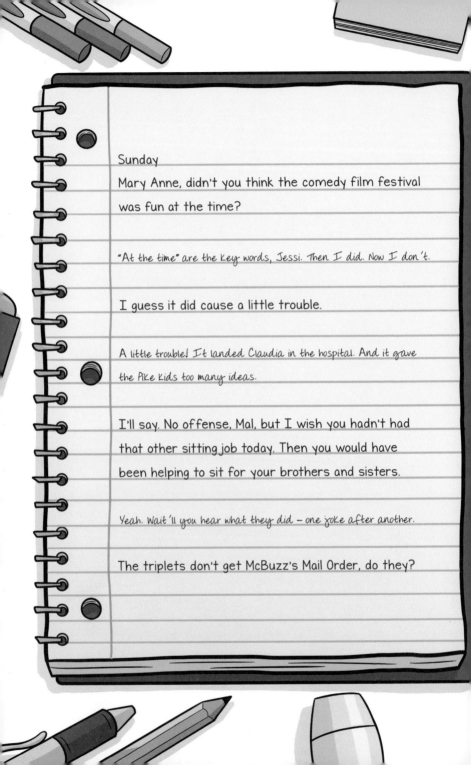

Sunday

Mary Anne, didn't you think the comedy film festival was fun at the time?

"At the time" are the key words, Jessi. Then I did. Now I don't.

I guess it did cause a little trouble.

A little trouble! It landed Claudia in the hospital. And it gave the Pike kids too many ideas.

I'll say. No offense, Mal, but I wish you hadn't had that other sitting job today. Then you would have been helping to sit for your brothers and sisters.

Yeah. Wait 'll you hear what they did — one joke after another.

The triplets don't get McBuzz's Mail Order, do they?

CHAPTER 7

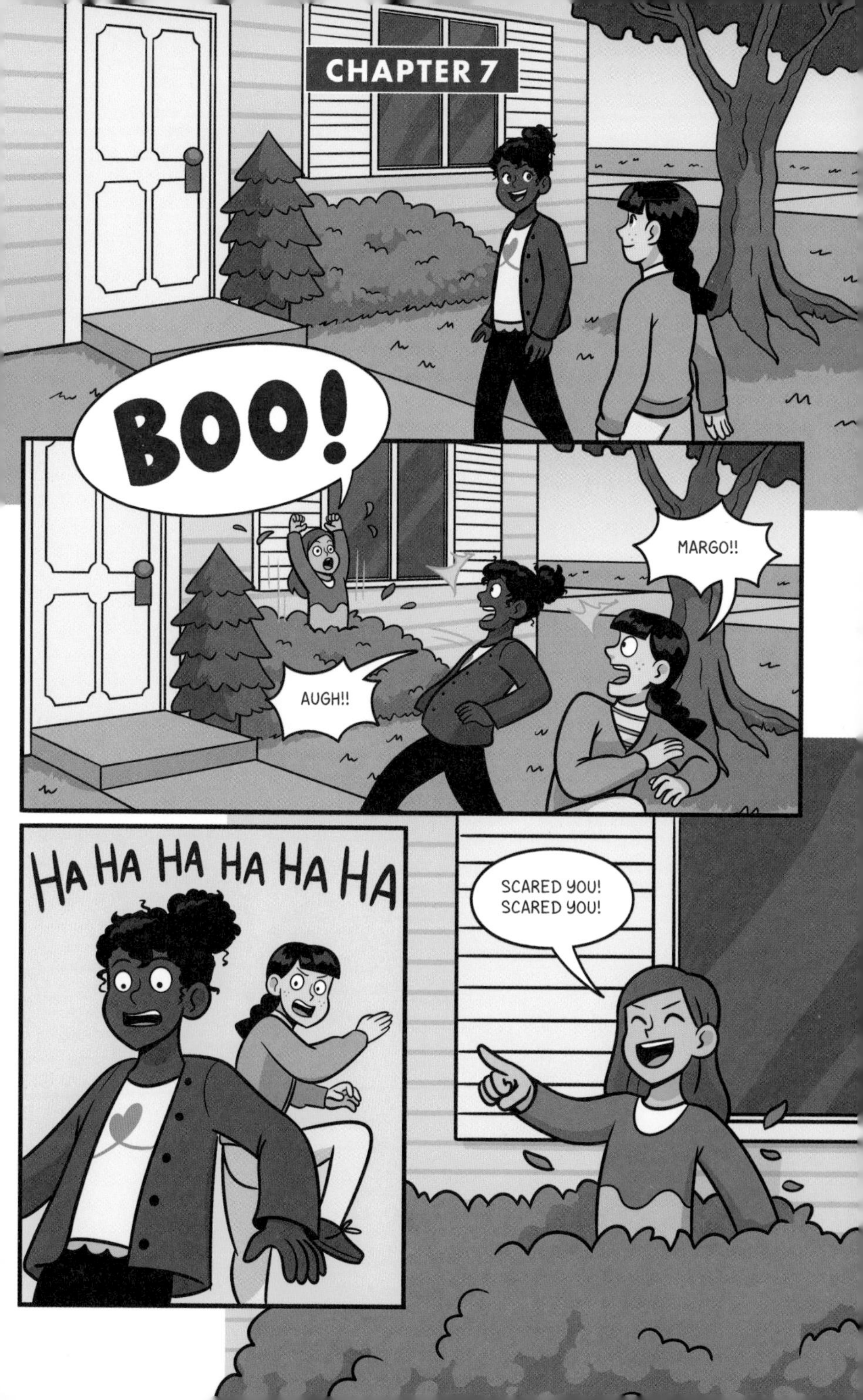
BOO!
MARGO!!
AUGH!!
HA HA HA HA HA HA
SCARED YOU!
SCARED YOU!

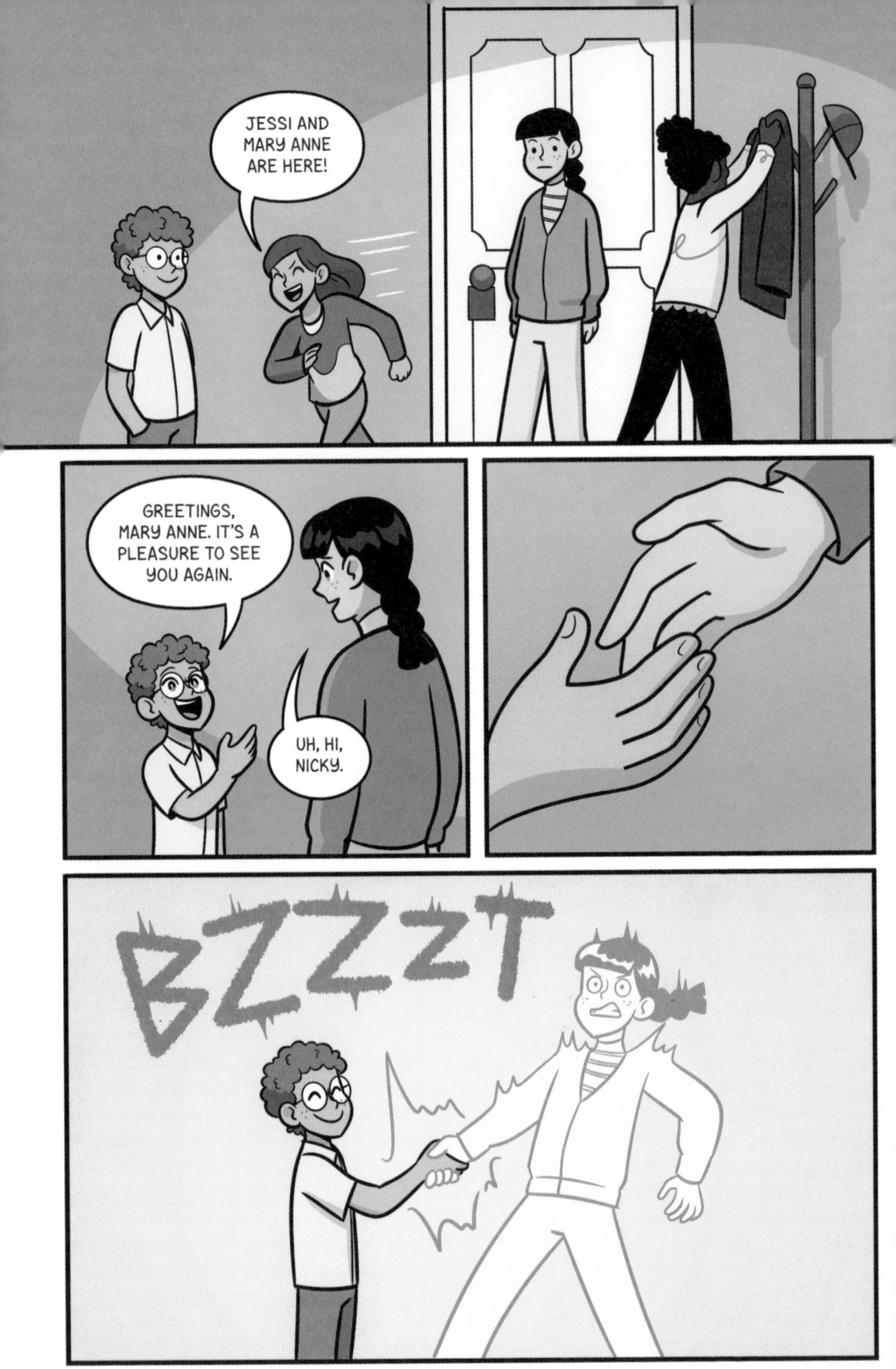
JESSI AND MARY ANNE ARE HERE!
GREETINGS, MARY ANNE. IT'S A PLEASURE TO SEE YOU AGAIN.
UH, HI, NICKY.
BZZZT

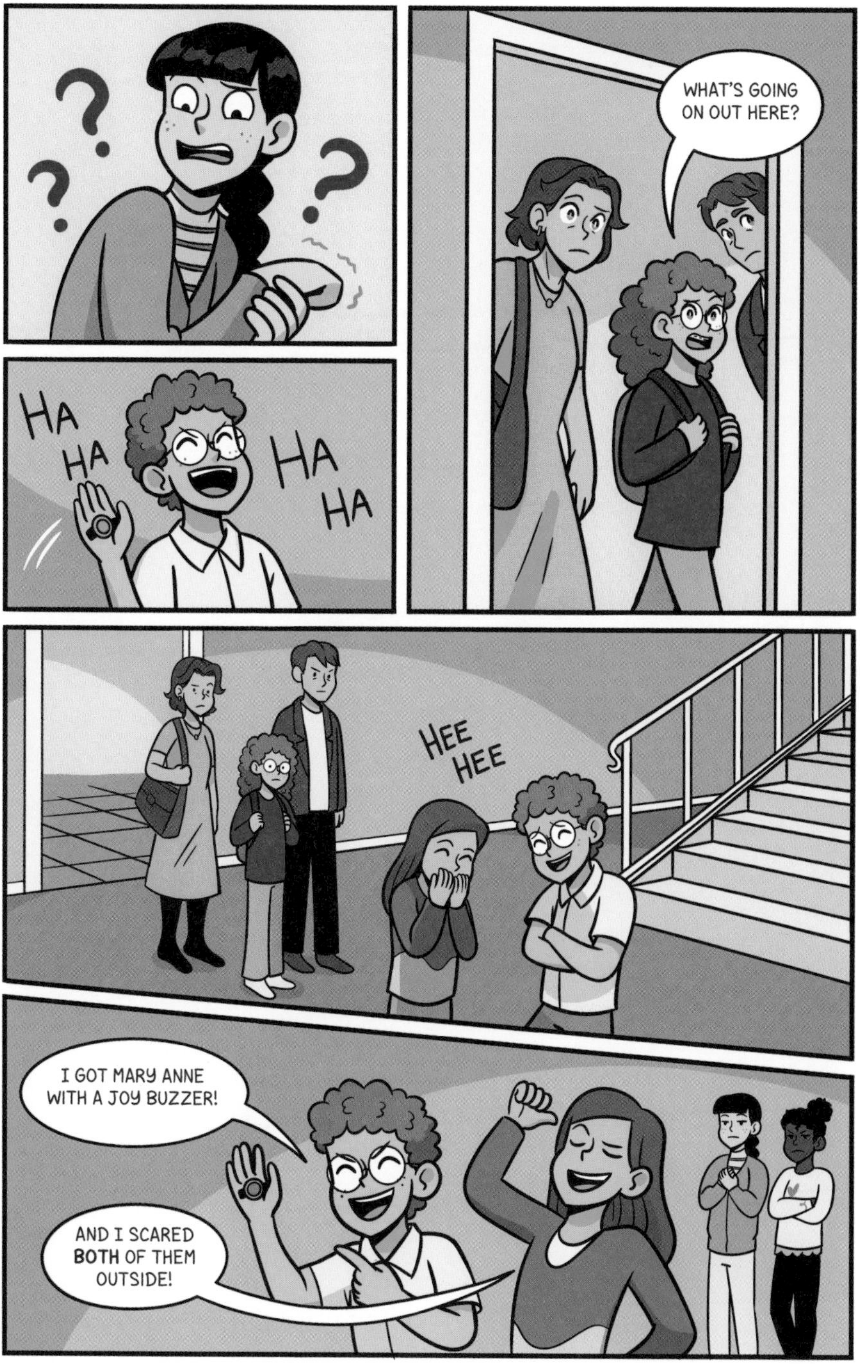
?
?
?
WHAT'S GOING ON OUT HERE?
HA HA HA HA
HEE HEE
I GOT MARY ANNE WITH A JOY BUZZER!
AND I SCARED **BOTH** OF THEM OUTSIDE!

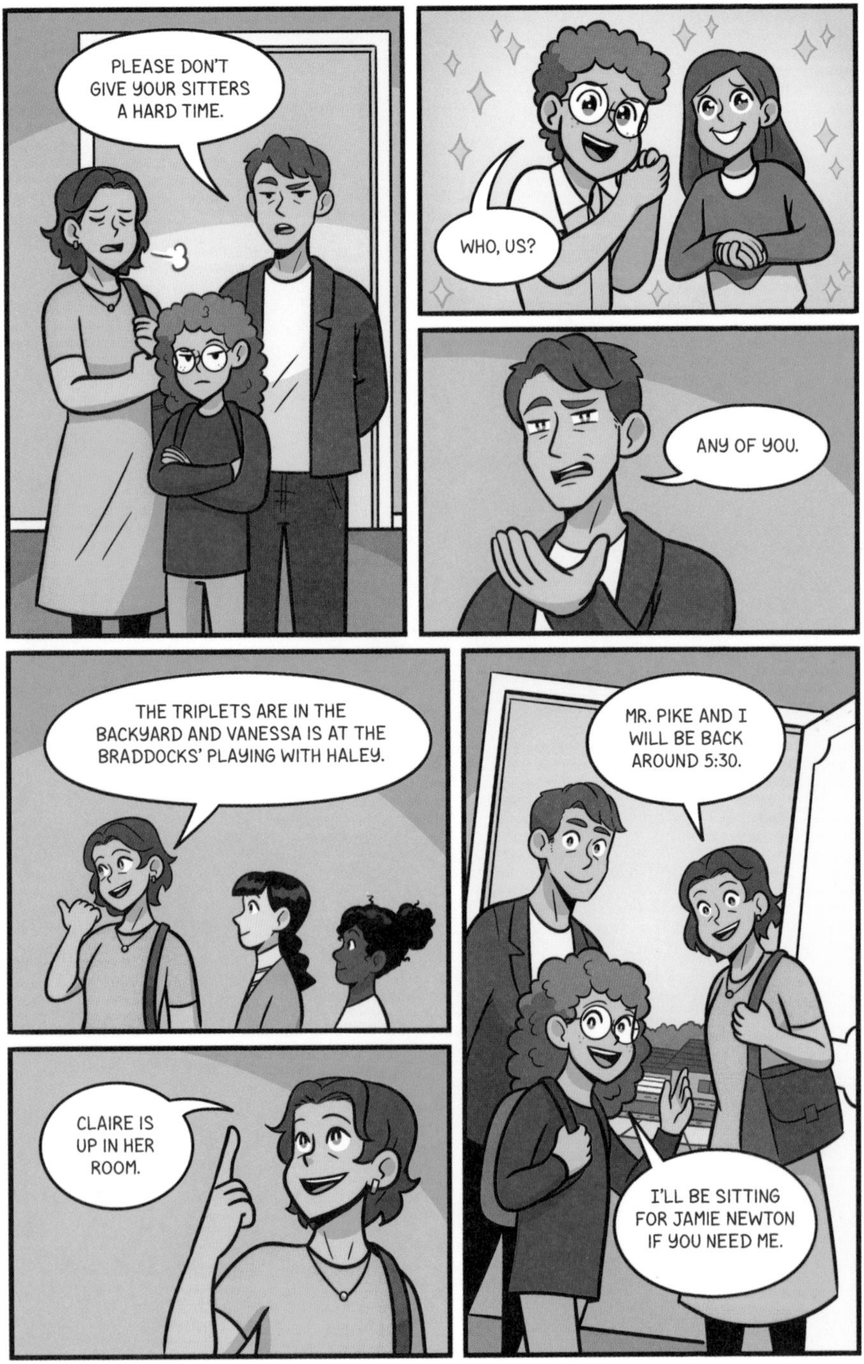
PLEASE DON'T GIVE YOUR SITTERS A HARD TIME.
WHO, US?
ANY OF YOU.
THE TRIPLETS ARE IN THE BACKYARD AND VANESSA IS AT THE BRADDOCKS' PLAYING WITH HALEY.
CLAIRE IS UP IN HER ROOM.
MR. PIKE AND I WILL BE BACK AROUND 5:30.
I'LL BE SITTING FOR JAMIE NEWTON IF YOU NEED ME.

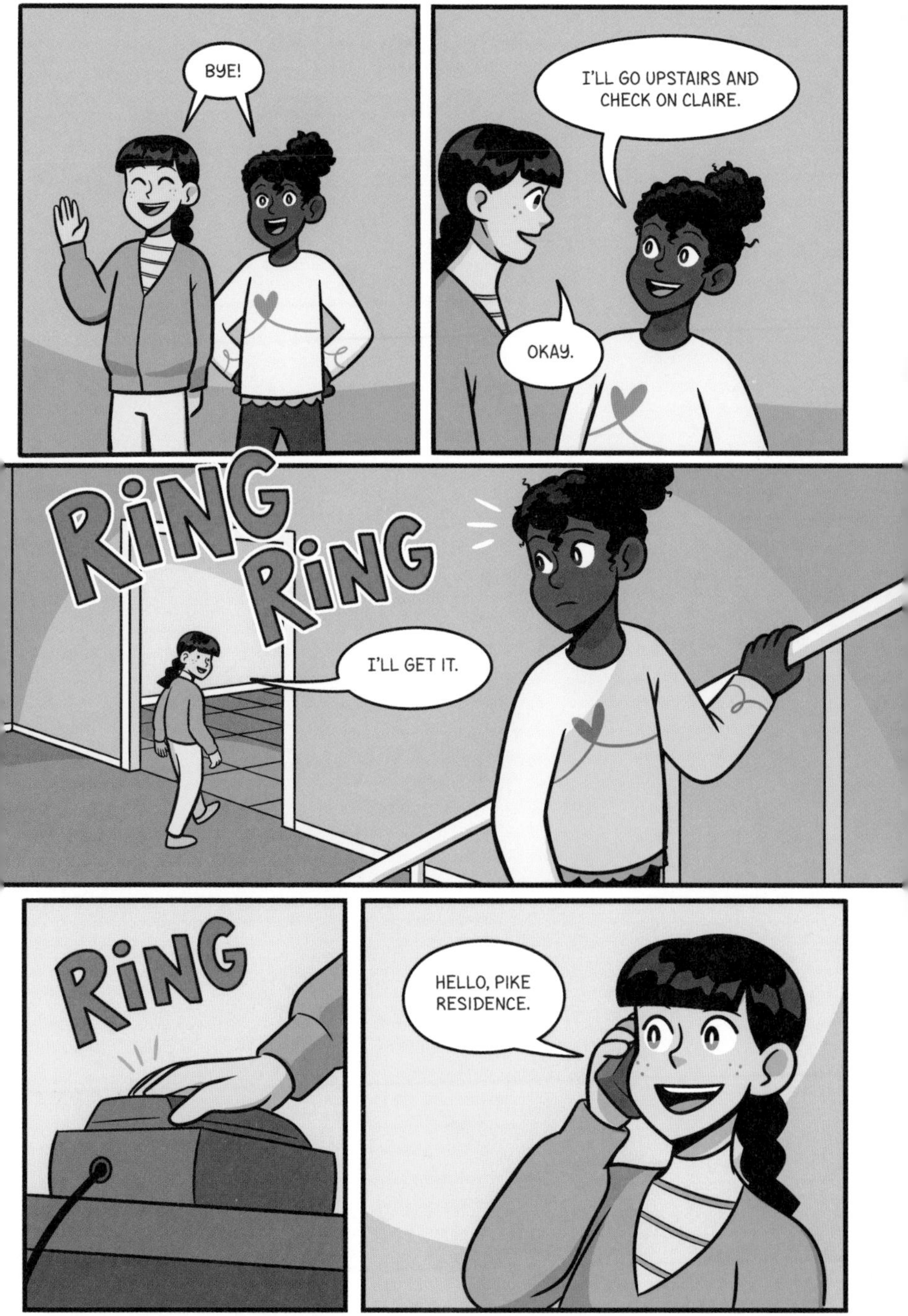
BYE!
I'LL GO UPSTAIRS AND CHECK ON CLAIRE.
OKAY.
RING RING
I'LL GET IT.
RING
HELLO, PIKE RESIDENCE.

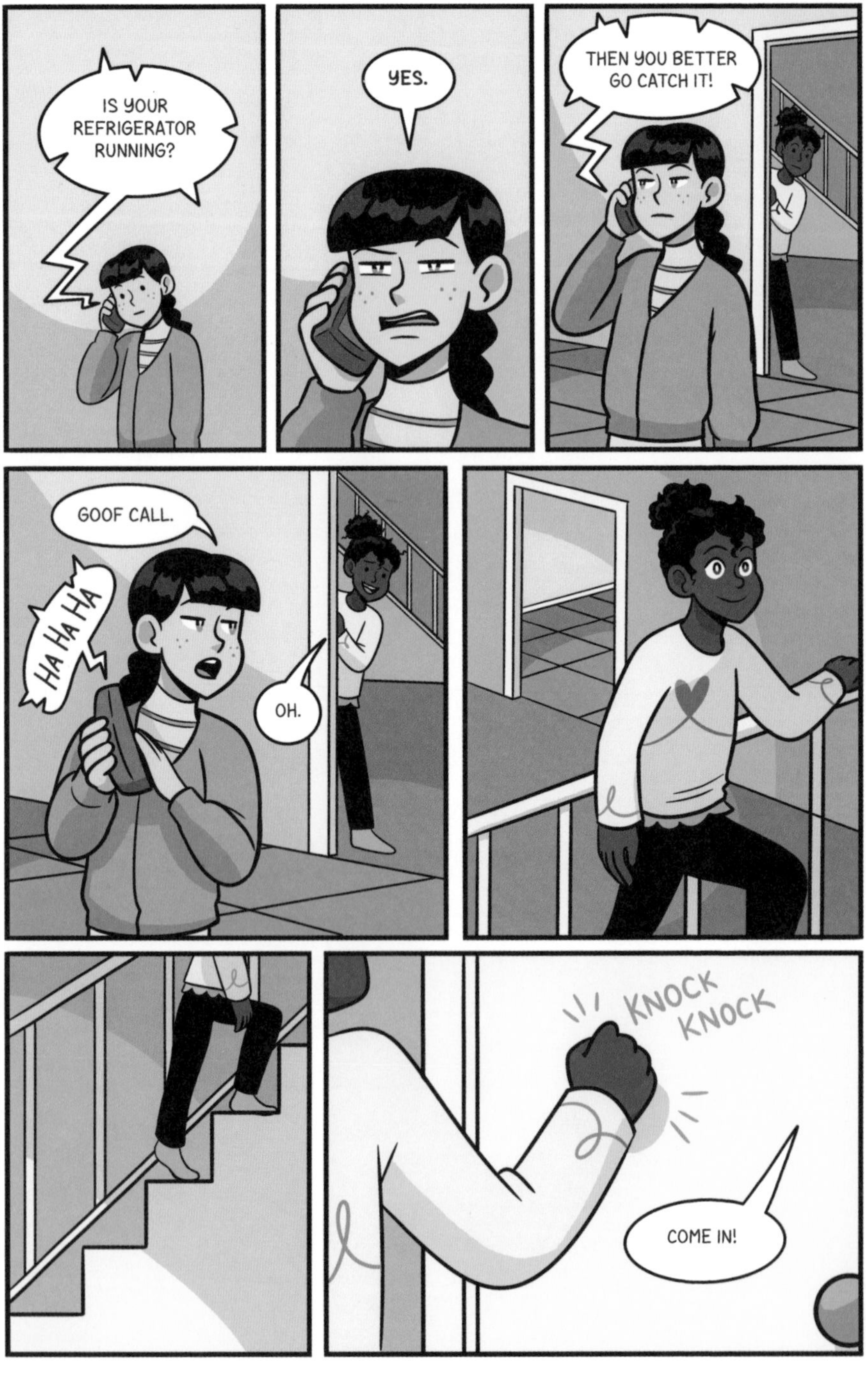

IS YOUR REFRIGERATOR RUNNING?
YES.
THEN YOU BETTER GO CATCH IT!
GOOF CALL.
HA HA HA
OH.
KNOCK KNOCK
COME IN!

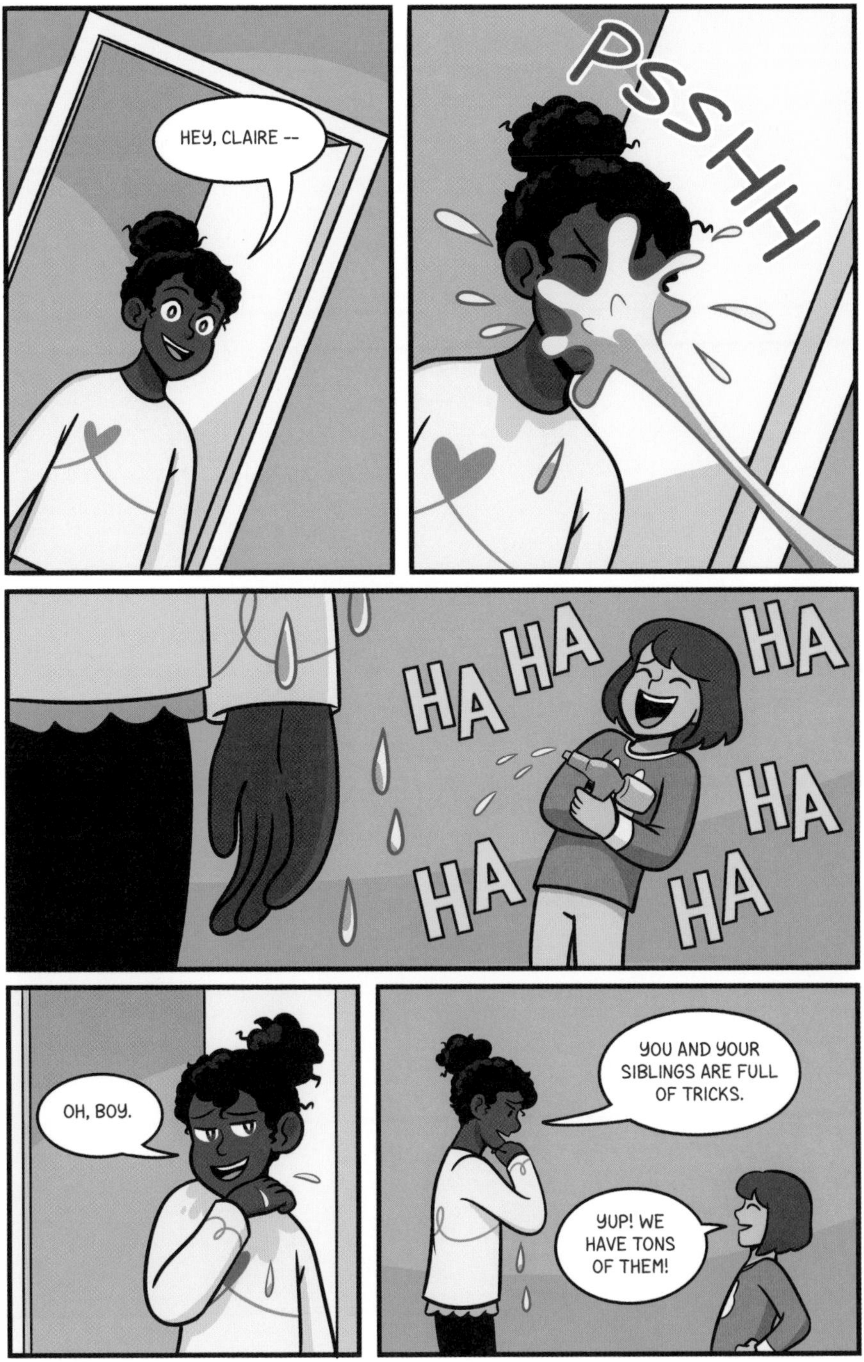
HEY, CLAIRE --
PSSHH
HA HA HA HA HA HA HA
OH, BOY.
YOU AND YOUR SIBLINGS ARE FULL OF TRICKS.
YUP! WE HAVE TONS OF THEM!

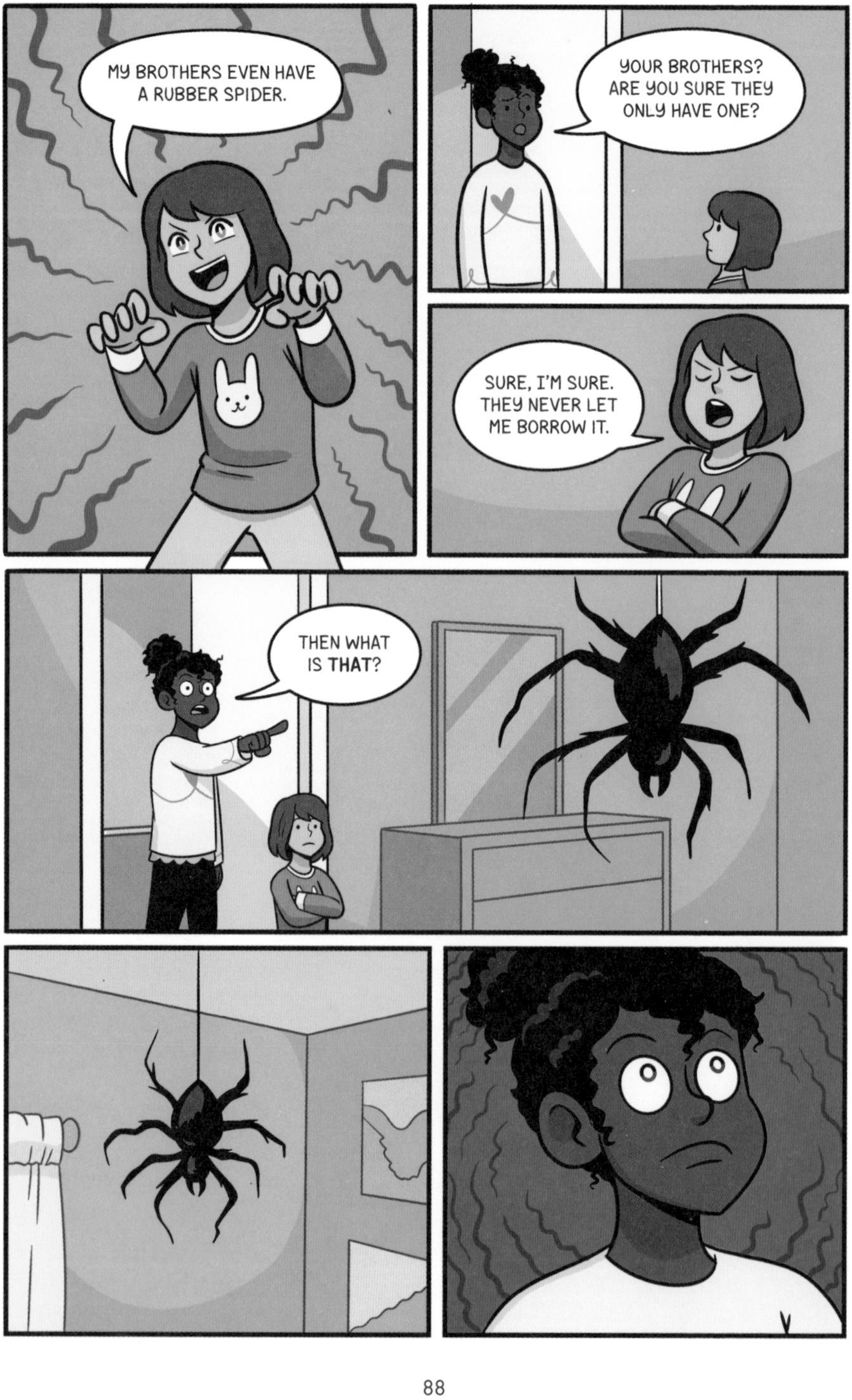
MY BROTHERS EVEN HAVE A RUBBER SPIDER.
YOUR BROTHERS? ARE YOU SURE THEY ONLY HAVE ONE?
SURE, I'M SURE. THEY NEVER LET ME BORROW IT.
THEN WHAT IS **THAT**?

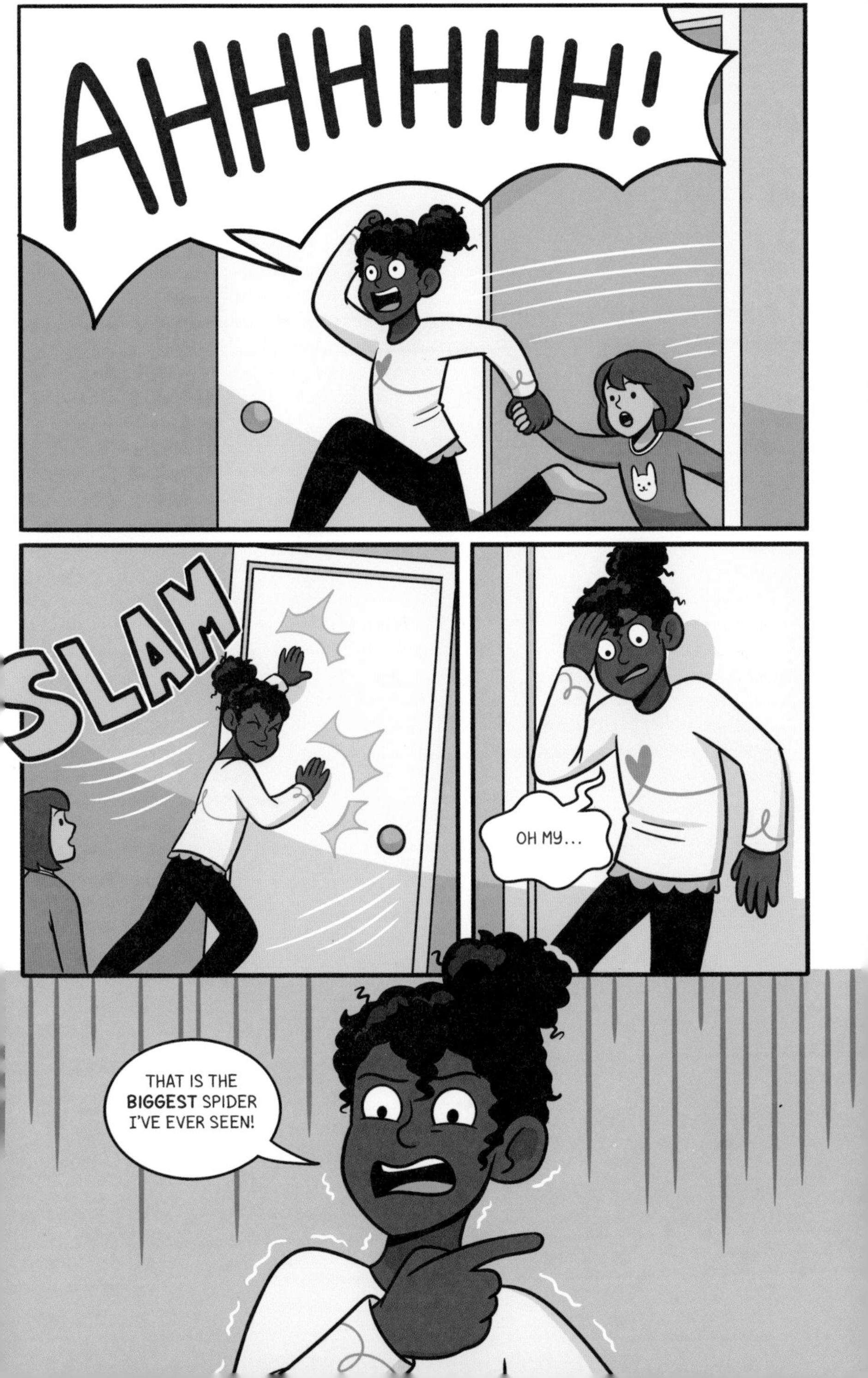
AHHHHHHH!
SLAM
OH MY...
THAT IS THE **BIGGEST** SPIDER I'VE EVER SEEN!

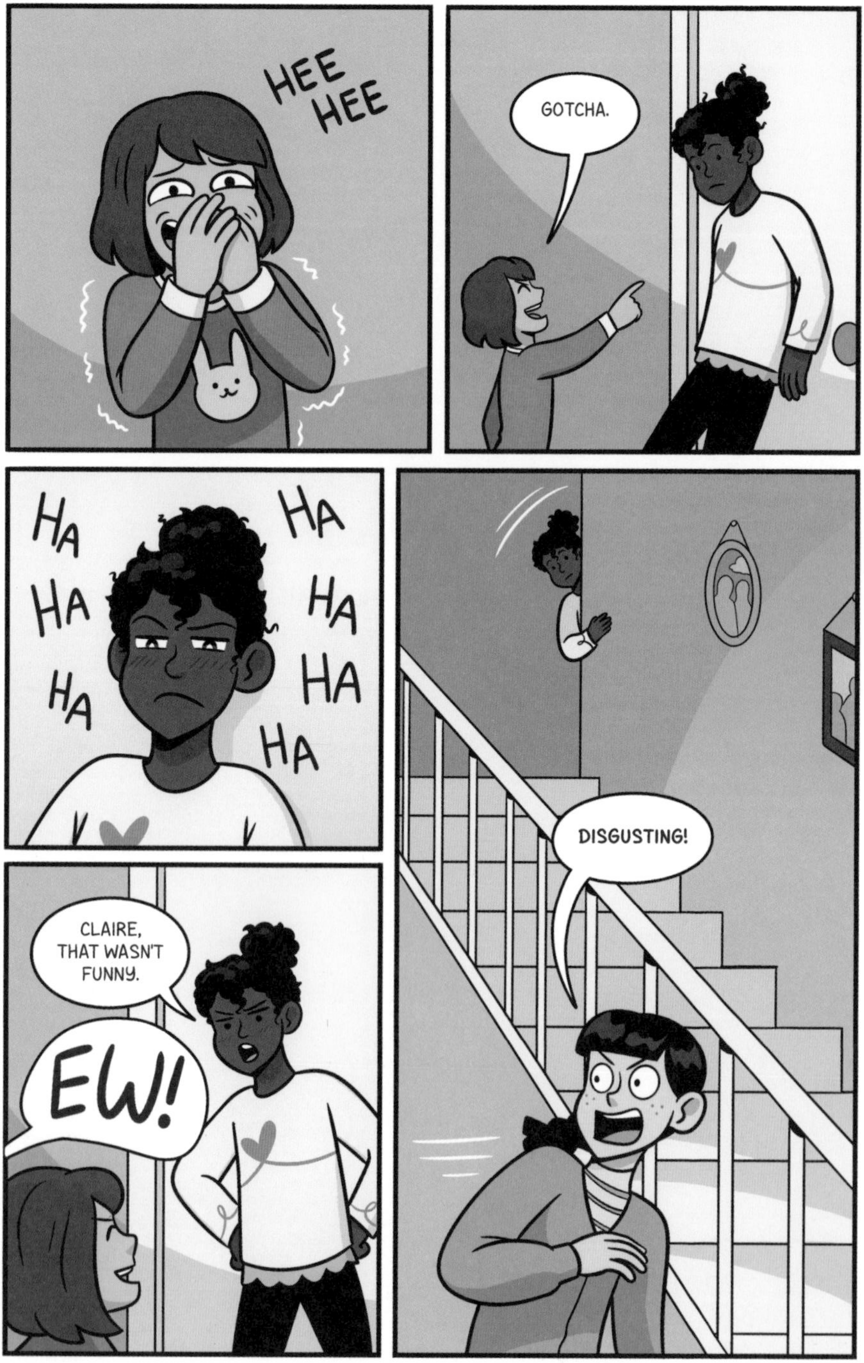
HEE
HEE
GOTCHA.
HA
HA
HA
HA
HA
HA
HA
CLAIRE, THAT WASN'T FUNNY.
EW!
DISGUSTING!

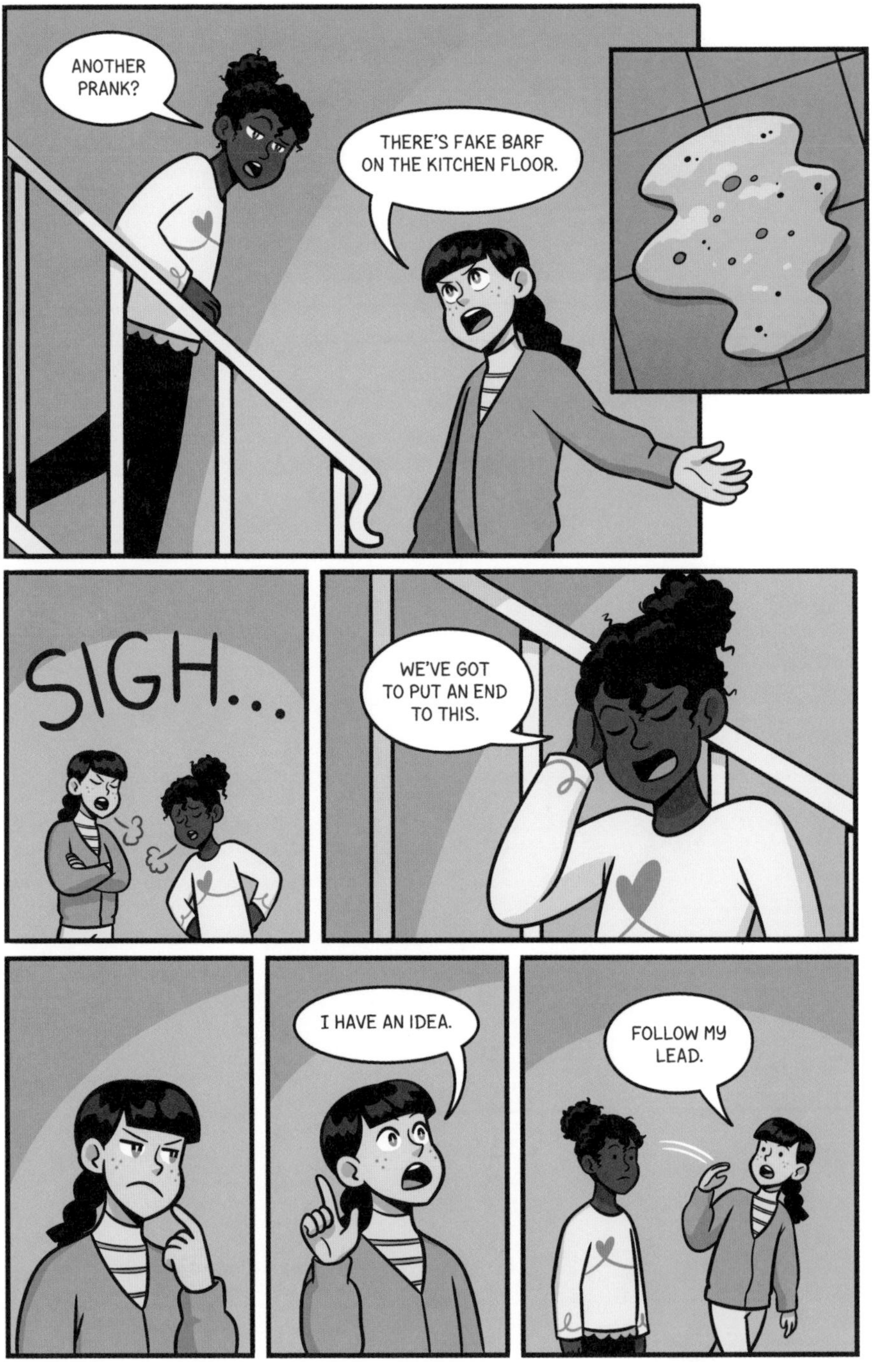
ANOTHER PRANK?
THERE'S FAKE BARF ON THE KITCHEN FLOOR.
SIGH...
WE'VE GOT TO PUT AN END TO THIS.
I HAVE AN IDEA.
FOLLOW MY LEAD.

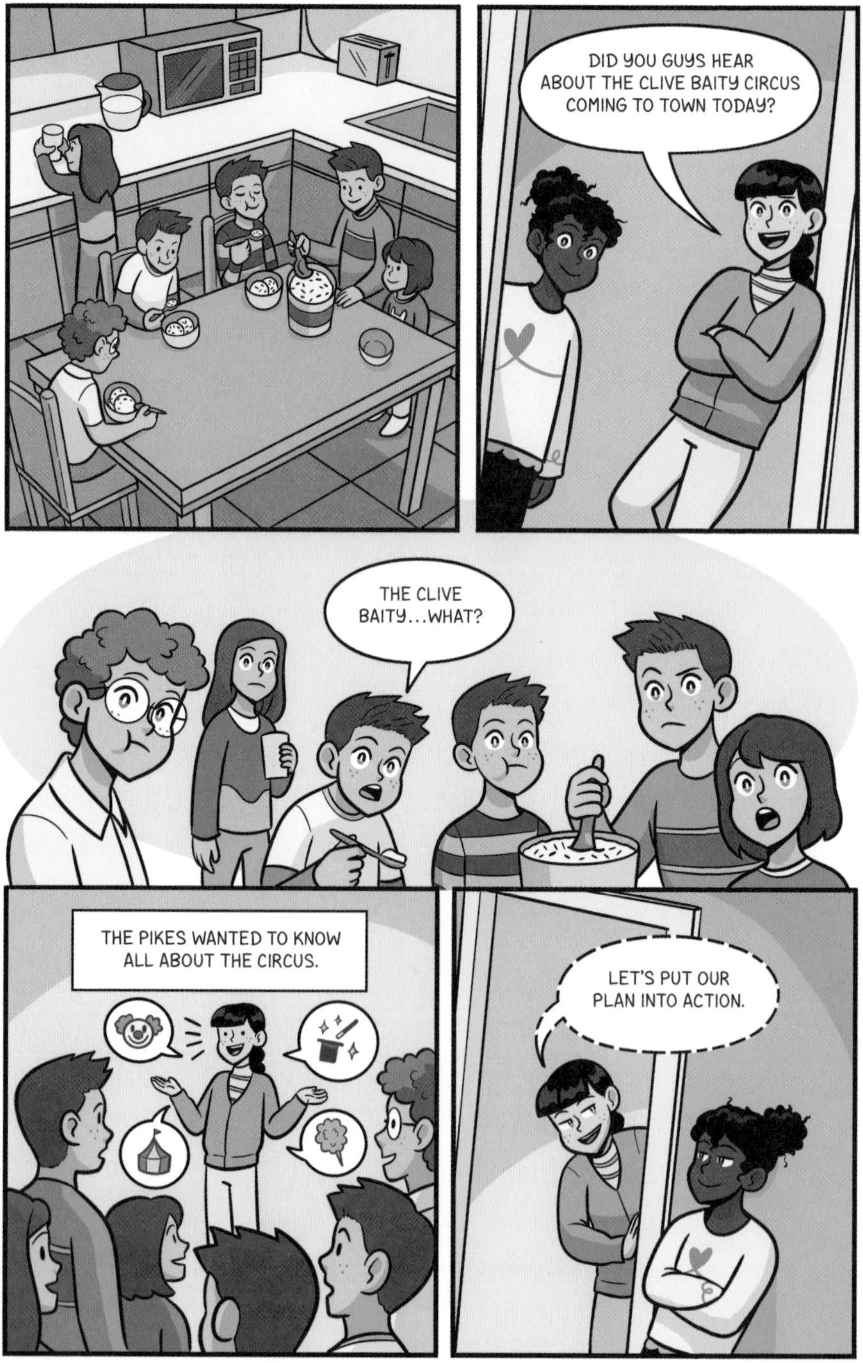

DID YOU GUYS HEAR ABOUT THE CLIVE BAITY CIRCUS COMING TO TOWN TODAY?
THE CLIVE BAITY...WHAT?
THE PIKES WANTED TO KNOW ALL ABOUT THE CIRCUS.
LET'S PUT OUR PLAN INTO ACTION.

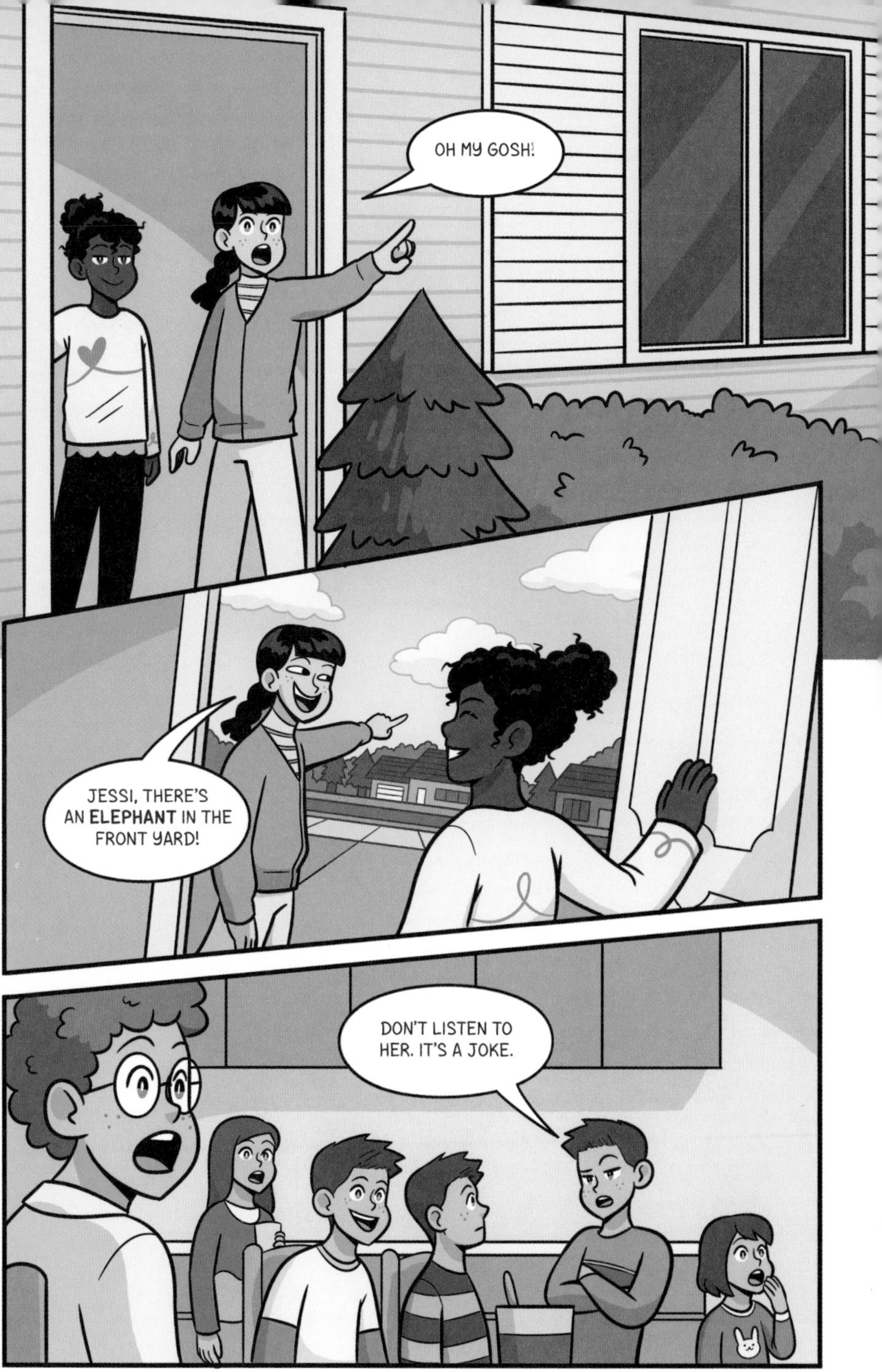
OH MY GOSH!
JESSI, THERE'S AN **ELEPHANT** IN THE FRONT YARD!
DON'T LISTEN TO HER. IT'S A JOKE.

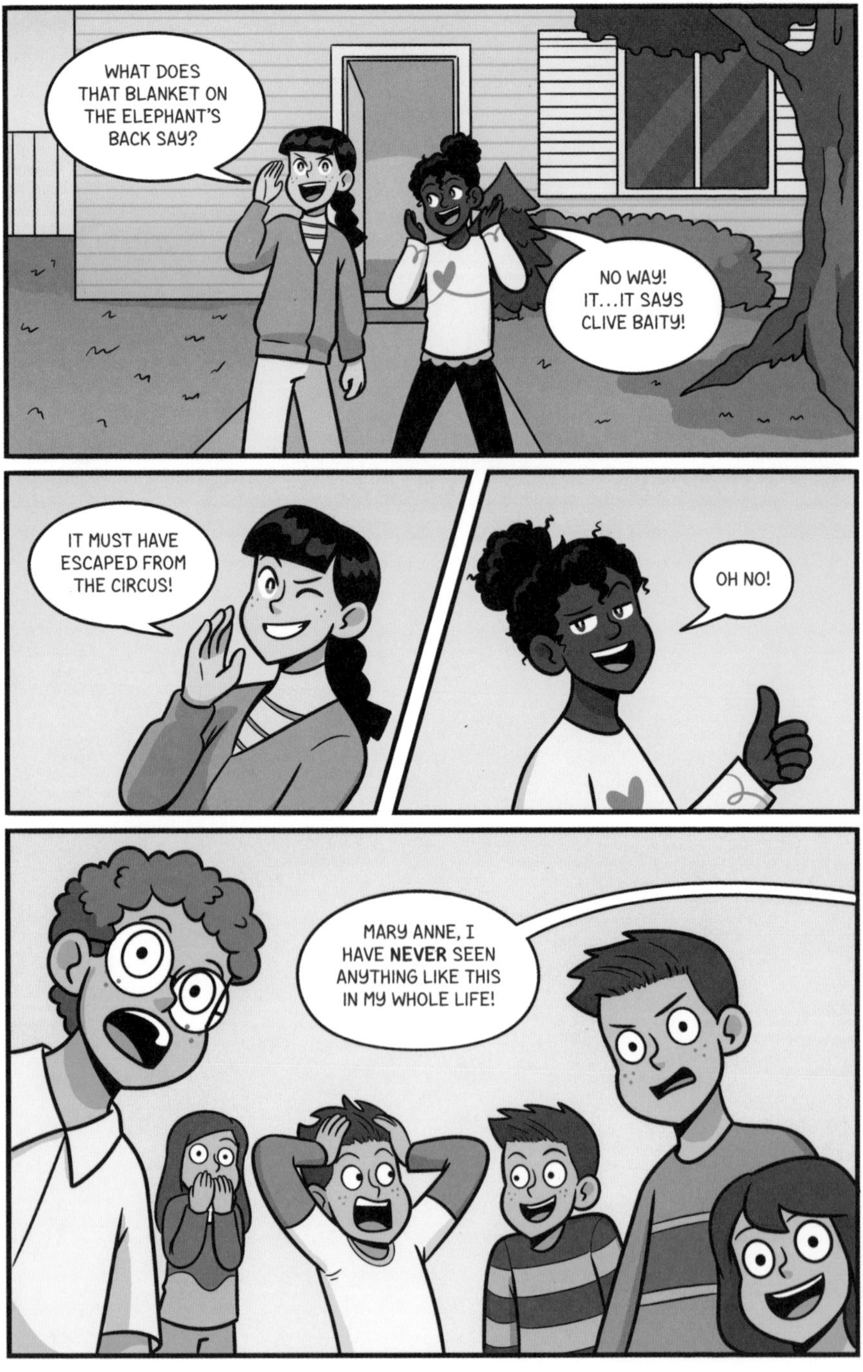
WHAT DOES THAT BLANKET ON THE ELEPHANT'S BACK SAY?
NO WAY! IT...IT SAYS CLIVE BAITY!
IT MUST HAVE ESCAPED FROM THE CIRCUS!
OH NO!
MARY ANNE, I HAVE **NEVER** SEEN ANYTHING LIKE THIS IN MY WHOLE LIFE!

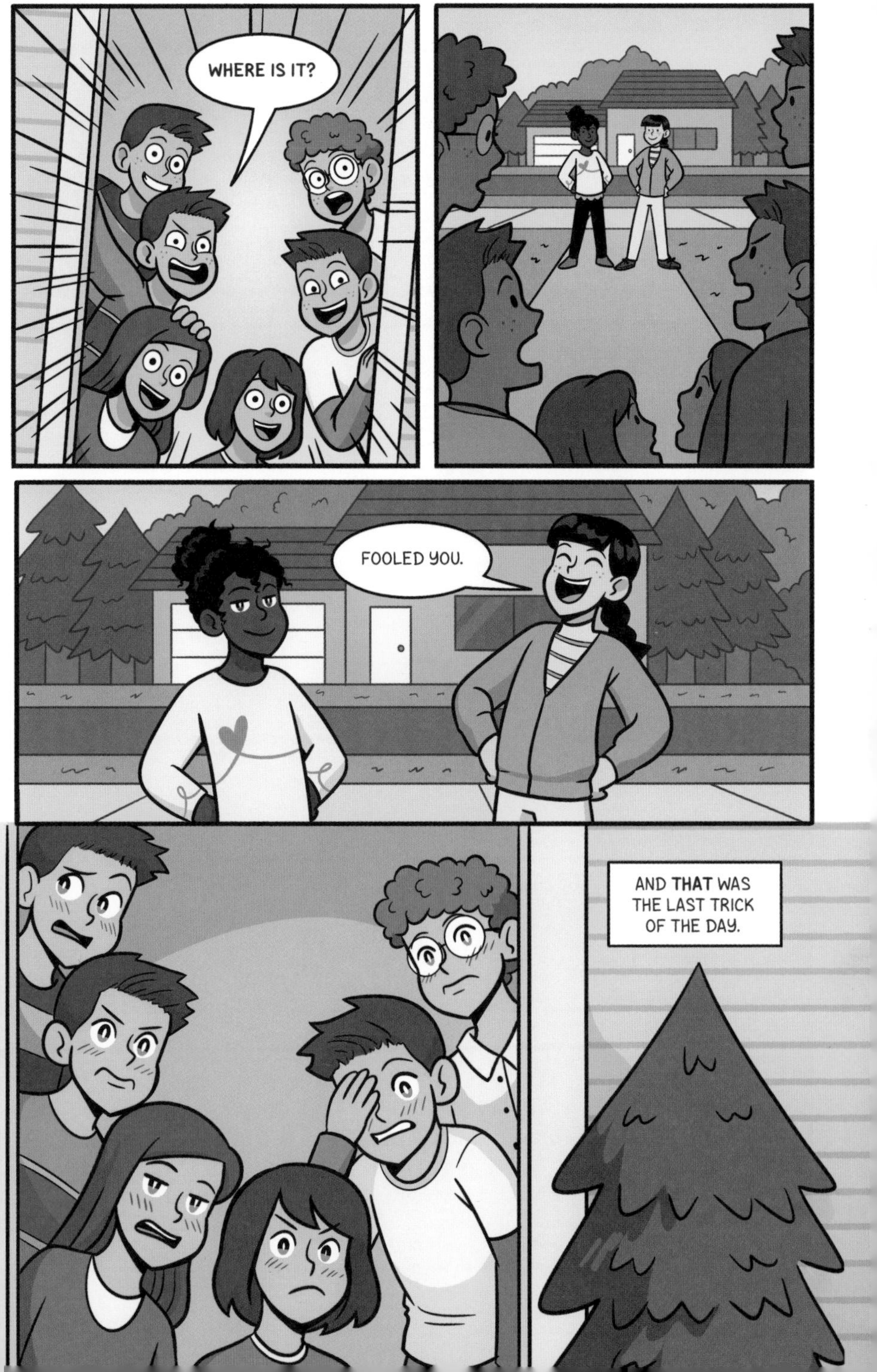
WHERE IS IT?
FOOLED YOU.
AND **THAT** WAS THE LAST TRICK OF THE DAY.

CHAPTER 8

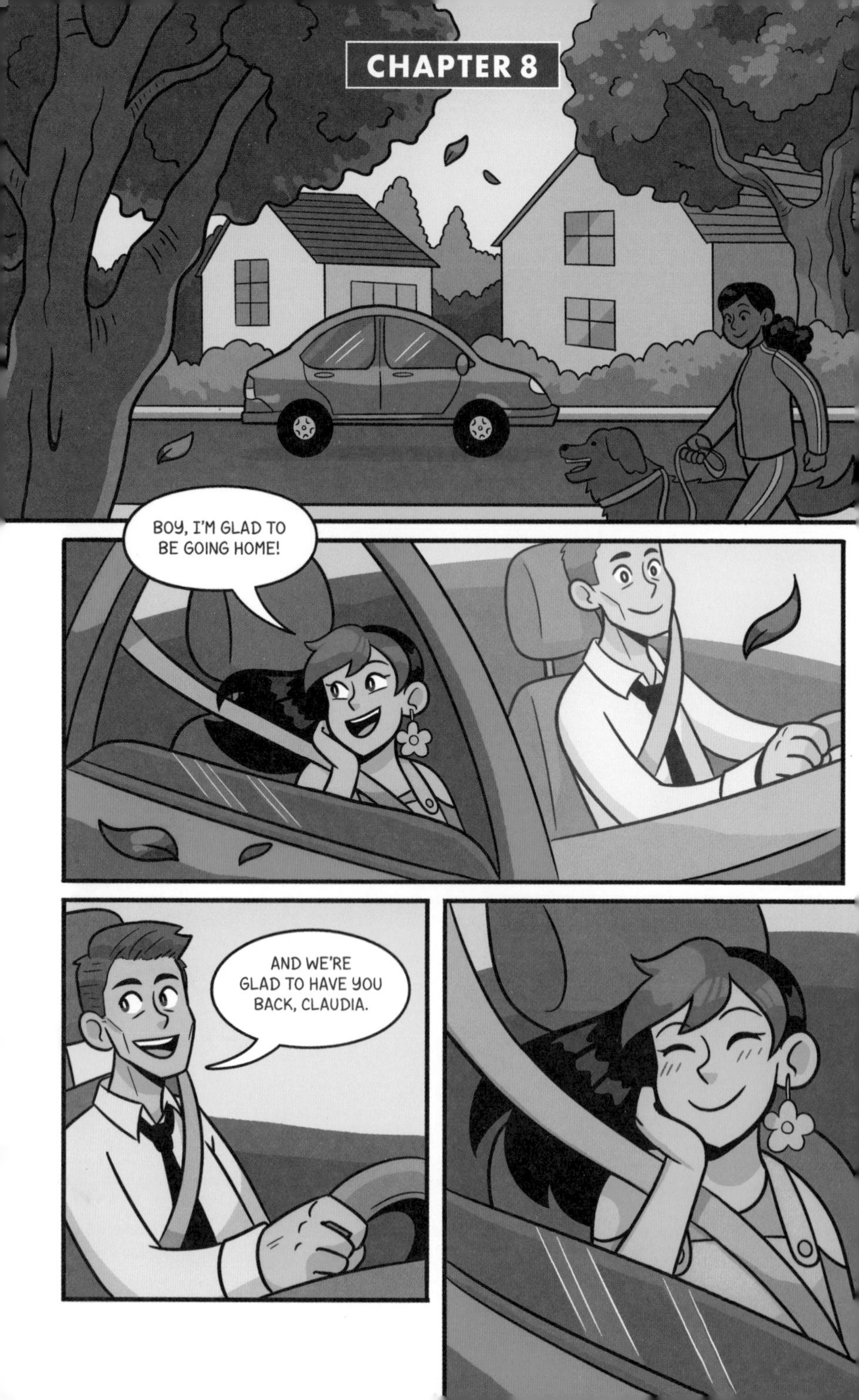
BOY, I'M GLAD TO BE GOING HOME!
AND WE'RE GLAD TO HAVE YOU BACK, CLAUDIA.

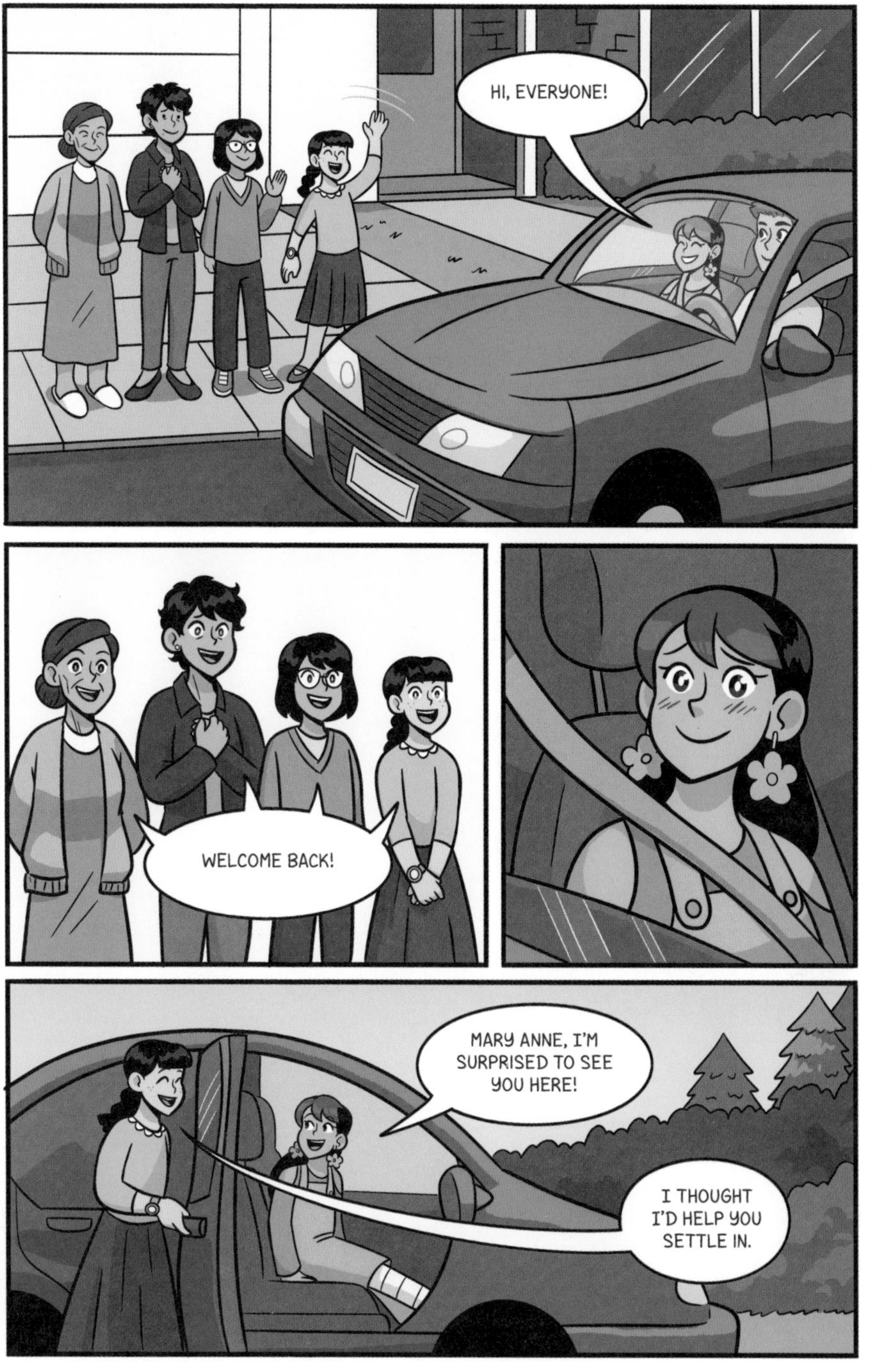
HI, EVERYONE!
WELCOME BACK!
MARY ANNE, I'M SURPRISED TO SEE YOU HERE!
I THOUGHT I'D HELP YOU SETTLE IN.

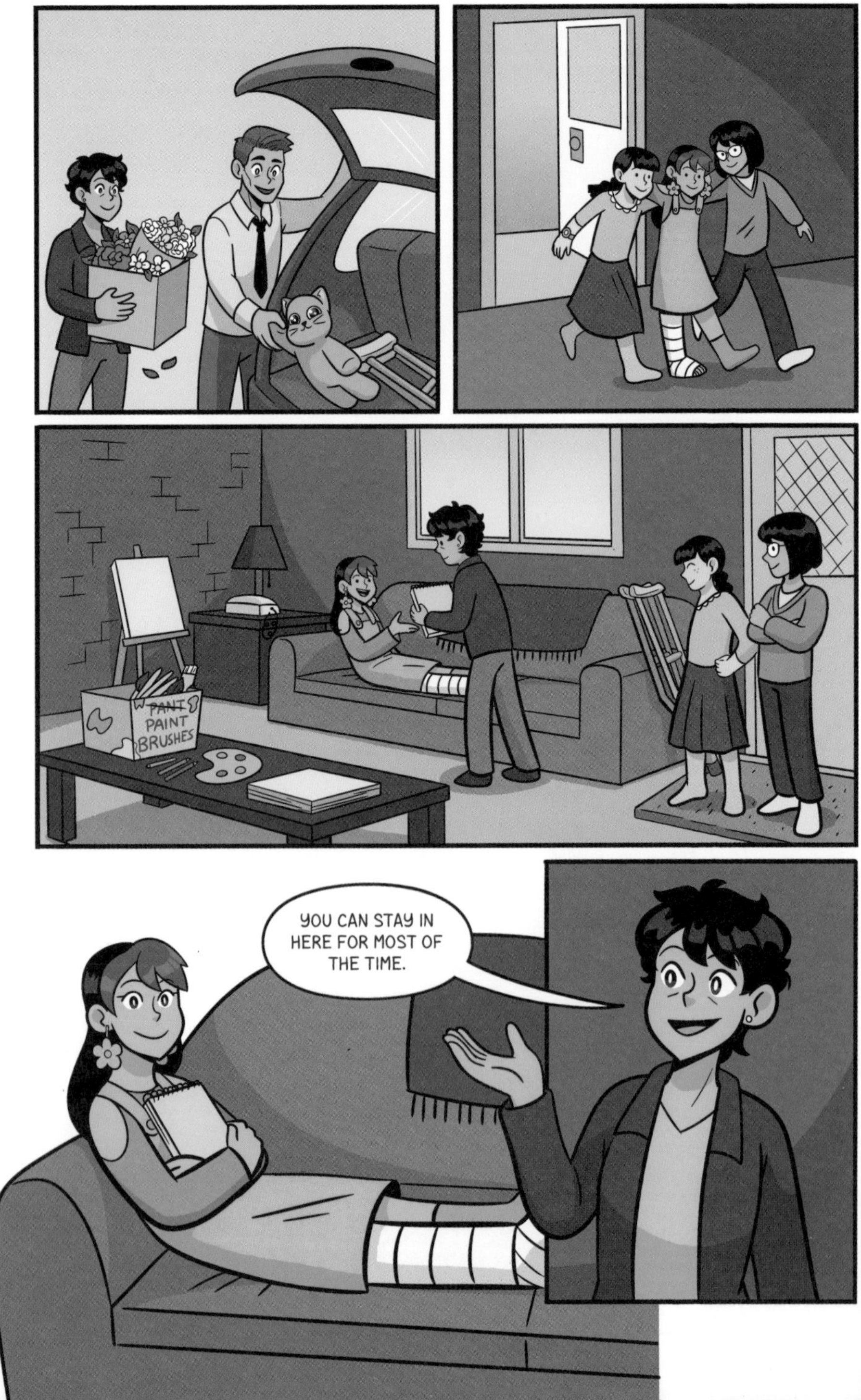
PANT
PAINT
BRUSHES
YOU CAN STAY IN HERE FOR MOST OF THE TIME.

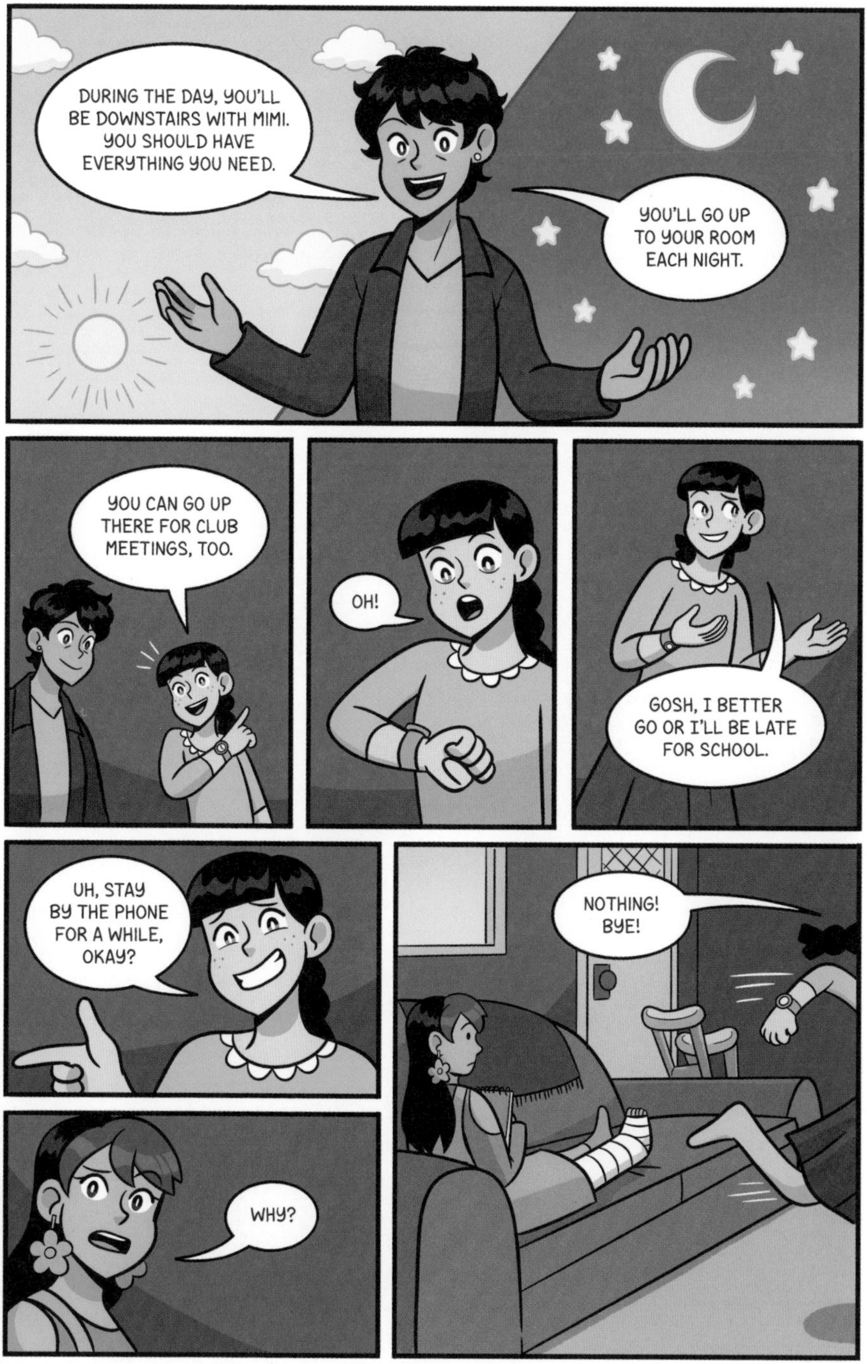
DURING THE DAY, YOU'LL BE DOWNSTAIRS WITH MIMI. YOU SHOULD HAVE EVERYTHING YOU NEED.
YOU'LL GO UP TO YOUR ROOM EACH NIGHT.
YOU CAN GO UP THERE FOR CLUB MEETINGS, TOO.
OH!
GOSH, I BETTER GO OR I'LL BE LATE FOR SCHOOL.
UH, STAY BY THE PHONE FOR A WHILE, OKAY?
WHY?
NOTHING! BYE!

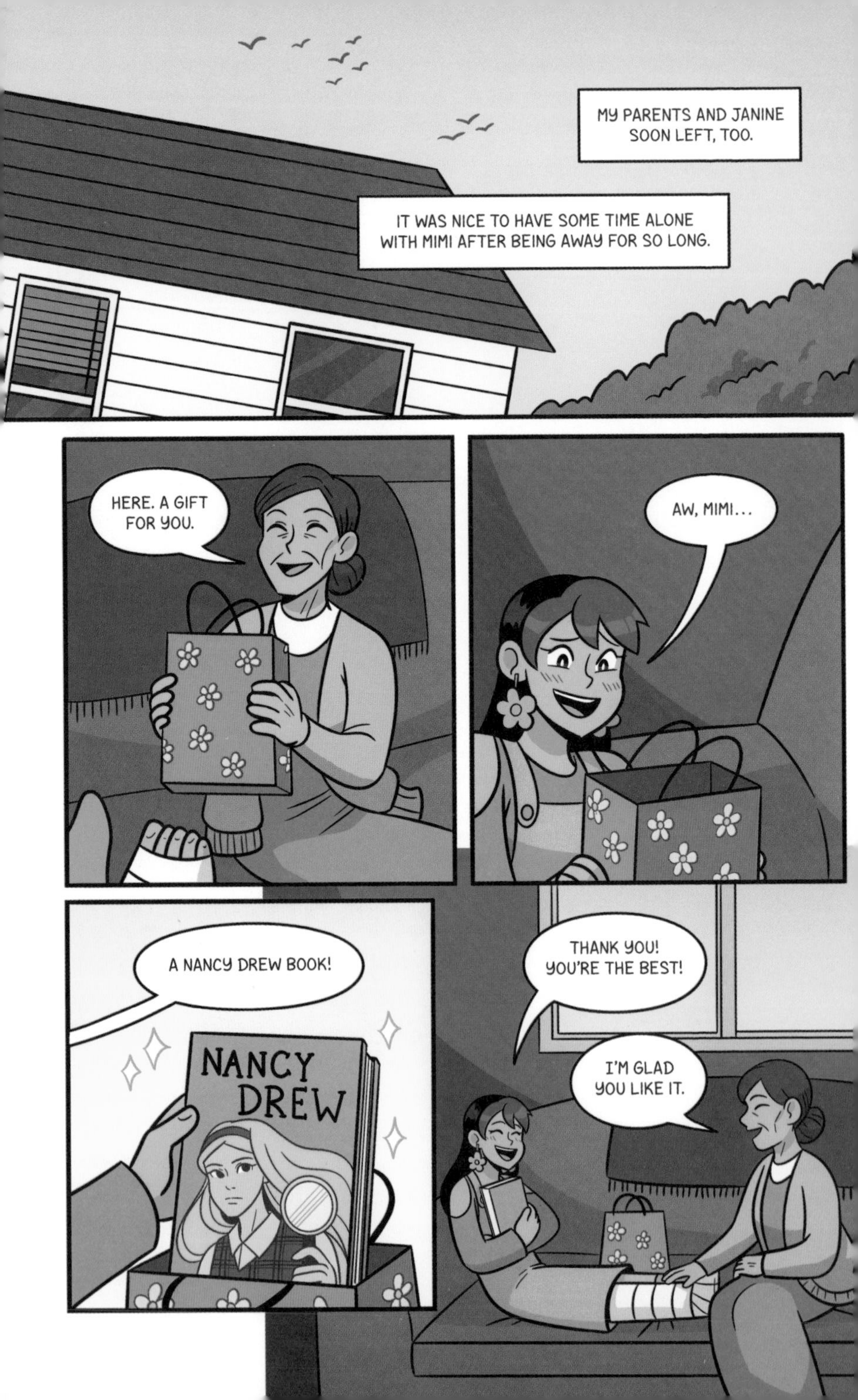
MY PARENTS AND JANINE SOON LEFT, TOO.
IT WAS NICE TO HAVE SOME TIME ALONE WITH MIMI AFTER BEING AWAY FOR SO LONG.
HERE. A GIFT FOR YOU.
AW, MIMI...
A NANCY DREW BOOK!
NANCY DREW
THANK YOU! YOU'RE THE BEST!
I'M GLAD YOU LIKE IT.

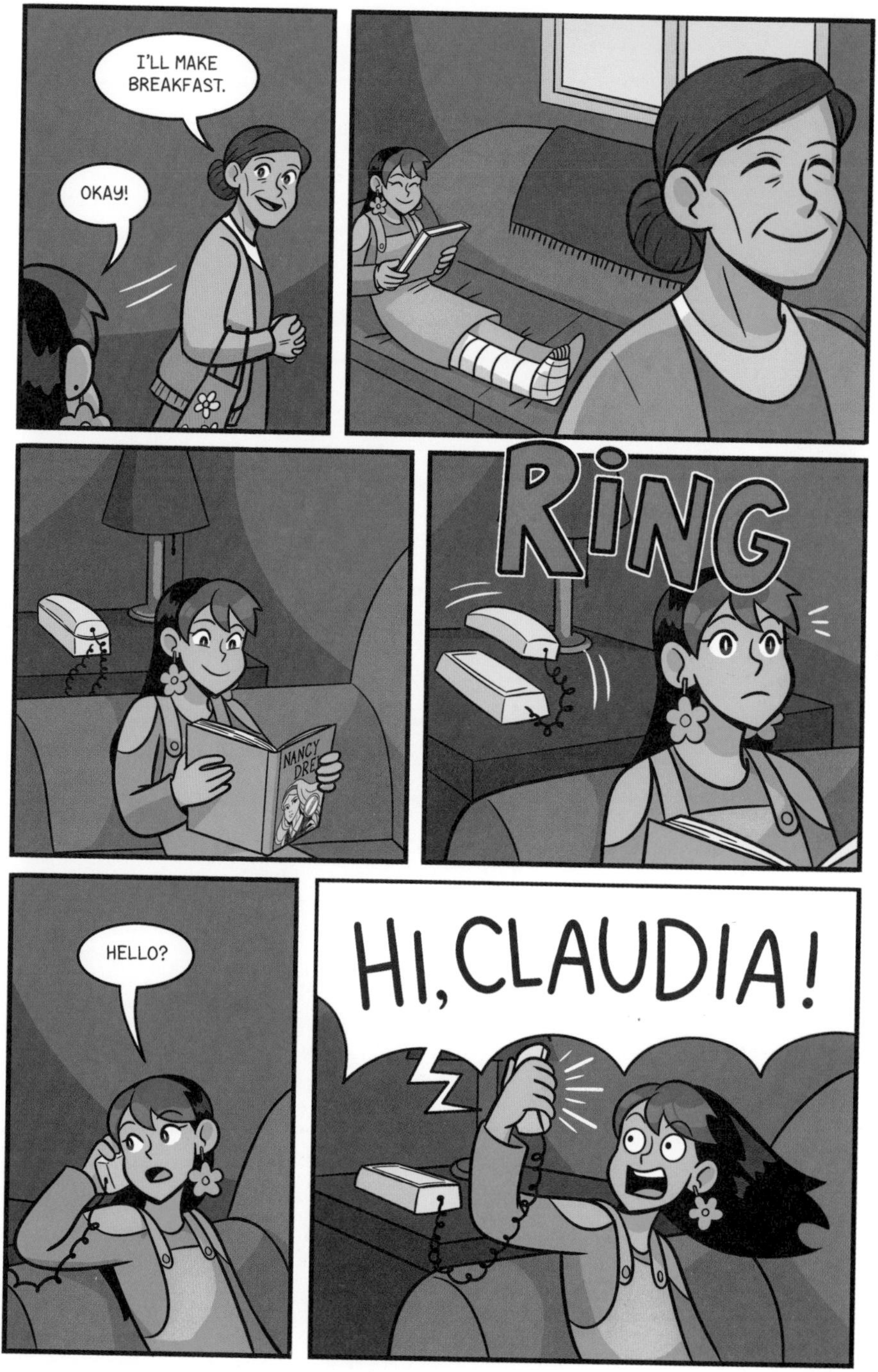
I'LL MAKE BREAKFAST.
OKAY!
RING
HELLO?
HI, CLAUDIA!
NANCY DRE

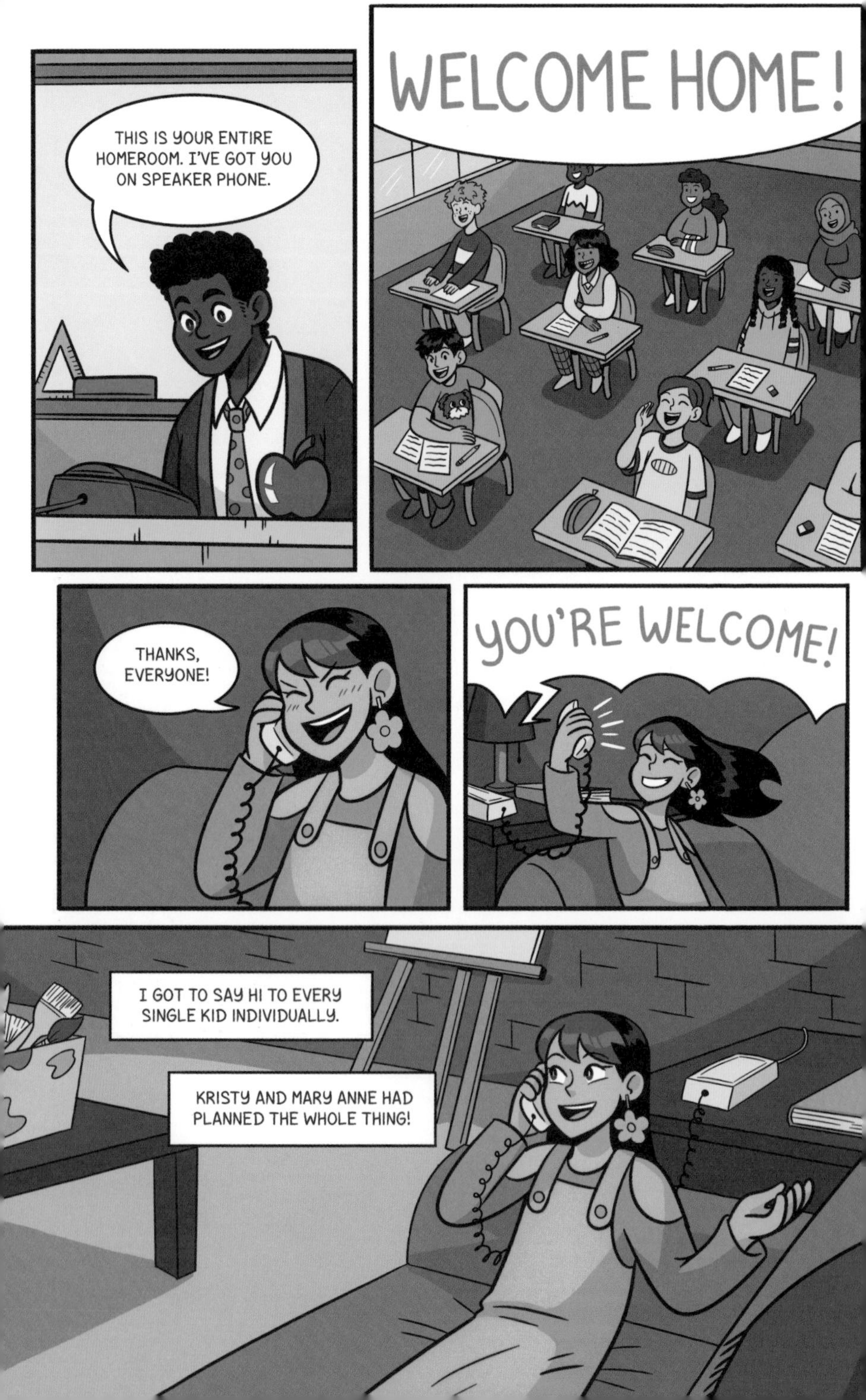
THIS IS YOUR ENTIRE HOMEROOM. I'VE GOT YOU ON SPEAKER PHONE.
WELCOME HOME!
THANKS, EVERYONE!
YOU'RE WELCOME!
I GOT TO SAY HI TO EVERY SINGLE KID INDIVIDUALLY.
KRISTY AND MARY ANNE HAD PLANNED THE WHOLE THING!

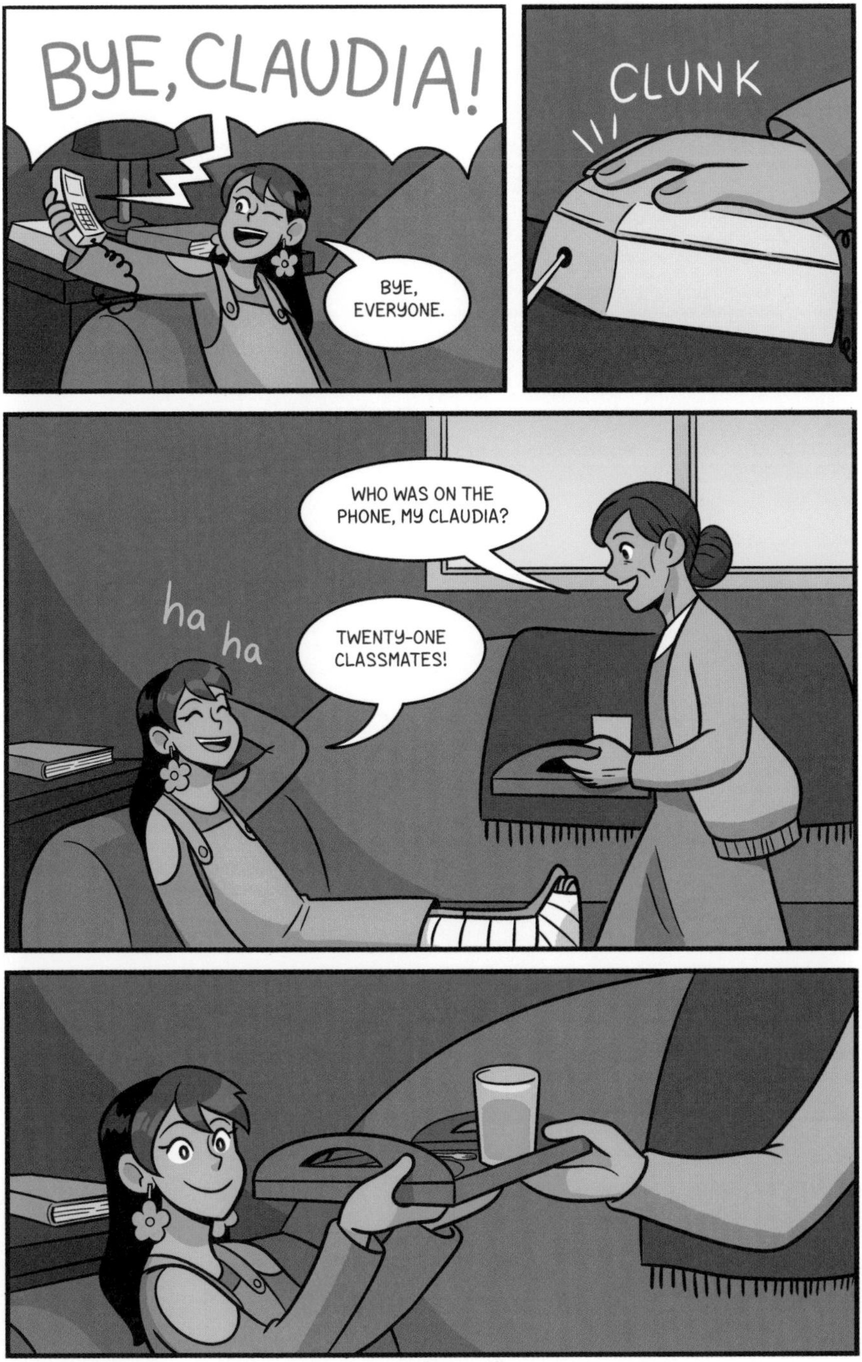

BYE, CLAUDIA!
BYE, EVERYONE.
CLUNK
WHO WAS ON THE PHONE, MY CLAUDIA?
ha ha
TWENTY-ONE CLASSMATES!

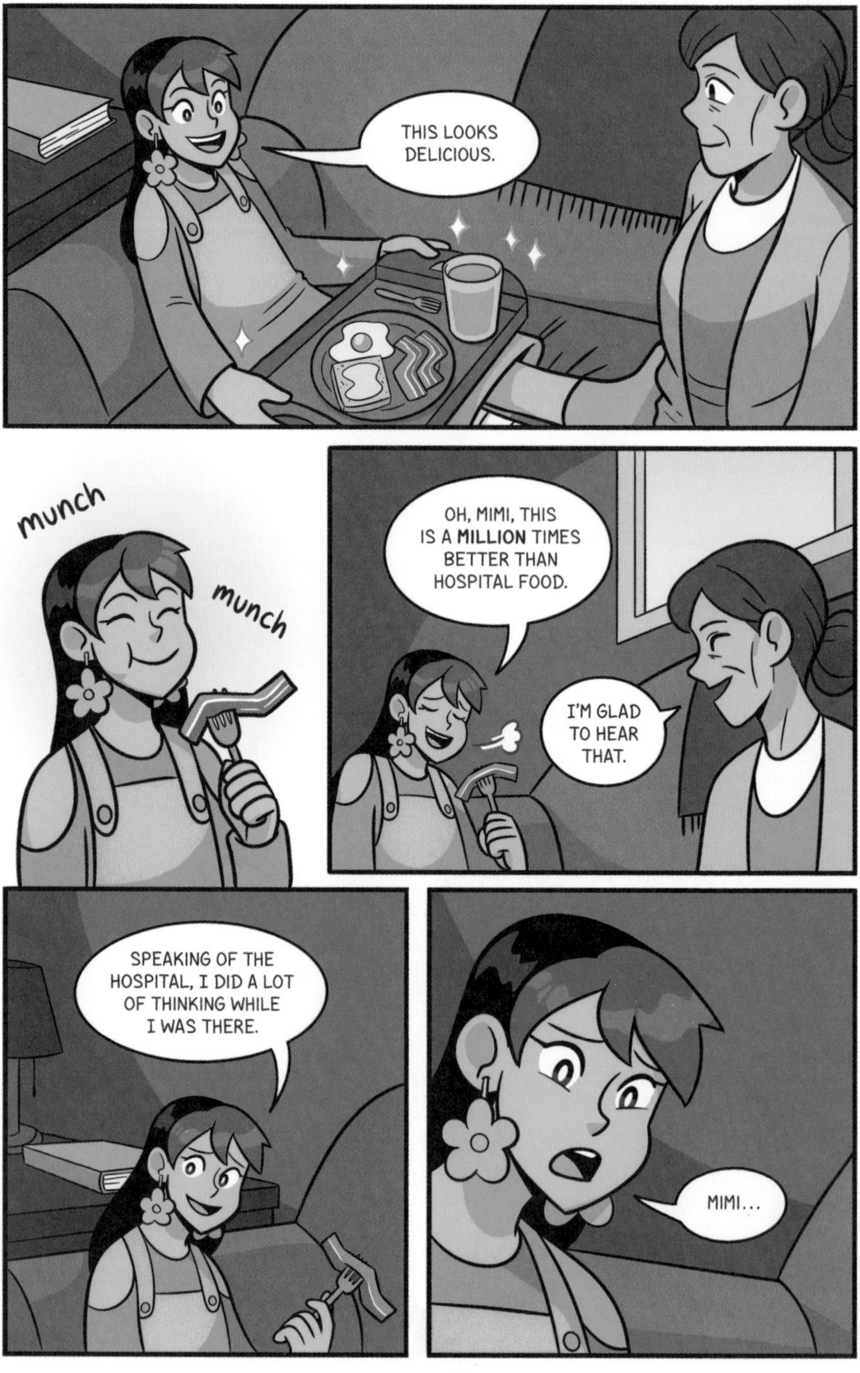
THIS LOOKS DELICIOUS.
munch
munch
OH, MIMI, THIS IS A **MILLION** TIMES BETTER THAN HOSPITAL FOOD.
I'M GLAD TO HEAR THAT.
SPEAKING OF THE HOSPITAL, I DID A LOT OF THINKING WHILE I WAS THERE.
MIMI...

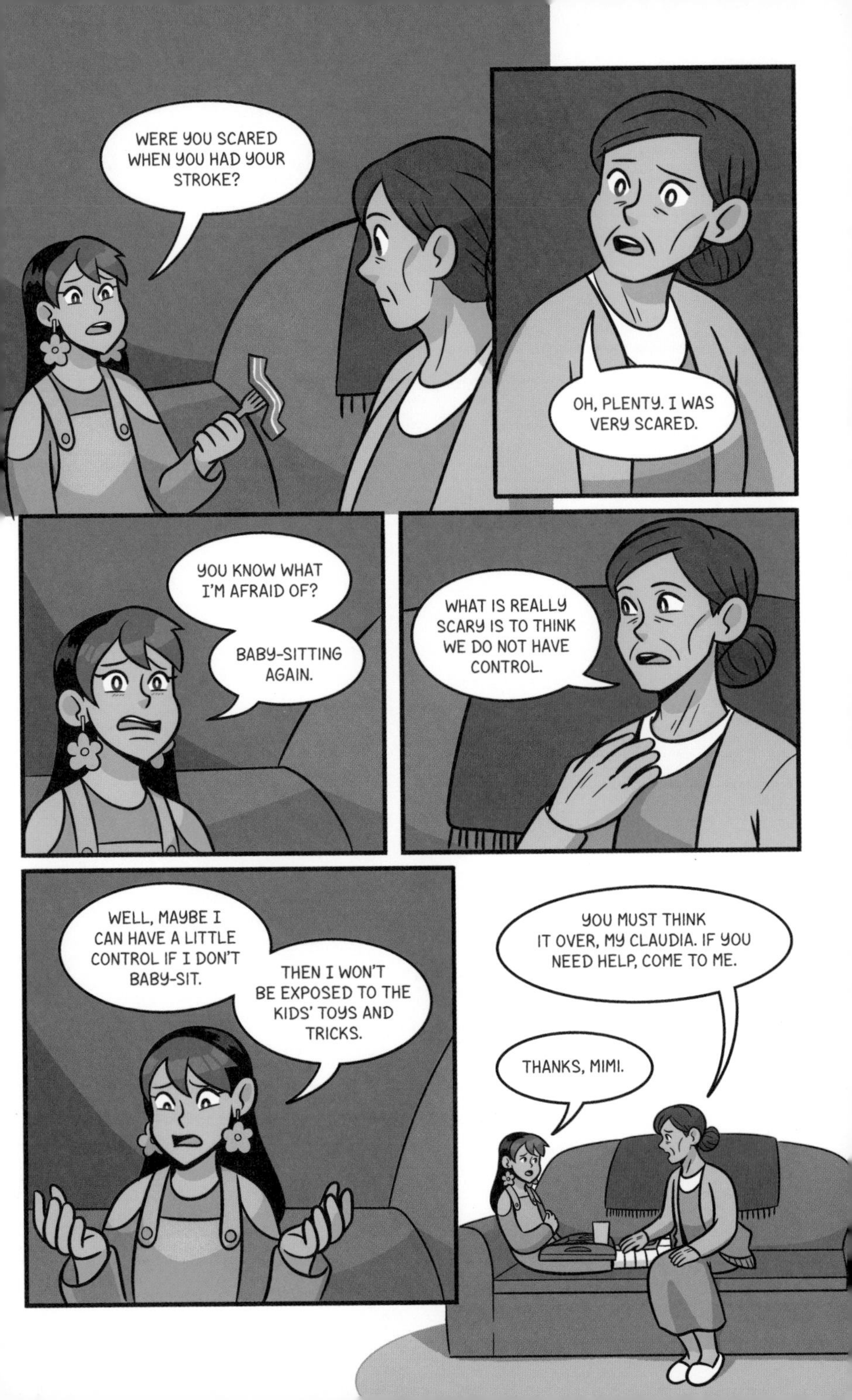
WERE YOU SCARED WHEN YOU HAD YOUR STROKE?
OH, PLENTY. I WAS VERY SCARED.
YOU KNOW WHAT I'M AFRAID OF?
BABY-SITTING AGAIN.
WHAT IS REALLY SCARY IS TO THINK WE DO NOT HAVE CONTROL.
WELL, MAYBE I CAN HAVE A LITTLE CONTROL IF I DON'T BABY-SIT.
THEN I WON'T BE EXPOSED TO THE KIDS' TOYS AND TRICKS.
YOU MUST THINK IT OVER, MY CLAUDIA. IF YOU NEED HELP, COME TO ME.
THANKS, MIMI.

CHAPTER 9

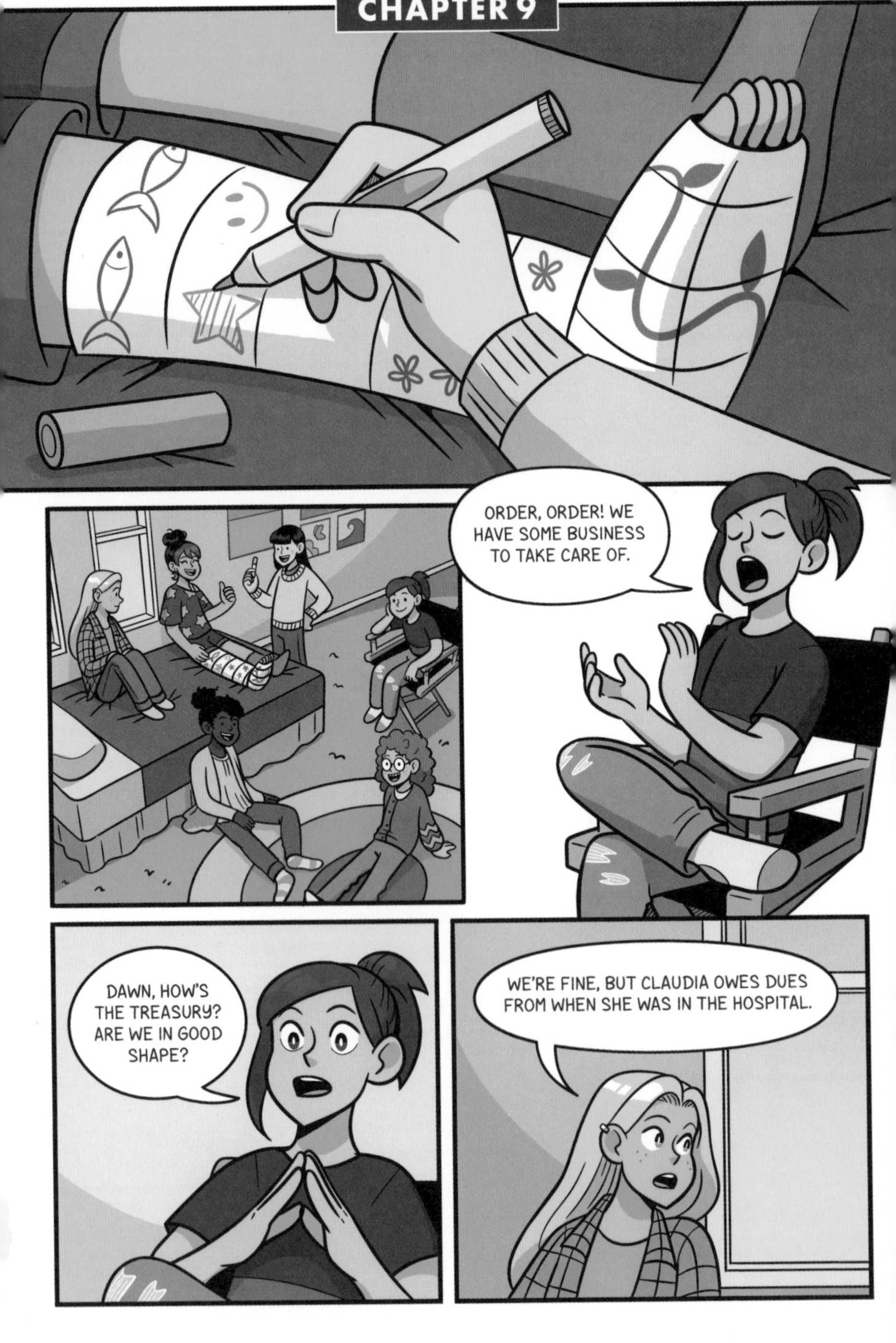
ORDER, ORDER! WE HAVE SOME BUSINESS TO TAKE CARE OF.
DAWN, HOW'S THE TREASURY? ARE WE IN GOOD SHAPE?
WE'RE FINE, BUT CLAUDIA OWES DUES FROM WHEN SHE WAS IN THE HOSPITAL.

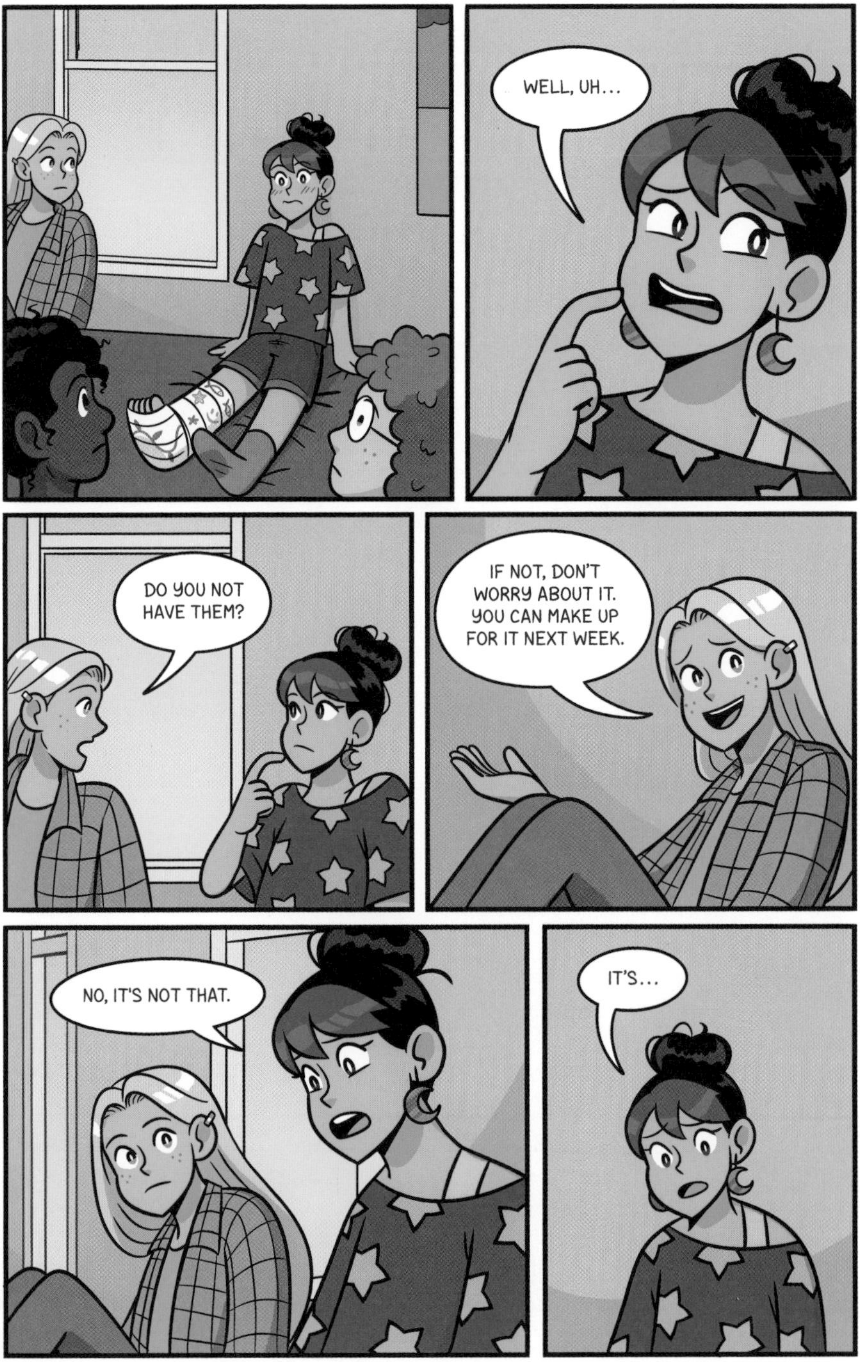
WELL, UH...
DO YOU NOT HAVE THEM?
IF NOT, DON'T WORRY ABOUT IT. YOU CAN MAKE UP FOR IT NEXT WEEK.
NO, IT'S NOT THAT.
IT'S...

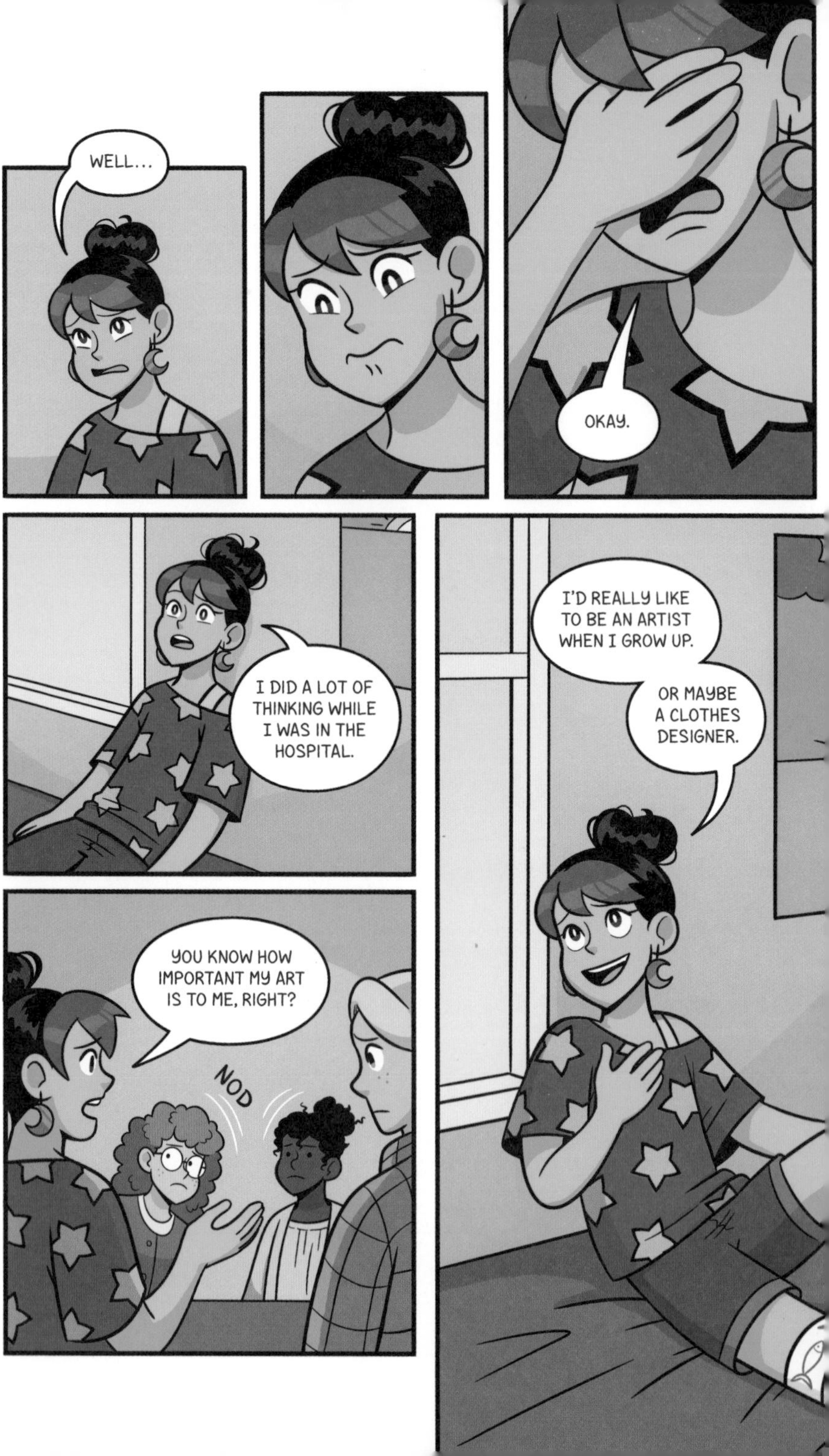
WELL...
OKAY.
I DID A LOT OF THINKING WHILE I WAS IN THE HOSPITAL.
I'D REALLY LIKE TO BE AN ARTIST WHEN I GROW UP.
OR MAYBE A CLOTHES DESIGNER.
YOU KNOW HOW IMPORTANT MY ART IS TO ME, RIGHT?
NOD

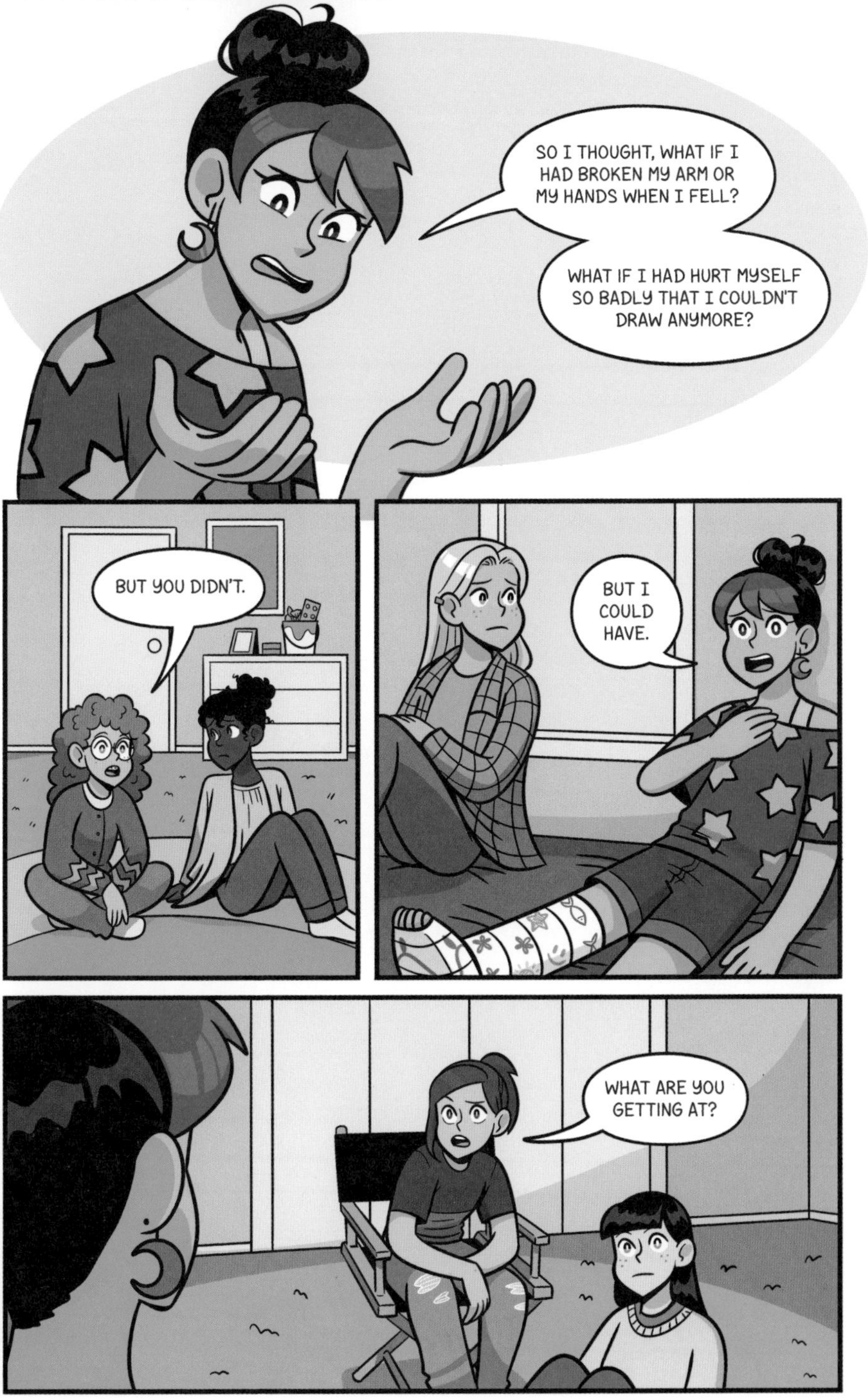
SO I THOUGHT, WHAT IF I HAD BROKEN MY ARM OR MY HANDS WHEN I FELL?
WHAT IF I HAD HURT MYSELF SO BADLY THAT I COULDN'T DRAW ANYMORE?
BUT YOU DIDN'T.
BUT I COULD HAVE.
WHAT ARE YOU GETTING AT?

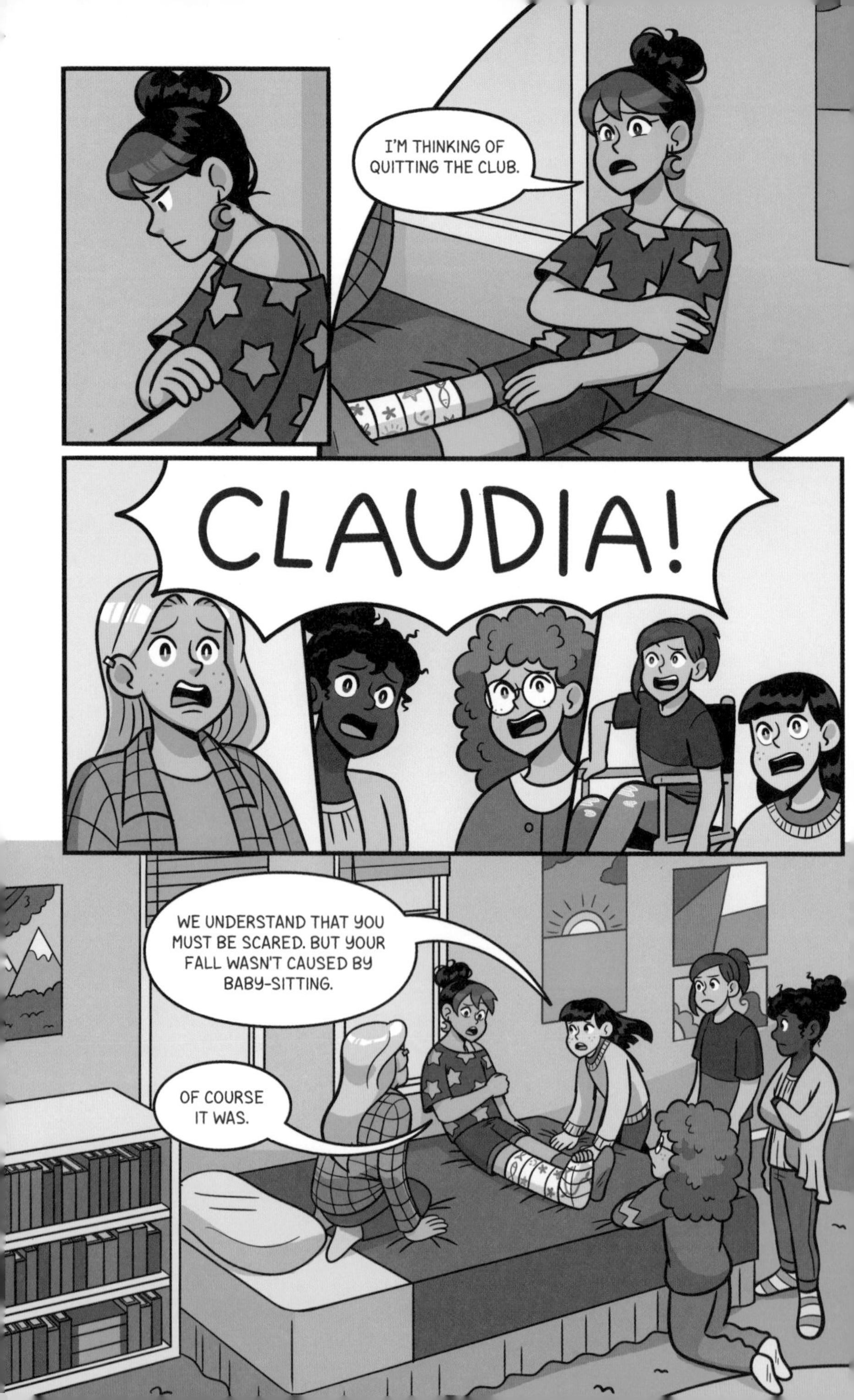
I'M THINKING OF QUITTING THE CLUB.
CLAUDIA!
WE UNDERSTAND THAT YOU MUST BE SCARED. BUT YOUR FALL WASN'T CAUSED BY BABY-SITTING.
OF COURSE IT WAS.

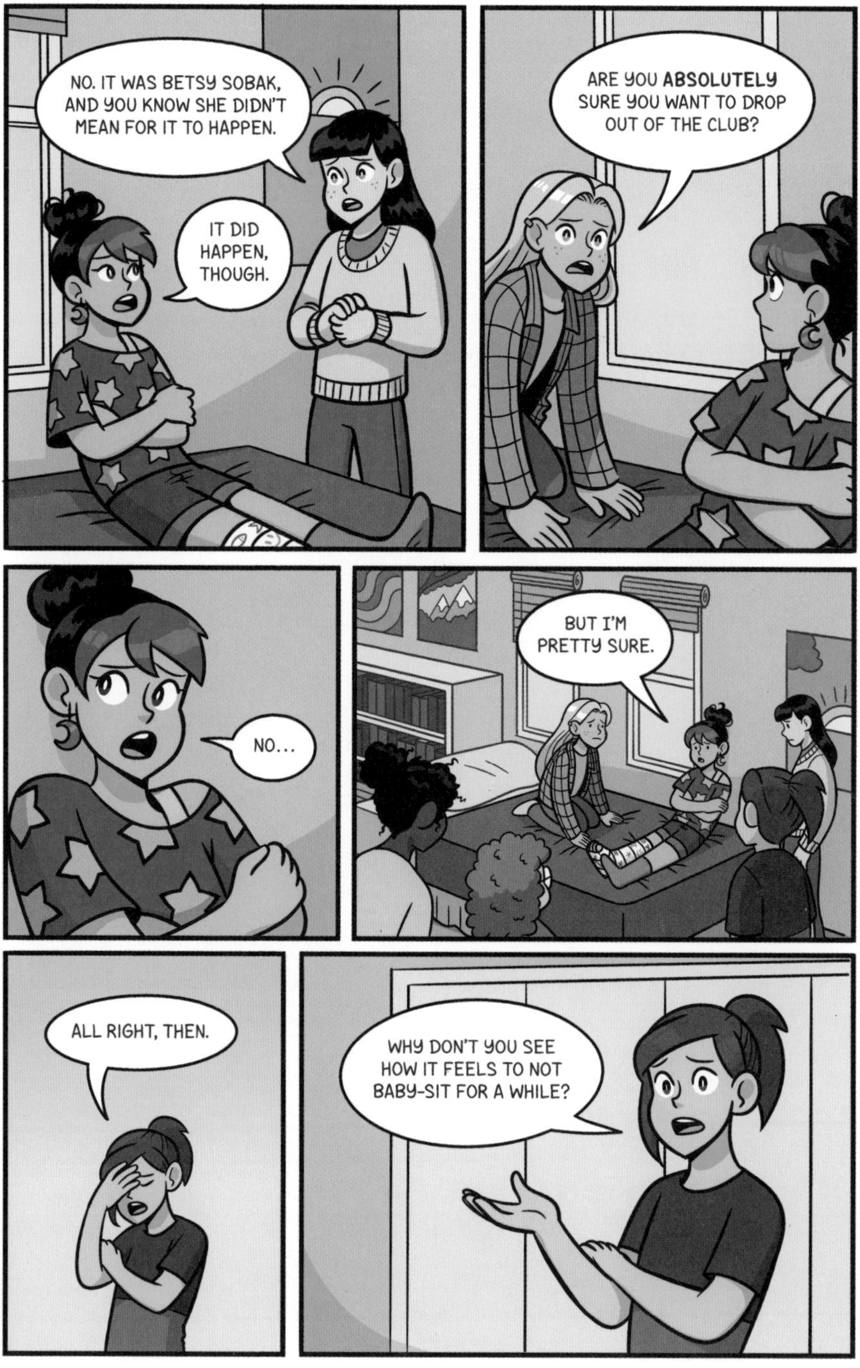
NO. IT WAS BETSY SOBAK, AND YOU KNOW SHE DIDN'T MEAN FOR IT TO HAPPEN.
IT DID HAPPEN, THOUGH.
ARE YOU **ABSOLUTELY** SURE YOU WANT TO DROP OUT OF THE CLUB?
NO...
BUT I'M PRETTY SURE.
ALL RIGHT, THEN.
WHY DON'T YOU SEE HOW IT FEELS TO NOT BABY-SIT FOR A WHILE?

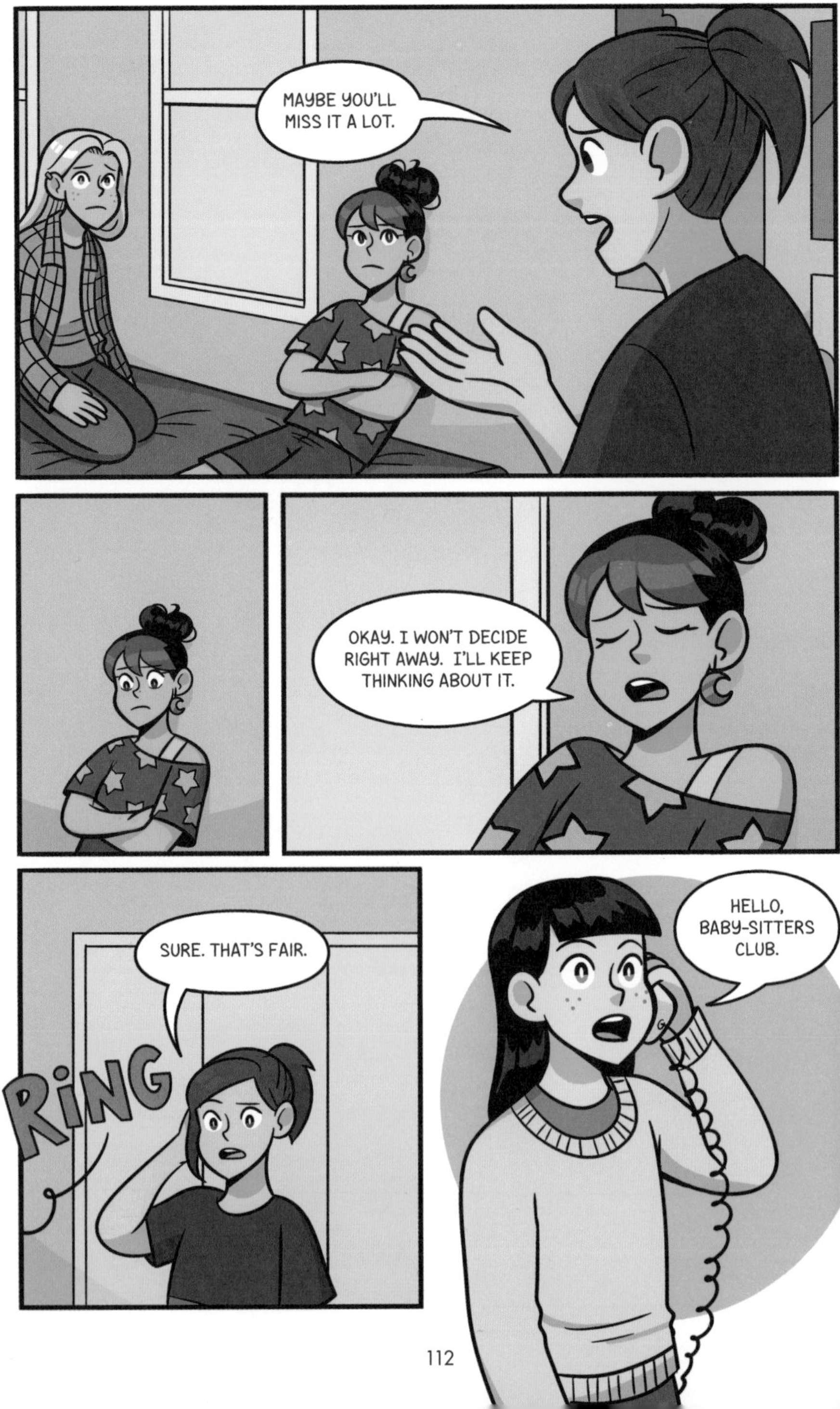
MAYBE YOU'LL MISS IT A LOT.
OKAY. I WON'T DECIDE RIGHT AWAY. I'LL KEEP THINKING ABOUT IT.
SURE. THAT'S FAIR.
RING
HELLO, BABY-SITTERS CLUB.

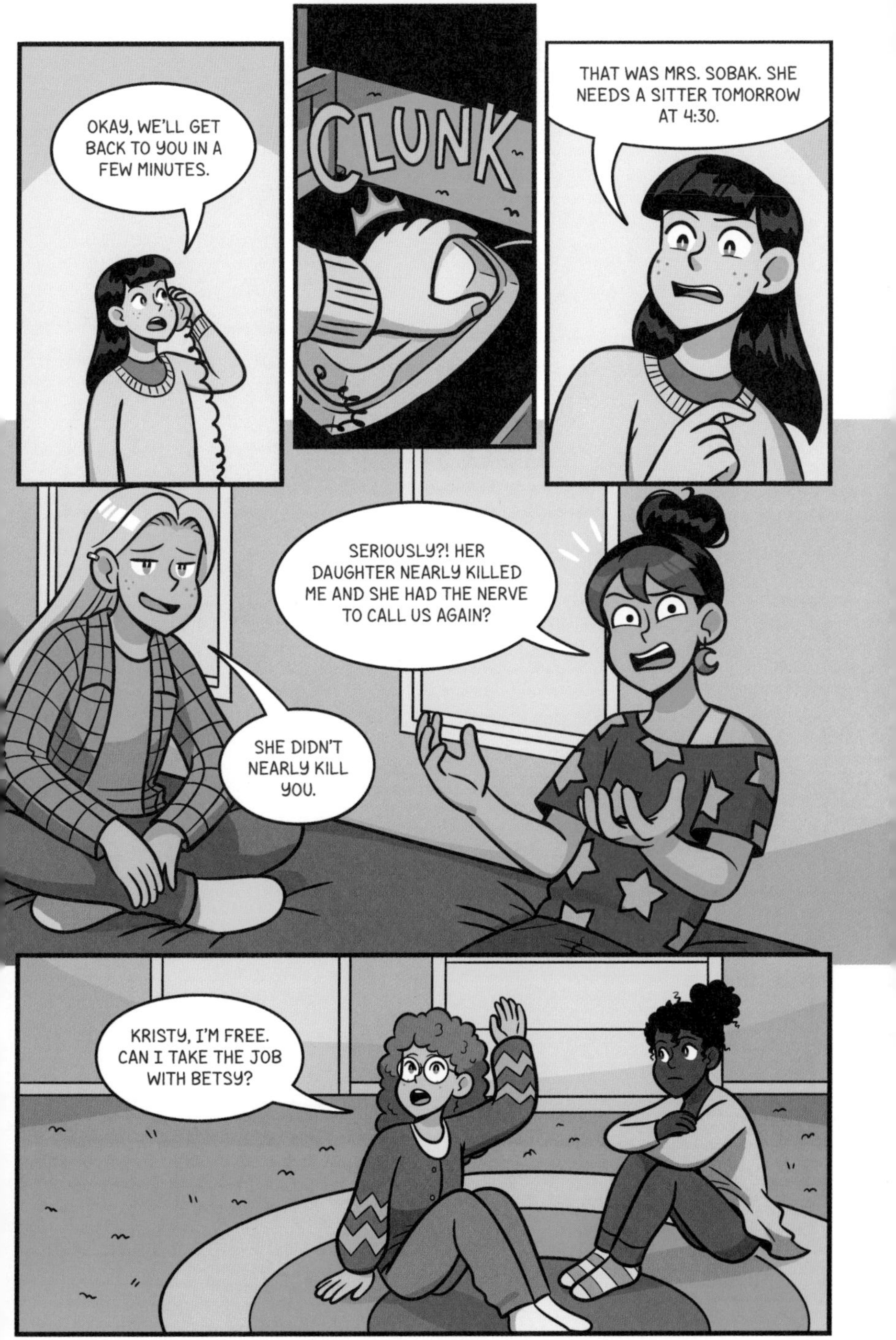
OKAY, WE'LL GET BACK TO YOU IN A FEW MINUTES.
CLUNK
THAT WAS MRS. SOBAK. SHE NEEDS A SITTER TOMORROW AT 4:30.
SERIOUSLY?! HER DAUGHTER NEARLY KILLED ME AND SHE HAD THE NERVE TO CALL US AGAIN?
SHE DIDN'T NEARLY KILL YOU.
KRISTY, I'M FREE. CAN I TAKE THE JOB WITH BETSY?

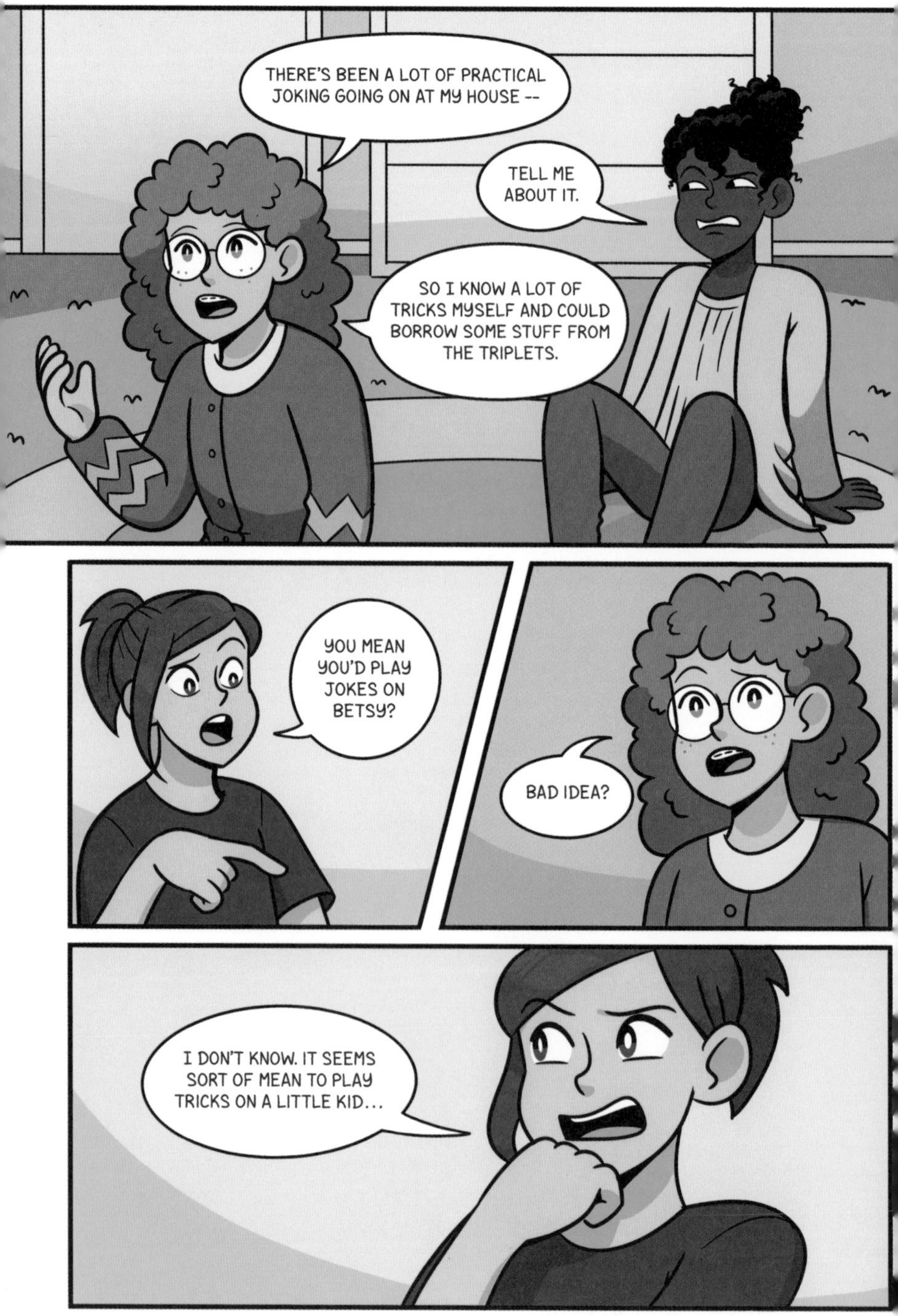
THERE'S BEEN A LOT OF PRACTICAL JOKING GOING ON AT MY HOUSE --
TELL ME ABOUT IT.
SO I KNOW A LOT OF TRICKS MYSELF AND COULD BORROW SOME STUFF FROM THE TRIPLETS.
YOU MEAN YOU'D PLAY JOKES ON BETSY?
BAD IDEA?
I DON'T KNOW. IT SEEMS SORT OF MEAN TO PLAY TRICKS ON A LITTLE KID...

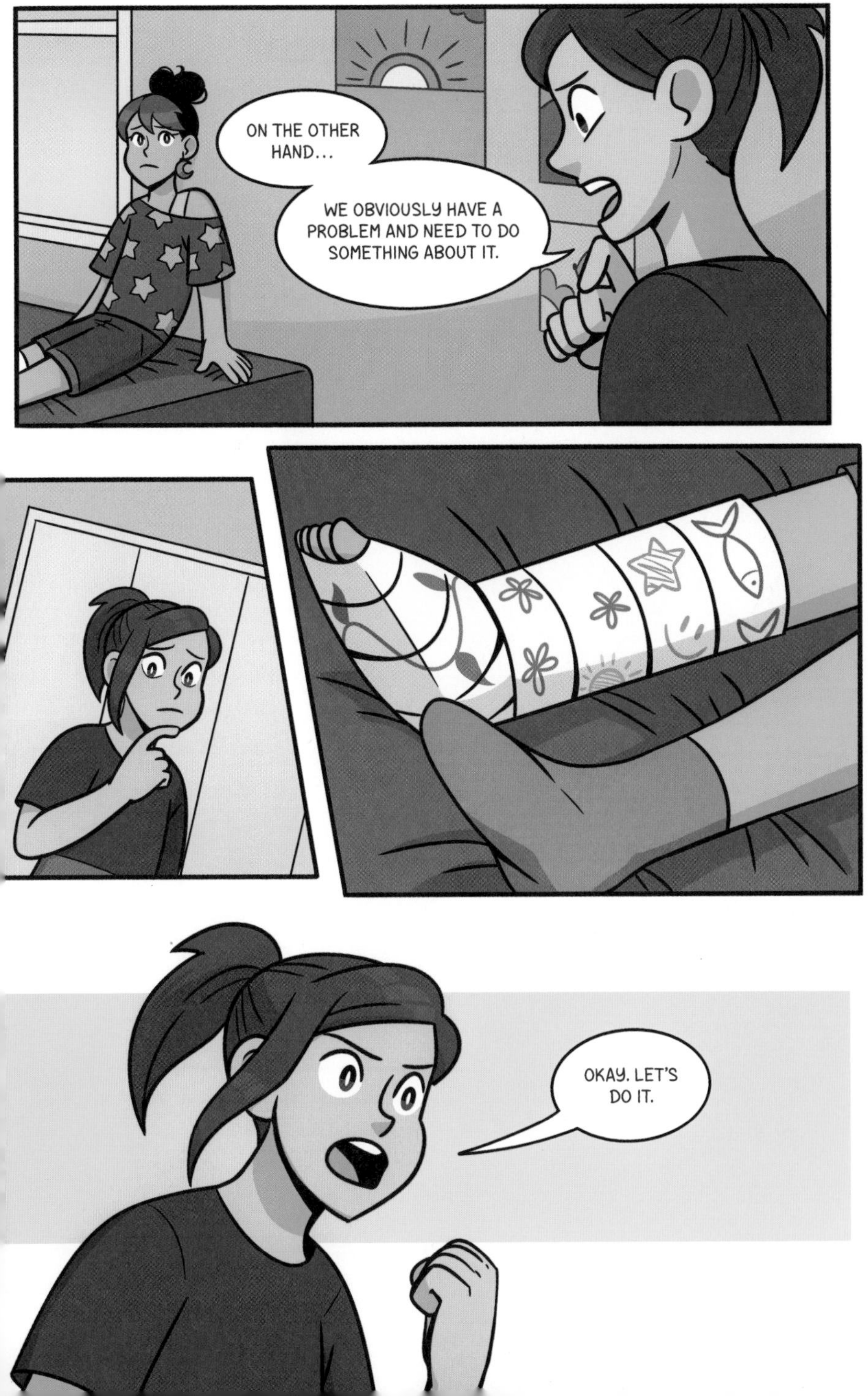
ON THE OTHER HAND...
WE OBVIOUSLY HAVE A PROBLEM AND NEED TO DO SOMETHING ABOUT IT.
OKAY. LET'S DO IT.

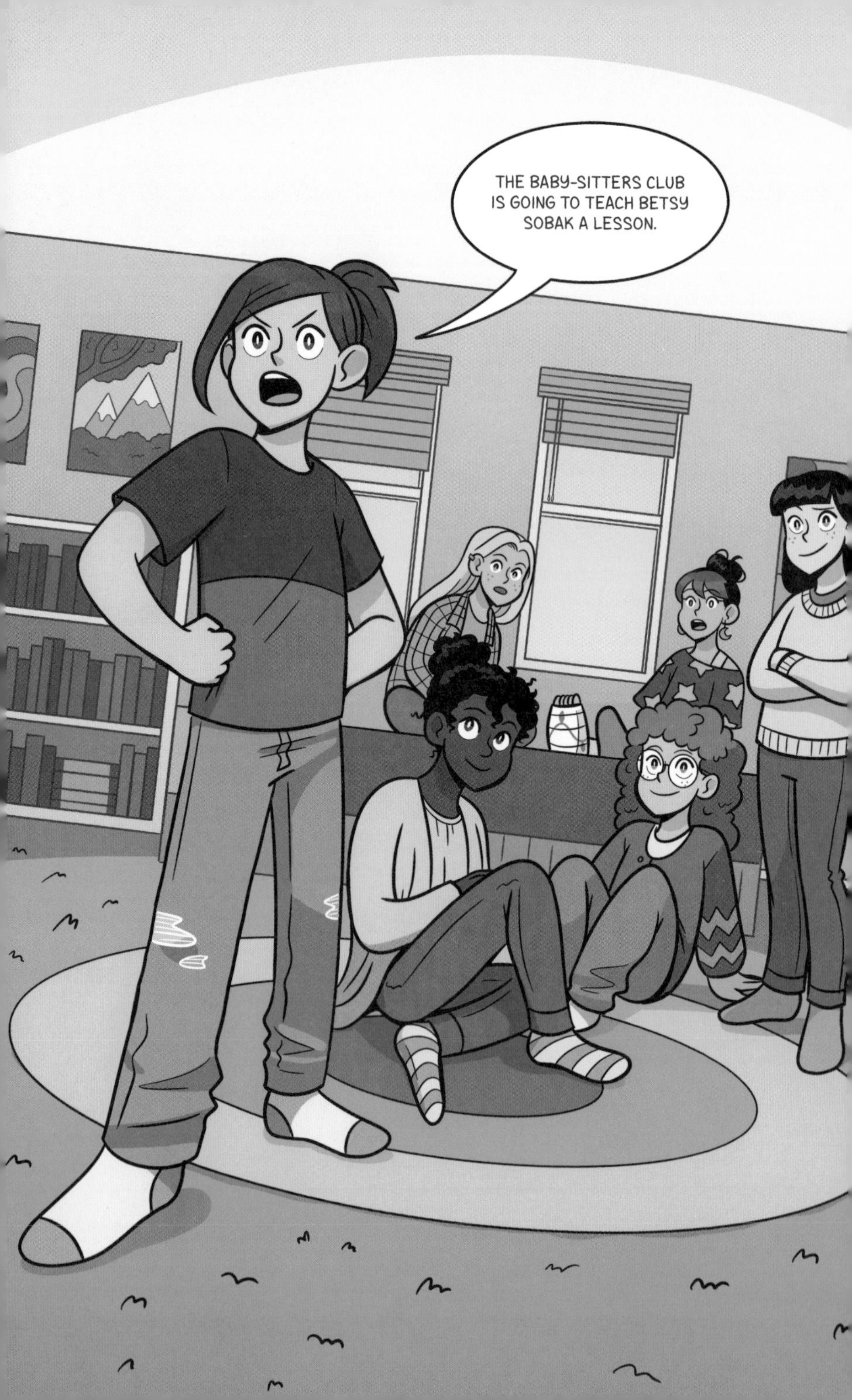
THE BABY-SITTERS CLUB IS GOING TO TEACH BETSY SOBAK A LESSON.

Thursday

When I went over to Betsy Sobak's, I had a package of sneezing powder, a rubber slug, and a very realistic-looking furry rat. I had rented them from the triplets for the afternoon. It cost me $3.00 — a dollar per triplet. Anyway, I was feeling pretty confident when I reached the Sobaks', but I was also jumpy. I knew I would have to be on my toes with Betsy . . .

— Mallory

Hey, Mallory, remind me at our next meeting that we should pay you back the $3.00 "rental" fee from the treasury.

— Kristy

CHAPTER 10

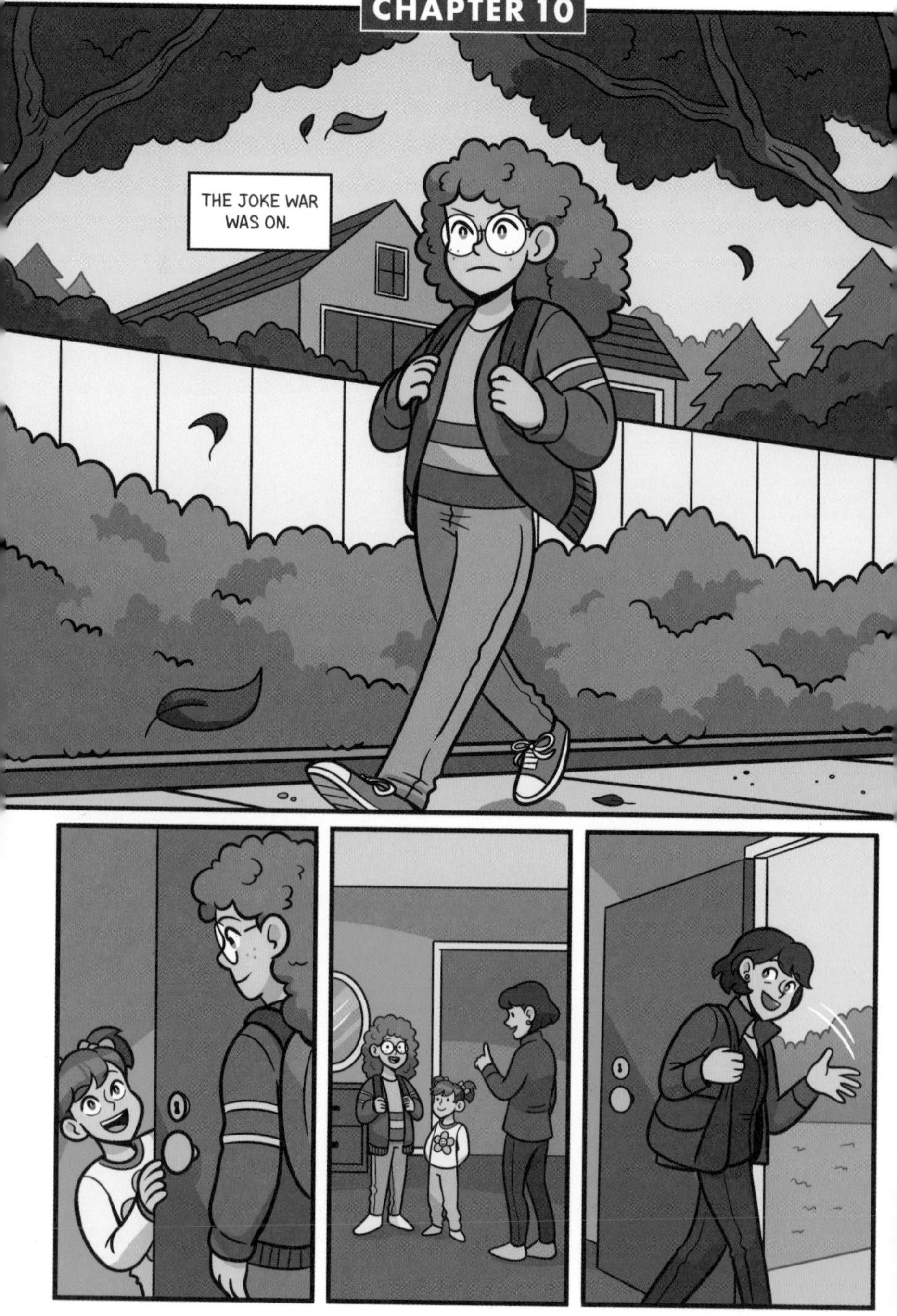
THE JOKE WAR WAS ON.

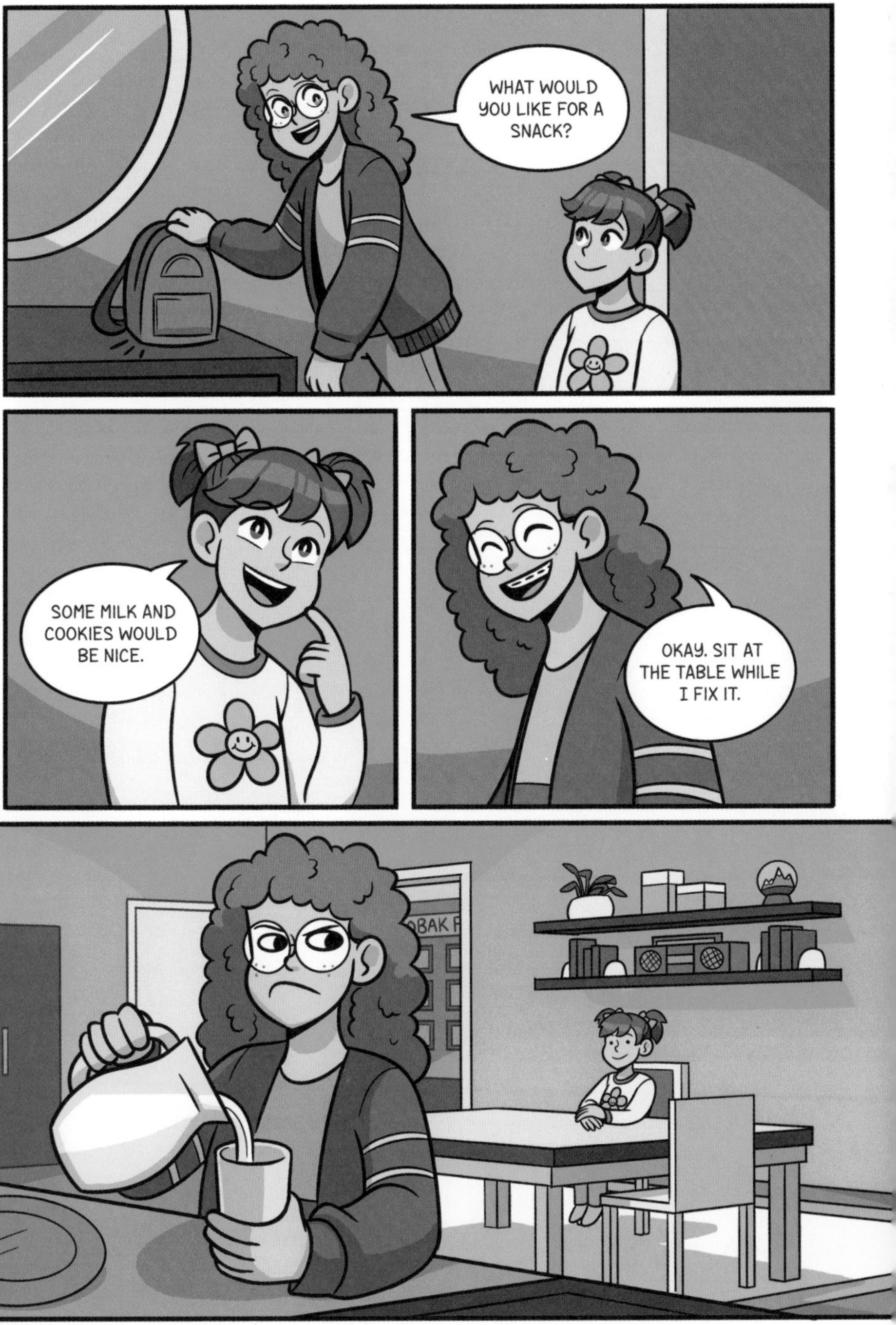
WHAT WOULD YOU LIKE FOR A SNACK?
SOME MILK AND COOKIES WOULD BE NICE.
OKAY. SIT AT THE TABLE WHILE I FIX IT.

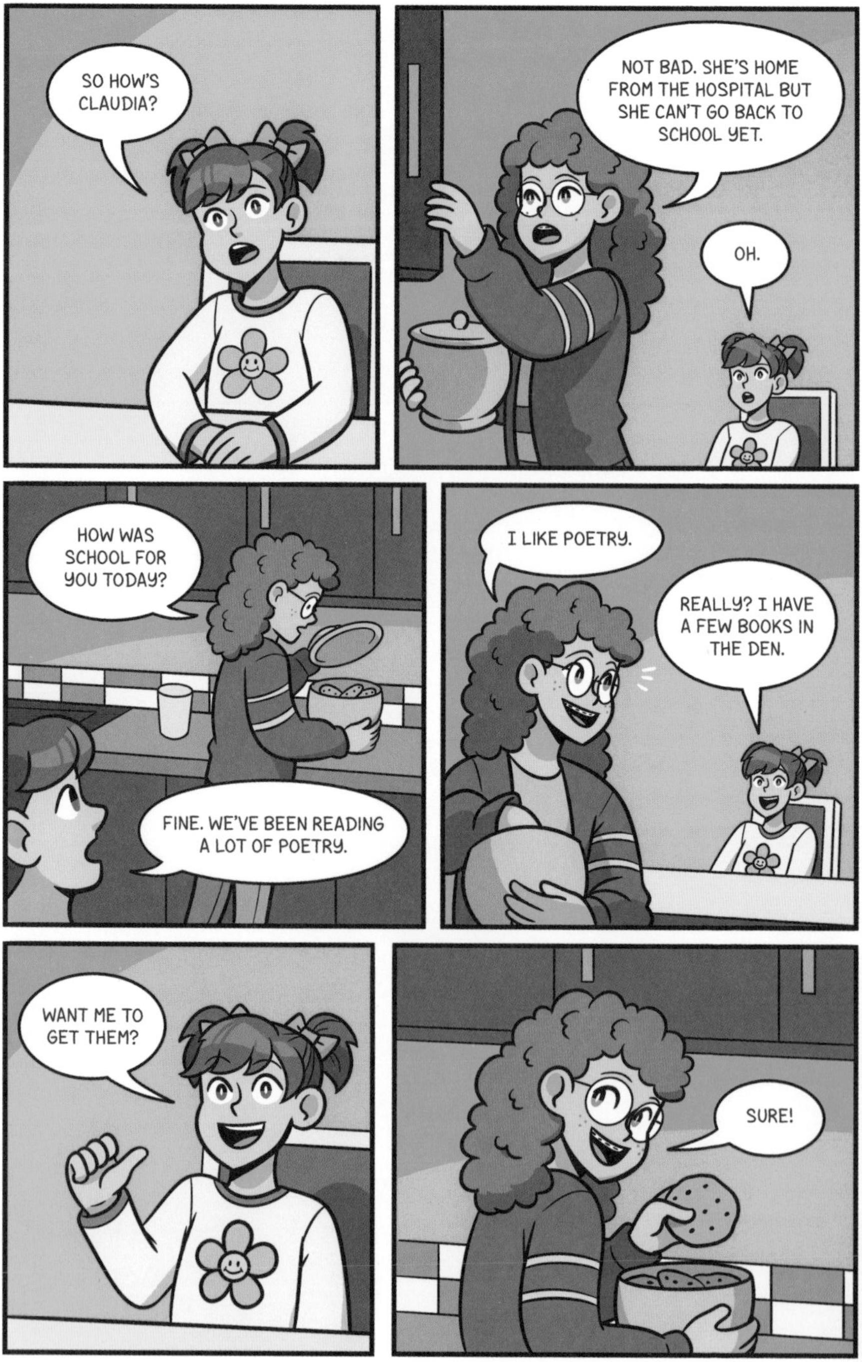
SO HOW'S CLAUDIA?
NOT BAD. SHE'S HOME FROM THE HOSPITAL BUT SHE CAN'T GO BACK TO SCHOOL YET.
OH.
HOW WAS SCHOOL FOR YOU TODAY?
FINE. WE'VE BEEN READING A LOT OF POETRY.
I LIKE POETRY.
REALLY? I HAVE A FEW BOOKS IN THE DEN.
WANT ME TO GET THEM?
SURE!

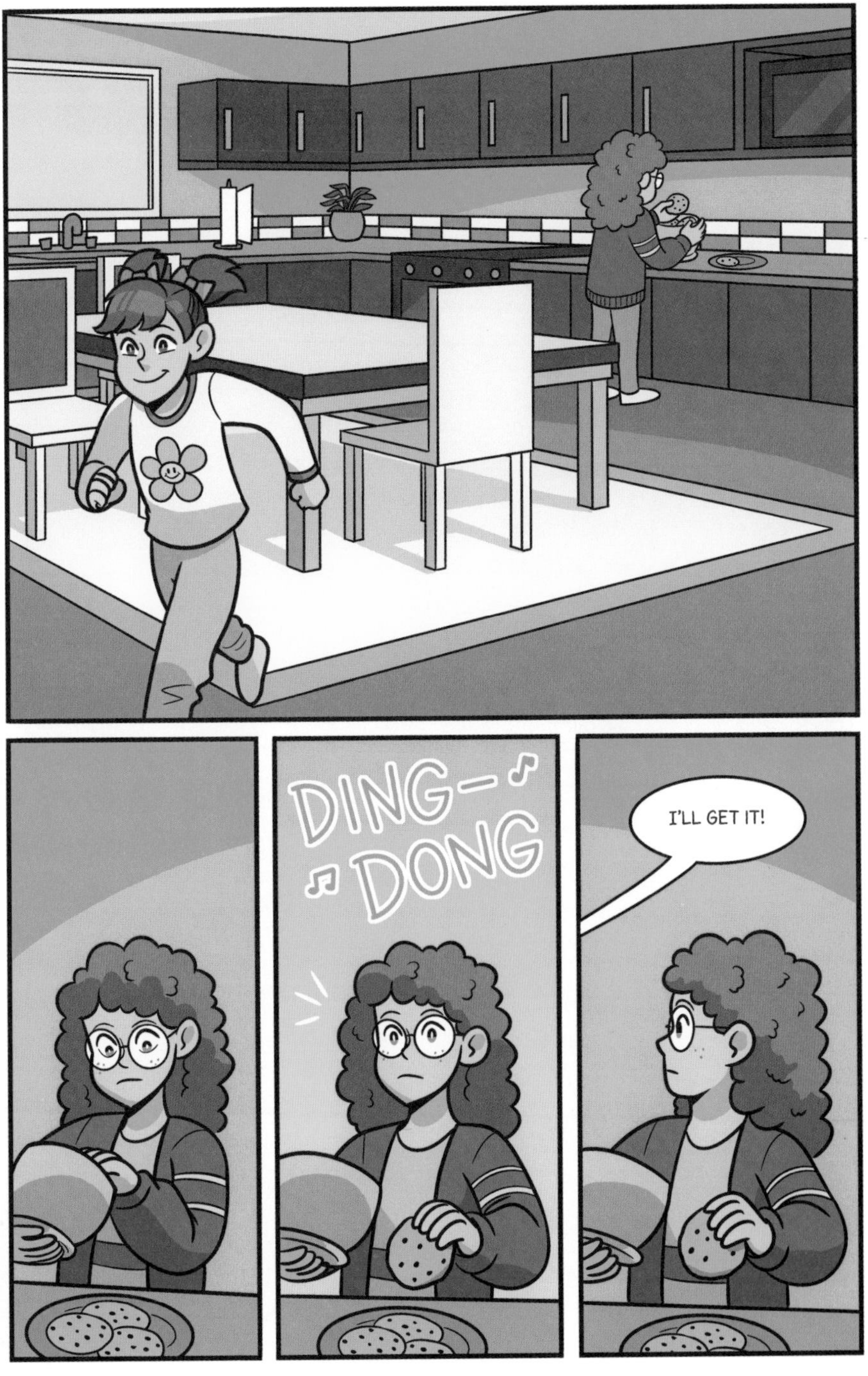
DING-DONG
I'LL GET IT!

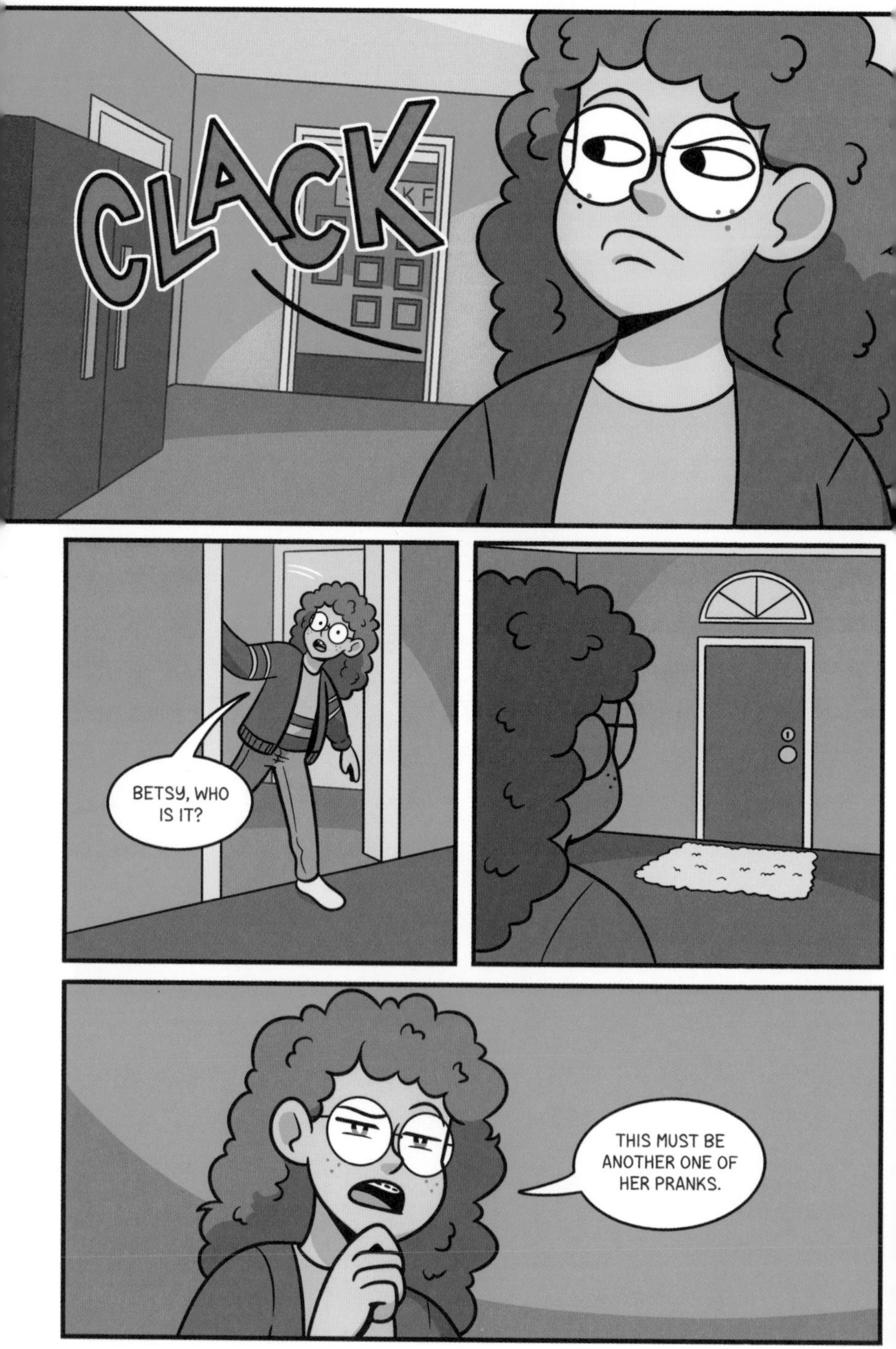
CLACK
BETSY, WHO IS IT?
THIS MUST BE ANOTHER ONE OF HER PRANKS.

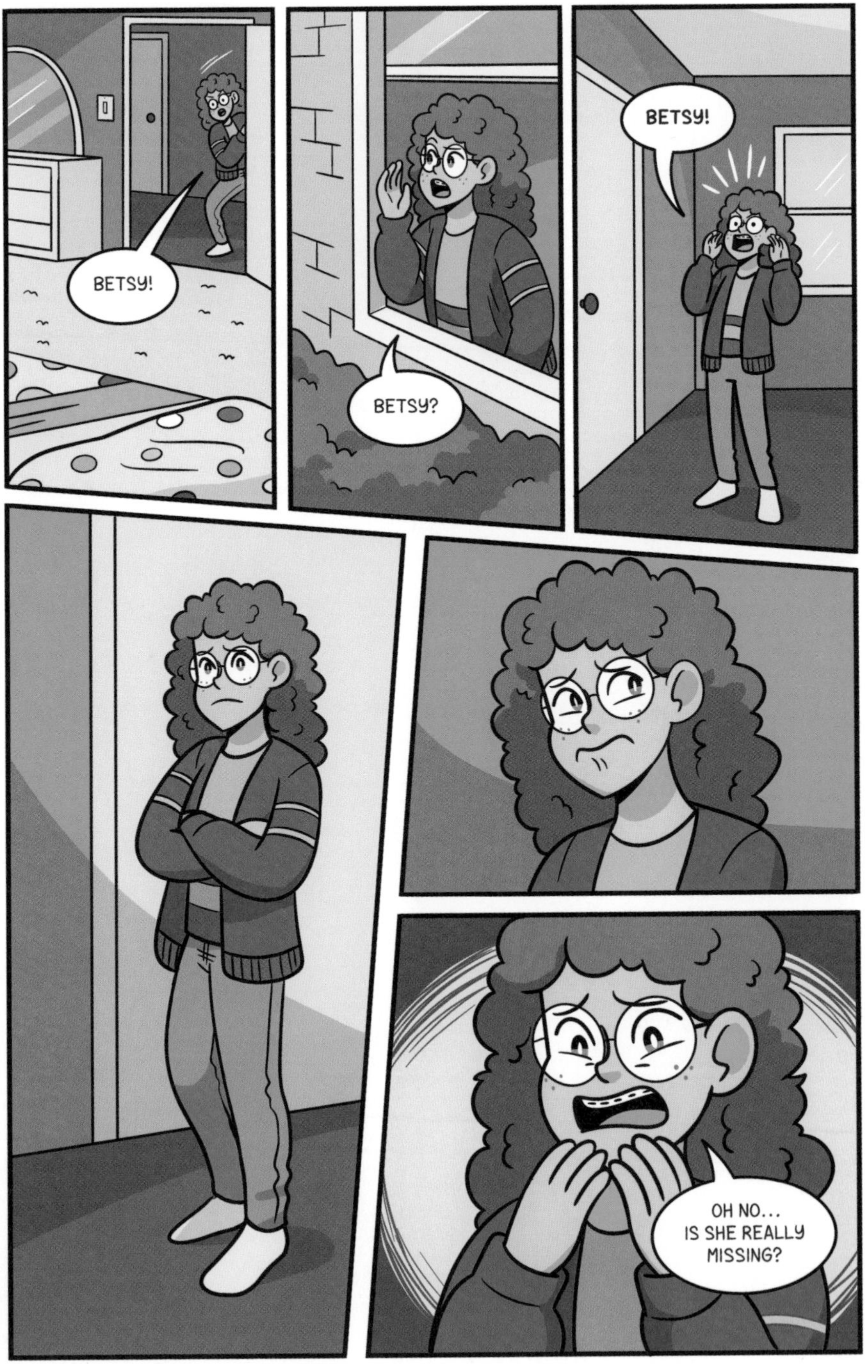
BETSY!
BETSY?
BETSY!
OH NO...
IS SHE REALLY
MISSING?

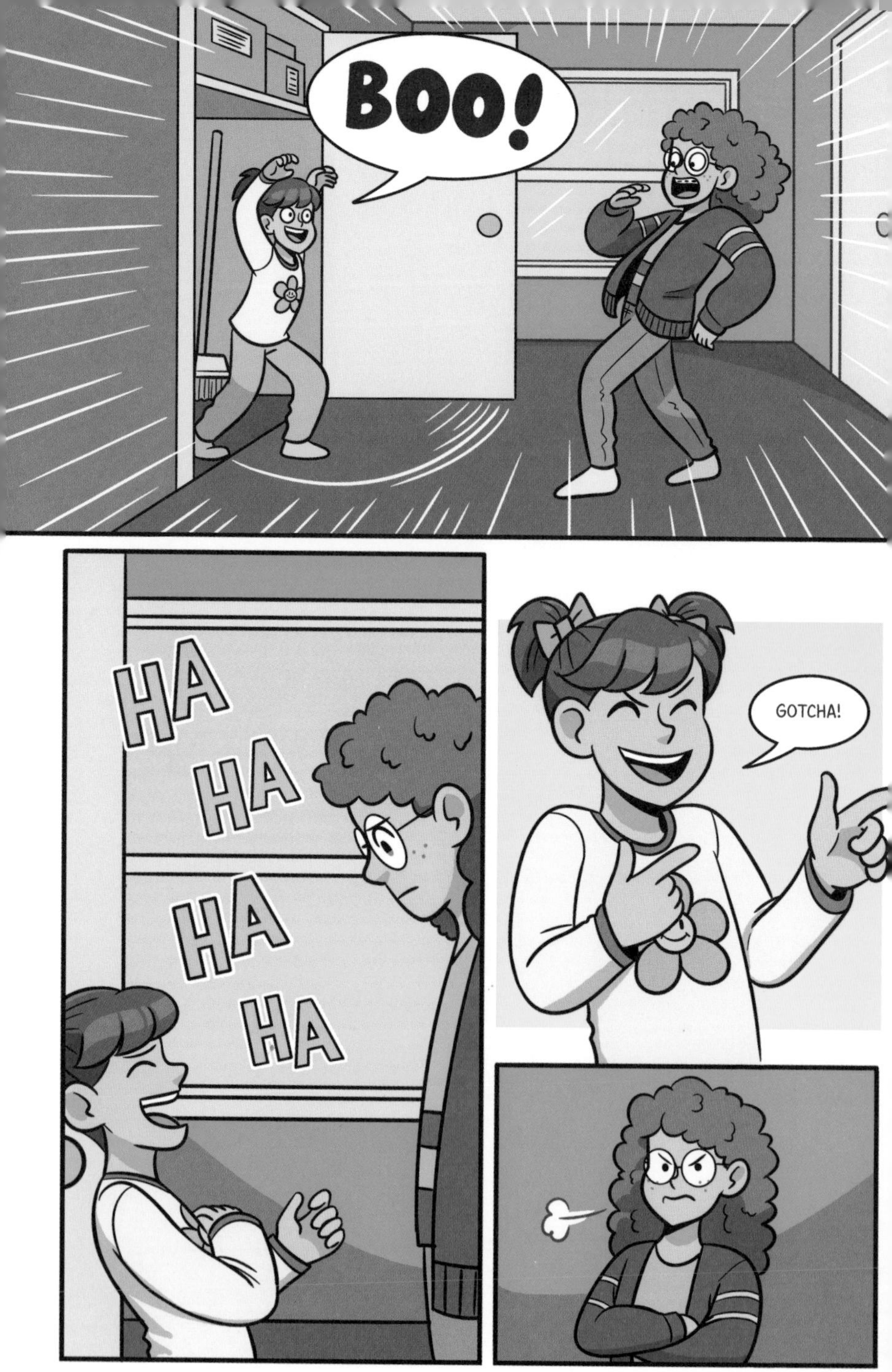
BOO!
HA
HA
HA
HA
GOTCHA!

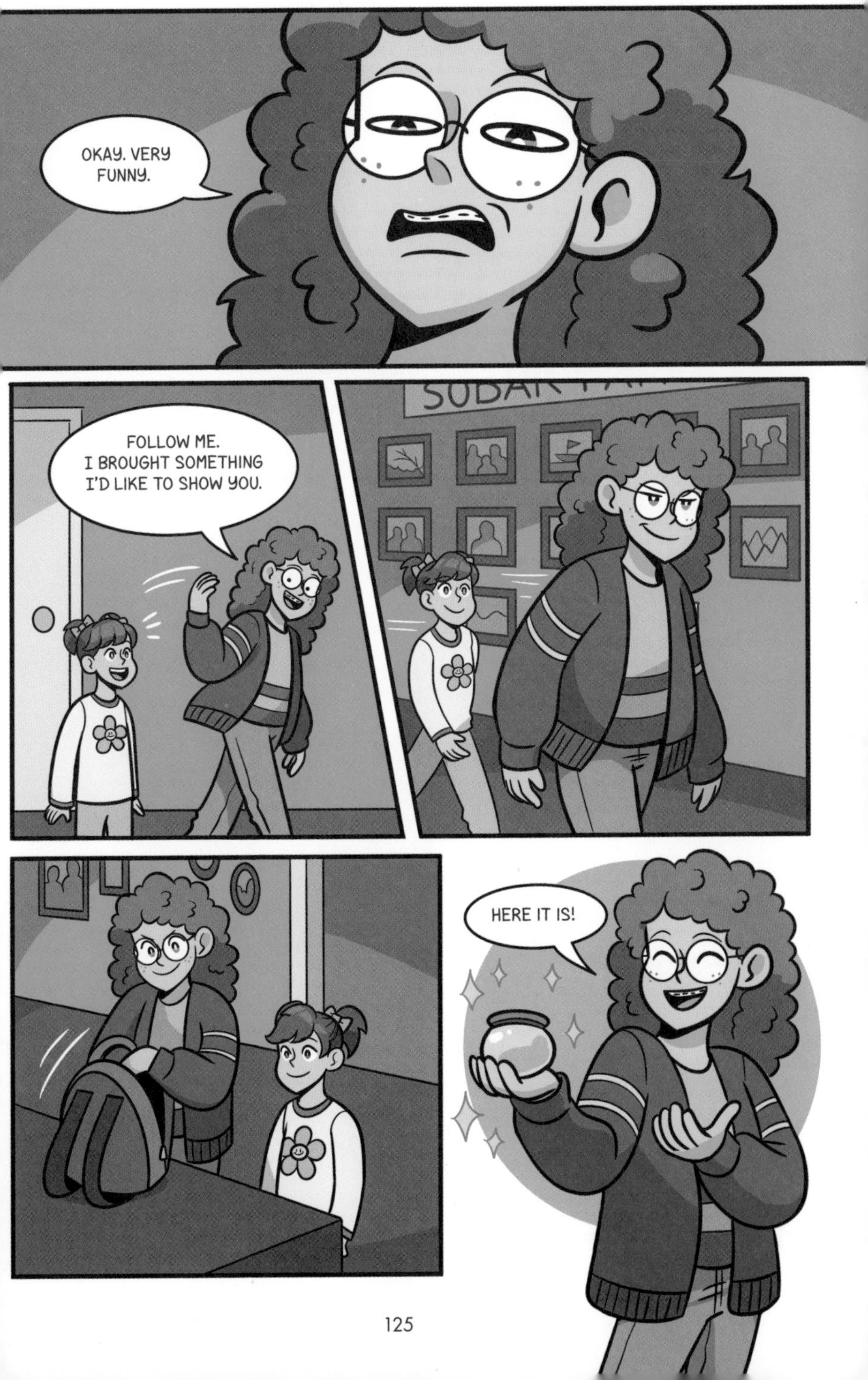
OKAY. VERY FUNNY.
FOLLOW ME. I BROUGHT SOMETHING I'D LIKE TO SHOW YOU.
HERE IT IS!

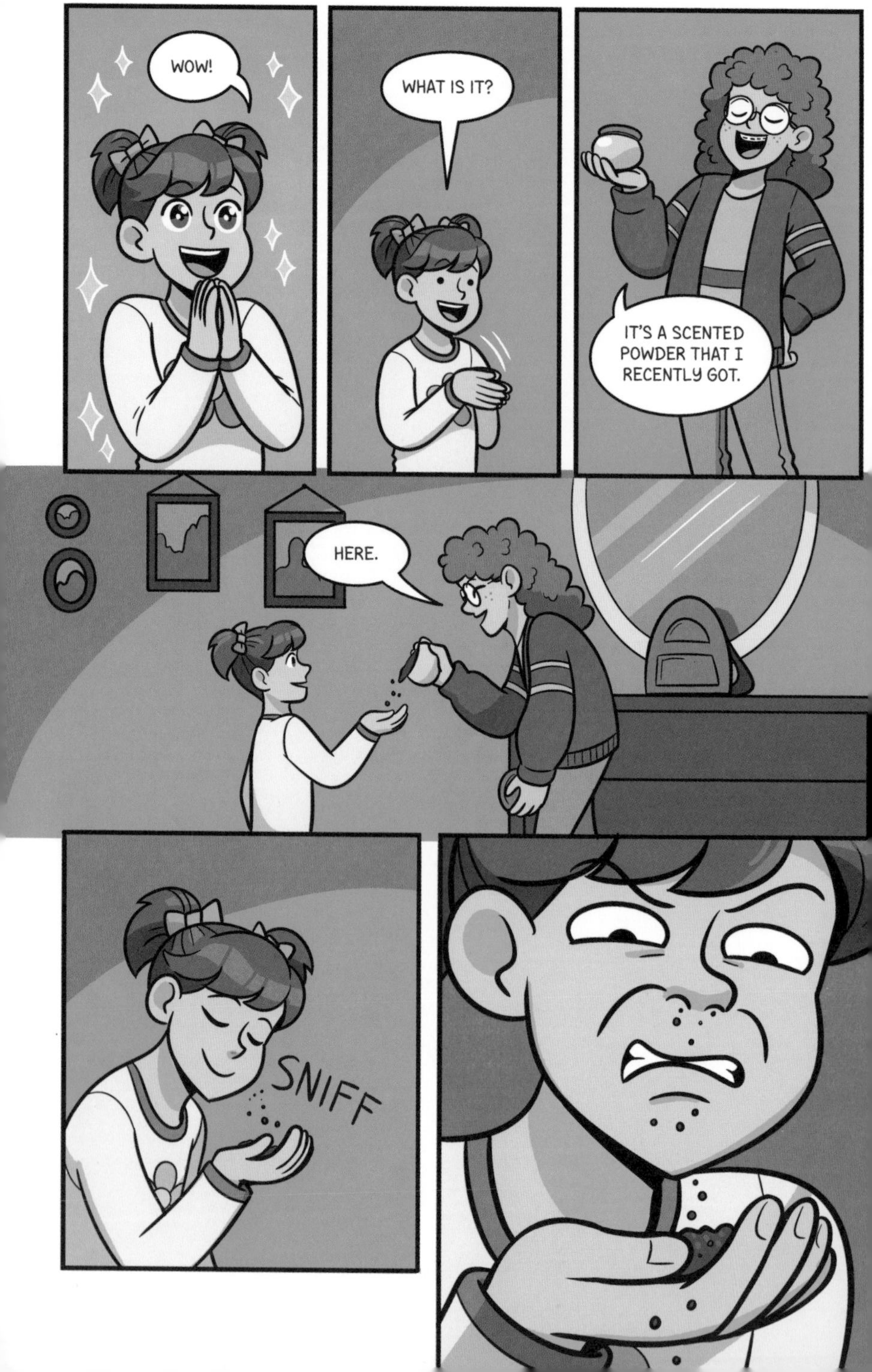
WOW!
WHAT IS IT?
IT'S A SCENTED POWDER THAT I RECENTLY GOT.
HERE.
SNIFF

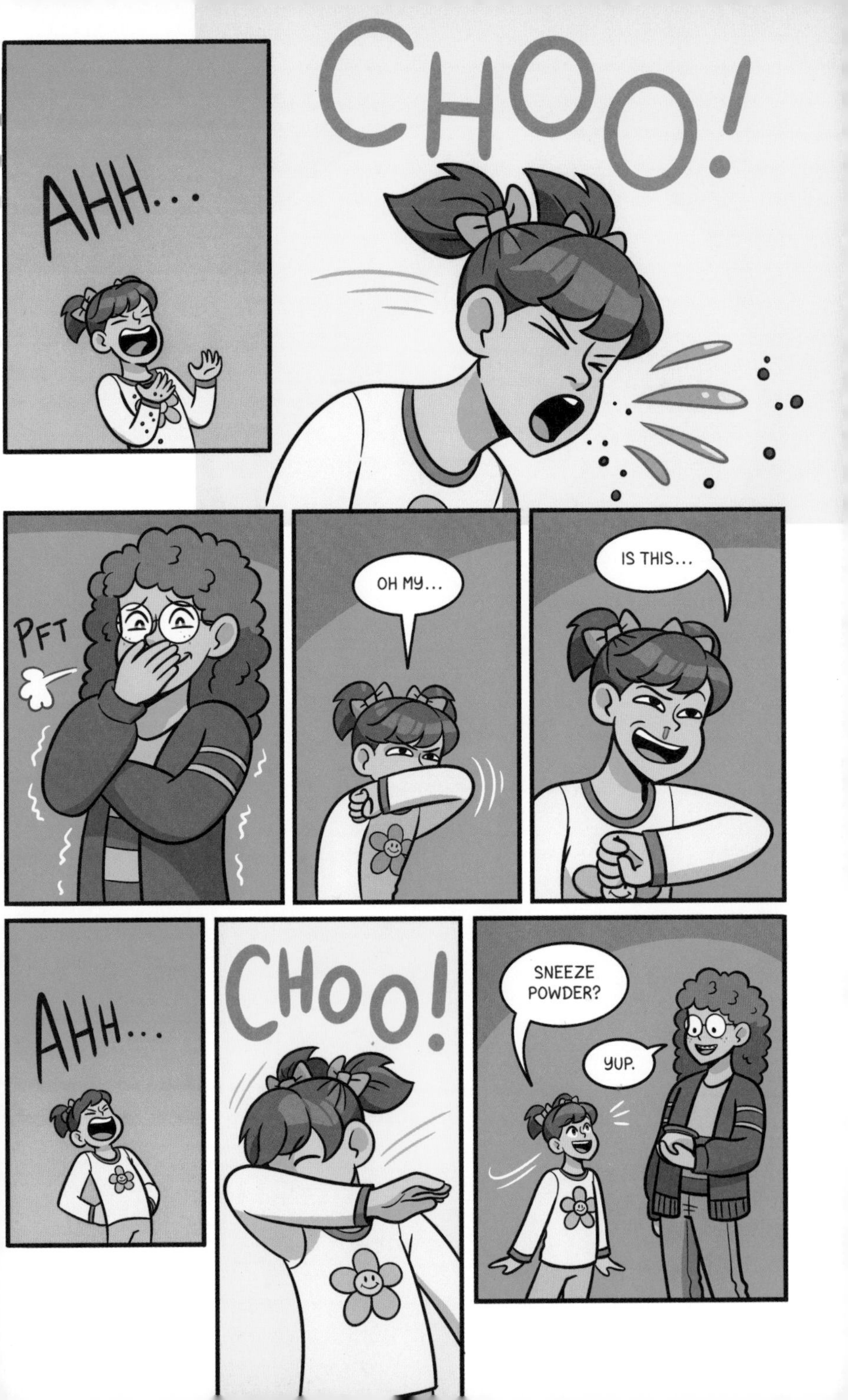
AHH...
CHOO!
PFT
OH MY...
IS THIS...
AHH...
CHOO!
SNEEZE POWDER?
YUP.

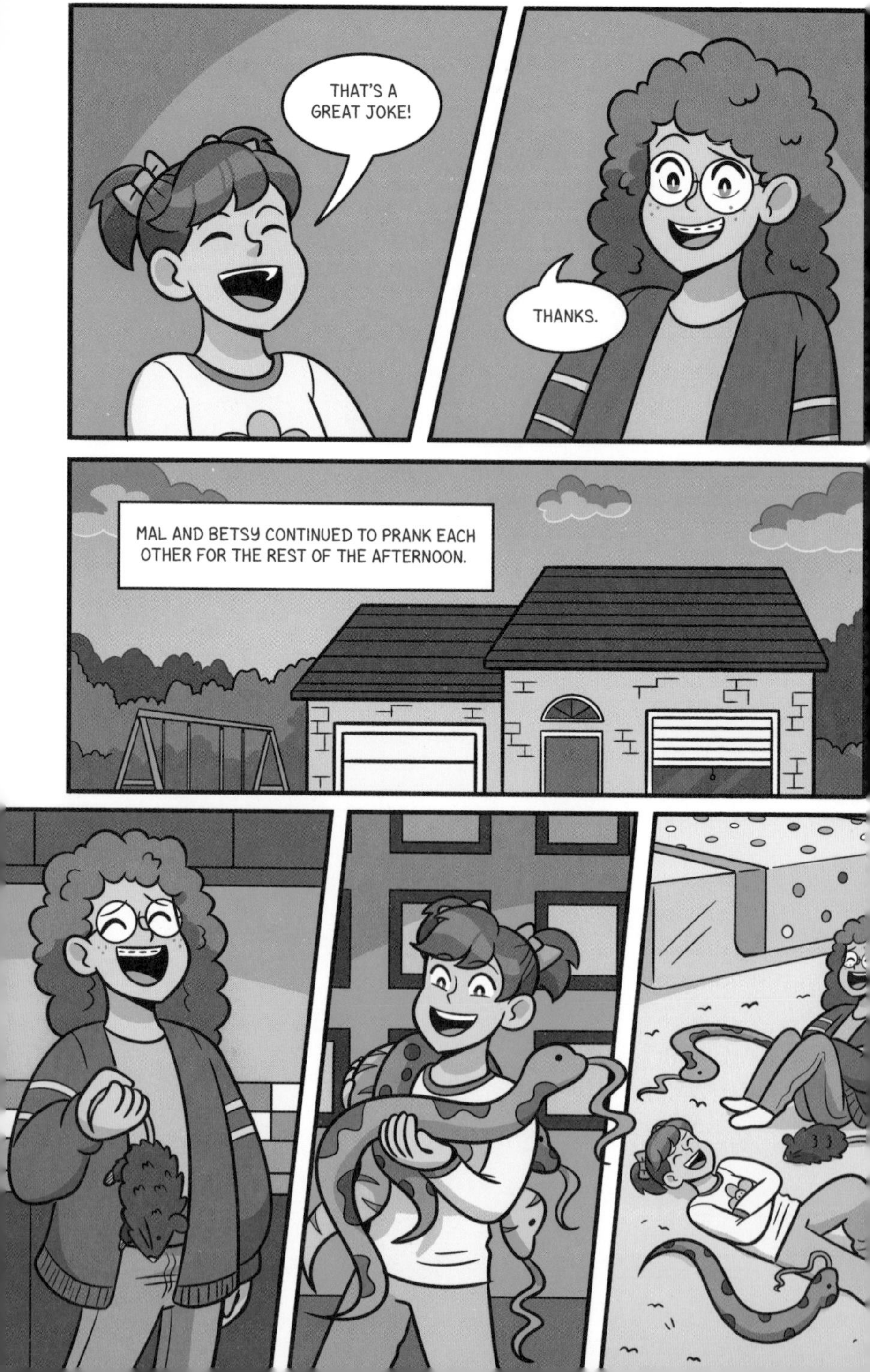
THAT'S A GREAT JOKE!
THANKS.
MAL AND BETSY CONTINUED TO PRANK EACH OTHER FOR THE REST OF THE AFTERNOON.

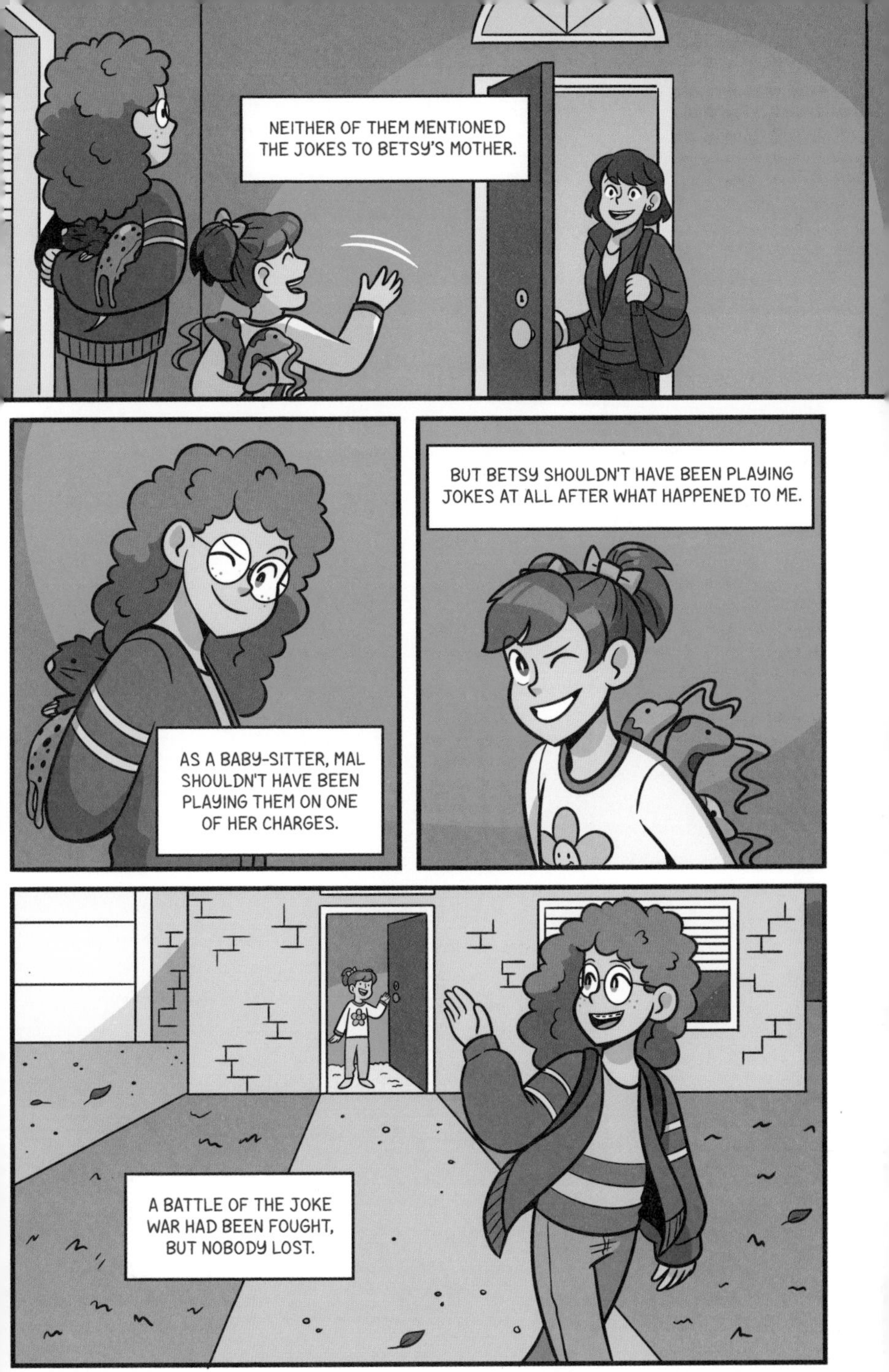
NEITHER OF THEM MENTIONED THE JOKES TO BETSY'S MOTHER.
AS A BABY-SITTER, MAL SHOULDN'T HAVE BEEN PLAYING THEM ON ONE OF HER CHARGES.
BUT BETSY SHOULDN'T HAVE BEEN PLAYING JOKES AT ALL AFTER WHAT HAPPENED TO ME.
A BATTLE OF THE JOKE WAR HAD BEEN FOUGHT, BUT NOBODY LOST.

JOKE WAR SCOR[E]
BSC | BETSY

SATURDAY

I PREPARED FOR MY SITTING JOB WITH BETSY BY CALLING MY BROTHER IN CALIFORNIA. WHEN I EXPLAINED TO JEFF WHAT WAS GOING ON, HE SAID "BOY, DAWN. AWESOME! YOU COULD SCARE HER WITH A RUBBER SPIDER! YOU COULD PRETEND THERE'S A MOUSE LOOSE IN THE HOUSE . . . OR A RAT! OR YOU COULD PRETEND TO FAINT, AND THEN WHEN SHE BENDS OVER TO SEE HOW YOU ARE, JUMP UP AND SCARE HER. OH, AND YOU COULD STUFF HER ROOM WITH WADDED-UP NEWSPAPER SO SHE CAN'T GET INSIDE!"

WELL, SOME OF JEFF'S IDEAS WERE GOOD. I WENT TO THE SOBAKS' WELL-PREPARED . . .

- DAWN

CHAPTER 11

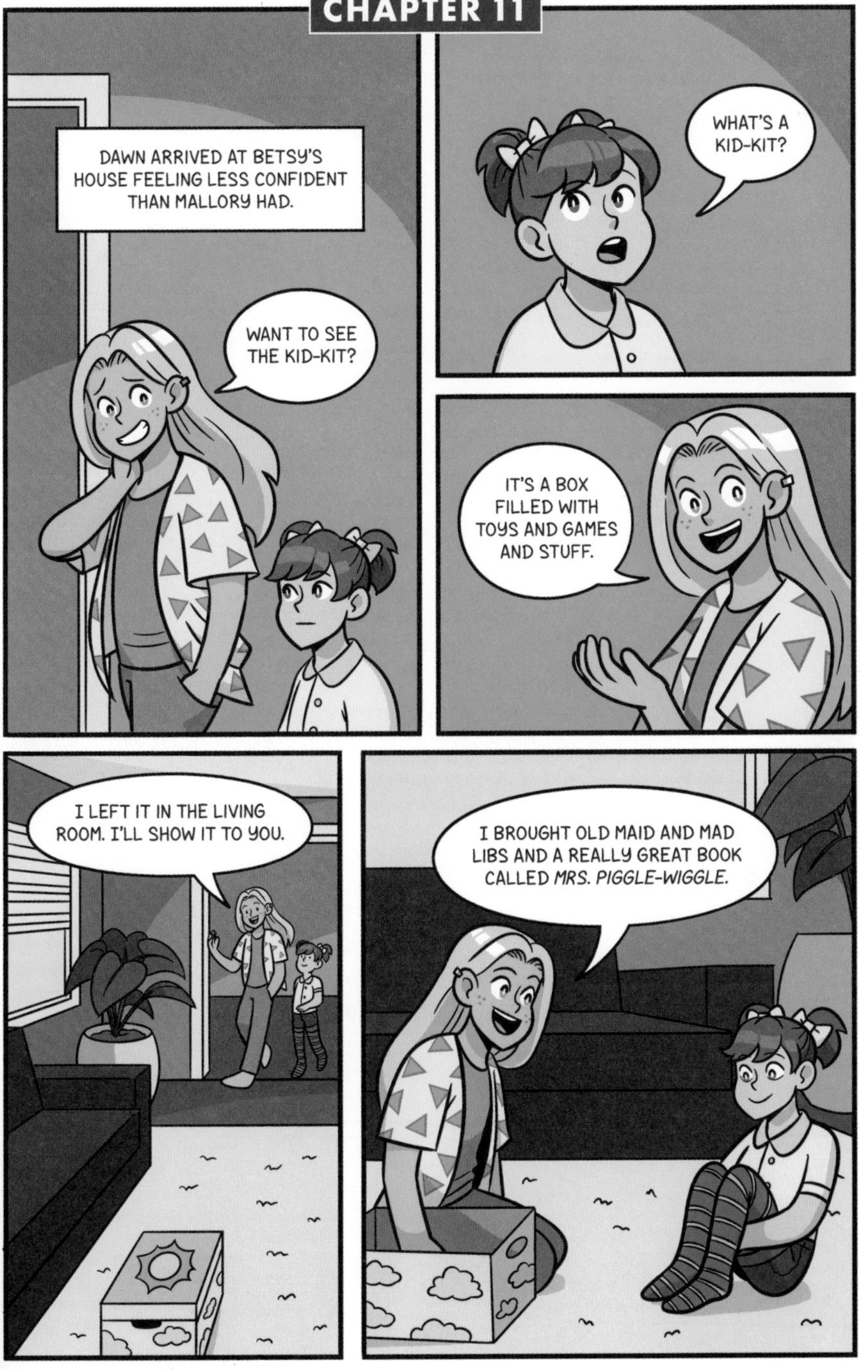

DAWN ARRIVED AT BETSY'S HOUSE FEELING LESS CONFIDENT THAN MALLORY HAD.
WANT TO SEE THE KID-KIT?
WHAT'S A KID-KIT?
IT'S A BOX FILLED WITH TOYS AND GAMES AND STUFF.
I LEFT IT IN THE LIVING ROOM. I'LL SHOW IT TO YOU.
I BROUGHT OLD MAID AND MAD LIBS AND A REALLY GREAT BOOK CALLED *MRS. PIGGLE-WIGGLE.*

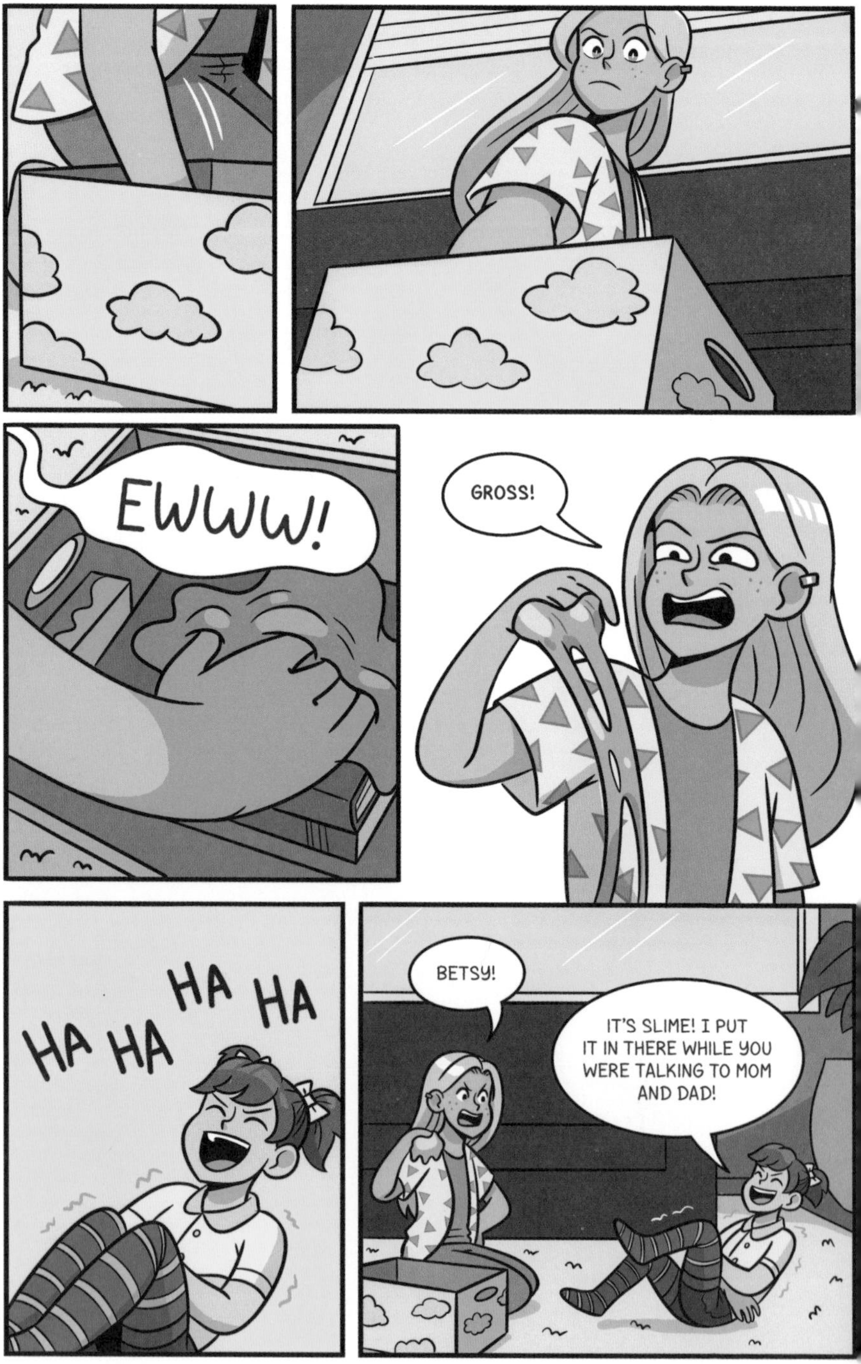
EWWW!
GROSS!
HA HA HA HA
BETSY!
IT'S SLIME! I PUT IT IN THERE WHILE YOU WERE TALKING TO MOM AND DAD!

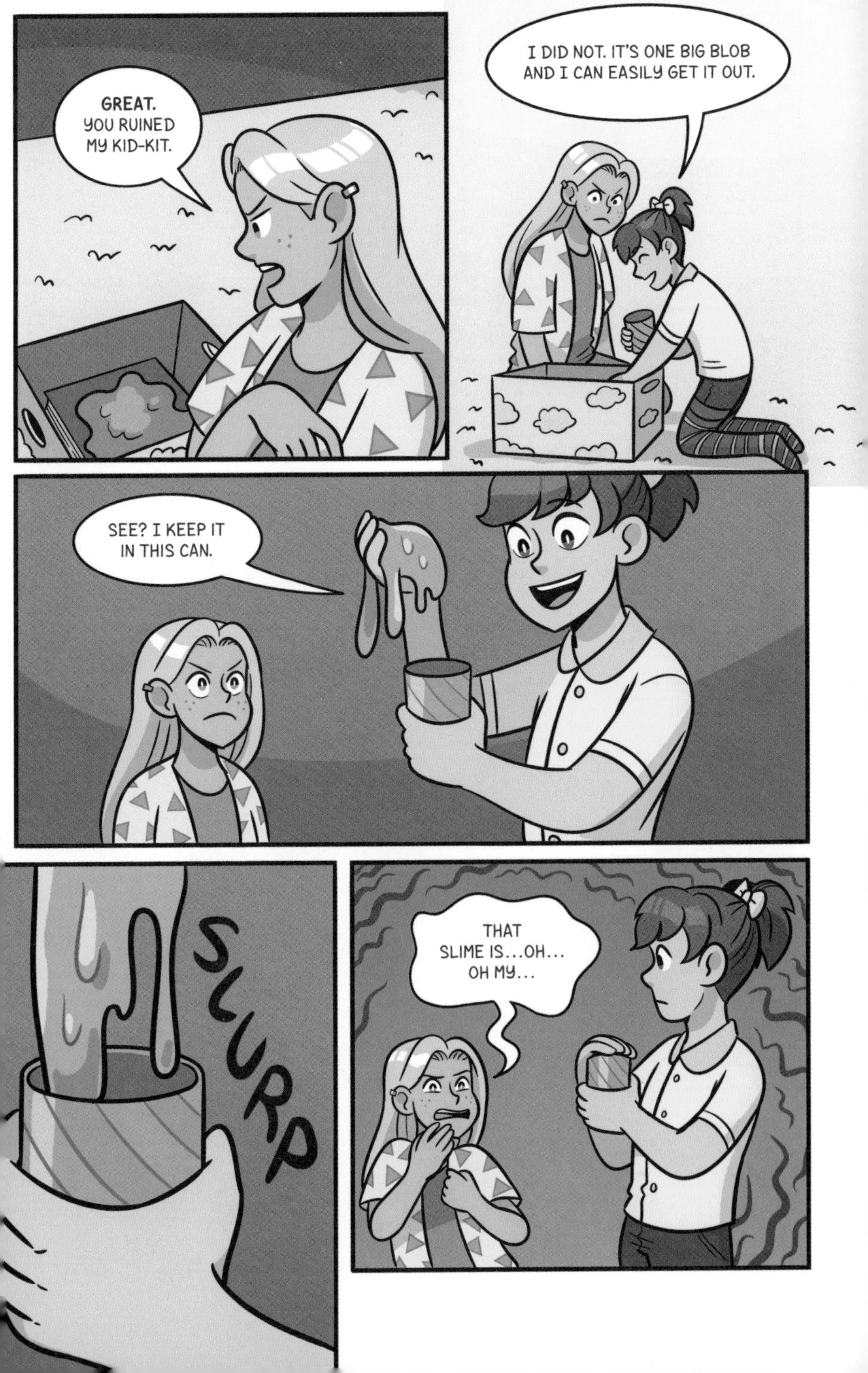
GREAT. YOU RUINED MY KID-KIT.
I DID NOT. IT'S ONE BIG BLOB AND I CAN EASILY GET IT OUT.
SEE? I KEEP IT IN THIS CAN.
SLURP
THAT SLIME IS...OH... OH MY...

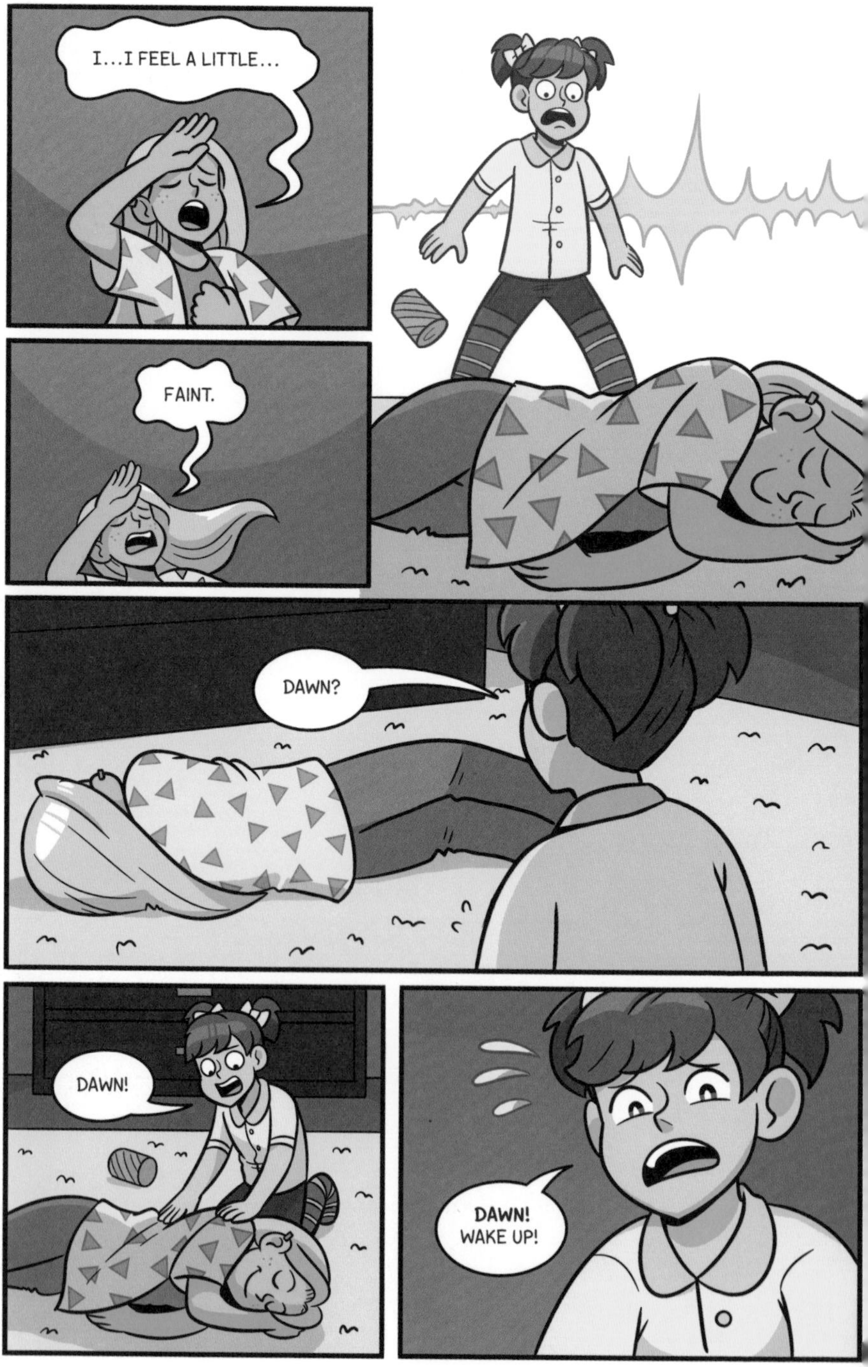
I...I FEEL A LITTLE...
FAINT.
DAWN?
DAWN!
DAWN!
WAKE UP!

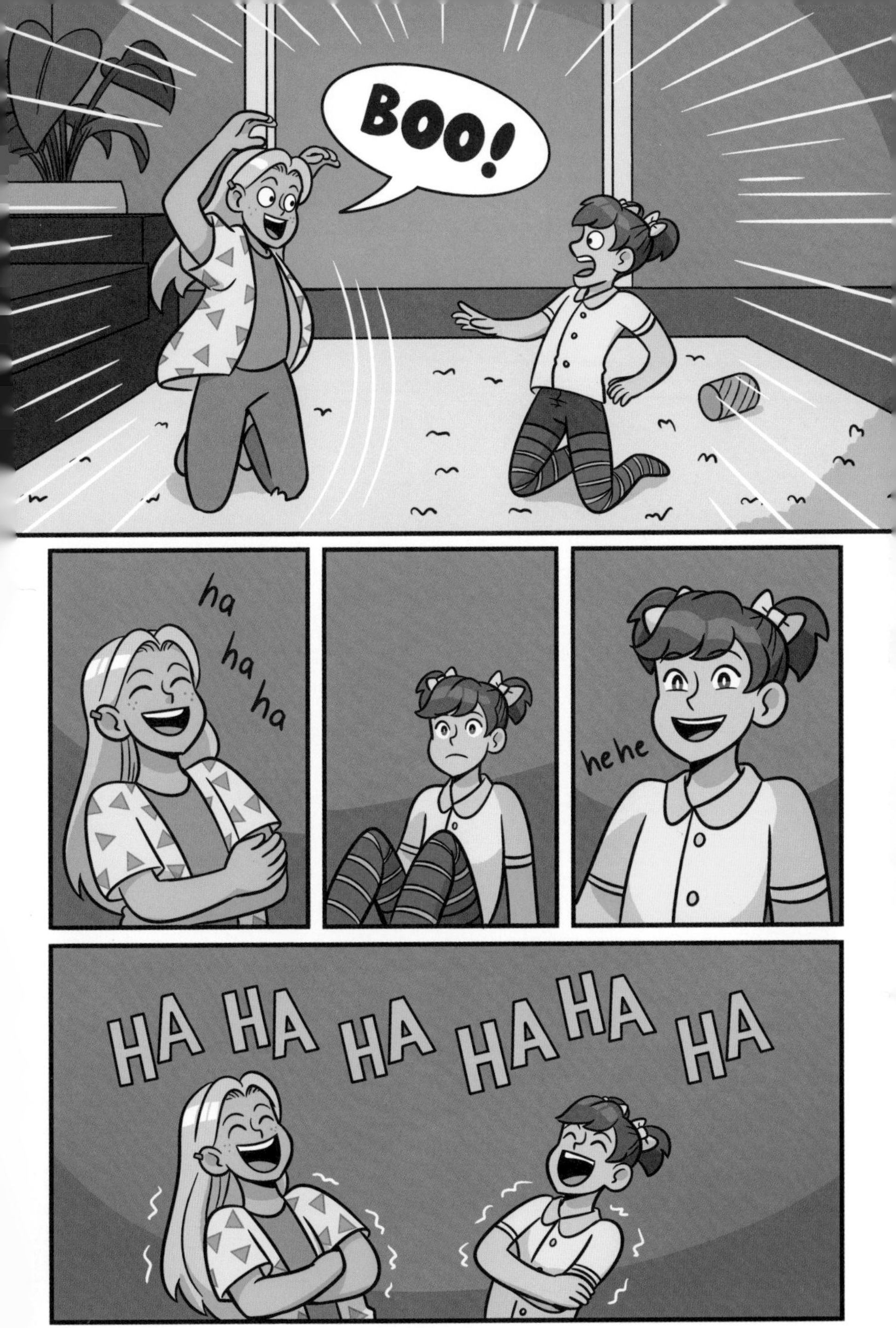
BOO!
ha
ha
ha
hehe
HA HA HA HA HA HA

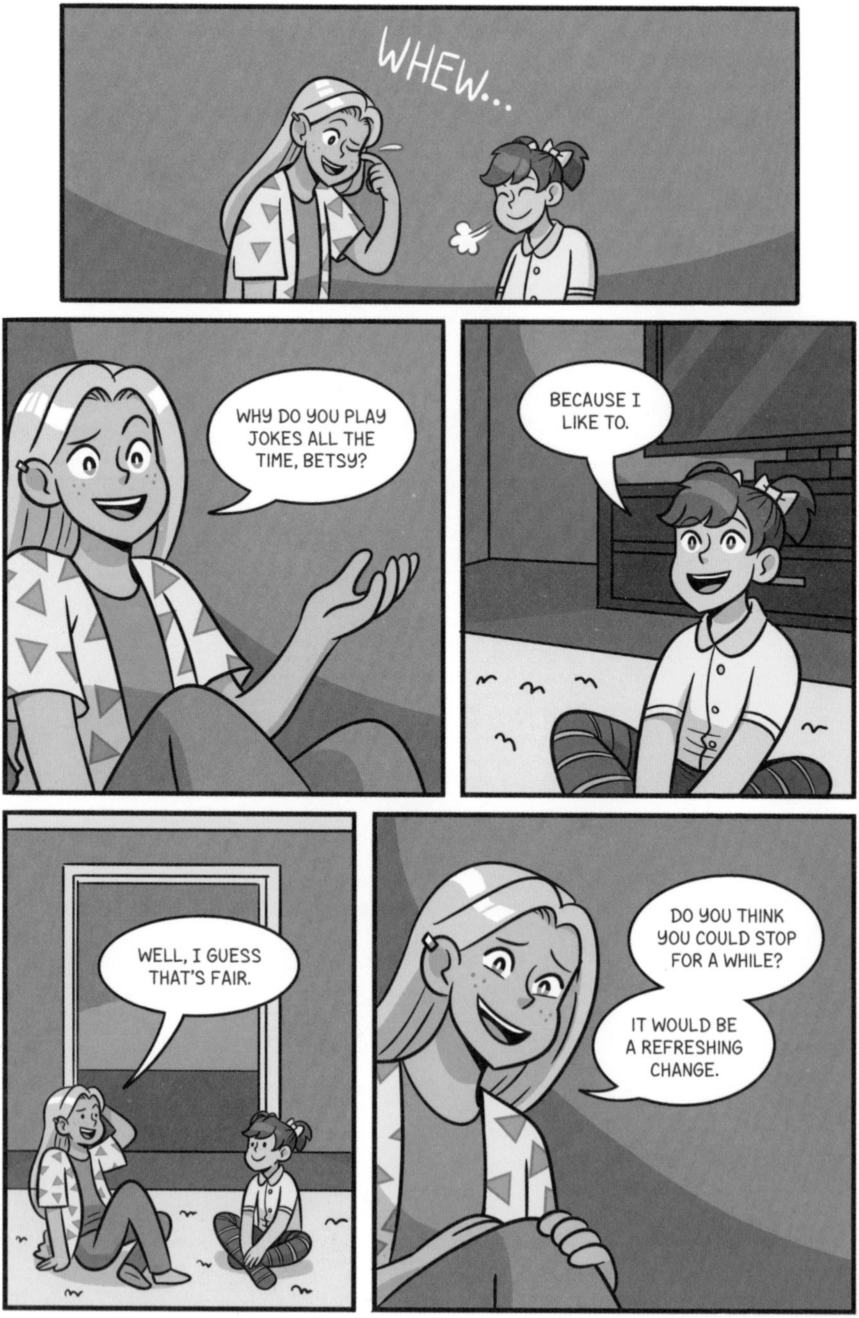
WHEW...
WHY DO YOU PLAY JOKES ALL THE TIME, BETSY?
BECAUSE I LIKE TO.
WELL, I GUESS THAT'S FAIR.
DO YOU THINK YOU COULD STOP FOR A WHILE?
IT WOULD BE A REFRESHING CHANGE.

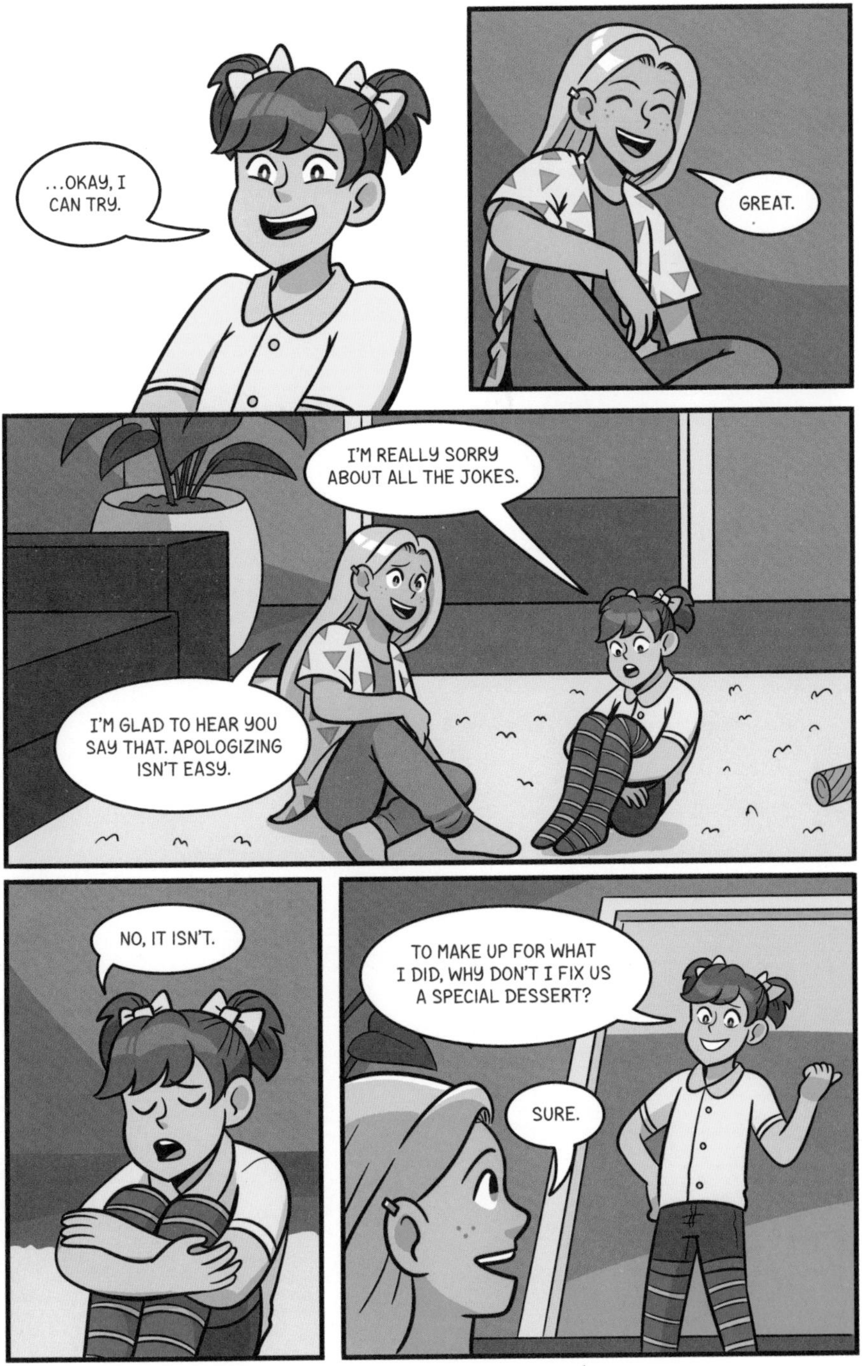
...OKAY, I CAN TRY.
GREAT.
I'M REALLY SORRY ABOUT ALL THE JOKES.
I'M GLAD TO HEAR YOU SAY THAT. APOLOGIZING ISN'T EASY.
NO, IT ISN'T.
TO MAKE UP FOR WHAT I DID, WHY DON'T I FIX US A SPECIAL DESSERT?
SURE.

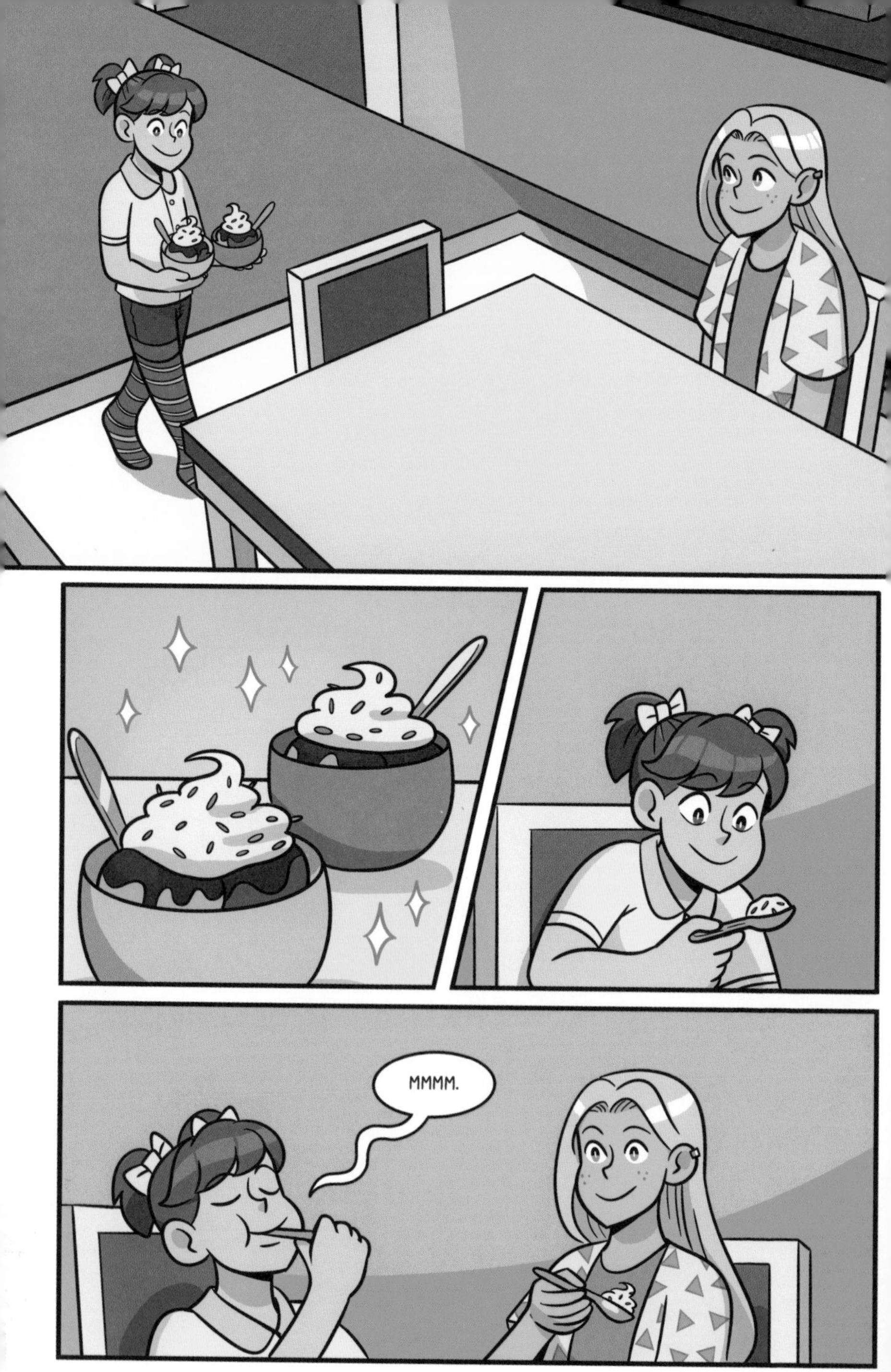
MMMM.

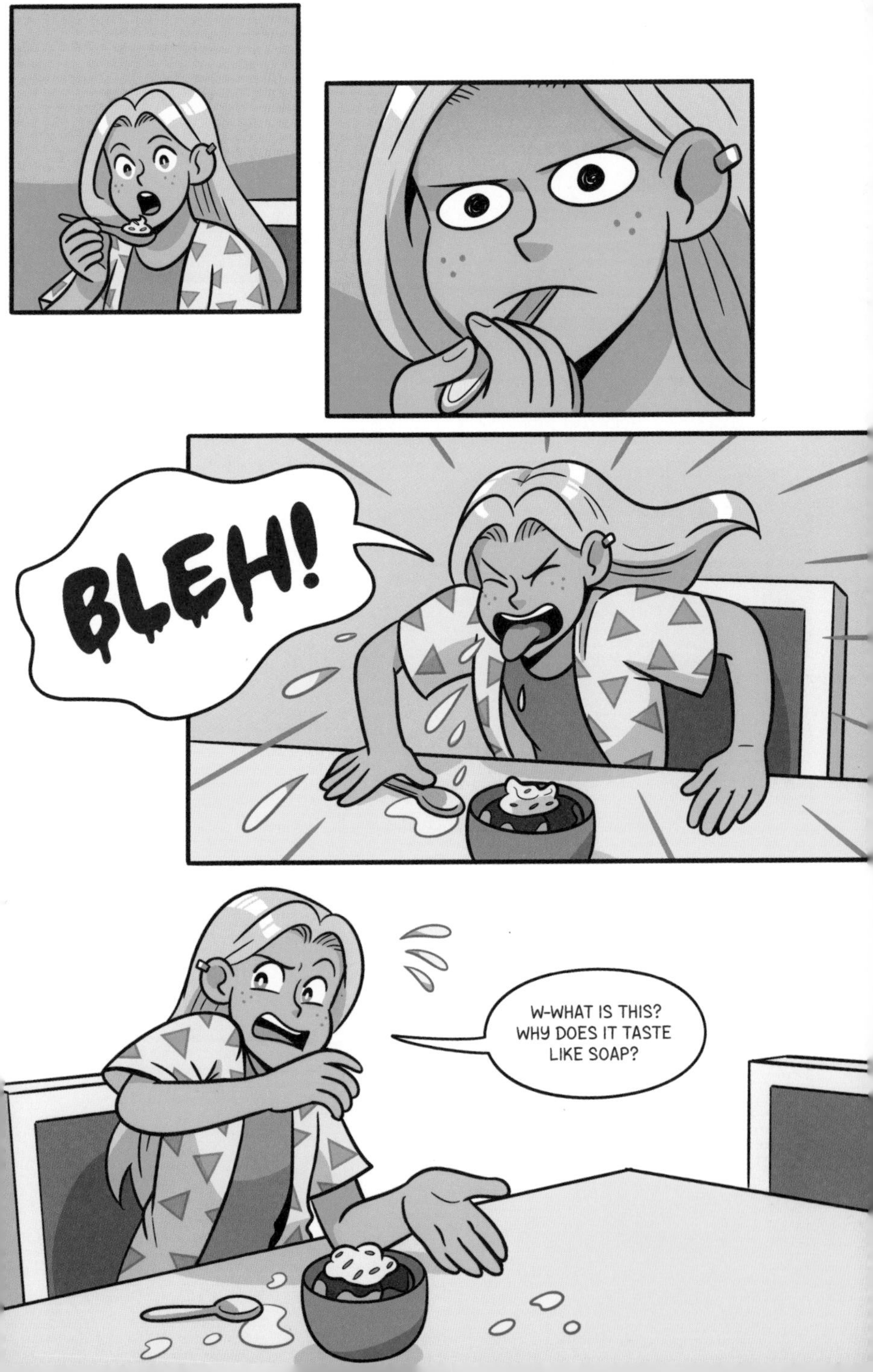
BLEH!
W-WHAT IS THIS? WHY DOES IT TASTE LIKE SOAP?

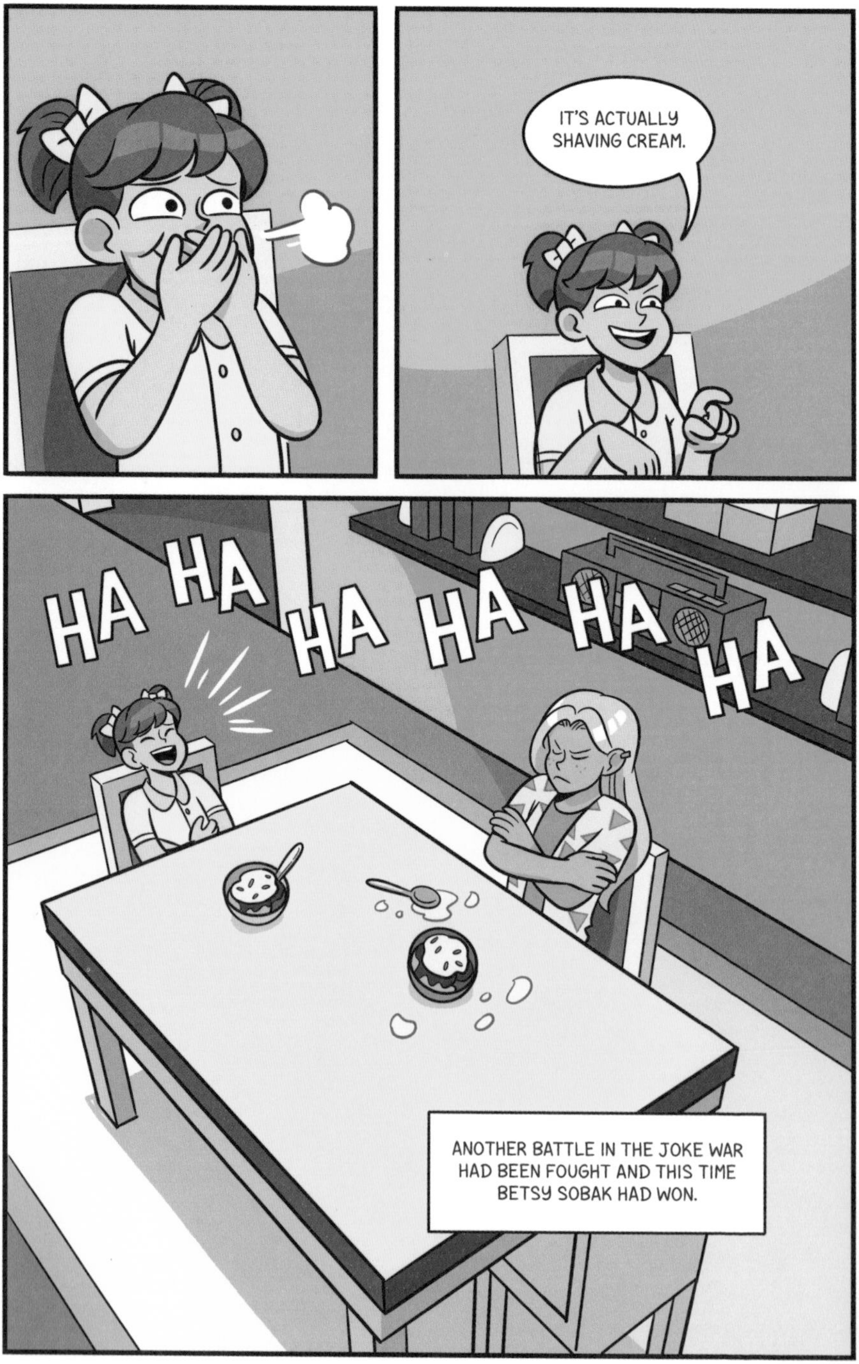
IT'S ACTUALLY SHAVING CREAM.
HA HA HA HA HA HA
ANOTHER BATTLE IN THE JOKE WAR HAD BEEN FOUGHT AND THIS TIME BETSY SOBAK HAD WON.

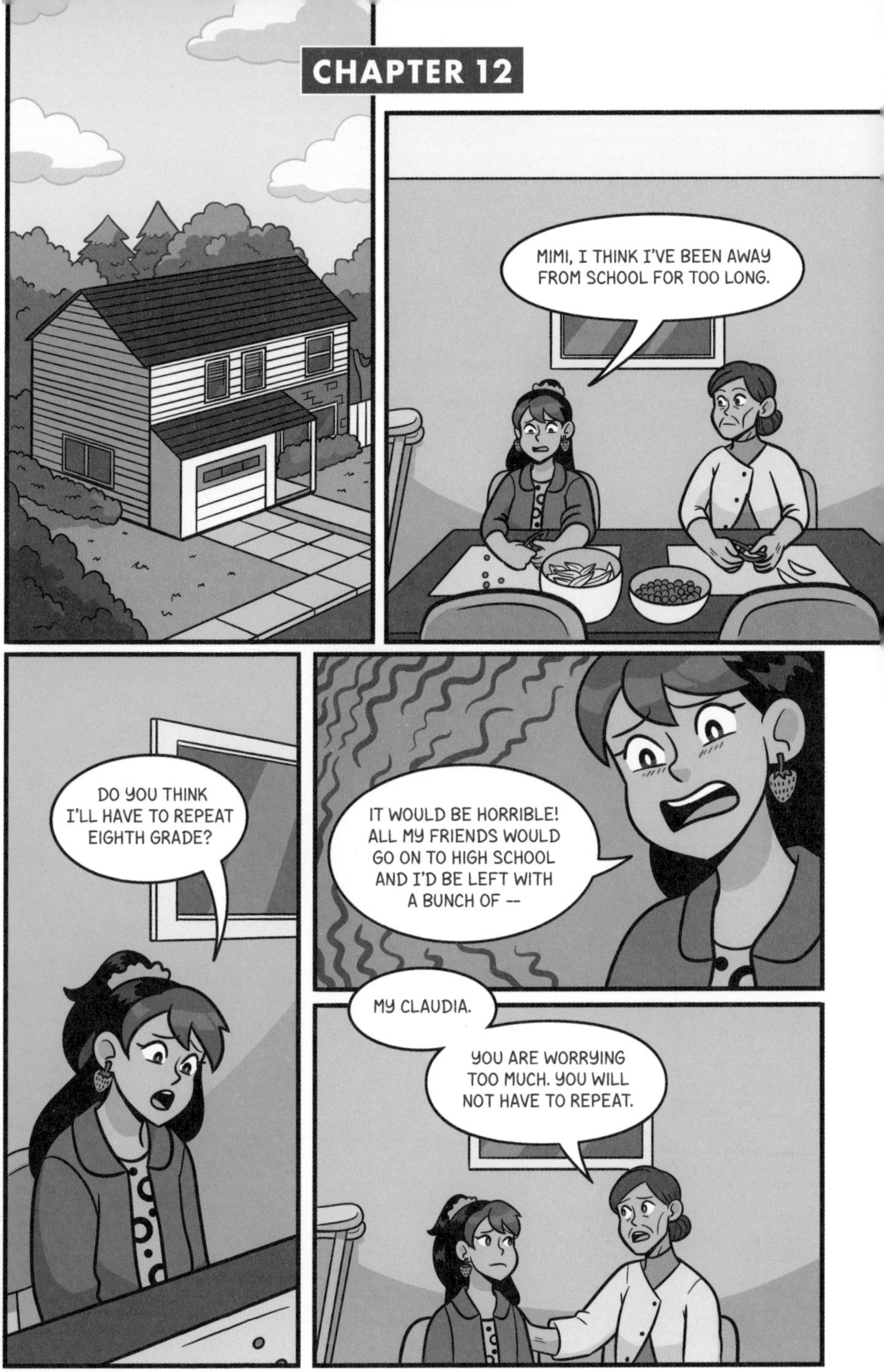
CHAPTER 12
MIMI, I THINK I'VE BEEN AWAY FROM SCHOOL FOR TOO LONG.
DO YOU THINK I'LL HAVE TO REPEAT EIGHTH GRADE?
IT WOULD BE HORRIBLE! ALL MY FRIENDS WOULD GO ON TO HIGH SCHOOL AND I'D BE LEFT WITH A BUNCH OF --
MY CLAUDIA.
YOU ARE WORRYING TOO MUCH. YOU WILL NOT HAVE TO REPEAT.

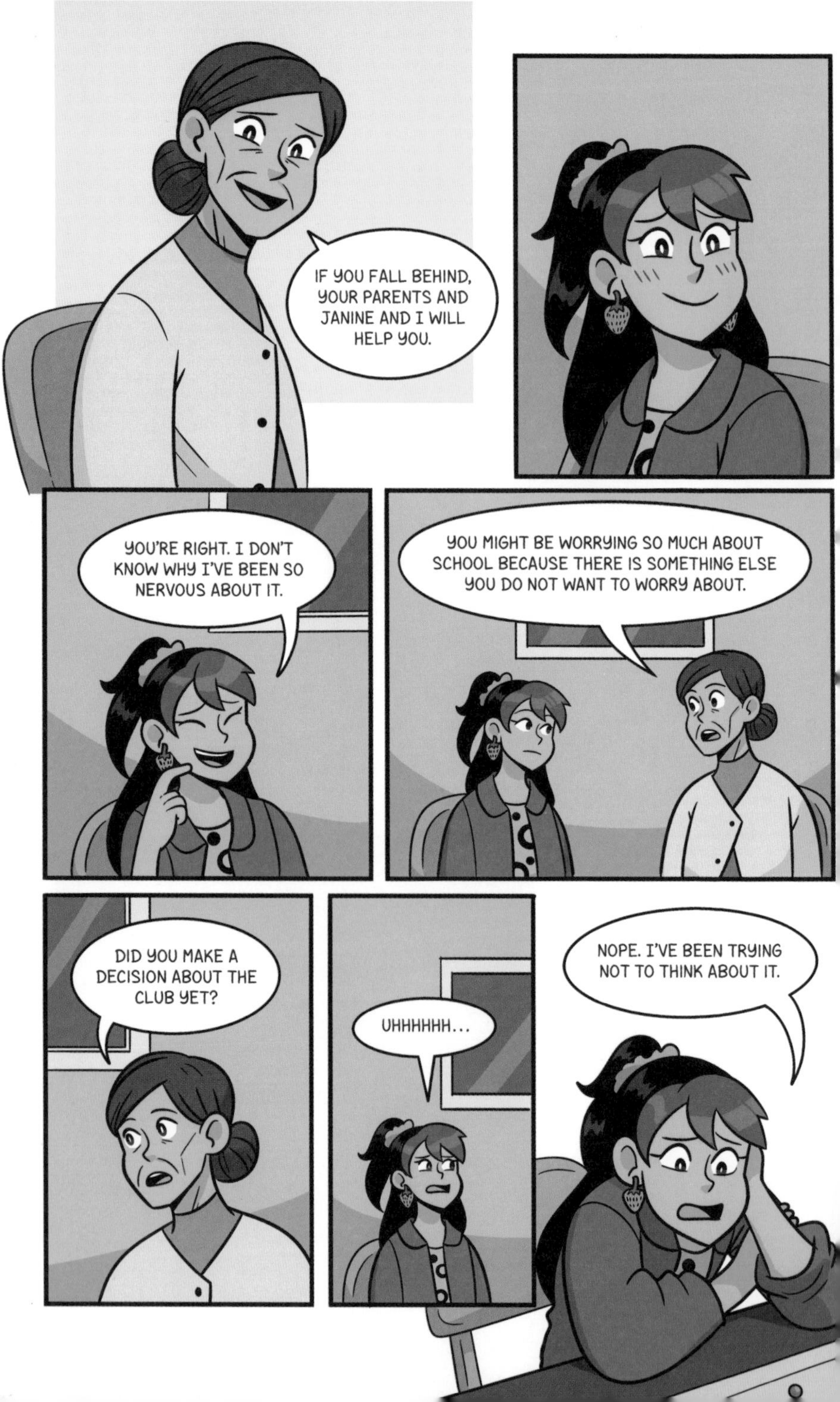
IF YOU FALL BEHIND, YOUR PARENTS AND JANINE AND I WILL HELP YOU.
YOU'RE RIGHT. I DON'T KNOW WHY I'VE BEEN SO NERVOUS ABOUT IT.
YOU MIGHT BE WORRYING SO MUCH ABOUT SCHOOL BECAUSE THERE IS SOMETHING ELSE YOU DO NOT WANT TO WORRY ABOUT.
DID YOU MAKE A DECISION ABOUT THE CLUB YET?
UHHHHHH...
NOPE. I'VE BEEN TRYING NOT TO THINK ABOUT IT.

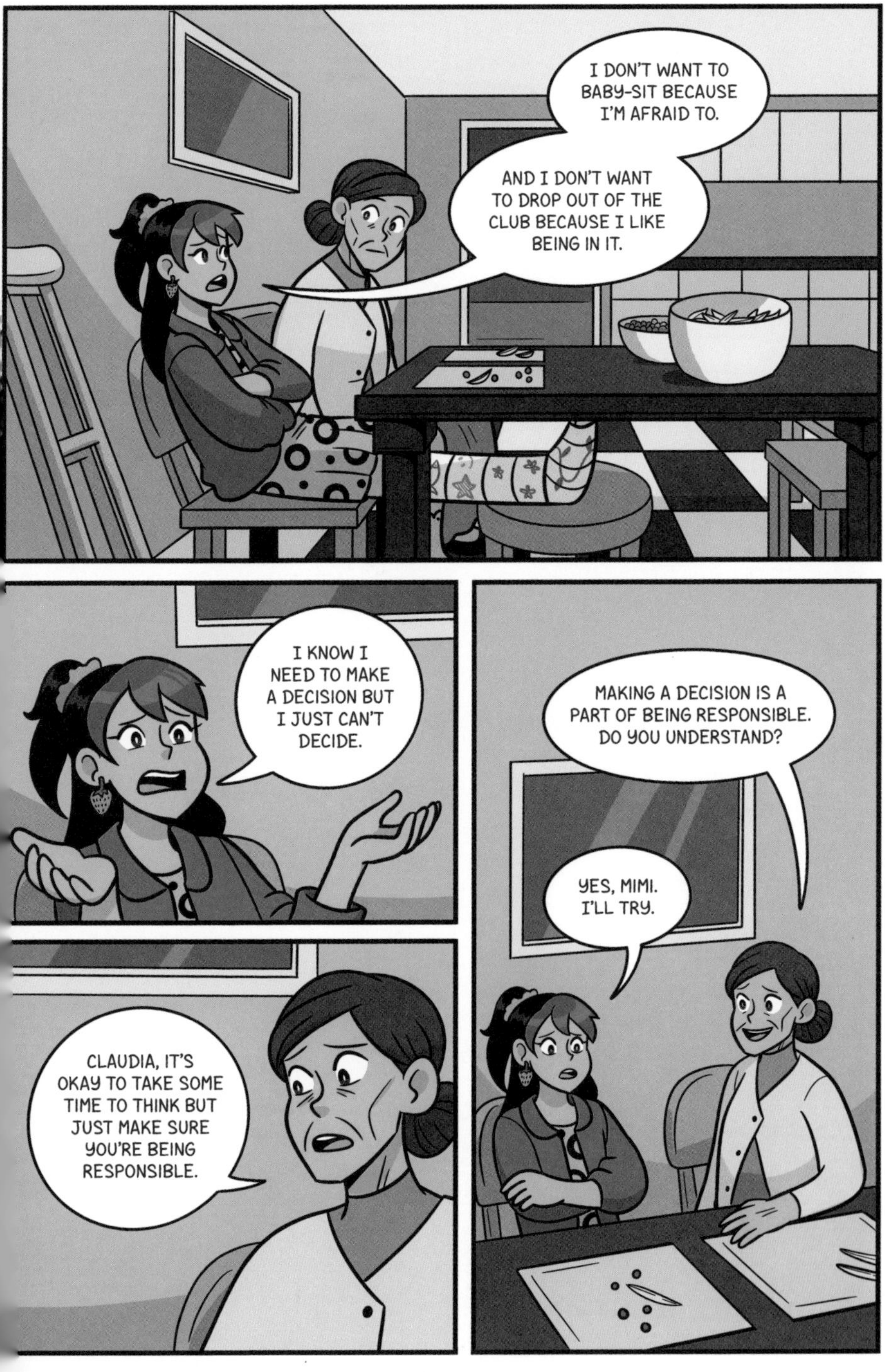
I DON'T WANT TO BABY-SIT BECAUSE I'M AFRAID TO.
AND I DON'T WANT TO DROP OUT OF THE CLUB BECAUSE I LIKE BEING IN IT.
I KNOW I NEED TO MAKE A DECISION BUT I JUST CAN'T DECIDE.
CLAUDIA, IT'S OKAY TO TAKE SOME TIME TO THINK BUT JUST MAKE SURE YOU'RE BEING RESPONSIBLE.
MAKING A DECISION IS A PART OF BEING RESPONSIBLE. DO YOU UNDERSTAND?
YES, MIMI. I'LL TRY.

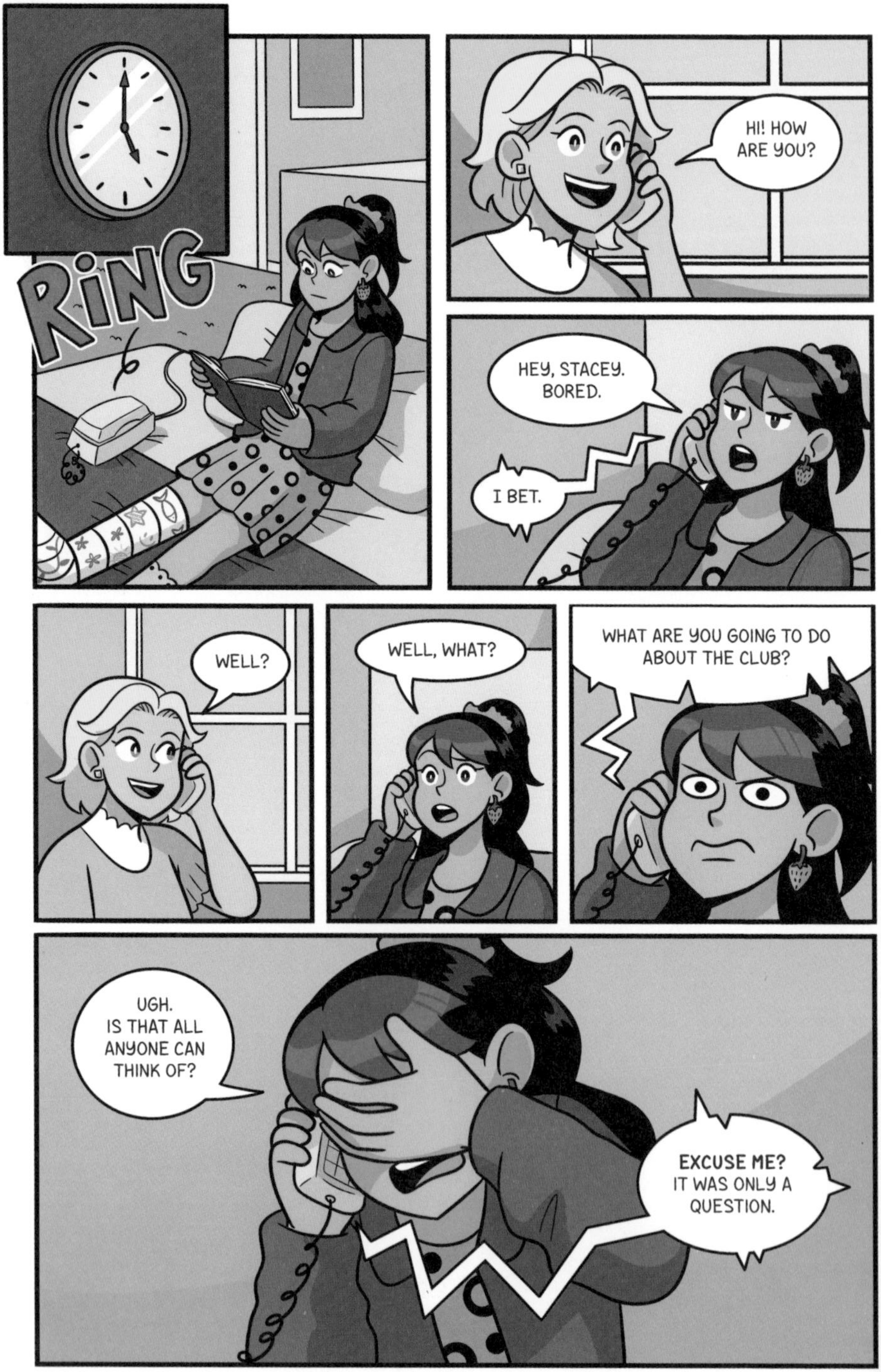
RING
HI! HOW ARE YOU?
HEY, STACEY. BORED.
I BET.
WELL?
WELL, WHAT?
WHAT ARE YOU GOING TO DO ABOUT THE CLUB?
UGH. IS THAT ALL ANYONE CAN THINK OF?
EXCUSE ME? IT WAS ONLY A QUESTION.

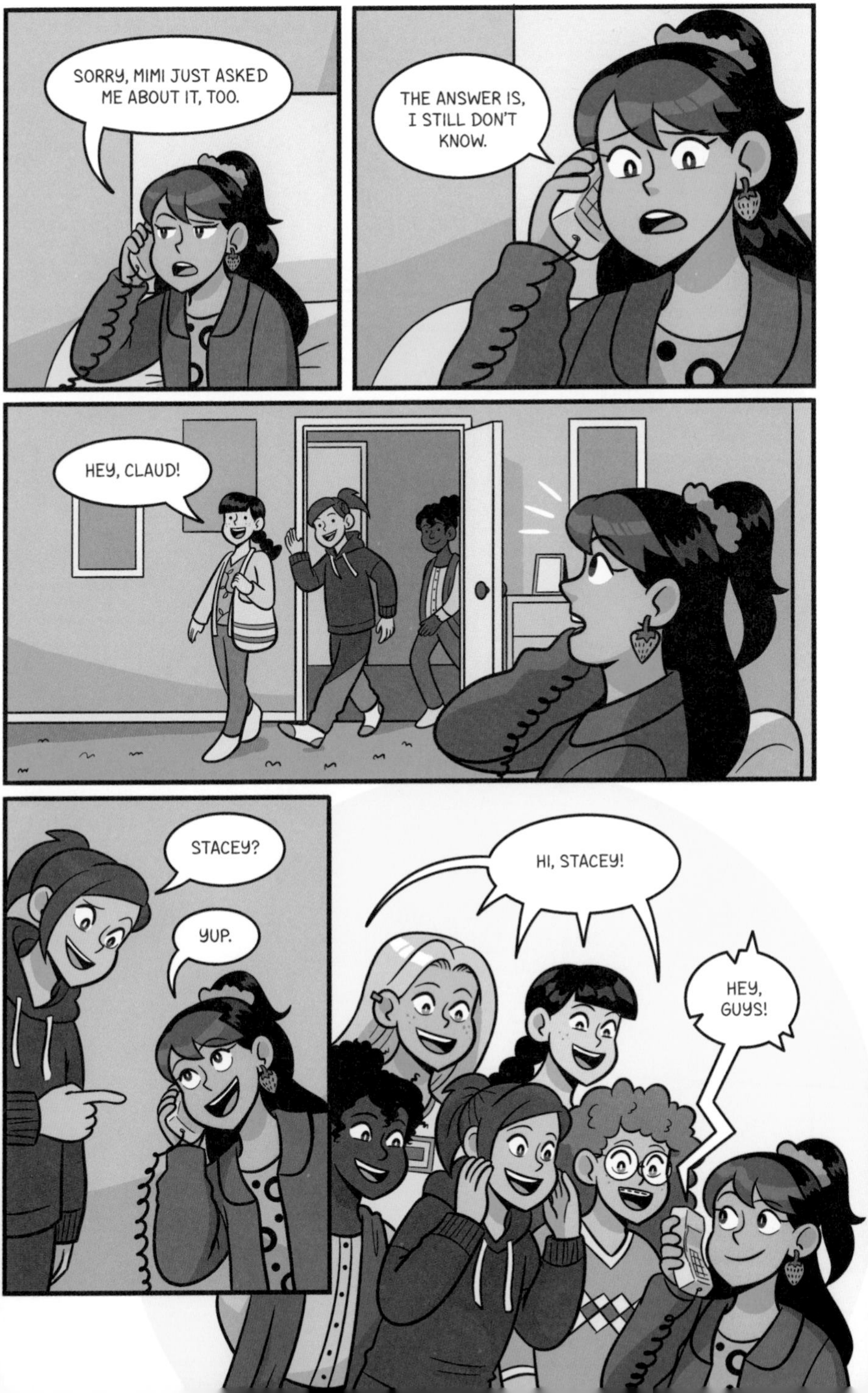
SORRY, MIMI JUST ASKED ME ABOUT IT, TOO.
THE ANSWER IS, I STILL DON'T KNOW.
HEY, CLAUD!
STACEY?
YUP.
HI, STACEY!
HEY, GUYS!

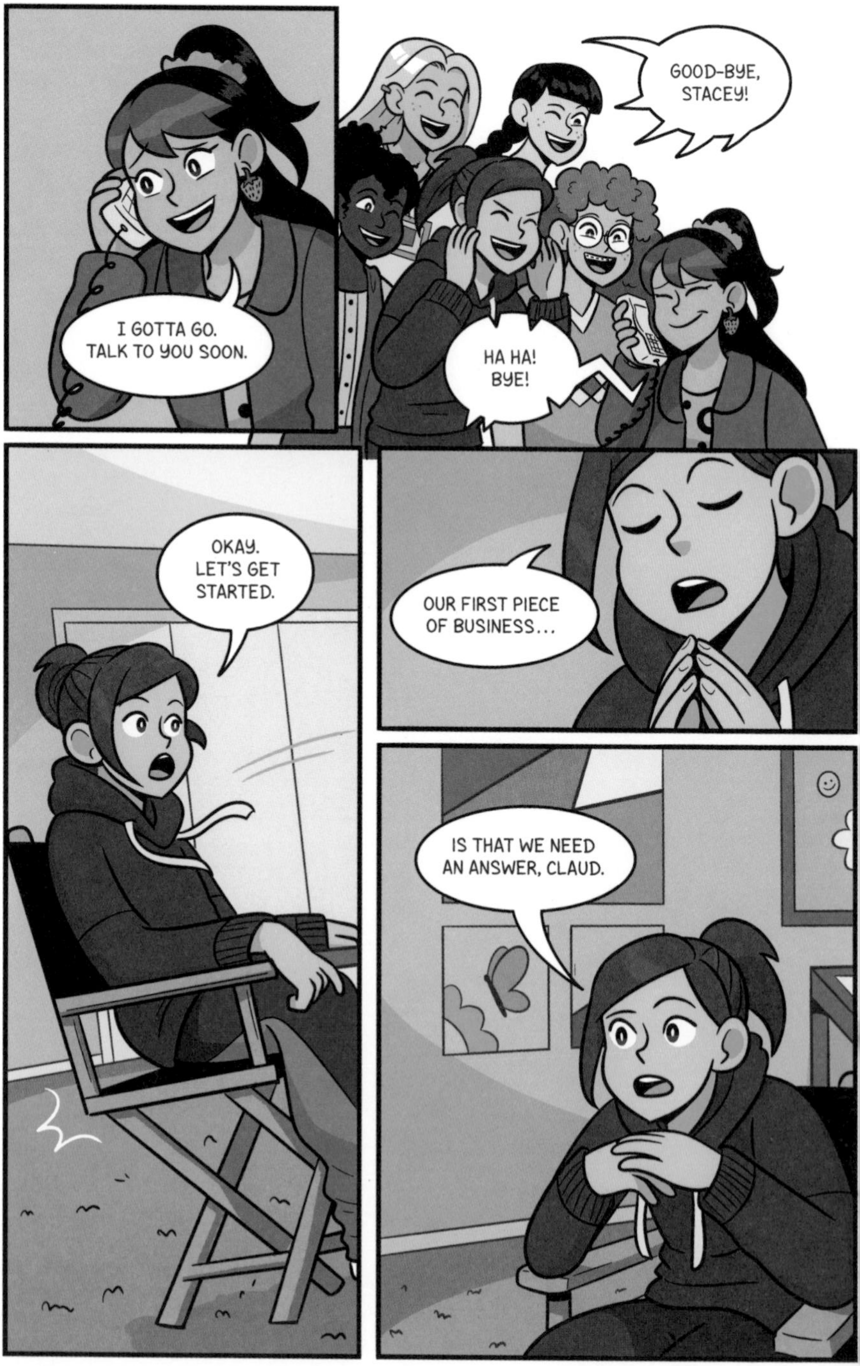
I GOTTA GO.
TALK TO YOU SOON.
GOOD-BYE, STACEY!
HA HA! BYE!
OKAY. LET'S GET STARTED.
OUR FIRST PIECE OF BUSINESS...
IS THAT WE NEED AN ANSWER, CLAUD.

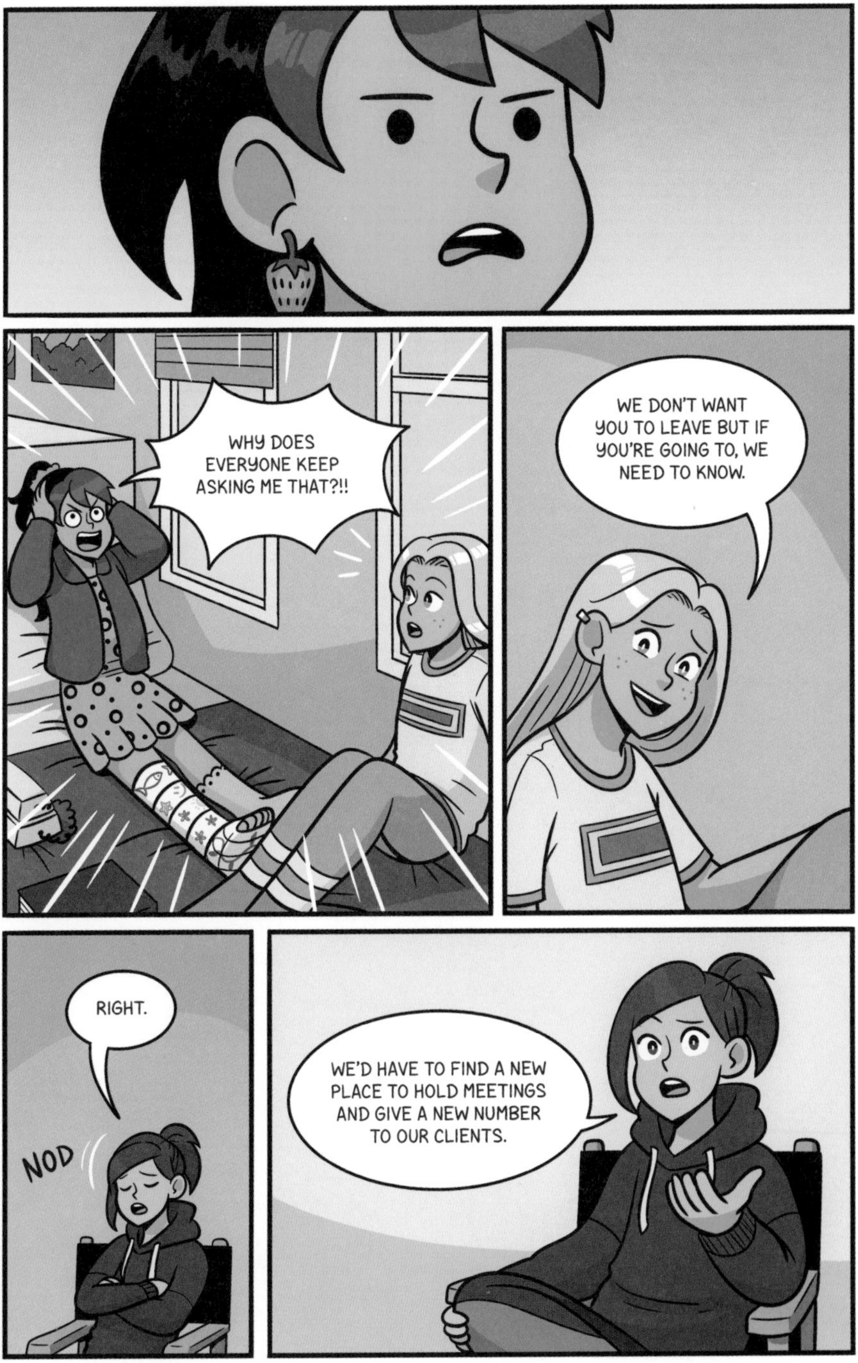
WHY DOES EVERYONE KEEP ASKING ME THAT?!!
WE DON'T WANT YOU TO LEAVE BUT IF YOU'RE GOING TO, WE NEED TO KNOW.
RIGHT.
NOD
WE'D HAVE TO FIND A NEW PLACE TO HOLD MEETINGS AND GIVE A NEW NUMBER TO OUR CLIENTS.

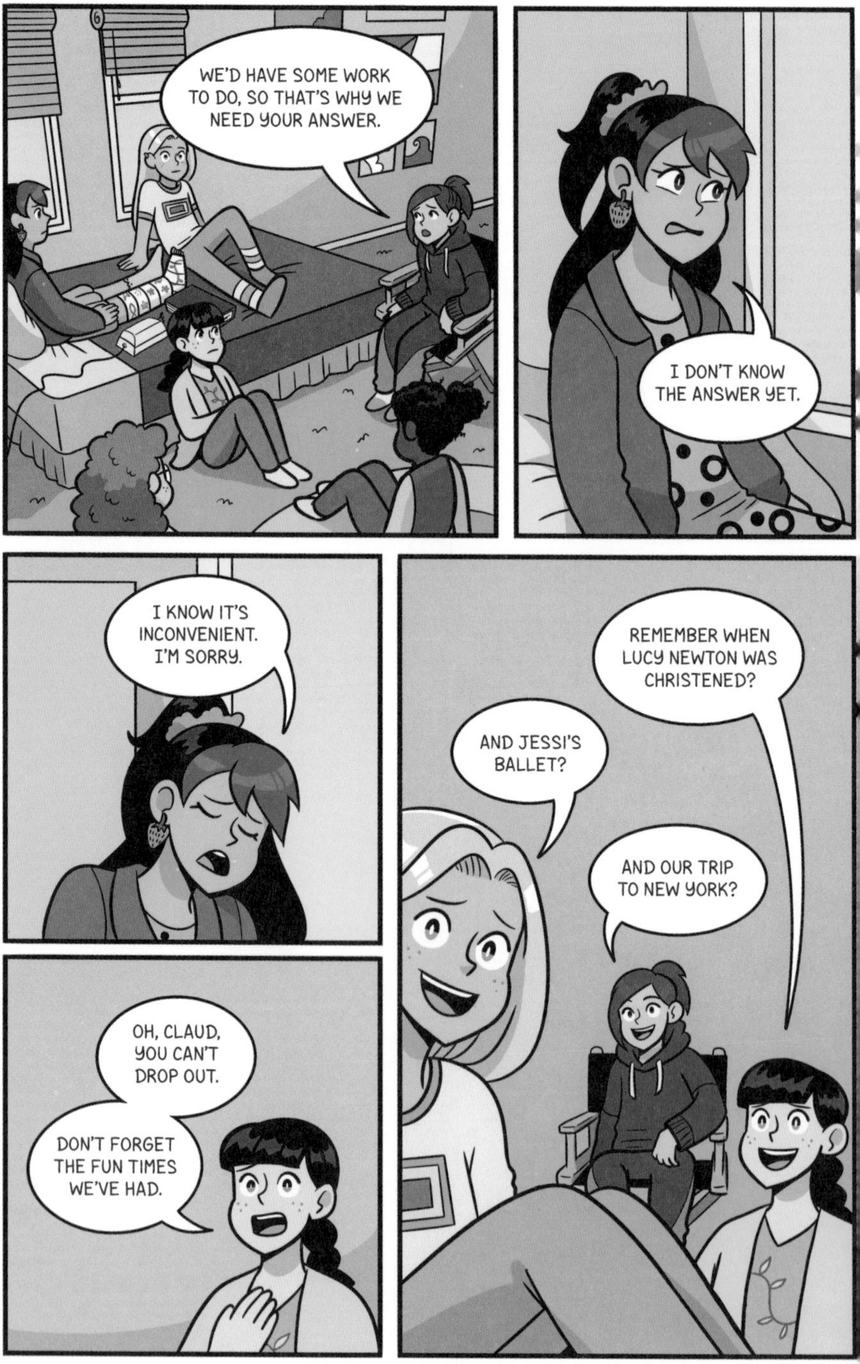
WE'D HAVE SOME WORK TO DO, SO THAT'S WHY WE NEED YOUR ANSWER.
I DON'T KNOW THE ANSWER YET.
I KNOW IT'S INCONVENIENT. I'M SORRY.
OH, CLAUD, YOU CAN'T DROP OUT.
DON'T FORGET THE FUN TIMES WE'VE HAD.
REMEMBER WHEN LUCY NEWTON WAS CHRISTENED?
AND JESSI'S BALLET?
AND OUR TRIP TO NEW YORK?

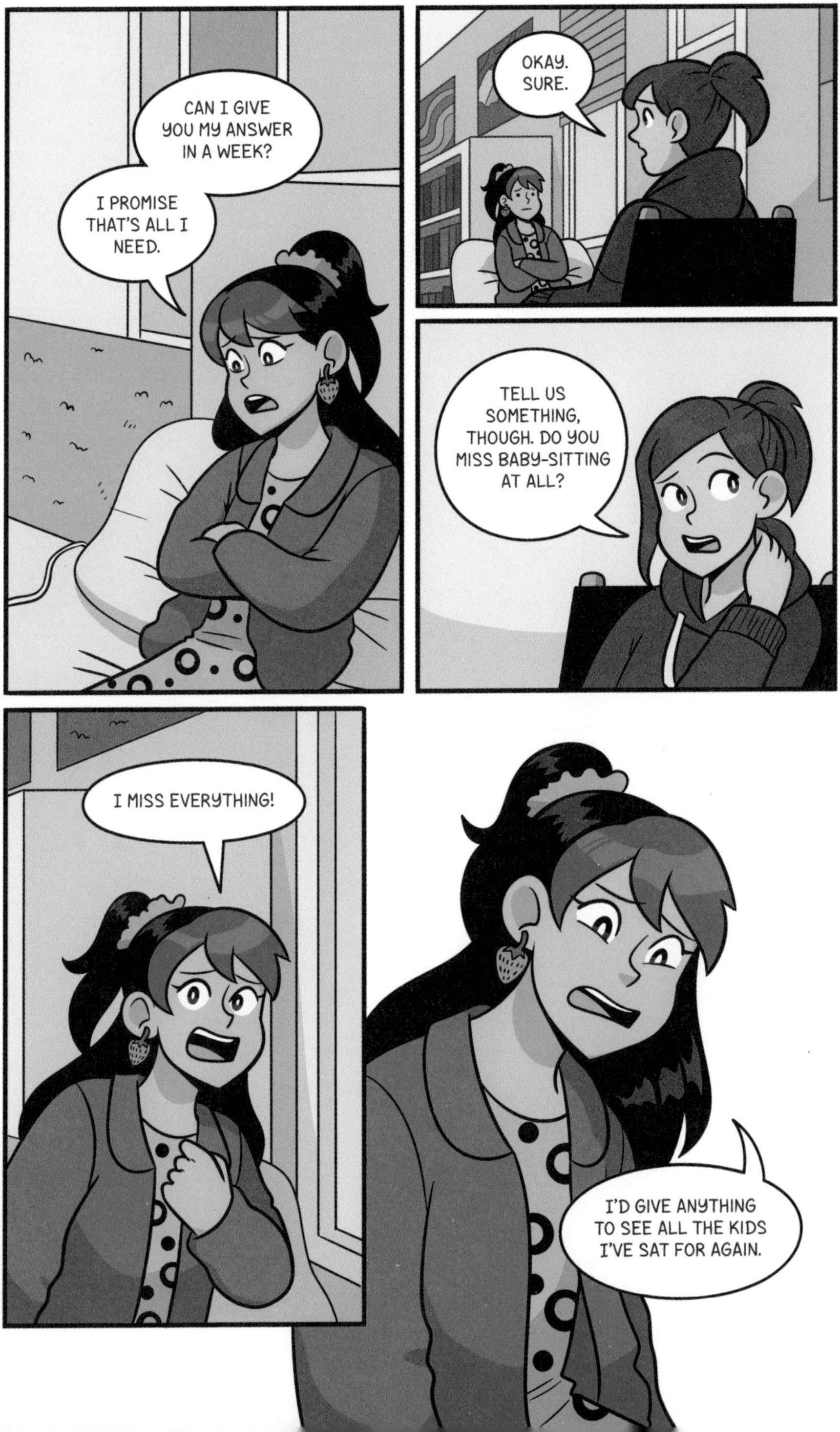
CAN I GIVE YOU MY ANSWER IN A WEEK?
I PROMISE THAT'S ALL I NEED.
OKAY. SURE.
TELL US SOMETHING, THOUGH. DO YOU MISS BABY-SITTING AT ALL?
I MISS EVERYTHING!
I'D GIVE ANYTHING TO SEE ALL THE KIDS I'VE SAT FOR AGAIN.

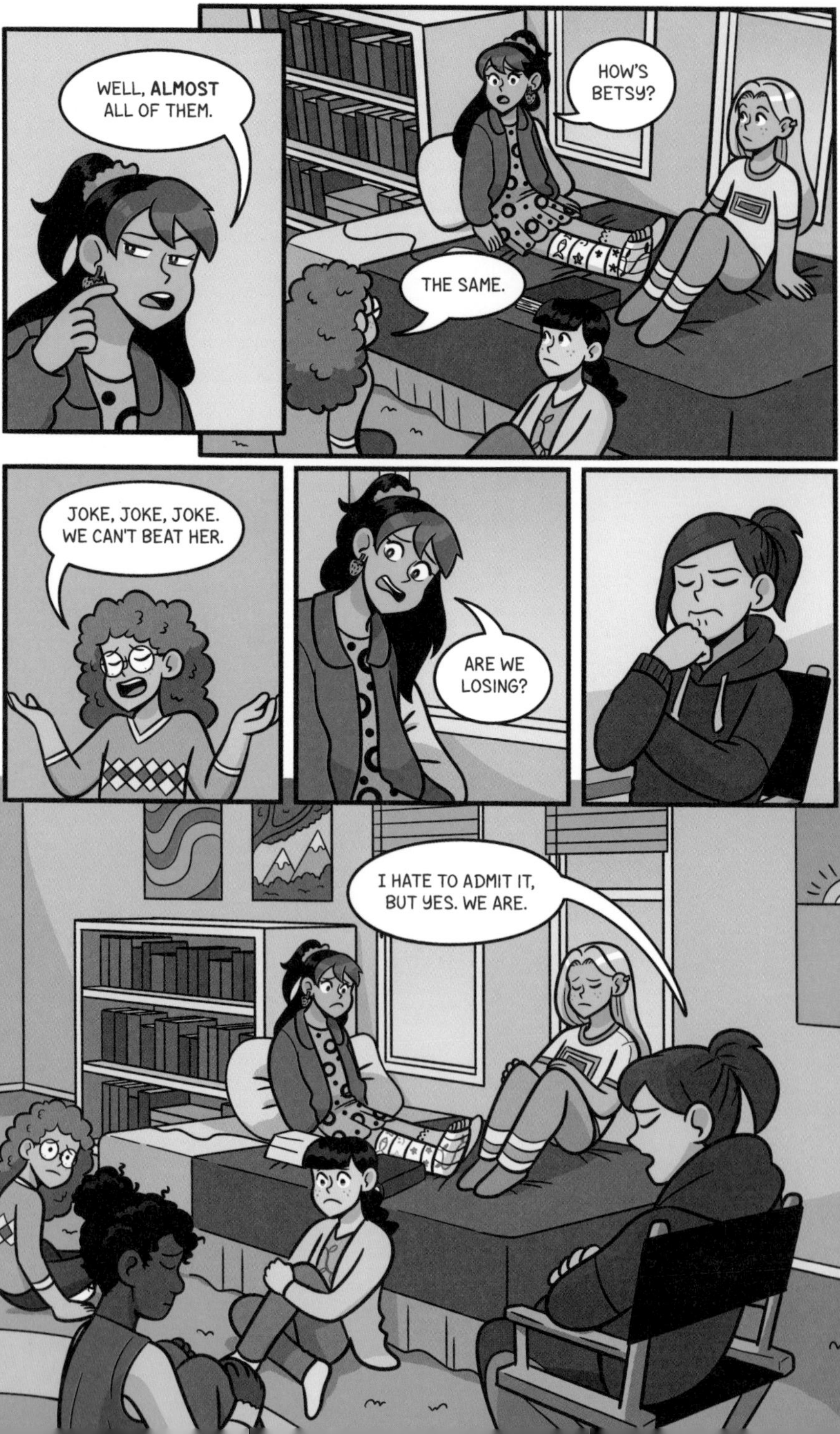
WELL, **ALMOST** ALL OF THEM.
HOW'S BETSY?
THE SAME.
JOKE, JOKE, JOKE. WE CAN'T BEAT HER.
ARE WE LOSING?
I HATE TO ADMIT IT, BUT YES. WE ARE.

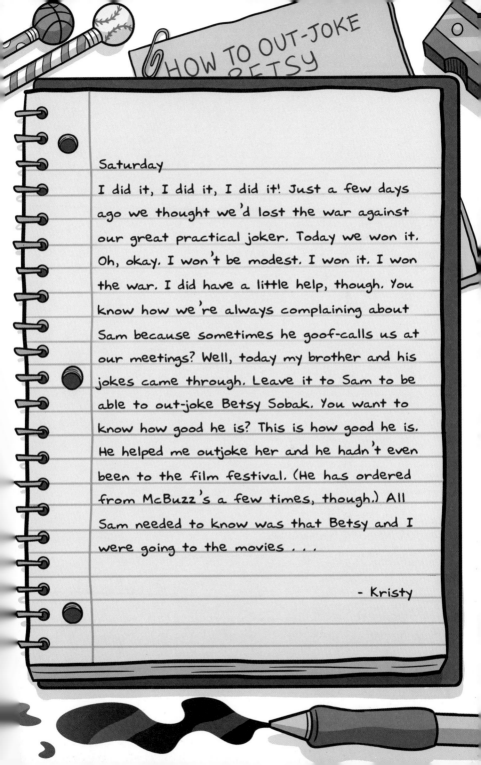

HOW TO OUT-JOKE BETSY

Saturday

I did it, I did it, I did it! Just a few days ago we thought we'd lost the war against our great practical joker. Today we won it. Oh, okay. I won't be modest. I won it. I won the war. I did have a little help, though. You know how we're always complaining about Sam because sometimes he goof-calls us at our meetings? Well, today my brother and his jokes came through. Leave it to Sam to be able to out-joke Betsy Sobak. You want to know how good he is? This is how good he is. He helped me outjoke her and he hadn't even been to the film festival. (He has ordered from McBuzz's a few times, though.) All Sam needed to know was that Betsy and I were going to the movies . . .

                                              - Kristy

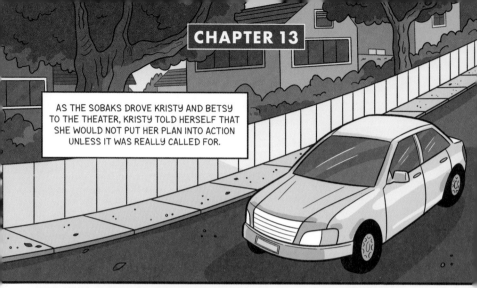

AS THE SOBAKS DROVE KRISTY AND BETSY TO THE THEATER, KRISTY TOLD HERSELF THAT SHE WOULD NOT PUT HER PLAN INTO ACTION UNLESS IT WAS REALLY CALLED FOR.

MR. SOBAK AND I WILL BE HOME AROUND FIVE.

YOU TWO CAN WALK TO OUR HOUSE AFTER THE MOVIE.

OKAY.

FWISHH

hee hee

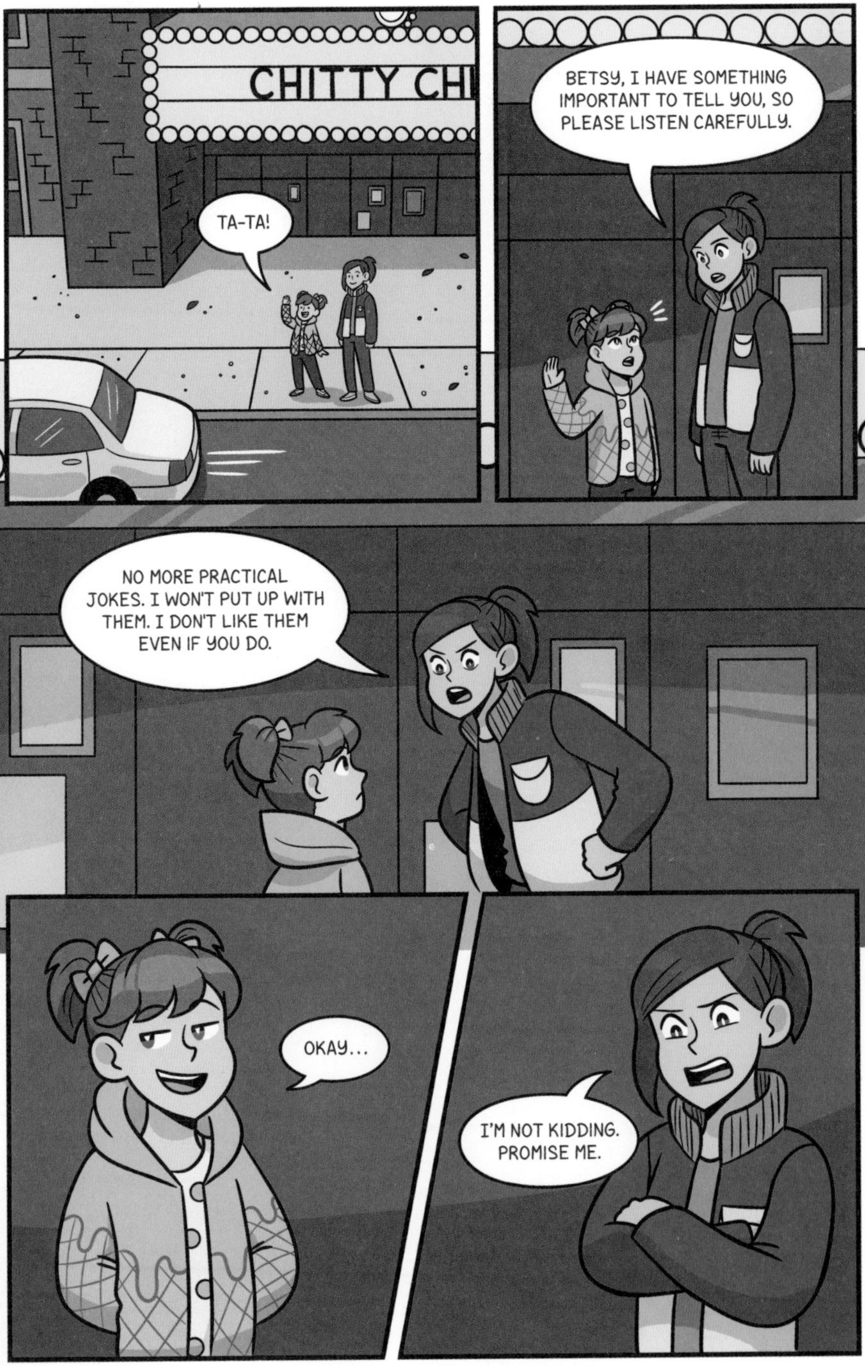
CHITTY CH
TA-TA!
BETSY, I HAVE SOMETHING IMPORTANT TO TELL YOU, SO PLEASE LISTEN CAREFULLY.
NO MORE PRACTICAL JOKES. I WON'T PUT UP WITH THEM. I DON'T LIKE THEM EVEN IF YOU DO.
OKAY...
I'M NOT KIDDING. PROMISE ME.

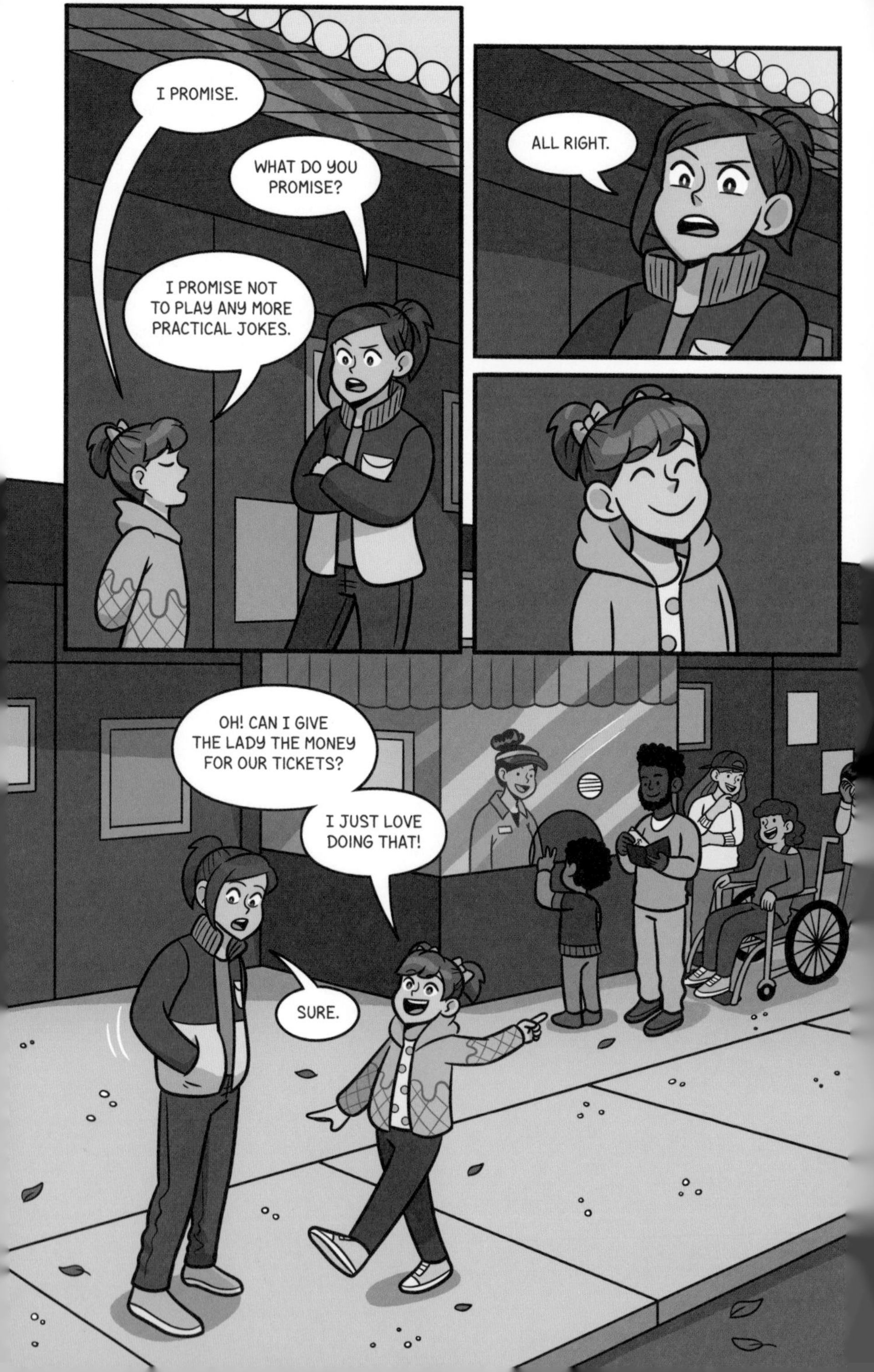
I PROMISE.
WHAT DO YOU PROMISE?
I PROMISE NOT TO PLAY ANY MORE PRACTICAL JOKES.
ALL RIGHT.
OH! CAN I GIVE THE LADY THE MONEY FOR OUR TICKETS?
I JUST LOVE DOING THAT!
SURE.

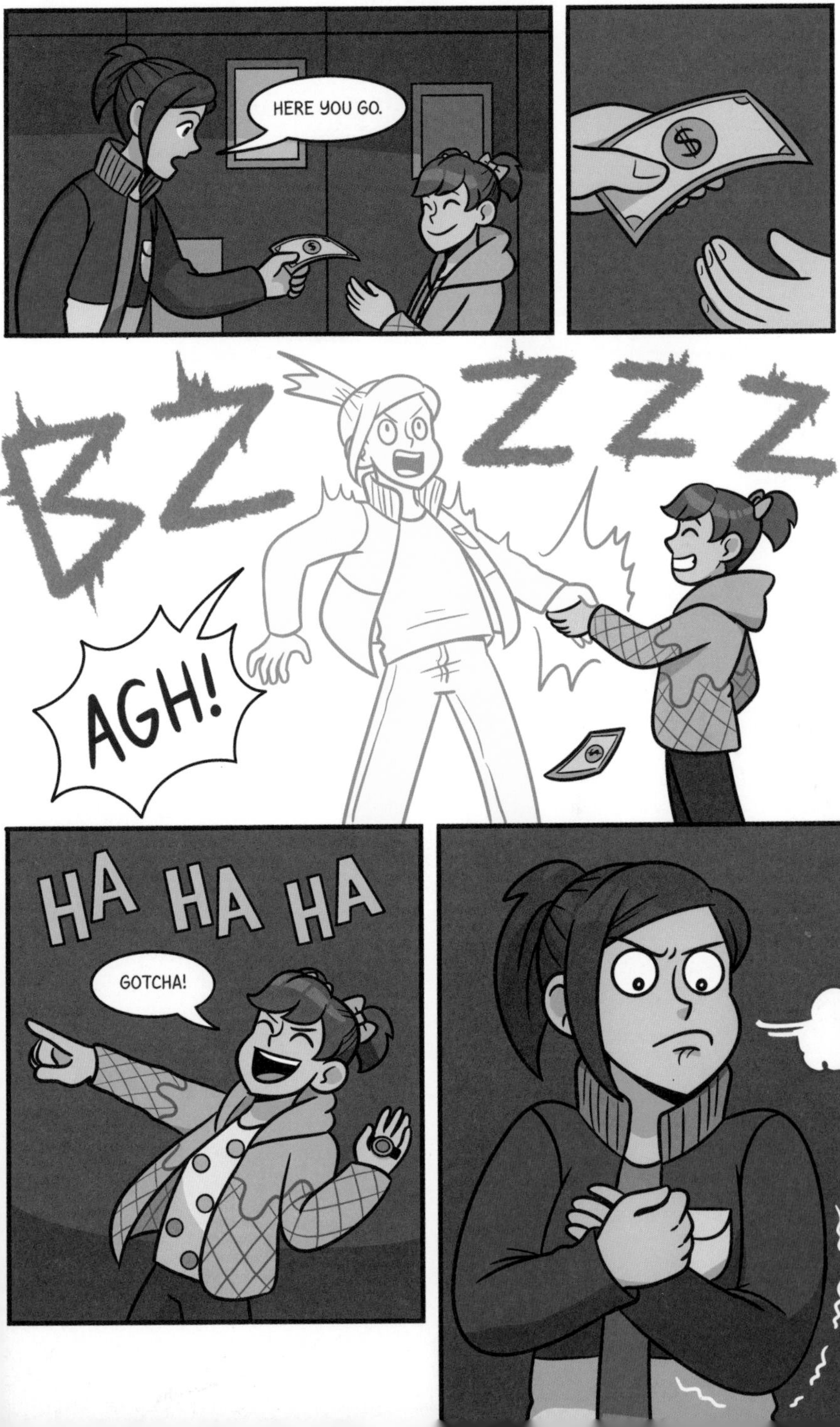
HERE YOU GO.
BZZZZ
AGH!
HA HA HA
GOTCHA!

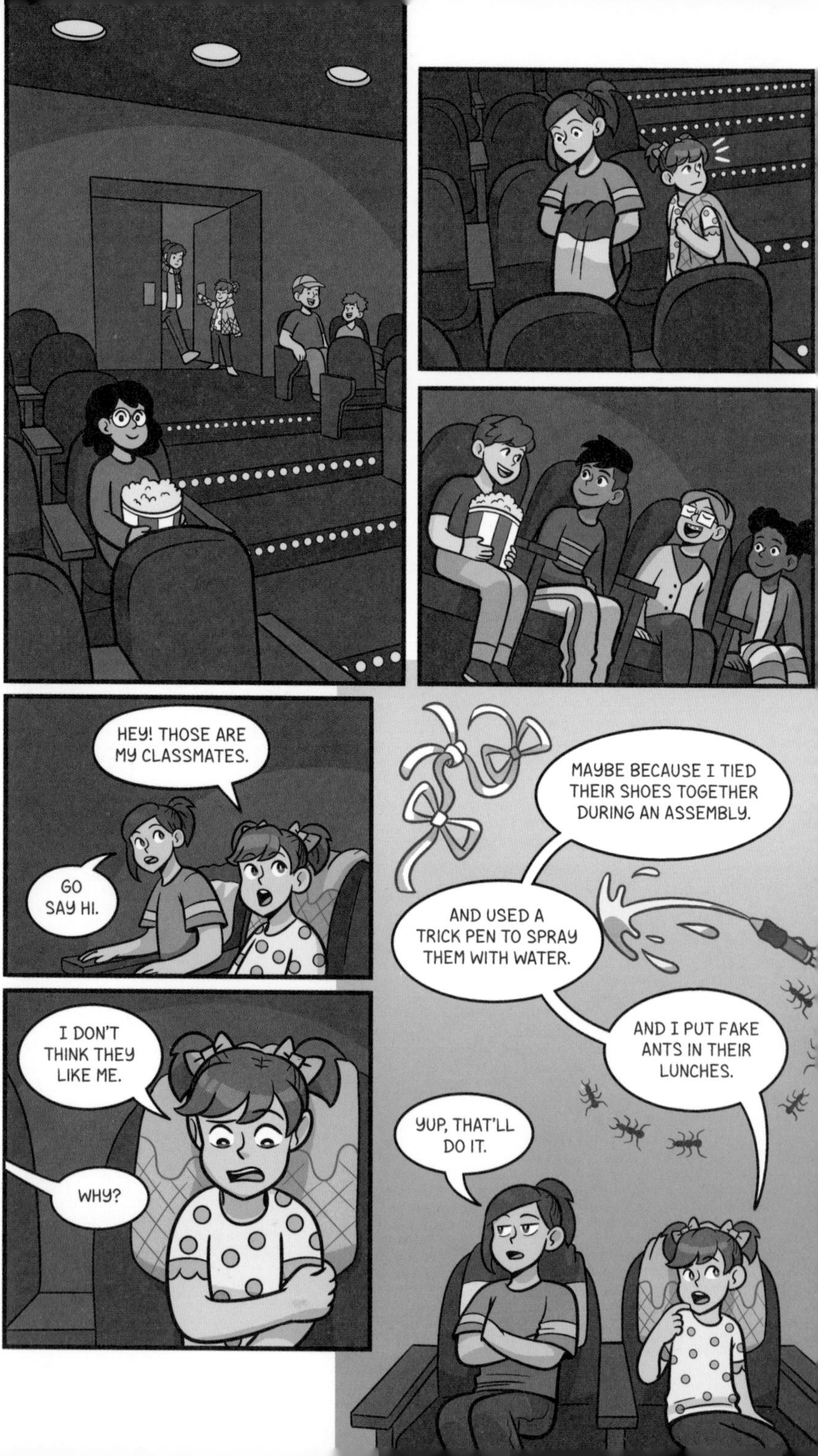
HEY! THOSE ARE MY CLASSMATES.
GO SAY HI.
I DON'T THINK THEY LIKE ME.
WHY?
MAYBE BECAUSE I TIED THEIR SHOES TOGETHER DURING AN ASSEMBLY.
AND USED A TRICK PEN TO SPRAY THEM WITH WATER.
AND I PUT FAKE ANTS IN THEIR LUNCHES.
YUP, THAT'LL DO IT.

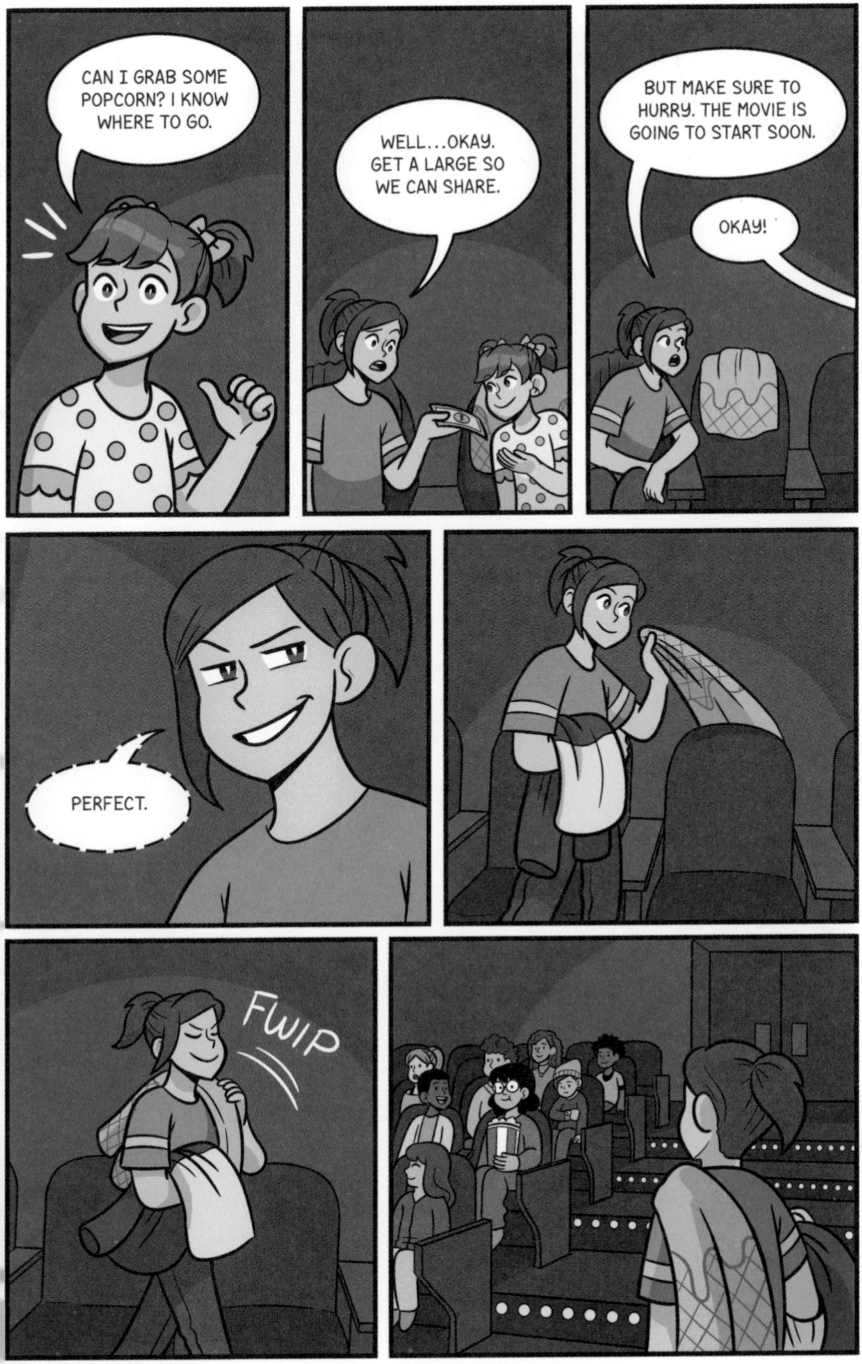
CAN I GRAB SOME POPCORN? I KNOW WHERE TO GO.
WELL...OKAY. GET A LARGE SO WE CAN SHARE.
BUT MAKE SURE TO HURRY. THE MOVIE IS GOING TO START SOON.
OKAY!
PERFECT.
FWIP

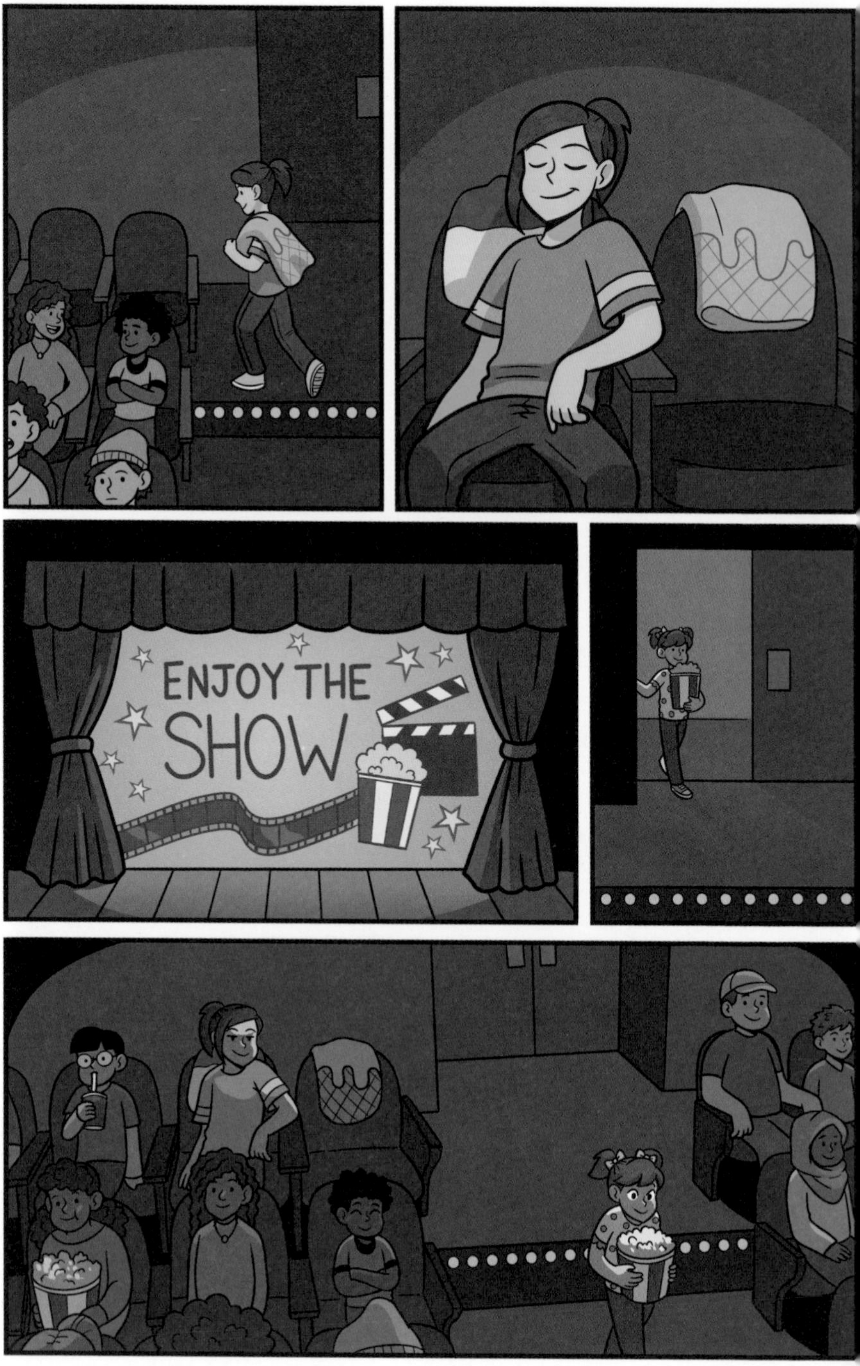
ENJOY THE
SHOW

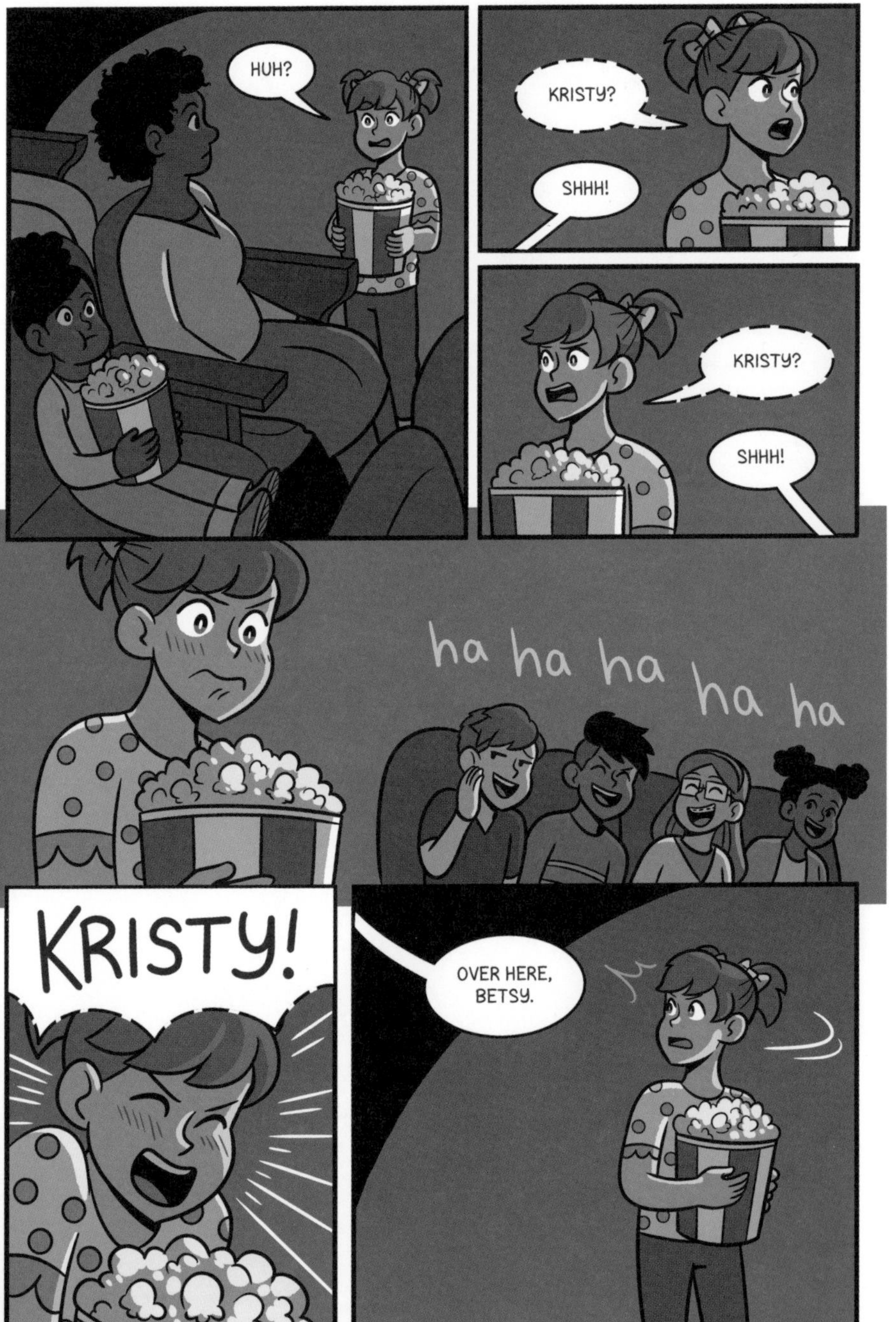
HUH?
KRISTY?
SHHH!
KRISTY?
SHHH!
ha ha ha ha ha
KRISTY!
OVER HERE, BETSY.

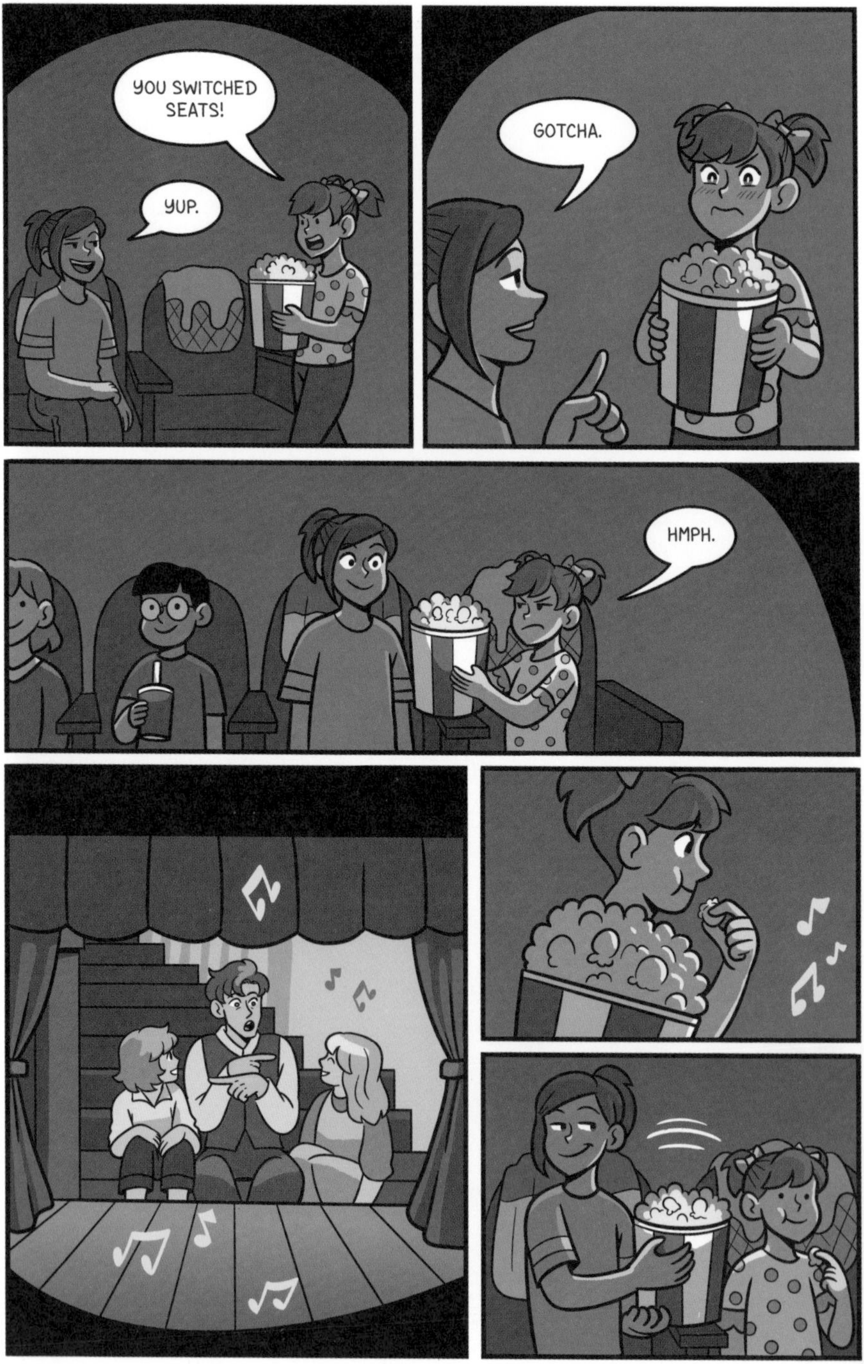
YOU SWITCHED SEATS!
YUP.
GOTCHA.
HMPH.

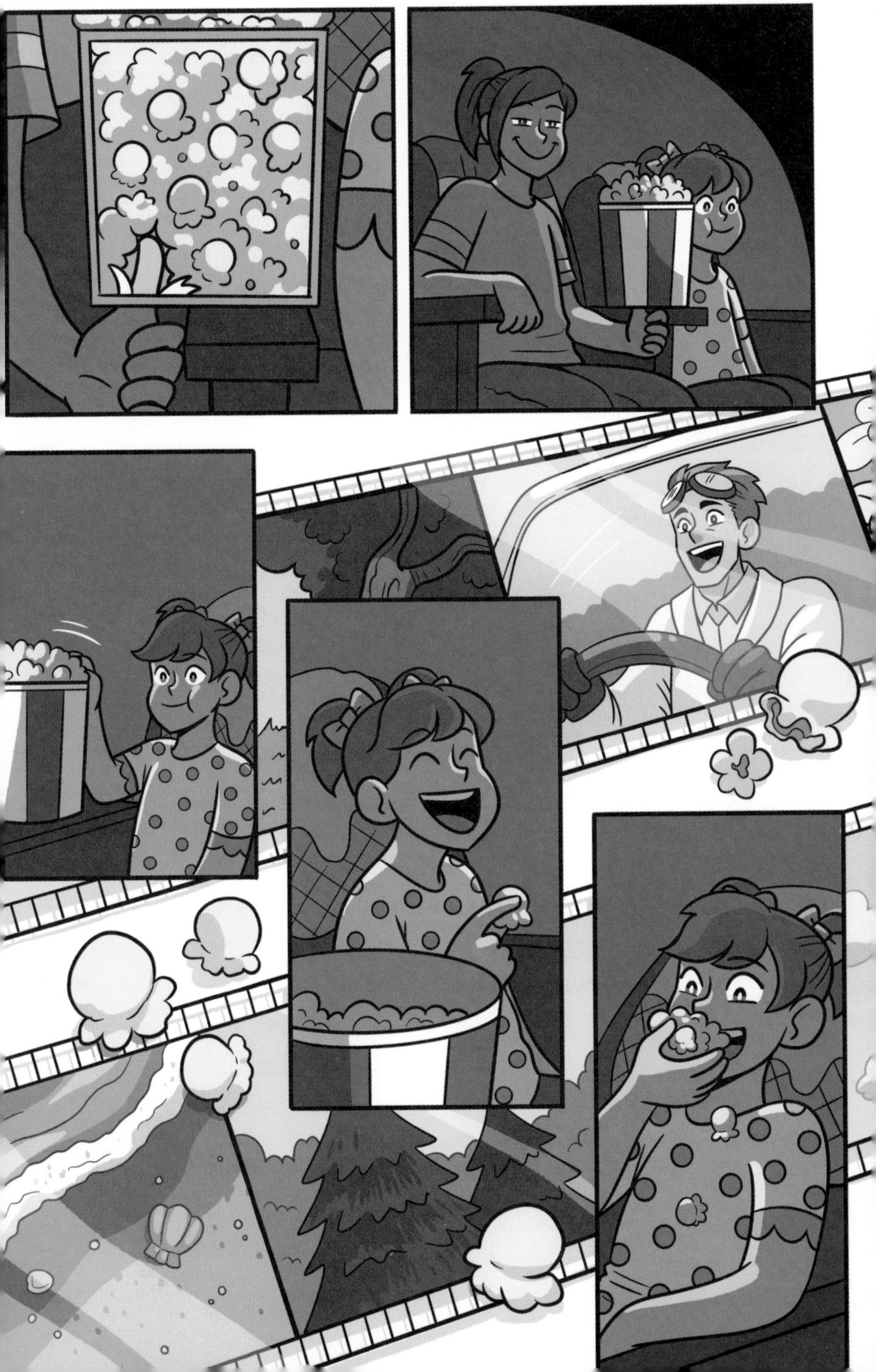

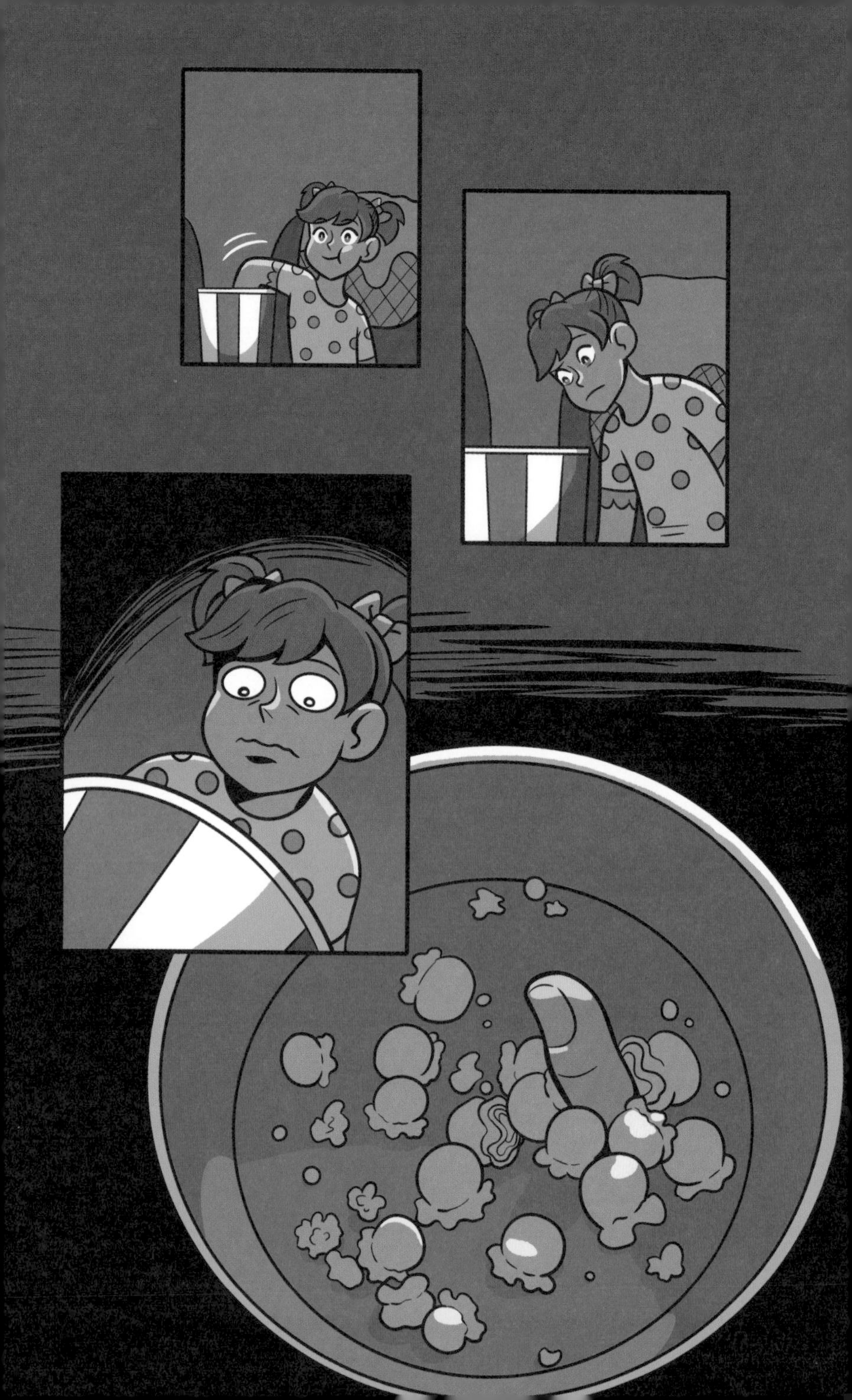

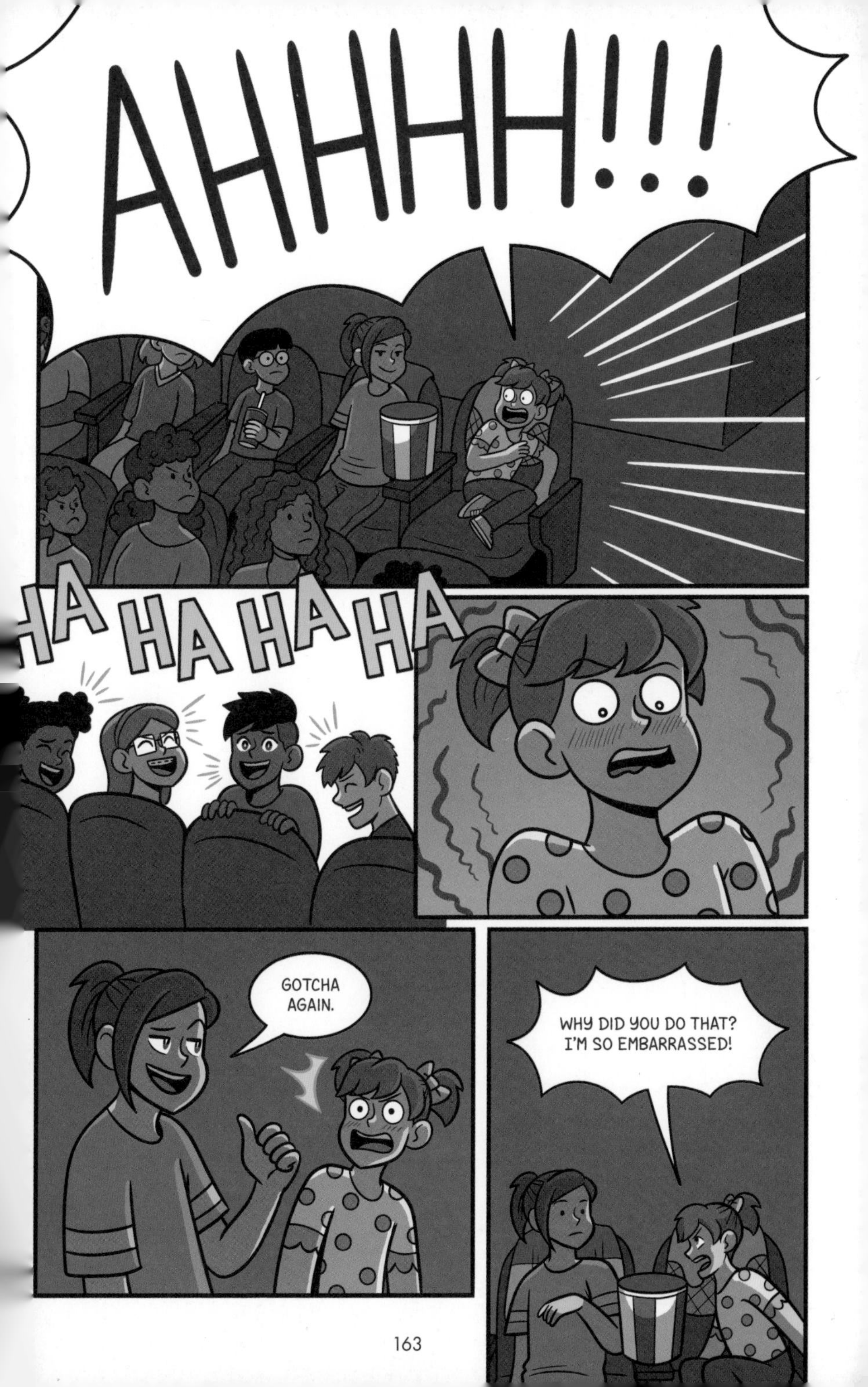
AHHHHH!!!
HA HA HA HA HA
GOTCHA AGAIN.
WHY DID YOU DO THAT? I'M SO EMBARRASSED!

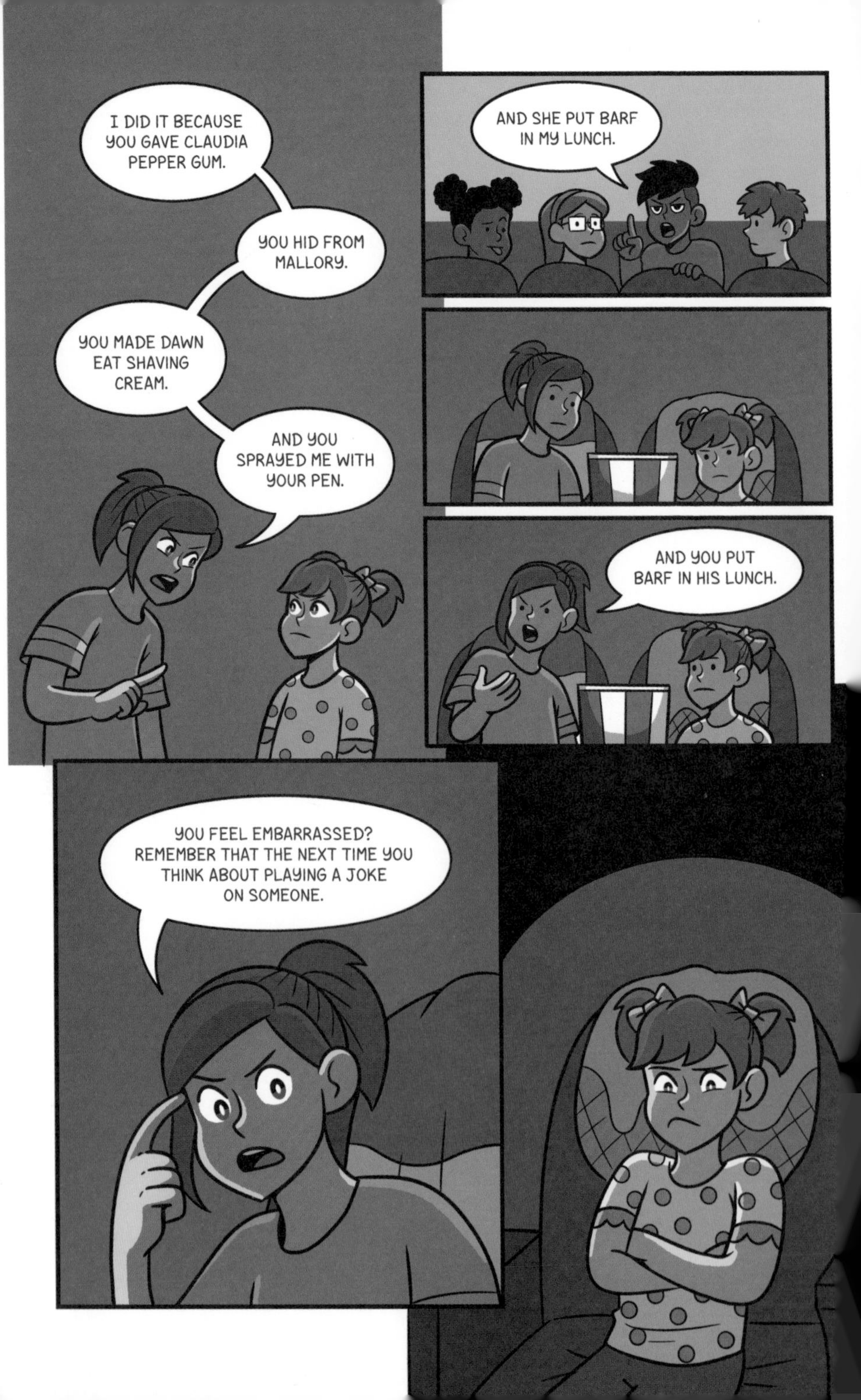
I DID IT BECAUSE YOU GAVE CLAUDIA PEPPER GUM.
YOU HID FROM MALLORY.
YOU MADE DAWN EAT SHAVING CREAM.
AND YOU SPRAYED ME WITH YOUR PEN.
AND SHE PUT BARF IN MY LUNCH.
AND YOU PUT BARF IN HIS LUNCH.
YOU FEEL EMBARRASSED? REMEMBER THAT THE NEXT TIME YOU THINK ABOUT PLAYING A JOKE ON SOMEONE.

CHAPTER 14

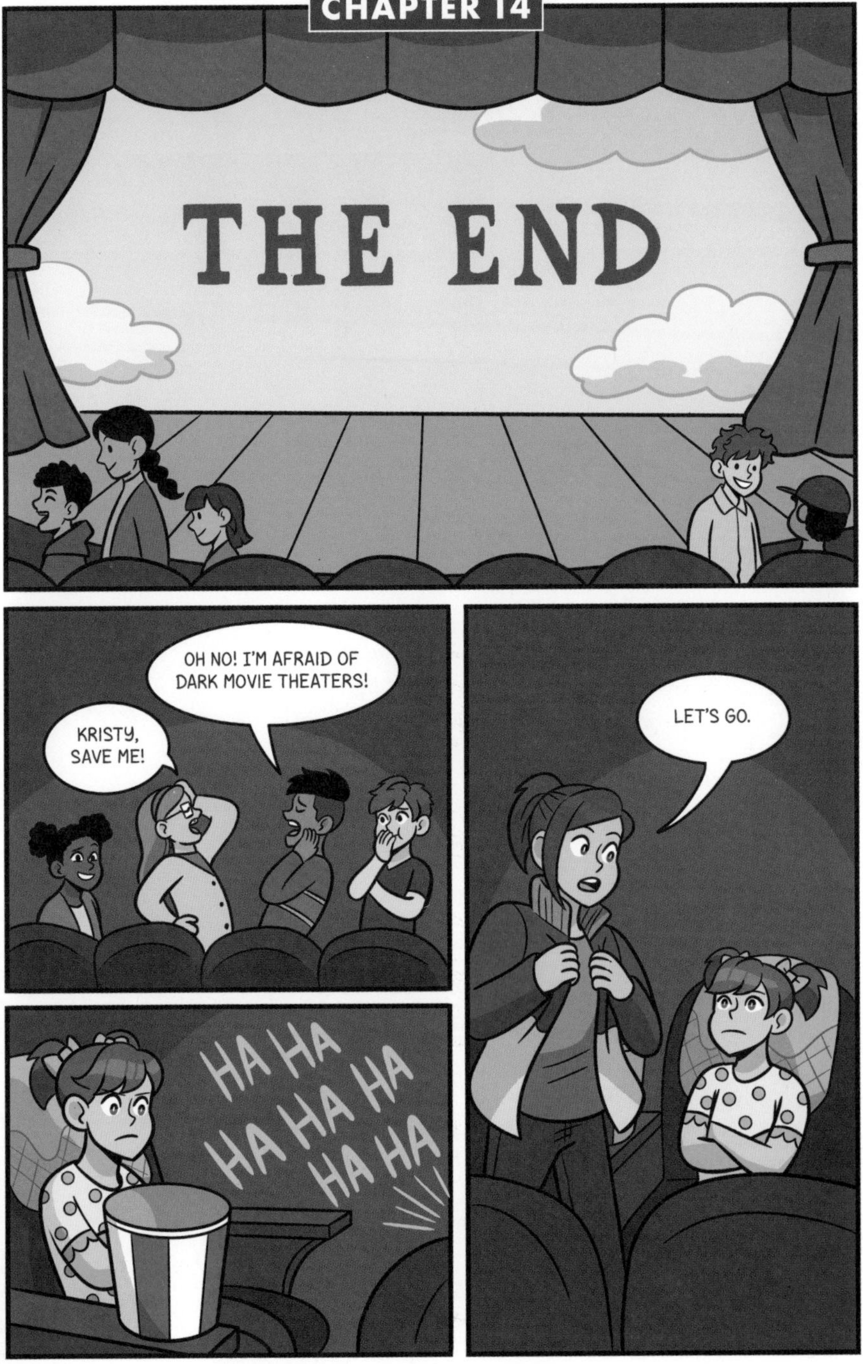
THE END
KRISTY, SAVE ME!
OH NO! I'M AFRAID OF DARK MOVIE THEATERS!
HA HA HA HA HA HA HA HA
LET'S GO.

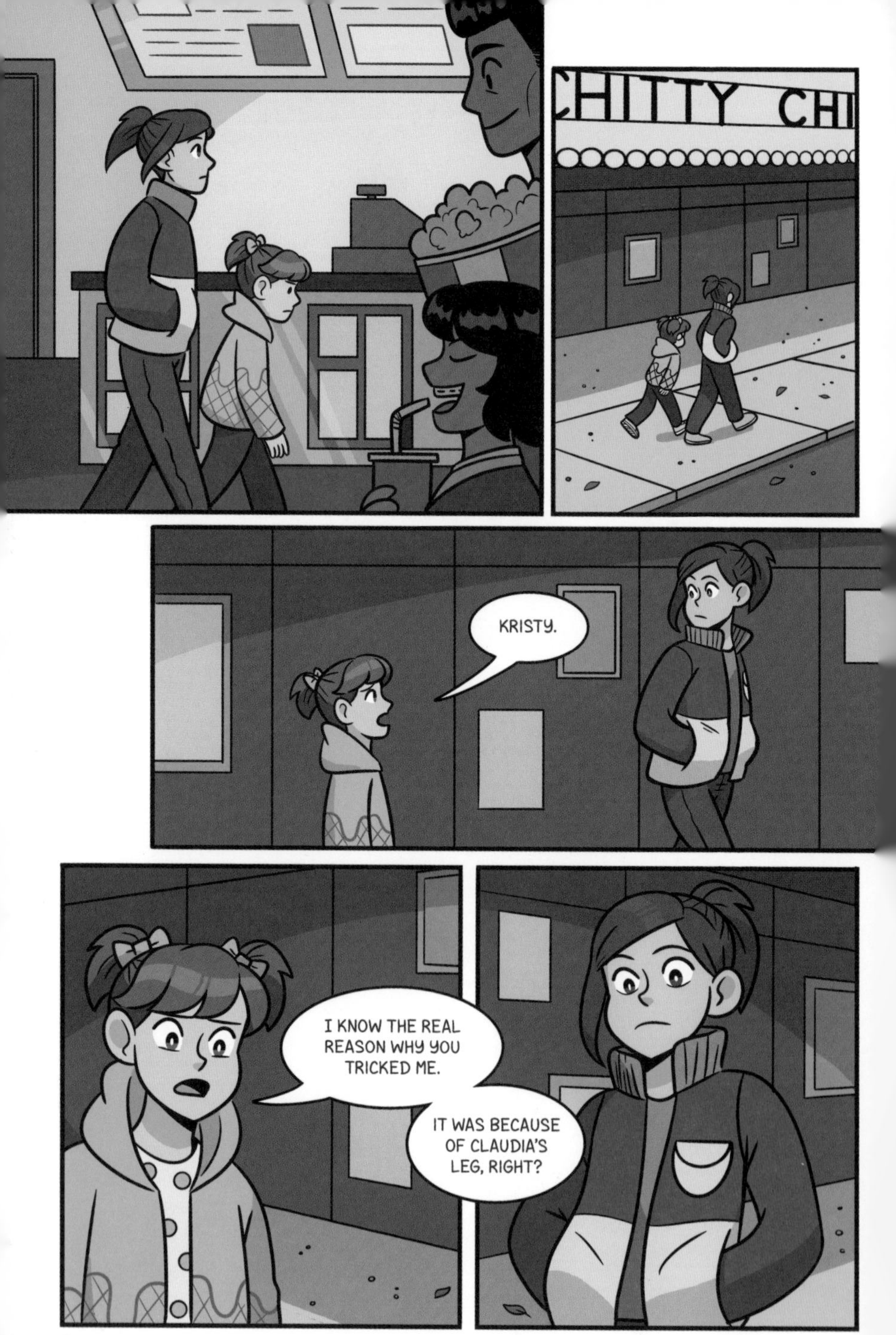
CHITTY CHI
KRISTY.
I KNOW THE REAL REASON WHY YOU TRICKED ME.
IT WAS BECAUSE OF CLAUDIA'S LEG, RIGHT?

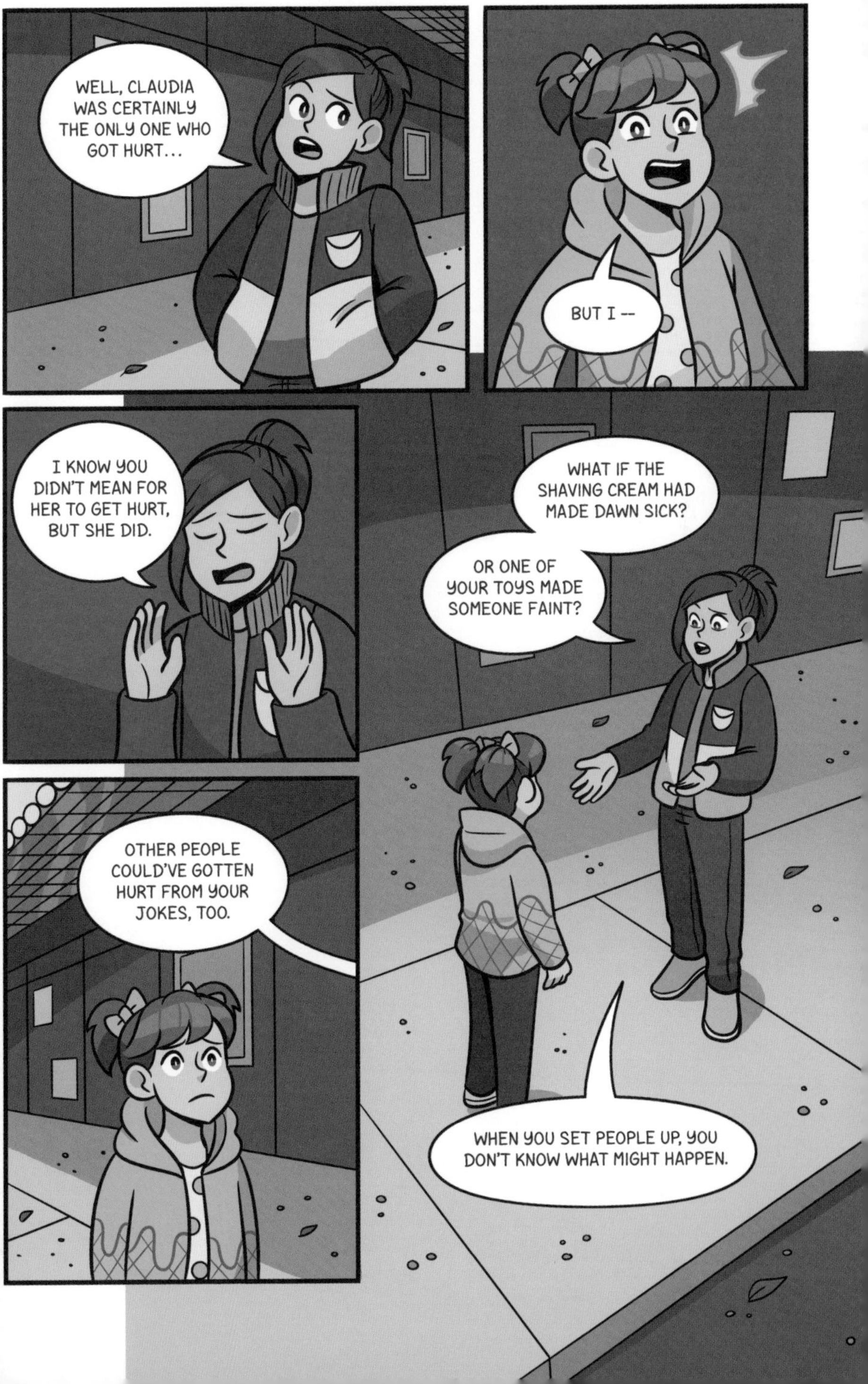
WELL, CLAUDIA WAS CERTAINLY THE ONLY ONE WHO GOT HURT...
BUT I --
I KNOW YOU DIDN'T MEAN FOR HER TO GET HURT, BUT SHE DID.
WHAT IF THE SHAVING CREAM HAD MADE DAWN SICK?
OR ONE OF YOUR TOYS MADE SOMEONE FAINT?
OTHER PEOPLE COULD'VE GOTTEN HURT FROM YOUR JOKES, TOO.
WHEN YOU SET PEOPLE UP, YOU DON'T KNOW WHAT MIGHT HAPPEN.

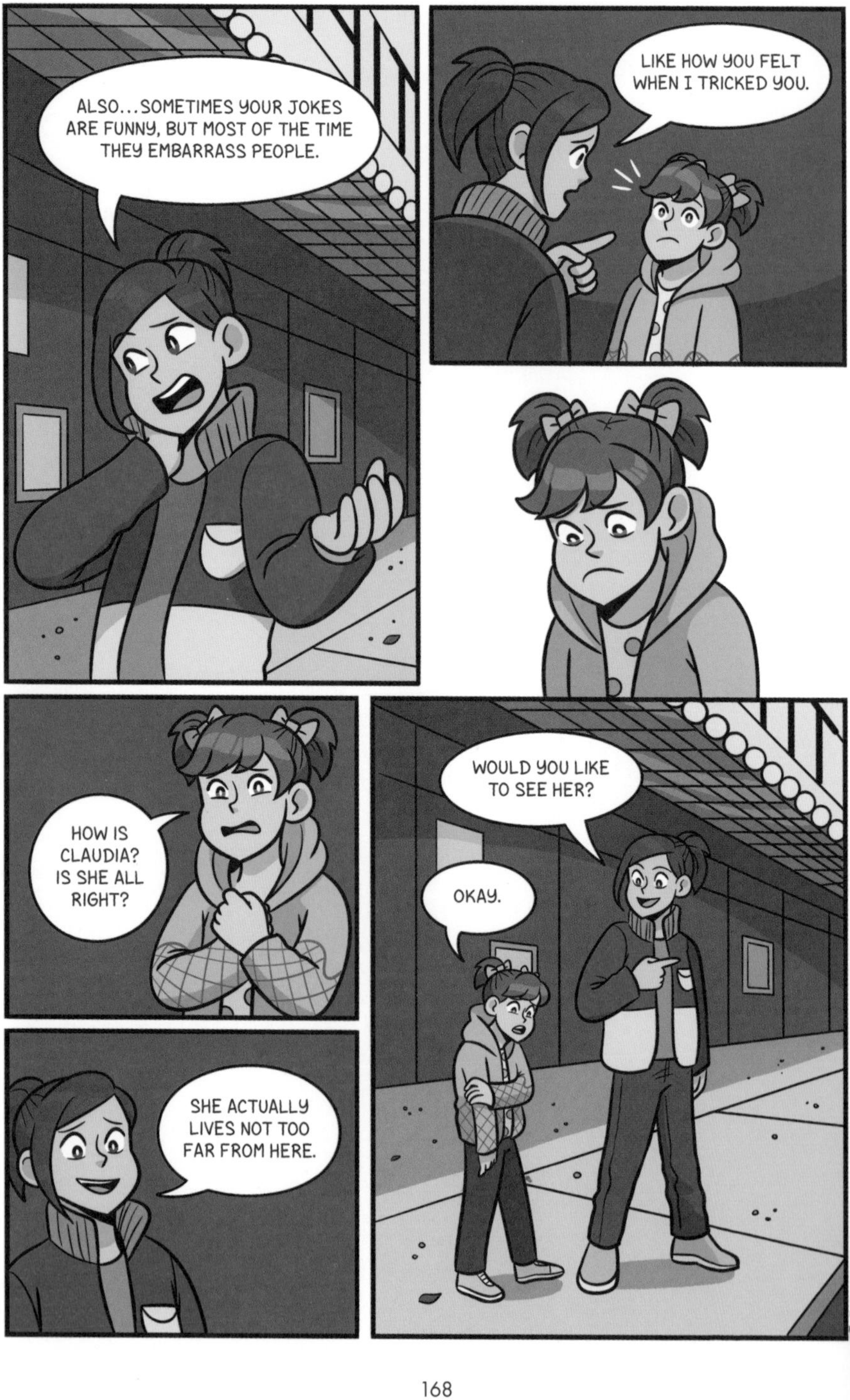
ALSO...SOMETIMES YOUR JOKES ARE FUNNY, BUT MOST OF THE TIME THEY EMBARRASS PEOPLE.
LIKE HOW YOU FELT WHEN I TRICKED YOU.
HOW IS CLAUDIA? IS SHE ALL RIGHT?
SHE ACTUALLY LIVES NOT TOO FAR FROM HERE.
WOULD YOU LIKE TO SEE HER?
OKAY.

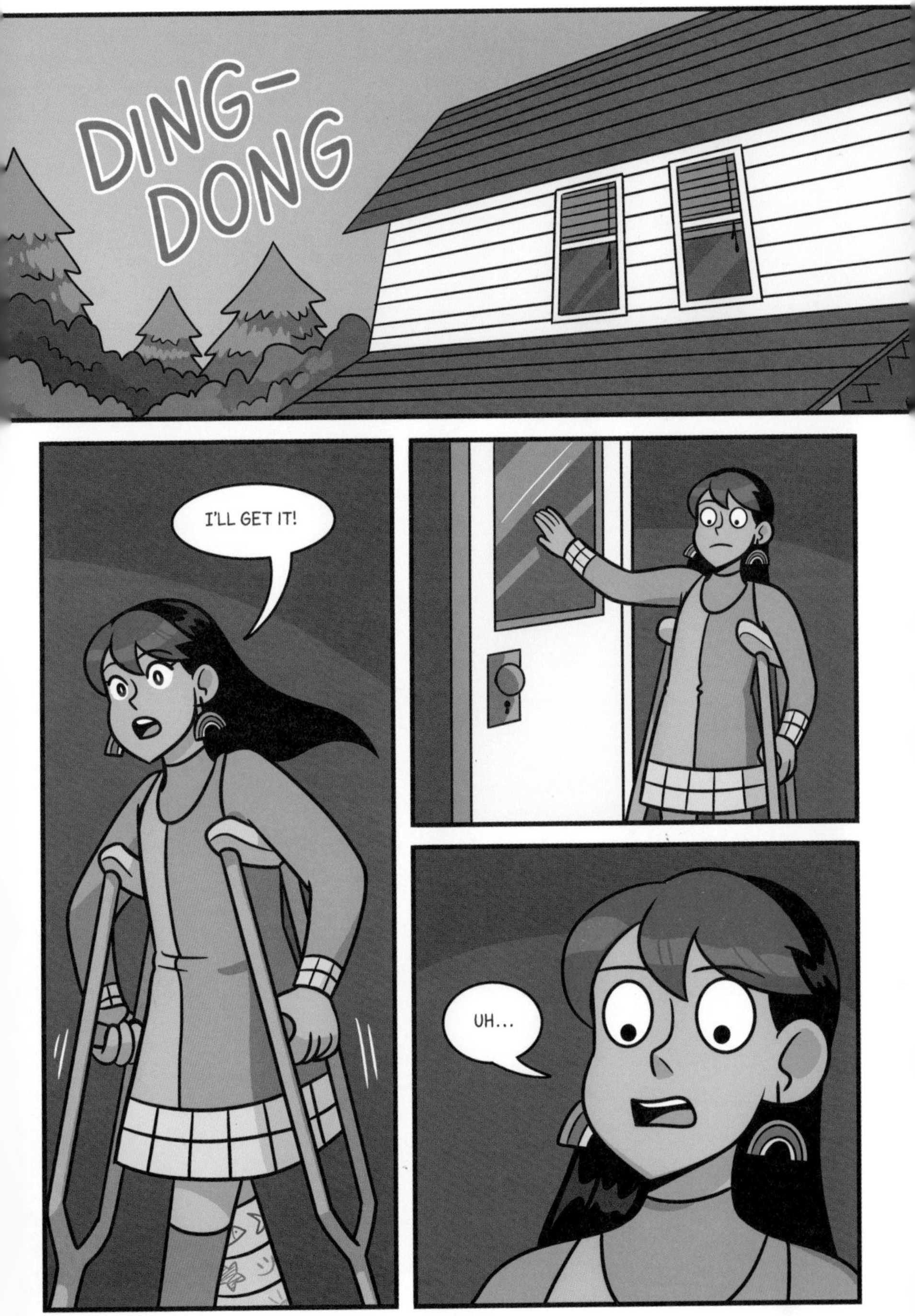
DING-DONG
I'LL GET IT!
UH...

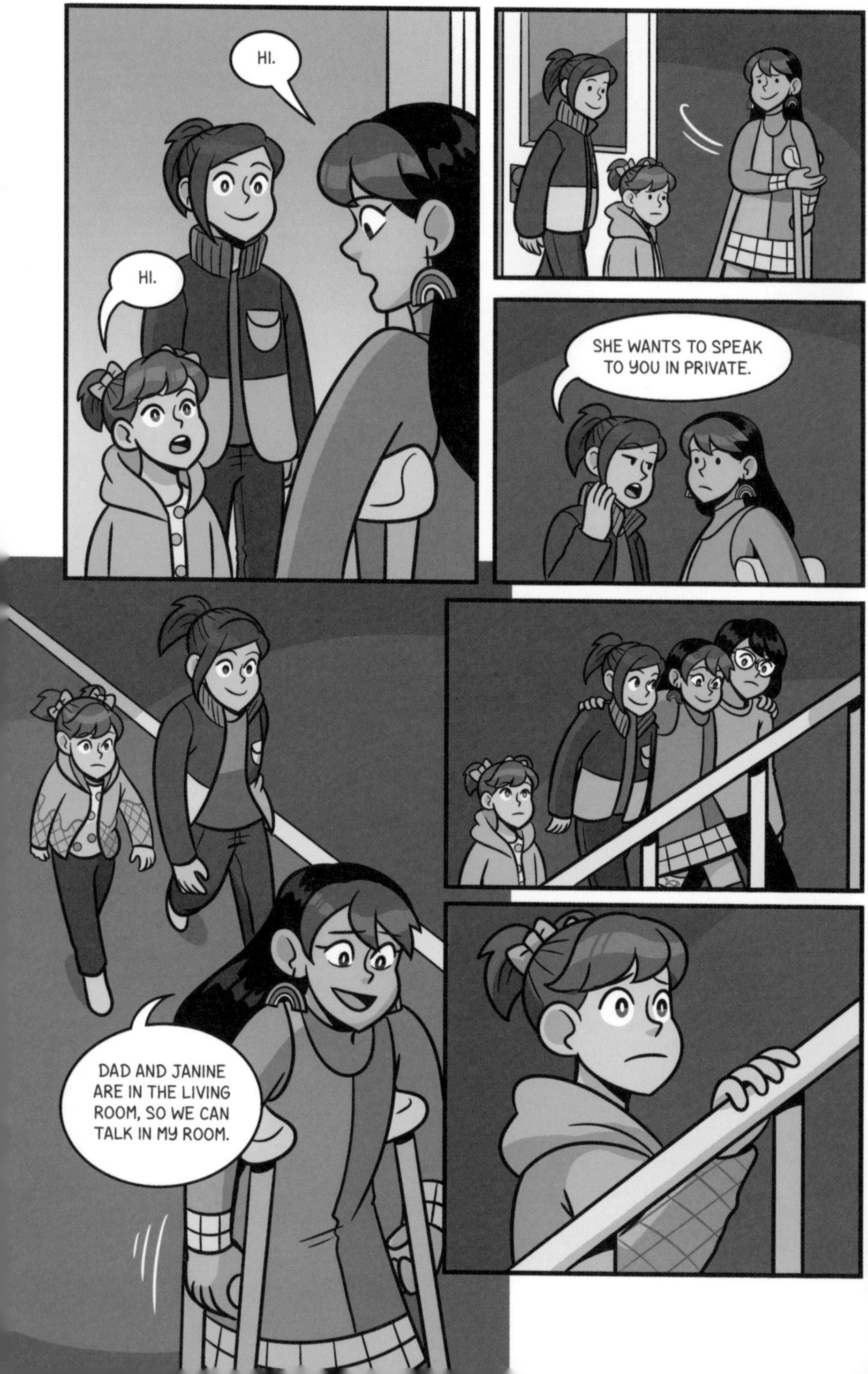
HI.
HI.
SHE WANTS TO SPEAK TO YOU IN PRIVATE.
DAD AND JANINE ARE IN THE LIVING ROOM, SO WE CAN TALK IN MY ROOM.

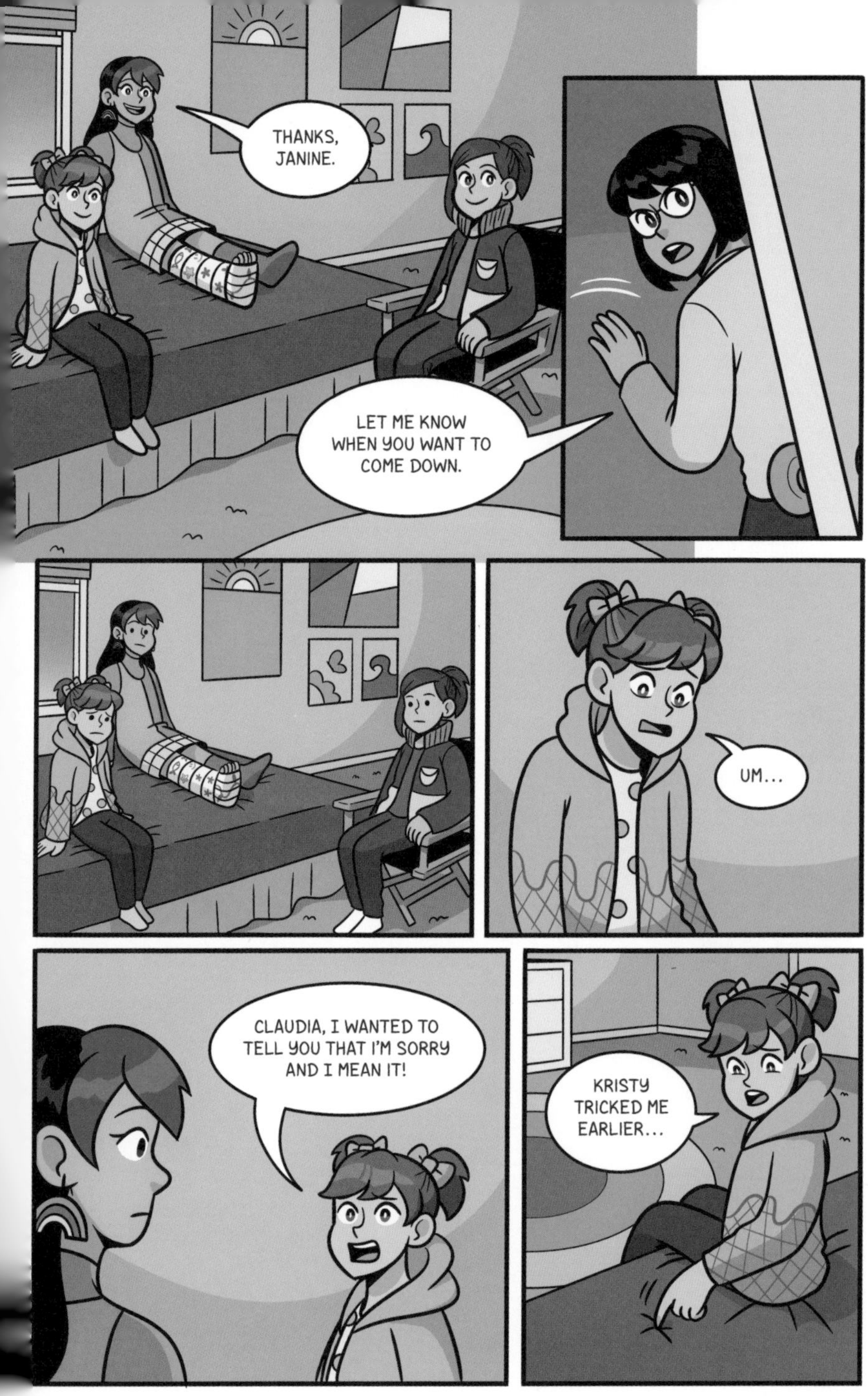
THANKS, JANINE.
LET ME KNOW WHEN YOU WANT TO COME DOWN.
UM...
CLAUDIA, I WANTED TO TELL YOU THAT I'M SORRY AND I MEAN IT!
KRISTY TRICKED ME EARLIER...

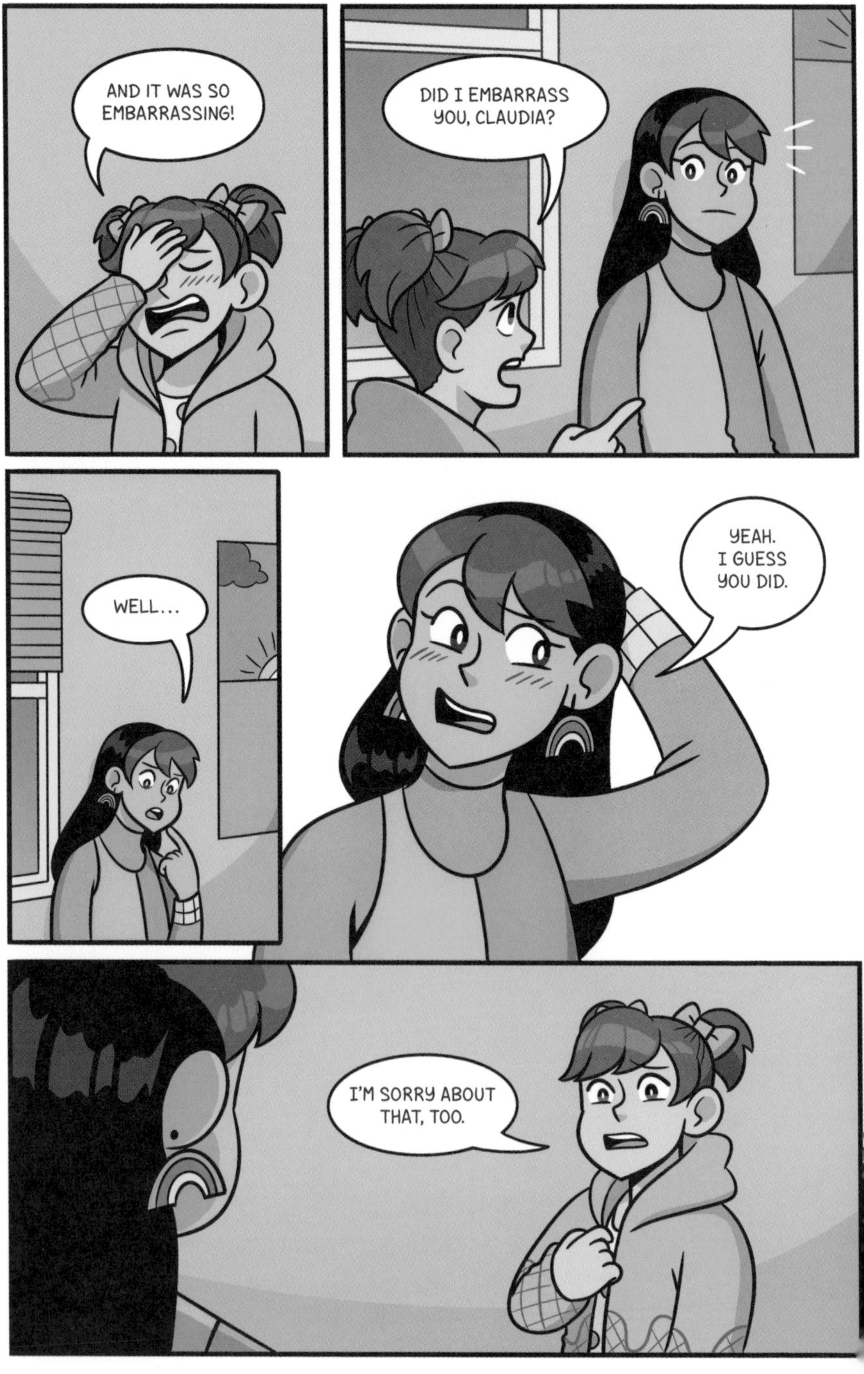
AND IT WAS SO EMBARRASSING!
DID I EMBARRASS YOU, CLAUDIA?
WELL...
YEAH. I GUESS YOU DID.
I'M SORRY ABOUT THAT, TOO.

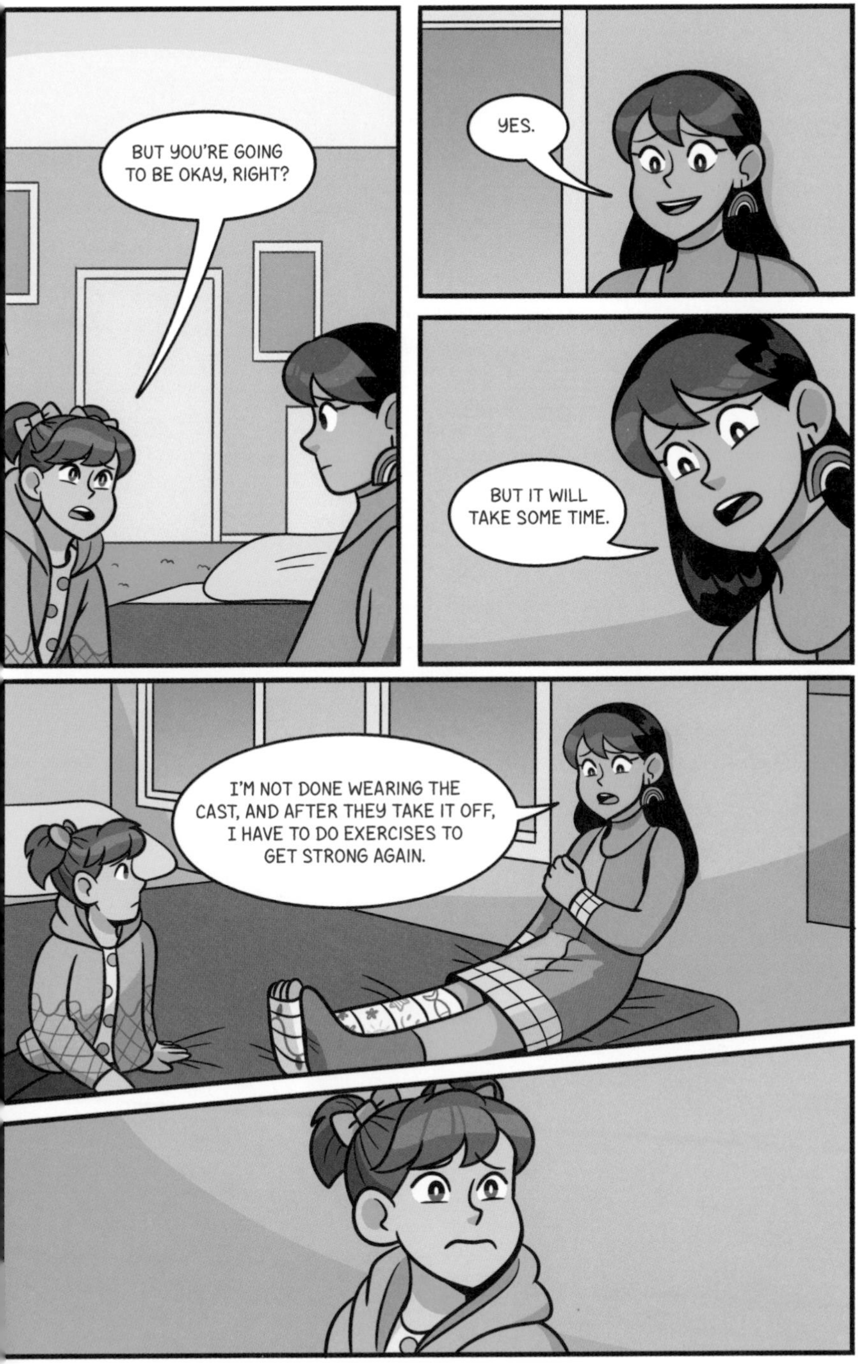
BUT YOU'RE GOING TO BE OKAY, RIGHT?
YES.
BUT IT WILL TAKE SOME TIME.
I'M NOT DONE WEARING THE CAST, AND AFTER THEY TAKE IT OFF, I HAVE TO DO EXERCISES TO GET STRONG AGAIN.

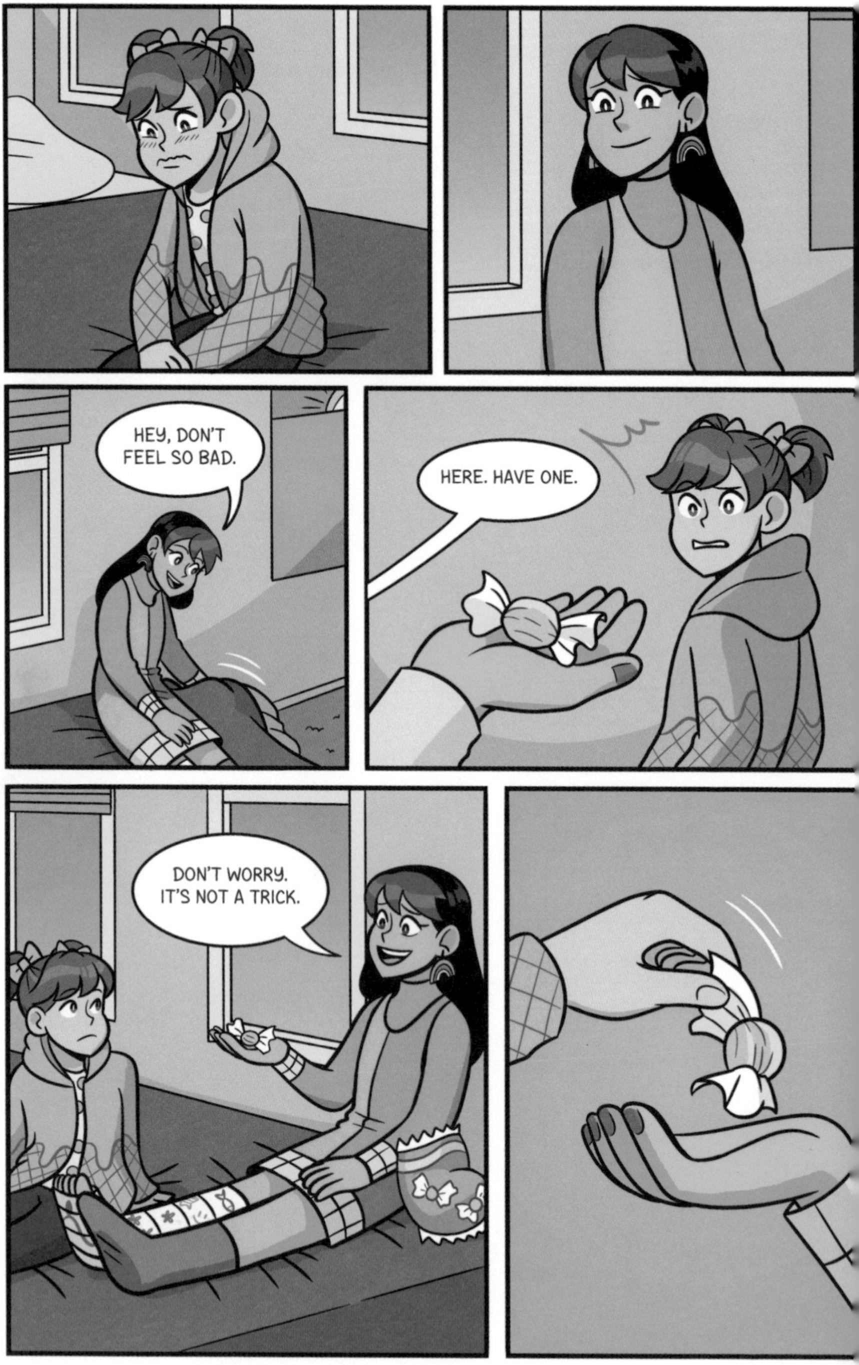

HEY, DON'T FEEL SO BAD.
HERE. HAVE ONE.
DON'T WORRY. IT'S NOT A TRICK.

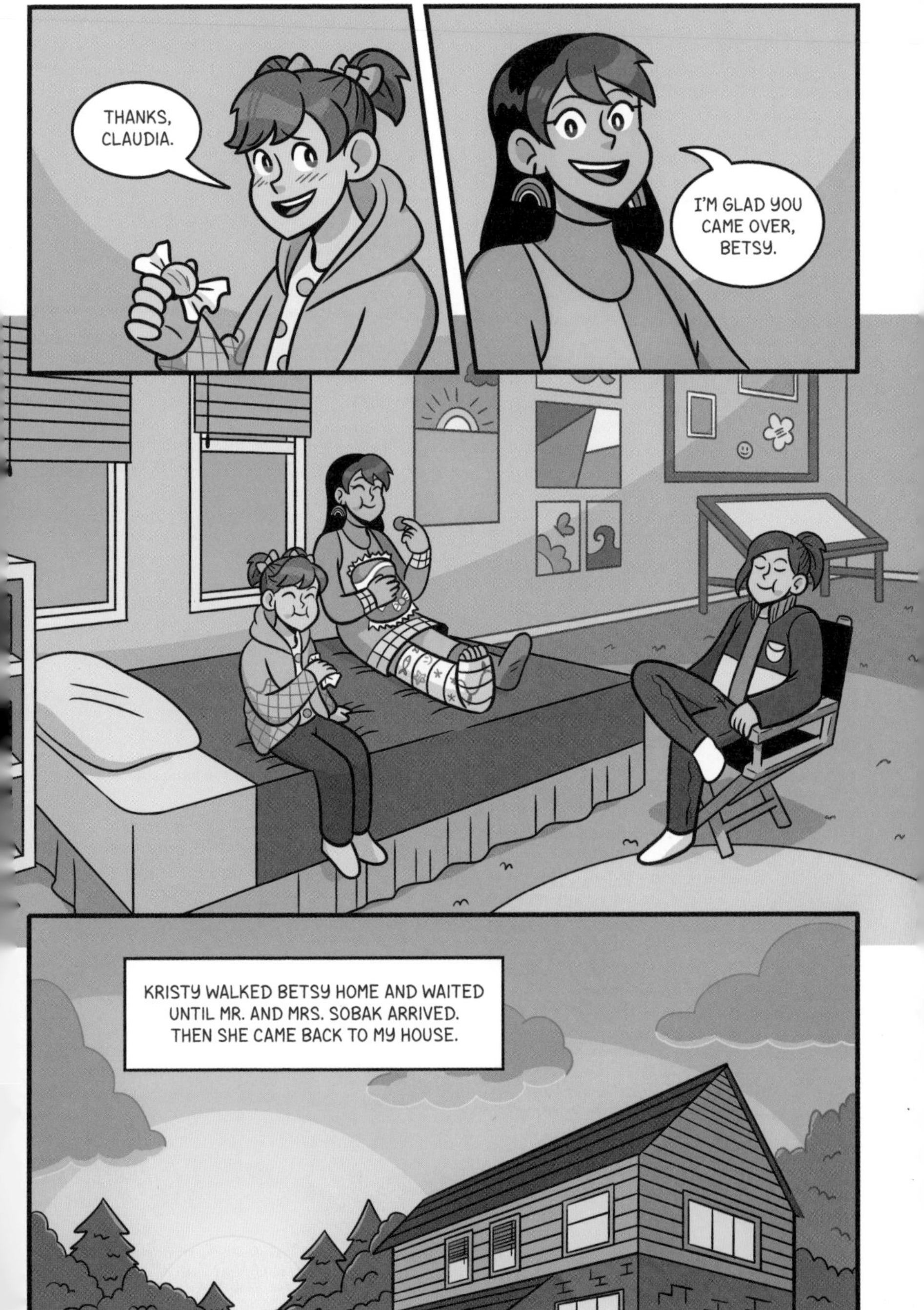
THANKS, CLAUDIA.
I'M GLAD YOU CAME OVER, BETSY.
KRISTY WALKED BETSY HOME AND WAITED UNTIL MR. AND MRS. SOBAK ARRIVED. THEN SHE CAME BACK TO MY HOUSE.

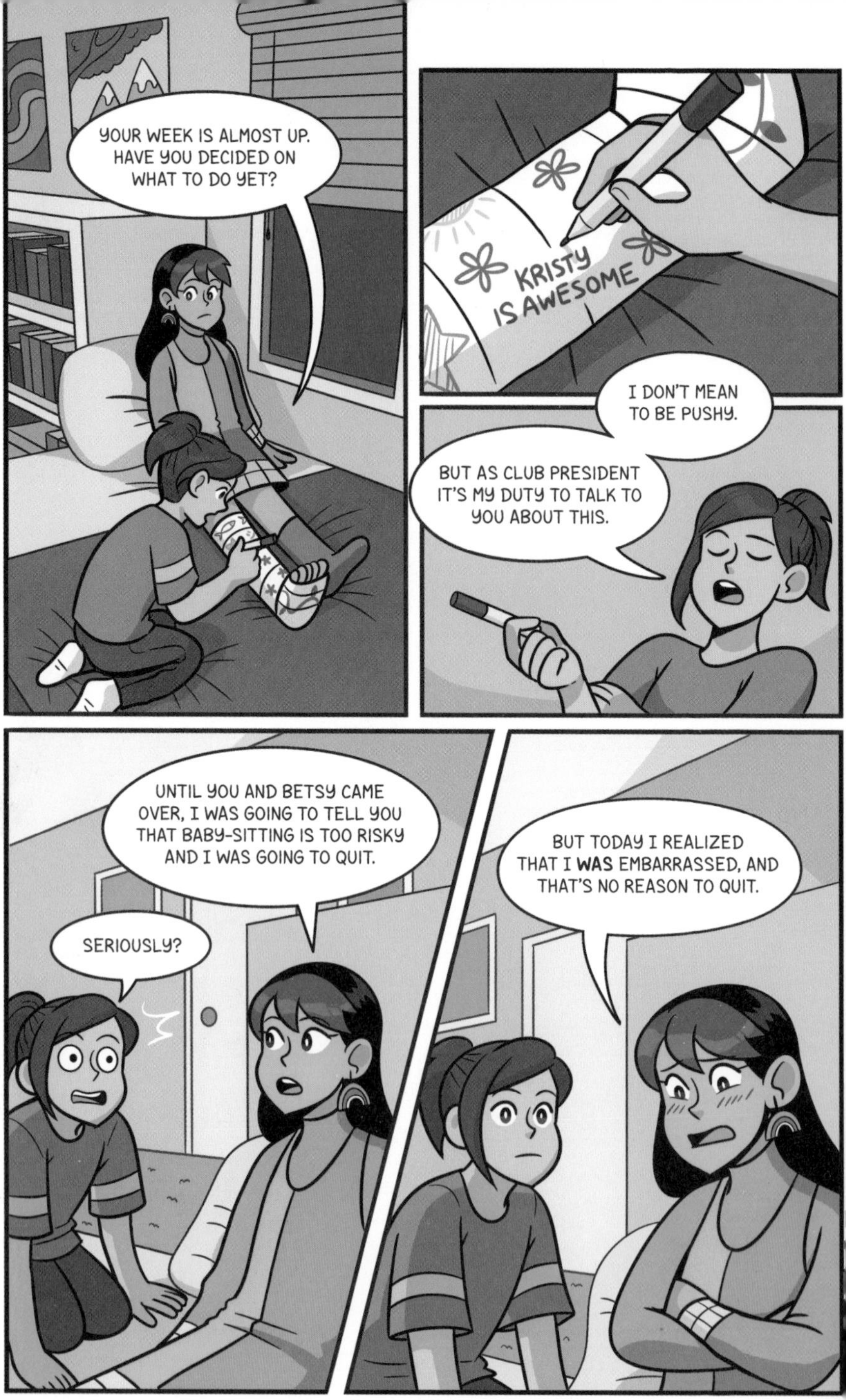
YOUR WEEK IS ALMOST UP. HAVE YOU DECIDED ON WHAT TO DO YET?
KRISTY IS AWESOME
I DON'T MEAN TO BE PUSHY.
BUT AS CLUB PRESIDENT IT'S MY DUTY TO TALK TO YOU ABOUT THIS.
UNTIL YOU AND BETSY CAME OVER, I WAS GOING TO TELL YOU THAT BABY-SITTING IS TOO RISKY AND I WAS GOING TO QUIT.
SERIOUSLY?
BUT TODAY I REALIZED THAT I **WAS** EMBARRASSED, AND THAT'S NO REASON TO QUIT.

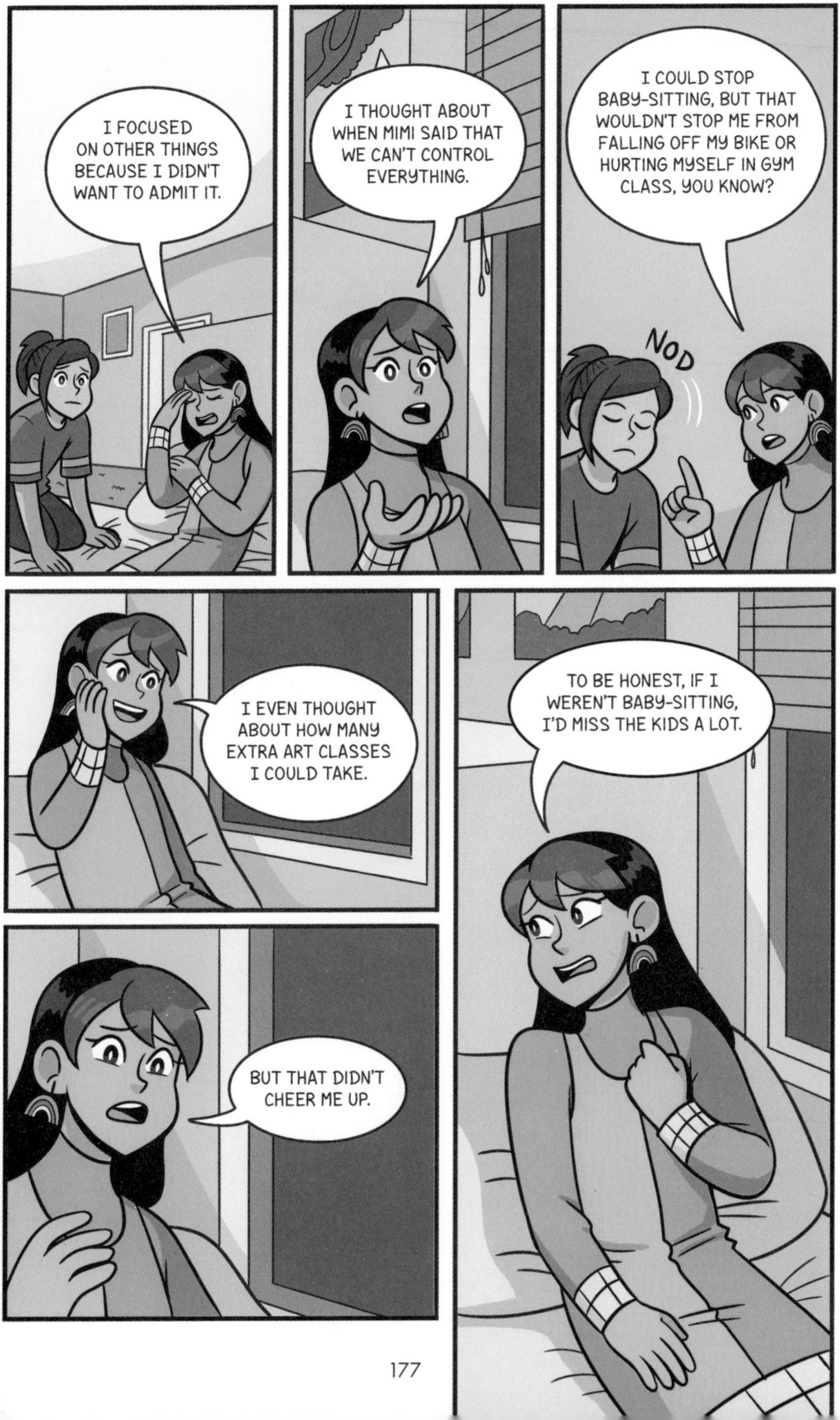
I FOCUSED ON OTHER THINGS BECAUSE I DIDN'T WANT TO ADMIT IT.
I THOUGHT ABOUT WHEN MIMI SAID THAT WE CAN'T CONTROL EVERYTHING.
I COULD STOP BABY-SITTING, BUT THAT WOULDN'T STOP ME FROM FALLING OFF MY BIKE OR HURTING MYSELF IN GYM CLASS, YOU KNOW?
NOD
I EVEN THOUGHT ABOUT HOW MANY EXTRA ART CLASSES I COULD TAKE.
TO BE HONEST, IF I WEREN'T BABY-SITTING, I'D MISS THE KIDS A LOT.
BUT THAT DIDN'T CHEER ME UP.

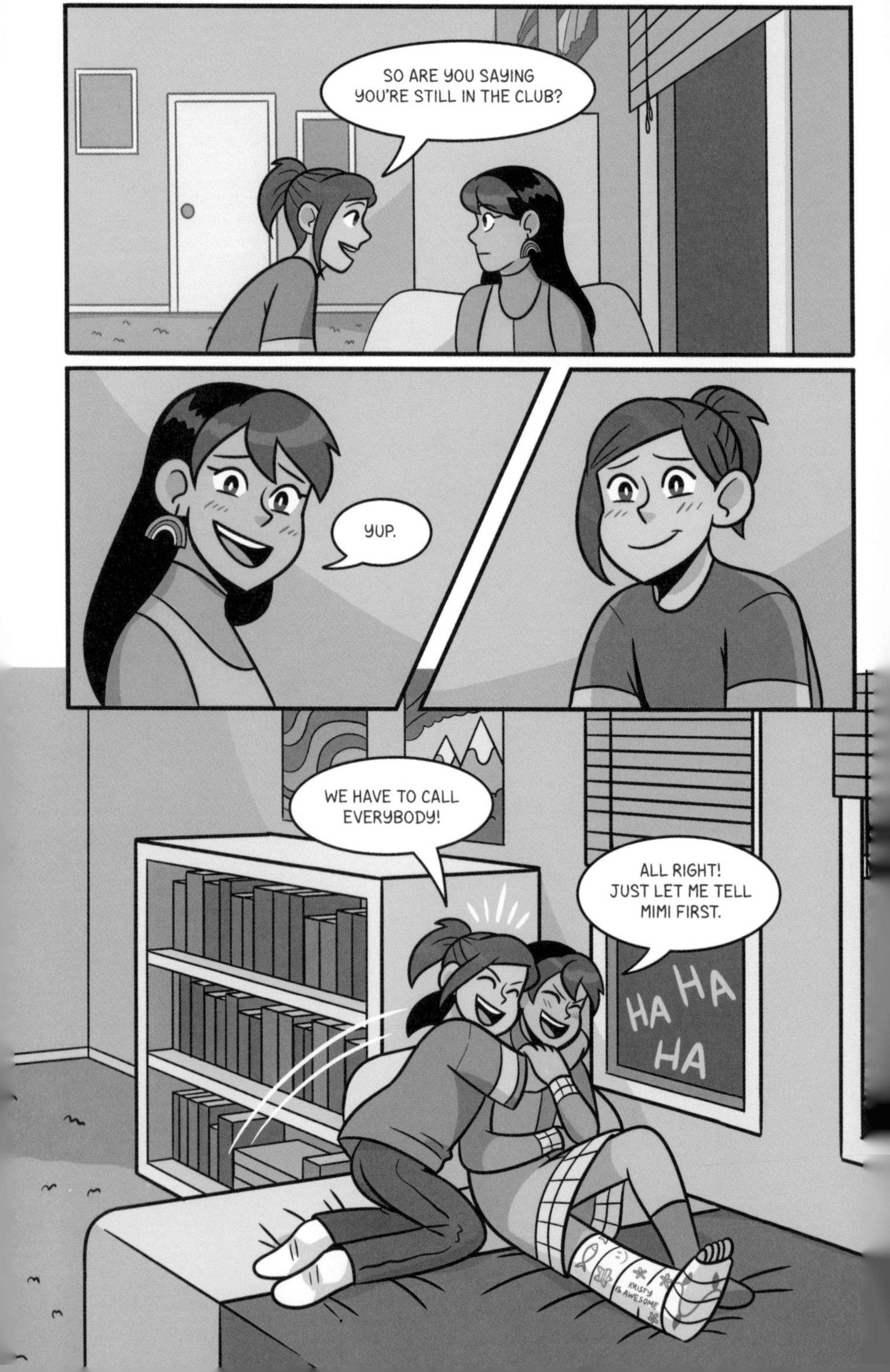
SO ARE YOU SAYING YOU'RE STILL IN THE CLUB?
YUP.
WE HAVE TO CALL EVERYBODY!
ALL RIGHT! JUST LET ME TELL MIMI FIRST.
HA HA HA
KRISTY IS AWESOME

CHAPTER 15

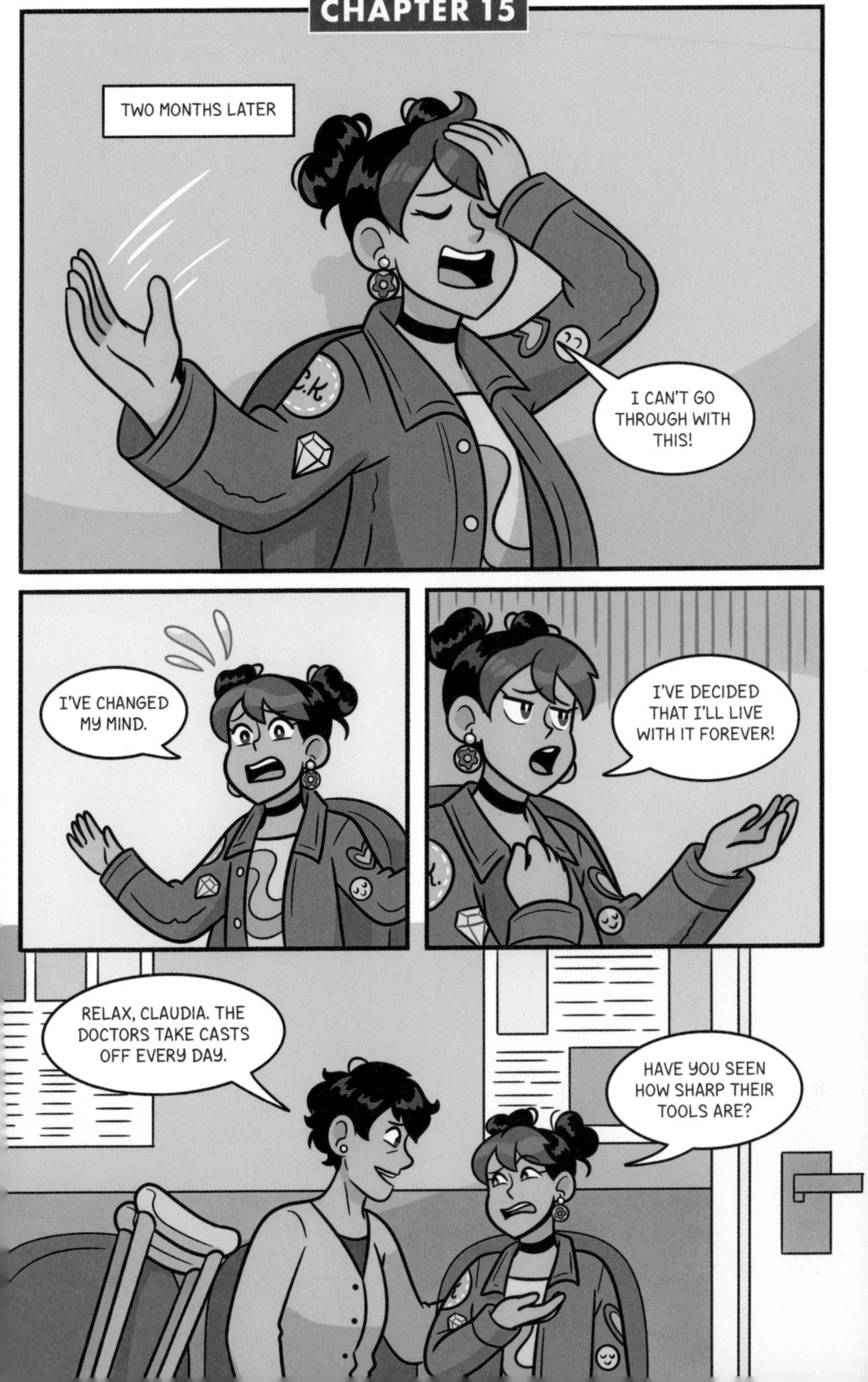
TWO MONTHS LATER
I CAN'T GO THROUGH WITH THIS!
I'VE CHANGED MY MIND.
I'VE DECIDED THAT I'LL LIVE WITH IT FOREVER!
RELAX, CLAUDIA. THE DOCTORS TAKE CASTS OFF EVERY DAY.
HAVE YOU SEEN HOW SHARP THEIR TOOLS ARE?

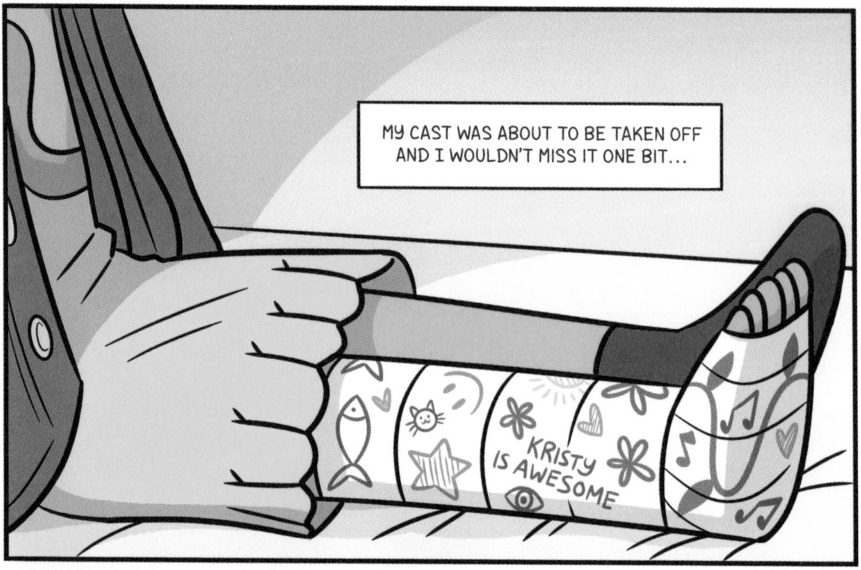
MY CAST WAS ABOUT TO BE TAKEN OFF AND I WOULDN'T MISS IT ONE BIT...
KRISTY IS AWESOME

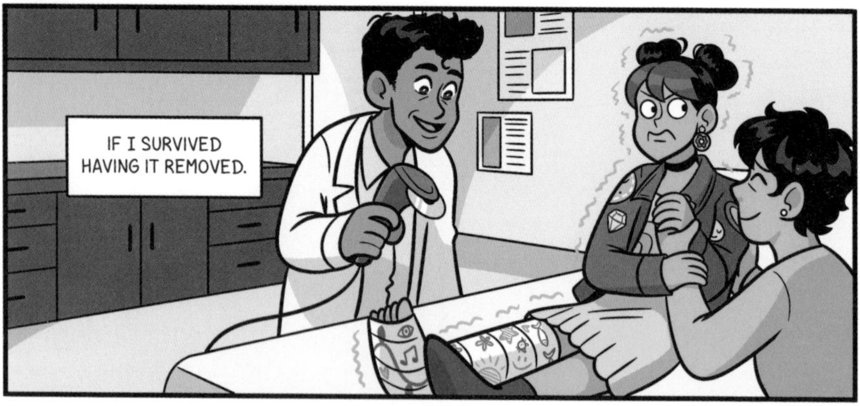
IF I SURVIVED HAVING IT REMOVED.

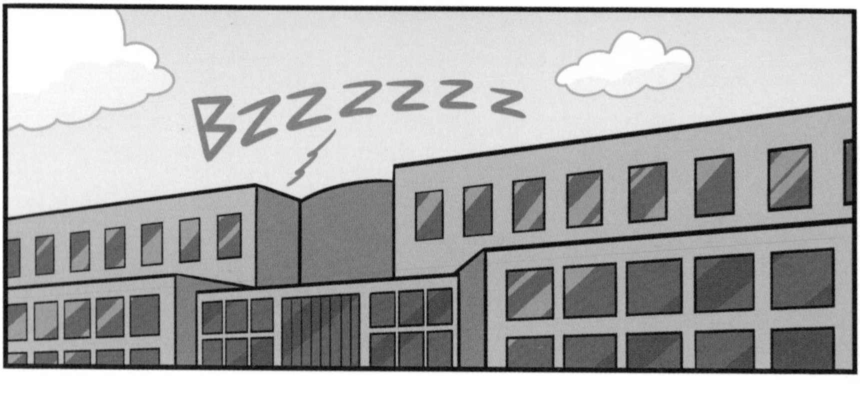
BZZZZZZ

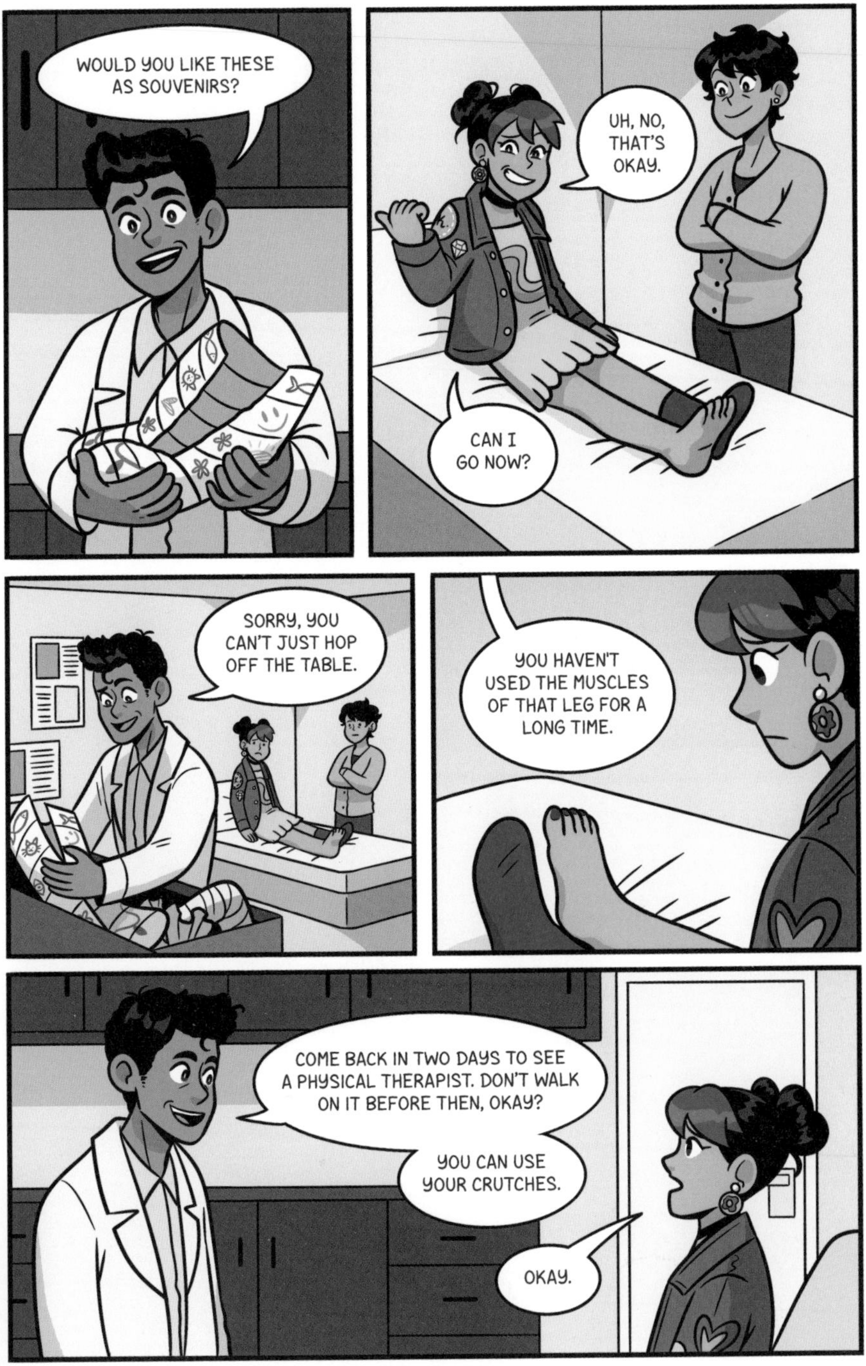
WOULD YOU LIKE THESE AS SOUVENIRS?
UH, NO, THAT'S OKAY.
CAN I GO NOW?
SORRY, YOU CAN'T JUST HOP OFF THE TABLE.
YOU HAVEN'T USED THE MUSCLES OF THAT LEG FOR A LONG TIME.
COME BACK IN TWO DAYS TO SEE A PHYSICAL THERAPIST. DON'T WALK ON IT BEFORE THEN, OKAY?
YOU CAN USE YOUR CRUTCHES.
OKAY.

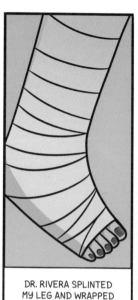

DR. RIVERA SPLINTED MY LEG AND WRAPPED A BANDAGE AROUND IT.

I WAS DISAPPOINTED. I KNEW I'D HAVE TO DO PHYSICAL THERAPY BUT I AT LEAST THOUGHT I WOULDN'T NEED THE CRUTCHES ANYMORE.

BUT I FELT A LOT BETTER WHEN I GOT HOME, JUST IN TIME FOR A MEETING OF THE BABY-SITTERS CLUB.

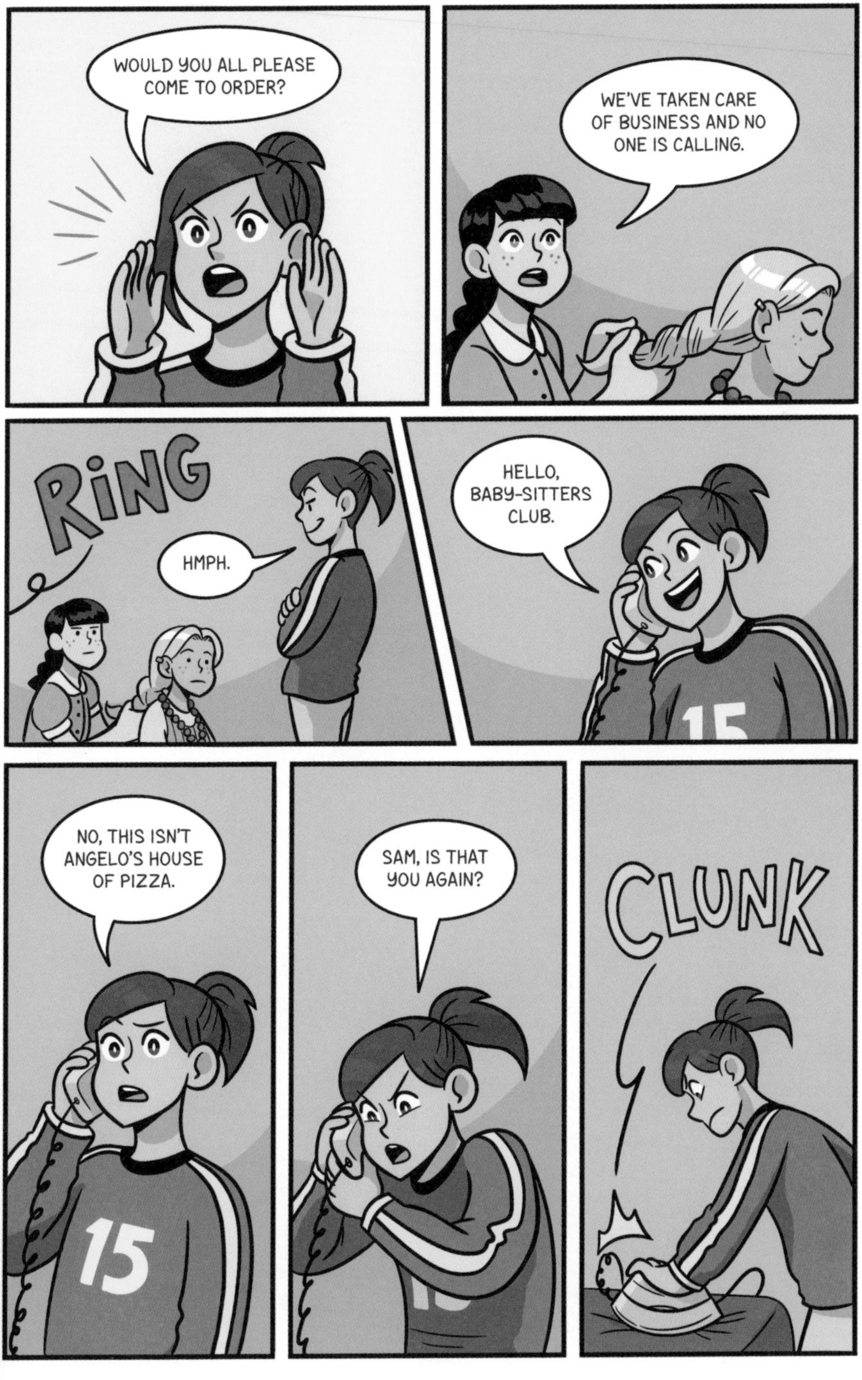
WOULD YOU ALL PLEASE COME TO ORDER?
WE'VE TAKEN CARE OF BUSINESS AND NO ONE IS CALLING.
RING
HMPH.
HELLO, BABY-SITTERS CLUB.
15
NO, THIS ISN'T ANGELO'S HOUSE OF PIZZA.
15
SAM, IS THAT YOU AGAIN?
CLUNK

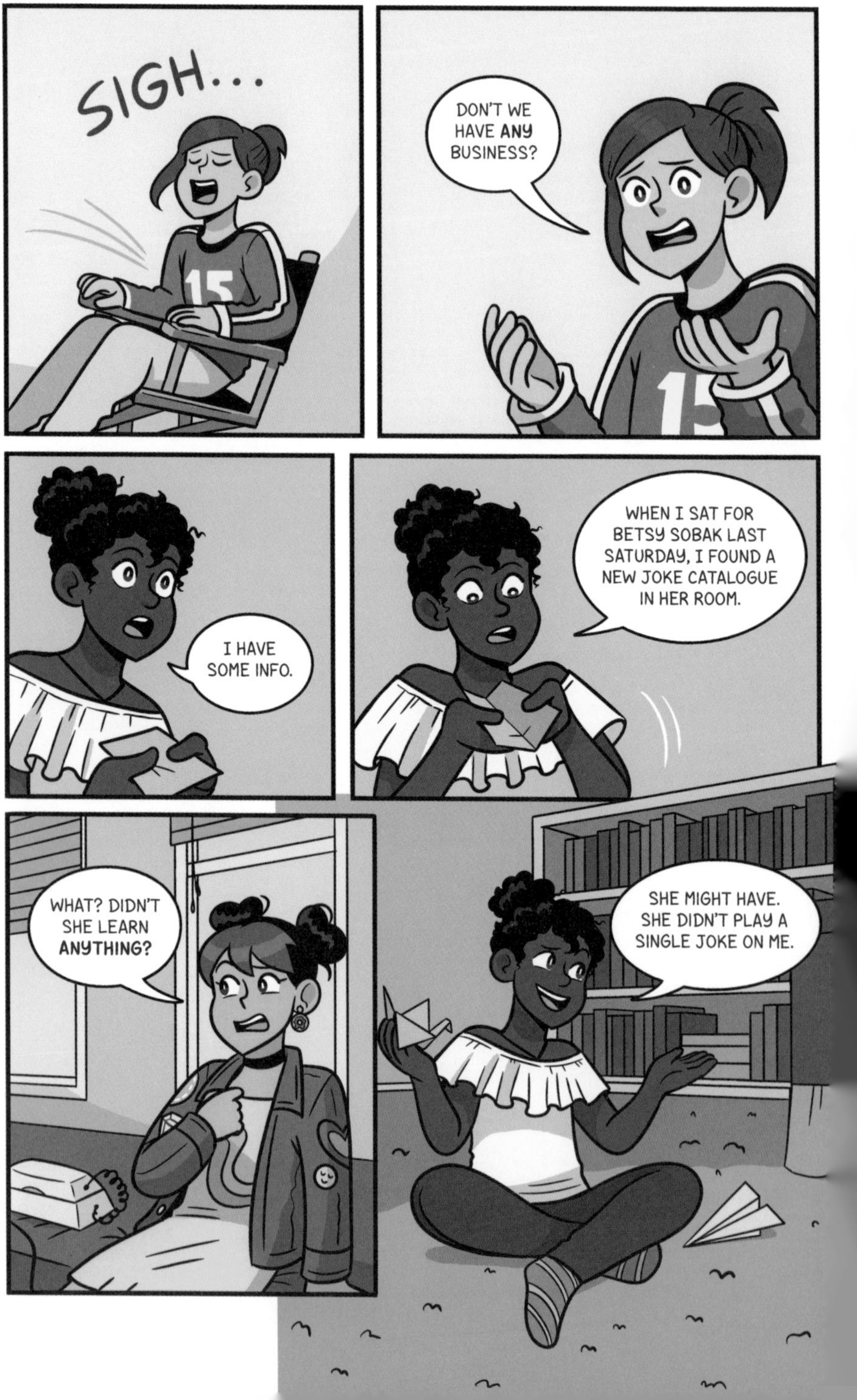
SIGH...
DON'T WE HAVE ANY BUSINESS?
I HAVE SOME INFO.
WHEN I SAT FOR BETSY SOBAK LAST SATURDAY, I FOUND A NEW JOKE CATALOGUE IN HER ROOM.
WHAT? DIDN'T SHE LEARN ANYTHING?
SHE MIGHT HAVE. SHE DIDN'T PLAY A SINGLE JOKE ON ME.

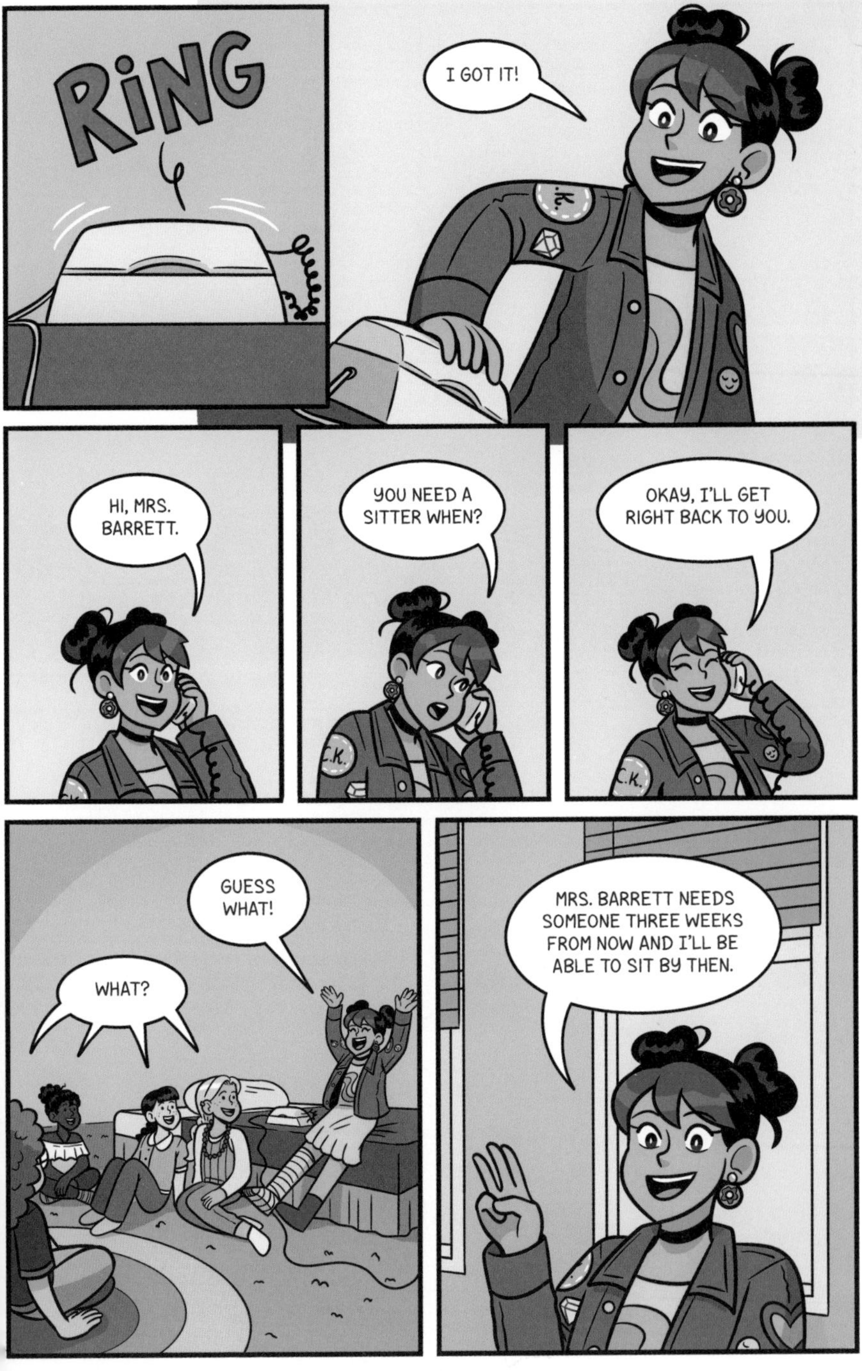
RING
I GOT IT!
HI, MRS. BARRETT.
YOU NEED A SITTER WHEN?
OKAY, I'LL GET RIGHT BACK TO YOU.
GUESS WHAT!
WHAT?
MRS. BARRETT NEEDS SOMEONE THREE WEEKS FROM NOW AND I'LL BE ABLE TO SIT BY THEN.

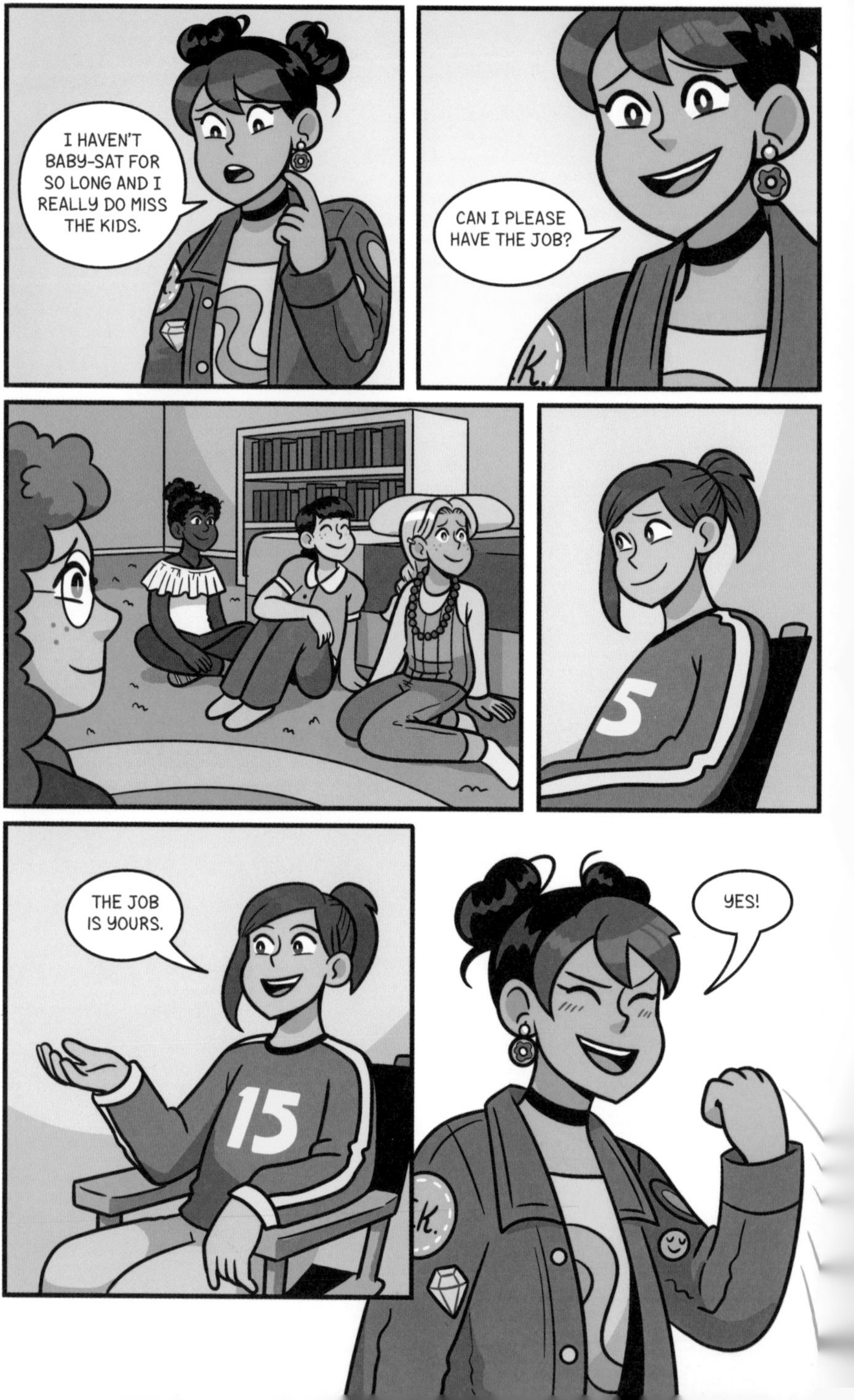
I HAVEN'T BABY-SAT FOR SO LONG AND I REALLY DO MISS THE KIDS.
CAN I PLEASE HAVE THE JOB?
THE JOB IS YOURS.
YES!

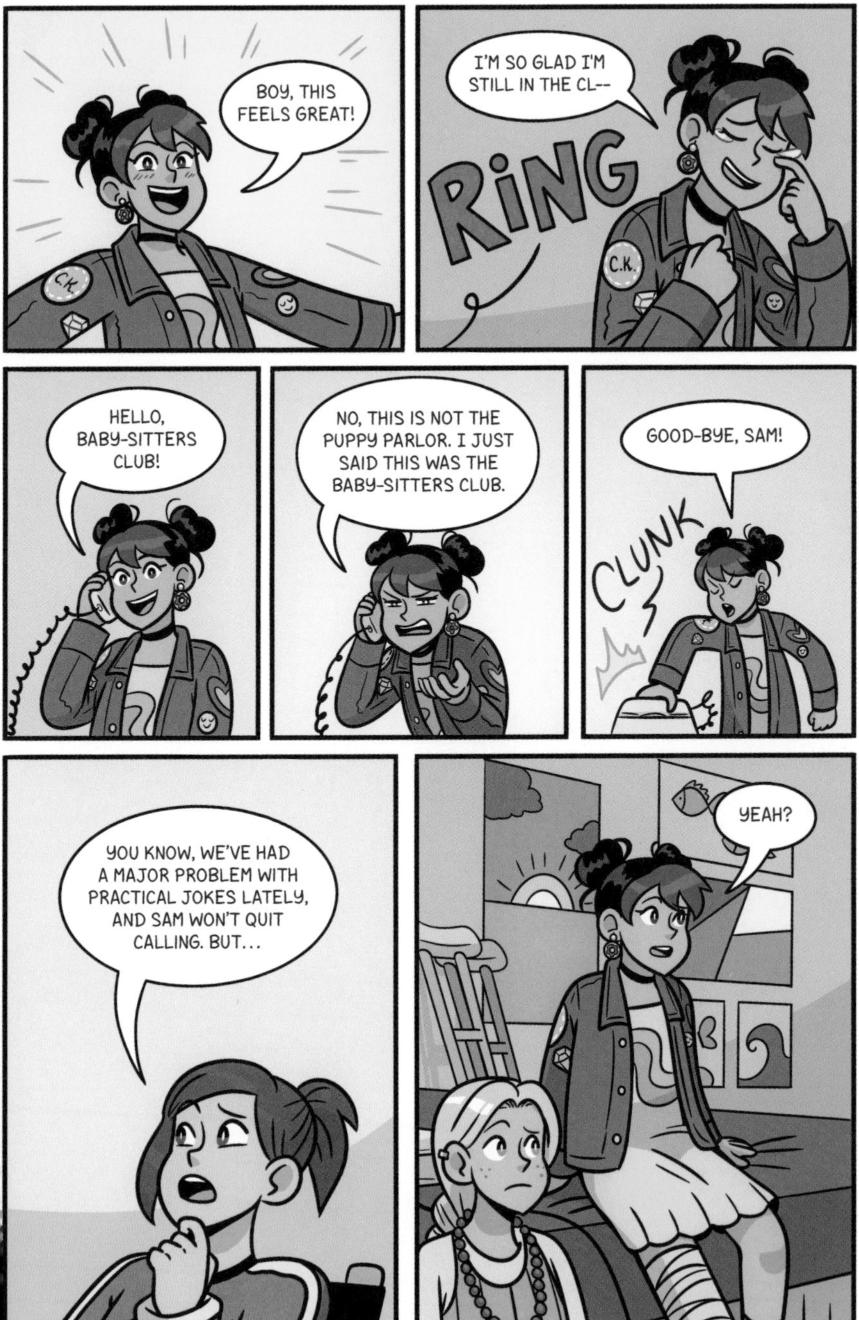
BOY, THIS FEELS GREAT!
I'M SO GLAD I'M STILL IN THE CL--
RING
HELLO, BABY-SITTERS CLUB!
NO, THIS IS NOT THE PUPPY PARLOR. I JUST SAID THIS WAS THE BABY-SITTERS CLUB.
GOOD-BYE, SAM!
CLUNK
YOU KNOW, WE'VE HAD A MAJOR PROBLEM WITH PRACTICAL JOKES LATELY, AND SAM WON'T QUIT CALLING. BUT...
YEAH?

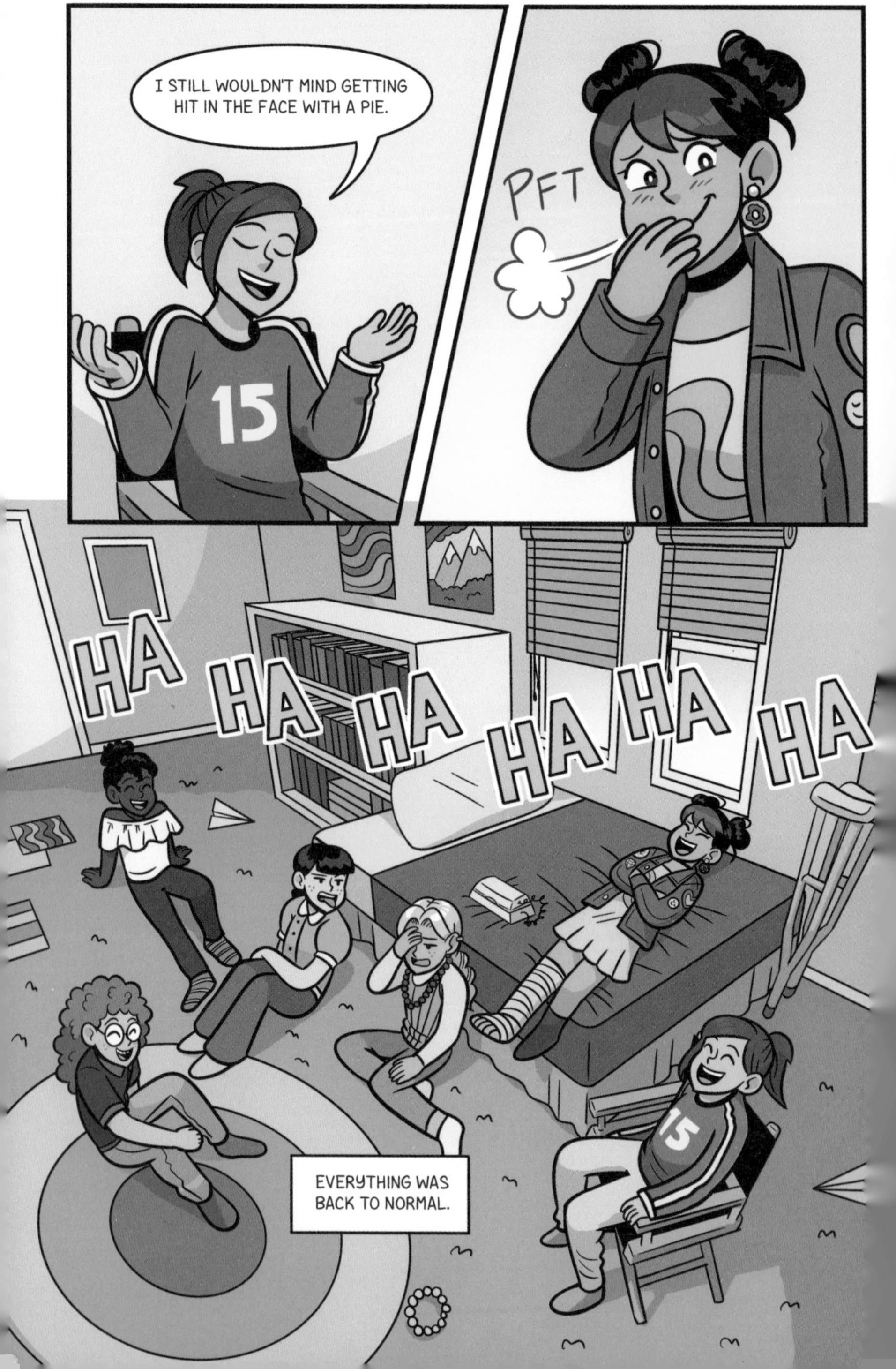
I STILL WOULDN'T MIND GETTING HIT IN THE FACE WITH A PIE.
PFT
HA HA HA HA HA HA
EVERYTHING WAS BACK TO NORMAL.